Untitled by Shen Chen Hsieh
Digital collage and illustration, 6.5 inches by 8 inches. 2022.

Moon City Review
2022

Moon City Review is a publication of Moon City Press, sponsored by the Department of English at Missouri State University, and is distributed by the University of Arkansas Press. Exchange subscriptions with literary magazines are encouraged. The editors of *Moon City Review* contract First North American Serial Rights, all rights reverting to the writers upon publication. The views expressed by authors in *Moon City Review* do not necessarily reflect the opinions of its editors, Moon City Press, or the Department of English at Missouri State University.

Submissions are considered at https://mooncitypress.submittable.com/submit. For more information, please consult www.moon-city-press.com.

Cover designed by Shen Chen Hsieh.
Text copyedited by Karen Craigo.

Copyright © 2022 Moon City Press
All rights reserved
Printed in the United States of America

moon city press
Department of English
Missouri State University

Staff

Editor
Michael Czyzniejewski

Poetry Editor
Sara Burge

Nonfiction Editor
John Turner

Assistant Nonfiction Editor
Jennifer Murvin

Fiction Editor
Joel Coltharp

Graphic Narrative Editor
Jennifer Murvin

Assistant Editors

Daniel Abramovitz	Madison Hart	Bridgette Noland
Taylor Barnhart	Rebekah Hartensveld	Sarah Padfield
Steve Booker	Abigail Jensen	Marianne Prax
Shane Brooks	Elizabeth King	Sujash Purna
Nicole Brunette	John King	Anne Roberts
Alexandria Clay	Mikaela Koehler	Hannah Rowland
Anna Edwards	Jueun Lee	Eli Slover
Alex Elleman	Sarah Lewis	Shannon Small
Julia Feuerborn	Alyssa Malloy	Cam Steilen
Jessica Flanigan	Rachel McClay	Sean Turlington
Amy Gault	Katie McWilliams	Jessica Weaver
Janel Haloupek	Mikaela Mohrmann	Sierra Welch
Rebecca Harris	Alyssah Morrison	Grace Willis

Student Editors

Mya Berry	Savannah Franklin	Abby McCord
Acacia Boerboom	Bethany Gott	Sidney Miles
Simone Cunningham	Tamara "Nic" Keel	Tinsley Merriman
Garrett Dudley	Anna Kleier	Meg Spring
Kelsey Embree	Amelia Kotulski	Claire Roberts
Erica Felmlee		Alex Wallace

Advisory Editors
James Baumlin   W.D. Blackmon   Lanette Cadle   Marcus Cafagña

Table of Contents

Derek Otsuji

Standoff at Oura-Henoko Bay

What else *was* there to do? The bay, the reef,
     blue coral groves and clown fish alleyways,
the thrumming pink and green anemones,
     sea turtles and cucumbers, sponges, crabs,
conch, Venus comb, the worm called Christmas tree—
     snuffed by red blanketing sand, slabbed concrete.
For what? A shiny airbase to blot bight's
     bend, turquoise lagoons bequeathed to landfill—
the sky, to harpies' metallic screeches
     invading silence to the very marrow.
No, I refuse. Their politic logic,
     spending packages with dainty wrappings.
Their obscene wars' unreckoned rationales.
     And offer what I have—my flesh, my will.
Our tactic: to interpose our bodies
     between the drills and body of the bay.
To sit on platform scaffolding and not
     move—in a contest of waiting and wills.
But how soon the hours stretched to weeks,
     the weeks to years. I had not thought that men
could be so hard, had not thought that standoff
     meant standstill, the litigations, the suits
and countersuits, endless maneuvering.
     The wind makes rags of colored ribbons tied
on concertina wire, the shredded voices
     of supporters whose ardor came and went.
Reporters with earnest faces ask and nod,
     get their statement, byline in nick of time.

But, mostly, we hang our bones on these gallows
       and watch the sea. The sun comes up, the same
goes down, the sloshed rocks break with winking lights,
       the day's wages. The watch is never done.
I will my flesh to the seafloor and grass,
       green-gold meadows where dugong tamely graze.

Robin Gow

Draft

A gun in the mail. A gun on a doorstep.

Give birth to more triggers.

Sixteen-year-old grandfathers. Life story.

Boys on boats. Great great great war.

Sleeping in army green. Tropical winter.

Brother on the moon. A flag to pierce the Earth's crust.

Ration dreams. Check radar.

Count the German words you know.

Write letters to machines.

Eat with your fingers and fly a kite.

Remember the rec room. The TV glow.

Telegram in the bloodstream.

A future will be fenced in. Your babies

are already in the works. A war is never waged

for mastery. Family's house turned to rust.

The gun, fused to your fingers,

you often point at targets

no one else can see. Your brother

is a ghost fisherman. He shoots

everyone directly between the eyes.

He thins so that he can sleep

between your bottom two ribs.

Jacob Griffin Hall

Buzzards

Before the war we knew the war
would last forever. We'd all go
to God or buzzards by the end.
Up late, we played with figurines
and *Southern Living* magazines,
made bunkers from the pages, taped
the plastic guns to plastic hands.
The news was full of desert wind.
We lined our soldiers up in rows
and slowly executed them—
their bodies falling from the couch,
revived and raised to die again.
We knew if we could keep awake
all night, the war would never end.

Noley Reid

The Mud Pit

It was the summer a flash storm flooded our back alley and all us kids got out our Big Wheels and skidded through the raging current that washed us down our alleyway and out the other end. Into the street if we were lucky, and if we weren't lucky enough to pedal and steer out in time, down into the muddy gulch fifteen feet wide and twenty feet deep on the other side of the road. Someone's dad had tied a rope around a nearby tree trunk there for the purpose of climbing out, years before we all were born. No one knew if it would work in a torrential downpour. Until that day. And then we did. Some of us did.

This was in Mineola, Texas, where our street shared an inclined alley that, during any normal rainstorm, made a perfect Big Wheels rain regatta for the eighteen elementary school kids on our block. But on the day of the flash flood, the oldest and coolest among us, Booth Russell, was on his Green Machine, the first to go screaming down through the new and dangerous course. He zoomed down the alley, hydroplaning left and right, then spun out spectacularly into the road and was washed over the curb and into the gulch in one swift kick of a wave.

The kids still waiting to go, standing at the top of the alley, could only see him disappear. Three of us stood next to the mudhole in our colored plastic ponchos like slick Tic Tacs, watching Booth pant and pick up his Green Machine out of the foot of muddy water and try to throw it all the way up to us.

"You OK?" said Corrine Butcher, the rain pounding so hard on her back it sounded like a doctor doing percussion to listen for pneumonia.

Booth didn't hear or chose not to answer. The Green Machine was an extra-long Big Wheel and made for an extremely unwieldy item to hoist so high overhead. Plus, he was twenty feet below ground. But he tried. Again and again, he tried, grunting each time he heaved it. It fell back down on him every time, growing heavier with muddy water in the wheels and seat. And each time, I remember thinking he would start yelling like my mom in the kitchen when something burned or I left a sticky drink ring off a coaster. But he was quiet.

"Just leave it," I called to him. "Just leave it!"

Booth looked up at me or maybe just into the hot rain blowing. He opened his mouth but remained silent.

"Is he drinking the rain?" said Corrine, pushing matted brown hair back up inside the hood of her blue poncho—the blue so pretty, it matched her eyes. I slipped my wet hand in hers. We were best friends.

"He's thinking," said Jeb Gordy.

Booth went to the rope then. He put a hand on the first knot, his other hand on the second knot, and began to pull himself up, all the way to the top of the gulch like that, slipping just a couple of times but catching himself so the only real damage was the blisters on his hands and the mud covering him from neck to toe. As well as the fact that his Green Machine was now lost forever at the bottom of the mud pit, quickly filling with water.

Nobody spoke. We just looked at him—the rain was washing fresh blood from his knees and shin—us waiting to see, was it worth it? Was he sorry?

"Holy shit." Booth didn't blink for a whole minute, even with the rain pounding at him.

Corrine and I looked at each other. She giggled, so I did, too.

Jeb Gordy said, "Oh, man!"

The four of us walked back up the alley: three of us dragging our Big Wheels, one of us back from war, triumphant. All the other kids looked up to Booth already. He never said much, but whatever he did, you could trust. He had a big dog who walked around the neighborhood with him at his side, no leash at all, that was just her deal; Kizzy wouldn't leave his side for anything. Booth was nine and would be in fourth grade in the fall, so older than the rest of us and with no younger siblings to take care of or have to be nice to, he could take us or leave us whenever he wanted. When he told them the following, the kids listened:

"Are you ready to lose your Big Wheels?"

They looked at one another, at me, at their Big Wheels.

"I just had the coolest ride ever," said Booth. "It's gonna be worth it."

"I don't want to lose my Big Wheel!" cried Abigail Fish, who was only four. She ran to her big sister Wendy, who told her to go home if she was going to be a baby, so she went back to her Big Wheel.

Booth went on, making his voice big to be heard through the rain. "So, here's what you're gonna do: You're gonna pedal all out, fast as you can, down the alley, into the street, then the cross-current will spin you so fast it won't even matter if you try to brake; you can't stop even if you try. You'll get thrown into that gulch so fast you won't know what hit you. We'll need someone down there to signal up here when it's safe for the next person to go—you know, once the last one's climbed out of the mud pit. There's a rope to climb out. Did I say that? Yeah, there's a rope. It's easy—just watch out for your hands. Ouch!" He held up his palms.

The kids made a hushed *ooh*, though there was little to see through that rain.

I nudged Booth. "Tell them that's where they'll lose their Big Wheel. I don't think they get it."

"Yeah, so that's where your Big Wheel will stay, I guess, forever."

"In the mud pit," I said really loud.

The little ones said, "Oh," and "Huh?" and "No."

"Kayla's right. But you don't have to do this," Booth said. "It's just the coolest ride and will probably never be possible ever again after today."

"I don't want to do it," said Clark Wills.

"Hey, man. No biggie," said Booth. He had this way of talking like a grown man.

"Me, either."

"Me, neither."

"I wanna do it," said Darcie Lynn.

"Cool," said Booth. "You'll love it."

"Me, too," said Arthur Beckwith.

"Yeah," said Booth.

"Me, too."

"Me, too."

"Me, too."

"Me, too."

And then it was everyone. Even Clark Wills and all the other naysayers.

Without Booth's Green Machine, the task of demonstration fell to me and my Big Wheel. And just like Booth said, I pedaled madly, sloshing down our alley, worrying maybe the rain had let up, that there wouldn't be enough to get me across the road. But just then, I hit the cross-current of the street and spun out into it. My stomach flipped sideways, and I thought I might throw up but in a good way. Up over the curb I went, in a wave that picked me up and washed me down fast with a slam into the mud pit. My innards felt stirred around and my bones felt like they'd been jumbled up then rammed back in all the wrong places. The water was now about up to my waist. I got to my feet and tried throwing my Big Wheel out of the pit a couple of times then gave up. The pit was too deep, the trike too heavy with water and mud filling the hollow wheels and seat, and the last time it landed on Booth's Green Machine, the handlebars locked with his steering sticks. I found the rope, now blending well into the wall of mud, and started climbing. Once out, I waved my arms at the top of the alley, so they sent someone else down.

On and on it went like this, until the pit was so full of water and Big Wheels that we saw Corrine fly into the pit but didn't see her blue ponchoed head bob back up. We yelled for her, but with the rain, who even knew if she heard us.

I would like to tell you I jumped in, swam through all the Big Wheels to find the person, the girl, the human being, my very best friend, and that she'd only been momentarily stunned beneath the surface of all that molded plastic. That I scooped up her head and brought it to the surface and patted her back enough to clear her airway and she breathed then climbed the mud-slimed rope to the surface and we sat huddled there a while, reclaiming our strength but more alive than ever we were.

I would like to tell you that.

What I have to tell you is that we yelled for Corrine and yelled for her, and I felt sick to my stomach and hoarse, knowing I needed to jump in. Seeing how deep the water was now, I thought of snakes and even alligators because the water was pitch black. I crept slowly down the rope, inching, inching precious time away. When I reached the water, I felt for her with arms stretched out across the surface of the water as if playing Marco Polo at the Y. Finally, I had to put a hand below the surface, and she was there, right in front of me. Fingers, an elbow. Her head. Her mouth wide open. I screamed because I knew.

She was dead.

By now, there were more kids at the top of the pit. Dozens of shiny eyeballs peering down at me. I pulled Corrine up onto a stack of Big Wheels in the water to lift her to the surface, but then it shifted and she went back under. I had to touch her again. Her shoulder. I dragged her back up again, and again I floated her on top of another stack of Big Wheels. I held her in place by the billowed blue poncho. "Someone, go get Booth!" I screamed up into the rain. The eyeballs only blinked.

What could he do, anyway? She was bigger, heavier, more unwieldy than a Big Wheel.

I climbed out.

Some put their arms around me. Some stood back.

Someone said, "We shouldn't have done this. I knew it was a bad idea."

"It's Booth's fault."

"I want my Big Wheel back."

"Me, too."

"Me, too."

I walked up the alley now, feeling each pelting raindrop and the hot wind. Back up to the starting line, where Booth had been waiting with all the kids before sending them on their way down the alley. "Booth," I said when I looked up and he smiled at me. "I need you."

His knees and shin were badly scraped and bloody, and the blood had dripped into his right sock and shoe. Though the rain had cleaned his body of the mud by now, his clothing and shoes were still streaked with it, too. He told the three kids remaining to wait there, then said to me, "Come on." We ducked next door to his house, where there was a deck overhanging the garage to shelter us. He rubbed at his forearm. "Dang," he said. "Now with a break from it, I can feel just how much that rain stings."

My teeth began to chatter.

"Hold on." He went inside his house. I looked down the alley at the pit. All those kids had left by now. I looked across the alleyway to the Butchers' house. Their living room light and the kitchen light were on. I wondered what Corrine would have had for supper that night. Her favorite was tacos and strawberry shortcake.

Booth was back. "Here," he said, pushing a Kilgore College sweatshirt at me.

I took off my poncho and pulled the sweatshirt over my head. "Why did you give me this?"

"You're cold, right?"

I shook my head. It was probably in the mid 80s.

"Your teeth?"

"Oh," I said, holding my clattering jaw still. "Didn't anyone run up here and tell you—Corrine?"

He just looked at me.

"In the mud pit," I said.

"Can't she climb out?"

"I think she's dead."

"She's not dead."

"She is."

"She's not," he said, and I don't know why or how but I believed him for a minute and so I shut my eyes and realized my heart had been hurt and who knew if it could go on beating much longer like that, but now I was sure it would be OK again. Until he said, "What happened?"

And I saw it all unfold before me one more time: Corrine on her Big Wheel, Corrine spinning out in the street, Corrine flying through the air, Corrine falling into the mud pit, Corrine never coming up for air. Corrine, Corrine, Corrine.

So, I told him every bit of it, from the snakes and alligators to feeling my way to finding her open mouth in the muddy water and climbing back out without her. Booth looked at me, then he leaned his head to mine so our wet foreheads touched, and we stood like this, forehead to forehead, eyes closed, all the while I saw stars inside my eyelids, me saying one word to him: *Corrine.*

When our eyes opened and our heads came apart, we were two people again. Booth said, "It will be OK." Then he went inside, where Kizzy tried to lick his bloody shin and knees, but he pushed her away and quickly ran right upstairs to tell his parents, tracking so much wet mud up the carpeted stairs.

I didn't want to go home. I went back to the mud pit and called out to Corrine. Then I just sat with her in the rain and let it bruise my back and head. Made a pact with the snakes that they could come for me, I deserved it. The gators, too.

By evening, someone had told someone else who told someone else who told Corrine's parents and they told mine and they all came to the mud pit with police and a rescue crew to remove Corrine from the gulch.

Her parents wept. My parents cried. I cried. Booth and Kizzy came and watched and other parents came and some cried and others shook their heads or their children.

All these years later, mud still stains Booth's stairs and he and I are together, which my parents hate because he dropped out of high school and hasn't even gotten his GED, and I'm on my way to nowhere if I marry him, they say. And probably they're right, because I'm twelve days late and he waits tables at Gordo's, coming home stinking of taco chips and sloshed margaritas.

Mrs. Butcher moved away about eight years ago. Mr. Butcher still lives across the alley. Booth and I still live next door to each other. We're saving our money, especially now, though I haven't told him about the baby. I haven't told anyone.

I work at the Brookshire's grocery and the library and I'm going to start studying online next fall to get a B.A. and then my master's in library science. I'll probably only take one or two classes a semester, so it's going to take twelve years, but I'll do it.

This afternoon, I'm reshelving books when I come upon Mr. Butcher in 155.937 Grief/Death. He looks up and his face looks just as stricken as it did at Corrine's funeral.

"Oh, I'm sorry," I say for interrupting him in a private moment.

He nods, his eyes retreating. He's unshaven, in wrinkled clothing, smelling stale and unclean.

"I really am so sorry."

"Of course," he says. He thumbs through the book in his hands.

"Mr. Butcher," I say, "she and I were friends, you know that." I touch his arm and he stops his riffling of the pages. "I'm pregnant," I say, and now I whisper, barely making any sound at all, "and I'm going to call the baby Corrine."

His eyes rise to mine for a moment then sink back down again. He leaves the book, turns, and goes.

Tonight, on my shift at Brookshire's, Booth stops in. I think to tell him about Mr. Butcher, but I don't want to say I'm pregnant over the conveyor belt checkout, so I wait. I ask my manager can I go pee again, and he thinks it's because Booth's here, but, seriously, I need to pee. Again. So, I tell Booth to go on home, and I go in the back and pee and make sure Mickey sees that Booth left. I do emergency pee runs two more times before my shift is over, buy a pee test on employee discount, then drive home, where my mother is waiting at the dinner table for me with a big box, despite it being past eleven.

"Kayla, come sit here with me," she says. She's been to the salon and has her weekly hairdo freshly poofed, a motorcycle helmet of strawberry-blond hair all standing equidistant around her head.

"Now?"

"What do you know about this box?" It's dusty and stained, real old. She turns it around so the front faces me. It reads: "CORRINE'S BABY CLOTHES."

My stomach tightens and I have to pee again.

"Mr. Butcher brought this by for you tonight."

I can't help it, I start to cry.

"What's going on, Kayla. Are you pregnant? You tell that awful man before you tell your mama?"

"*Awful?*"

"Don't turn this on me," she says. "He's been a drunk ever since his daughter's death and Norine left him. It's a wonder he hasn't killed someone, out driving like that."

I wipe my eyes. "Don't you feel any compassion for him?"

She pokes a long maroon fingernail up into the hair helmet to scratch her scalp. "Of course, I do. Or I did. There's only so long you can go on having a pity party for yourself, then you've got to get up and make something of your life."

"I killed his daughter," I say.

She removes her fingernail and lays both hands fanned out on the table, her many rings clacking against the lacquered wood. "Don't be melodramatic, Kayla. Are you pregnant?"

I swallow. "I'm not even sure."

"But you're late."

I nod.

"What are you going to do? How will you support it on your paychecks? And no insurance." She holds up her left hand, running the tips of the acrylic nails against her thumb, back and forth, up and down the row of them, over and over as she talks. "He said something idiotic about you naming the baby Corrine. You can't even know what sex the baby is right now, but even if it is a girl—you want to go and saddle her with a dead girl's name? That poor, poor child. You can't do that." Mom leaves the box and goes to bed.

I open one flap of the box and take out the first thing I see. It's a little yellow dress with squirrels sewn down at the hem. So small it almost fits in two cupped hands. I fold it gently and tuck it into my purse. I go next door.

Booth always leaves the downstairs door unlocked for me. His room is down here. I wait for my eyes to adjust to the darkness in here. Kizzy is white, so she glows from the foot of the bed. She lifts her snout but doesn't get up; she's old. Booth's asleep. I slip in behind him, underneath the covers, slide an arm between his arm and his stomach. I smell his hair, his ear, his stinky armpit and drink him all in, and I sleep like this until morning.

"Hey, there," says Booth, wiping drool off my face.

"Oooh, I got to pee!" I scramble so fast from the bed, Kizzy jumps up and follows me to the bathroom. "I'm sorry, girl," I say and shut the door in her face.

"You all right?" says Booth once I'm back.

I nod, knowing I'm about to say what I'm about to say and not knowing how to say it.

"You sure are smiley," he says. He kisses me on the nose.

"So," I say. "So …."

"Yes?"

I mush my lips around from one side then to the other side. I'm giddy with the hope of him loving me and this baby as much as I love it, her. "So."

"Yes?"

"So … I'm late."

"Late?" He looks at the digital clock by the bed. Then looks back at me. "Oh, late." He looks like someone who's just done math with the right formula. Someone who doesn't necessarily enjoy math but who has to take the class.

I nod. "Late."

"That's scary or, well, no—." He's looking at me and trying to see what I want from him. "I mean, what do you want to do?"

"I love you, Booth. Don't you love me?"

"You know I do."

I exhale hard. "Can't you just say it?"

"I love you, Kayla. You know I do."

"Right, but saying it and saying 'You know I do' are two different things. They make a big difference. Anyway, if we're in love, we have the baby. How could you even think we wouldn't? How could you even think that?"

"Sorry."

Kizzy stands up in her spot on the bed, walks a circle then lies down again in the exact same spot. She grinds her teeth.

"We should take a pee test."

"OK."

I get the box from my purse, careful not to let him see the dress, and we go to the bathroom. I pee on the stick, we wait, two lines appear. It's official. I tell Booth about Mr. Butcher in Grief/Death. I tell him I think the baby is a girl, but I stop there.

We don't tell Booth's dad for a week. Not until we see my mom and dad on their way over to talk and have to stop them, swearing his dad isn't home and he's had a really hard time at work lately, so many people being audited.

"For tax returns he prepared?" asks my dad.

I nod.

"That's not good," says my mom. "I hope everything's all right, Booth."

Dad tries to be tough on us for Mom's sake. He rolls his shoulders back and stands up taller than usual, saying, "A baby is about the last thing y'all need to be giving him, sounds like."

"Dad!" I say.

"Well, you'll let us know when things lighten up a bit for your daddy, Booth, OK?" she says. "So we can talk arrangements. We will not have three generations under one roof, and I bet he feels the same."

"You're kicking me out?" I say, running my hand over my girl.

"We can help get you started somewhere, but then it's sink or swim," says Mom, clicking her long nails.

Dad touches her shoulder, like maybe he's saying *Go easy* or maybe he's saying *I'm with you.*

I have a lump in my throat.

"That would be very kind of you, Mr. and Mrs. Davis," says Booth. He places his hand on my shoulder. "Kayla and I would really appreciate whatever help you can give us."

We go next door to his room, and I try to swallow, but all I can do is try to keep from crying. And it doesn't work. He puts his arm around me now. He looks at me and tells me it will be all right, and what comes out through all my tears is, "We're going to name her Corrine."

"Wait, what?" he says, pulling down his arm to his side. "That's not funny."

"I told Mr. Butcher I would name—"

"You don't get to decide that." He moves from the bed to sit on the floor, and Kizzy noses into his lap. He pets her face until she lies down all stiff-legged beside him.

"I thought," I say, "I thought we were the same about her. I thought we both wanted her back. And this was a way to pay a debt to … I don't know, the universe—"

"We're not paying a debt with our kid! Are you crazy?"

Kizzy rolls up on her elbows.

"I just mean that we could honor Corrine this way."

"That's not at all what you said." Booth hugs his knees. "You know what you said is totally fucked up, right? I mean *totally* fucked up."

We don't say anything for a while. Kizzy falls asleep, her paws flicking in a dream.

"We were kids," says Booth. "But of all of us, I was the oldest. I should have known better. It was my idea." He's never said this before, and he won't look at me, just down at Kizzy.

"There's no way you could have foreseen it," I say. "And we were just kids. I'm the one who should have jumped in. I should have swum beneath the surface of the water, feeling for her. I should have tried CPR."

"You didn't know CPR."

"I should have tried to get her out."

"Right, you were going to fireman-carry her up the rope. Where were all the parents?" he says. "It was practically a hurricane. Why did they let us all play out back and down into the street with no supervision? We could have been run over."

"All those fucking Big Wheels," I say.

"I know, OK?" Still hugging his knees, Booth starts rocking now.

"She'd have been fine if she hadn't hit her head on those fucking Big Wheels."

"Just shut up," he says.

I give it a minute then go to him on the floor. "I'm sorry," I say. "It wasn't your fault. It wasn't." I kiss him and whisper, "We'll call her Corrine and bring her back."

Booth takes on double shifts at Gordo's to sock away money for the baby and for a place of our own. I keep on at the library and Brookshire's, adding hours at the latter when girls call in sick or Mickey gets corporate to approve extra checkout lanes. Booth and I see each other only in our sleep and groggy morning goodbyes. We don't talk about Corrine. We don't talk.

Two weeks pass like this. Booth's dad leaves us a card on the bed one night. I'm home before Booth, and there's no way I can stay awake until he gets here, so I slide the card out of its envelope. On it is a picture of a pregnant belly with two hands on it, a woman's and a man's. It says, "Congratulations!" Inside, Booth's dad has written, "This may not have been planned, but what a blessing this baby will be. I'm here for you always. Love, Granddaddy Ford." I set the card on the nightstand and curl up with Kizzy in the bed, my hands on my girl.

In the morning, I dress for my shift at the library. I come back in the bedroom to kiss Booth goodbye. I whisper in his ear, "Did you see the card?"

He groans and turns over. Kizzy lifts her head to me.

"Booth," I say. I squeeze his shoulder. "Honey, did you see your dad's card?"

His eyes flap open. "Card? Yeah."

"Wasn't it sweet?"

"Uh." He rolls over again, and Kizzy lowers her head back down and sighs.

"Maybe we don't have to leave here quite so fast. Maybe we can save a bit longer, until we can afford something nicer. For the baby, you know."

Booth doesn't answer.

I go to work.

This is our life for several more weeks. Now I'm eight weeks pregnant and call to schedule my first prenatal appointment. I work. Booth works. His dad wants to take us out to dinner to celebrate, but we don't have an evening off together unless we trade shifts, and Booth doesn't want to do that.

But this Sunday morning, we can sleep in, then walk Kizzy together. We start down the alley, Kizzy right in step with us, with Booth. He takes my hand. My other hand is on my girl. It's a pretty spring day, with crocus bulbs wide open and hyacinths just having sprung. The air is crisp for Mineola, high 60s. So many of the kids we used to play with have moved on to college or moved away years ago and been replaced with new kids out now, playing on swing sets in their yards with moms in the kitchen windows, watching. It's hard to believe we ever did what we did. Or had the freedom to do it.

I squeeze Booth's hand. "Let's not walk all the way down, OK?"

"We can turn back," he says. "Come on, Kiz."

She turns with us. But she coughs. Then she stumbles. And then she's on the ground.

"Kizzy!" Booth says, and he's on the ground with her, lifting her head, but it's lifeless and falls back to the pavement. He pushes on her chest hard, and air comes out through her lips, but none goes back in. He opens her mouth and looks inside. He runs his finger around the back of her throat. He pushes her chest again, over and over, and the air moves through her but not really into her. He sets his mouth to hers and blows his own air inside her, but she does not take it. Her eyes are open, but they're not looking.

I kneel beside Kizzy and Booth, watching him try to resurrect his dog and fail again and again. And, finally, I touch his arm. "I think she's gone," I say softly.

"She can't be," he says. "I've had her since … I've known myself."

"I'm so sorry, love."

He scoops her up, this big, white, beautiful dog, and carries her across his arms back to his house. Every few steps, her body makes grunting sounds, and he lays her down gently and checks her out all over again, but it must only be the way he's carrying her creating movement and compression like breathing, so he scoops her back up again and continues. When we finally reach his house, he lays her down beneath a tall burr oak in the backyard, sets his ear against her heart, and tries chest compressions again. But there is no sound from her. No hope. He gets a shovel. I go for his dad, who comes with another shovel. They work without a word, just digging and wiping the sweat from their temples and brows. When the hole is four feet down and three feet long by two feet wide, Booth takes off her collar, and they lower her down gently, curled as if sleeping. Then they start filling the hole.

Booth calls in sick to Gordo's, so I call Brookshire's, too. He showers then collapses into bed, holding Kizzy's collar. He rolls towards the wall, so I sit beside him, my hand on his back. I can feel him crying.

"At least she didn't suffer," I say, feeling stupid for saying anything.

He nods.

I lie down next to him and fall asleep with him, but when I wake up needing to pee, I do it and then take my purse and drive to the mall in Tyler.

I go to Pea in the Pod and look at all the maternity clothes I'm about to be needing. I know I shouldn't, but I take one of their Velcro bellies and a couple of dresses in a fitting room and try them on to see how I'll look in six months. I fasten the belly's strap around my back and slip the first dress over my head. It's big flowers everywhere, so I look like a sofa, but I love it. I can't wait 'til my girl is this big, 'til she's here in this world, in my arms. My Corrine. I run my hands over the dummy belly, which feels strange because it isn't real, but it's sitting on top of my girl, so it presses on her when I press on it. I try on the other dress, an aqua fit-and-flare with small daisies all over it. I decide to get this one. I just need this in my closet. So, I get it and go home.

Booth is still in bed when I get back, but he's awake. I go in the bathroom and change into the dress. I ball up my shirt and jeans to make a belly and come out to show him.

"Like it?" I say.

He looks up from his pillow. "That's weird."

I try to smooth the lumps out of the belly. "It's how I'll look at six or seven months."

"OK. It's pretty."

"Thanks." I drop the clothes from the belly. "It was on sale," I lie. I unzip the dress and pull it over my head.

"When do you start to show?" He sits up in bed, rubbing at his red eyes.

"Should be any day now." I pull up my jeans and zip and button them.

"I guess you're lucky you can still wear all your clothes, huh?"

I grab my shirt and pull it on, too. "Yeah, I guess."

"Thanks for the show," he says.

I give a little bow and lean in and hug him. "How are you doing?"

"It'll sound ridiculous, but it's worse than when my mom left." He wipes at his eyes again to keep from crying.

"Oh, love. I'm so sorry. She was the best dog ever."

He nods. "She was." His voice cracks. "There can never be another dog like her. She knew exactly what I was thinking every second of the day—whatever I needed, she gave it. She was perfect in every way. Not just the no-leash thing, though that was cool, and you know I never trained her for that; she just did it on her own."

"I know."

"And if I was sad, she got goofy. If I was angry, she calmed me down. If I had a hard day, she relaxed me. If you and I fought, she'd lie on top of me. Whatever it was, she was there to fix me. How am I ever going to find another dog like that?"

"You will, if you want to. And if you don't, I can be goofy when you're sad and help relax you when you've had a hard day and all that."

"You can't be my safe haven from you," he says and pokes my nose.

"Um, OK."

"You know what I mean."

"Yeah, I do. I'm so sorry she's gone."

He wipes his eyes again and his nose. Booth takes a deep breath and lets it out. "OK, so when's your prenatal tomorrow?"

"At 8:15. You're still coming, right?"

"Of course."

Without feeding and walking Kizzy, Booth's morning routine has him sitting at the table over his empty bowl of granola, drumming his fingers long before I'm ready to go. But once we're in the car, he's less agitated. The doctor's waiting room is packed with pregnant women of all ages and all trimesters. I imagine myself as each one of them, with each of their baby bumps and popped-out bellybuttons. We wait forty minutes before the nurse calls us back. She has me first step on a scale then go in a bathroom and give a pee sample. Then Booth and I go with her into an exam room, where she takes my blood pressure and goes over my medical history and form of birth control. She asks the date of my last period and the age of my first. Then she asks me to undress and put on a gown with the opening to the front; she leaves, and I do so. Now, we wait again.

"Do you think she'll think it's weird I'm sitting where I can see right up into you?" says Booth.

"She'd probably think it was weirder if you didn't."

The doctor comes in, and she's short and cute as can be, with long brown hair, a round face, and rainbow-striped socks with her blue scrubs. "I'm Dr. Zelly," she says, pulling out the stirrups for the table and placing each of my feet in them. She runs through an initial exam: listening to my breathing, palpating my breasts, and doing a pelvic and cervical exam. "Are you experiencing any cramping?"

"No," I say.

She swabs my cervix, snaps the end of the swab into the specimen vial, and screws the jar shut.

"Any spotting or bleeding?"

"No."

The nurse comes back into the room with a big machine. Booth pulls his feet up out of the way.

"We're going to ultrasound." Dr. Zelly pulls the machine around to the other side of the table. She types into the machine then takes the wand out of its holster, squirts lube on it, and slides it into me. "Some pressure," she says. "Sorry, it's cold."

"It's OK," I say.

She's looking at the screen, her eyes sort of squinting.

I look at Booth, but he's looking at Dr. Zelly and the screen. She's moving the wand all around inside me to find things, then she stops the ultrasound picture and moves a cursor ball around on the machine to measure points across it. White zigs and zags arc the screen.

She does this all over me inside until she says, "I'm sorry, guys. We should be hearing a heartbeat if you were pregnant. There's no gestational sac."

"What?" I say, but I may not have made any sound.

"It's what we call a chemical pregnancy. When the embryo doesn't implant or grow."

"So, she's not pregnant," says Booth, leaning forward like to see the words on the screen.

"No, there's no pregnancy," says Dr. Zelly, looking at him then at me. "I'm sorry."

"Did I do something? To miscarry?" I ask.

"No," she says, "you didn't do anything to cause this. An embryo that never implants is just cells sloughing off, not a fetus."

"Why haven't I gotten my period?"

"There are all sorts of reasons that we can definitely pursue—being on birth control can sometimes cause …"

I look at the ceiling, which has posters of fat, happy babies in daisy fields with puppies, breastfeeding, and sleeping in a mother's arms.

"… even stops entirely for a while. There's also stress as a culprit. Thyroid issues. Low body …"

I look to the right wall, where there is a photograph of Dr. Zelly in surgical scrubs, holding triplets.

"… start with some blood panels and go from there. It's probably the pill and you're perfectly healthy and your period will return on its own, but we should check all the boxes we can to be sure."

She turns to Booth and back to me, but who I am, where I am, I don't know.

"You two should use condoms so you can get off the pill and give your body a break from the hormones, see if that solves the problem. Sound like a plan?"

My teeth start to quietly chatter.

She fills out the form I'm to take to the checkout window, then goes. The nurse cleans the ultrasound machine and wheels it out. I wipe away the lube and dress.

Booth is looking at me, but I don't look at him. I grab my purse and he stands. But he grabs my arm. "Wait," he says. He holds me now. Forehead to forehead, but I can't hear him think her name. When he's done, I walk out the door, feeling untethered—not quite floating, not quite weighted, just somewhere unknown in between.

At the checkout, I decline the tests and a follow-up appointment.

I drive Booth to Gordo's, unsure how we got here once we arrive.

"Let me call in again," he says.

"It's fine," I say. "You just did for Kizzy. We need the money, and, besides, I have to work, too."

"You're sure."

I give him a smile.

"I know that's not real." Still, he gets out of the car. "Just call if you change your mind. That's all you have to do. And I'm there." He leans back into the car and kisses me. "I love you," he says. "I love you."

I drive. But I don't go to my shift at the library. I go to his house. I park out front, and then I just walk along the street side of our houses, down to the cross street, down to the mud pit. Where I sit at the edge and I wait. I put my hand on my stomach, and, at first, I think I feel her. But I know how stupid that is.

I look over the edge of the hole. "Corrine," I say, "I've never had a best friend since you. Except for Booth, but that's different. And he had Kizzy." I think of us braiding each other's hair after school. Of us swapping sandwiches at lunch, peanut butter and jelly for salami and Swiss. Of us catching fireflies in pickle jars with nail holes hammered into the lids. "I've never even truly had a friend besides you and Booth." I'd thought maybe, just maybe, my girl could be that friend.

I think of the rain stinging our backs, our arms, our heads. All of us in our colored, plastic ponchos. The whooshing cross-current sending her up and over the curb and down into the pit so full of all our Big Wheels. The water so deep and black with mud. Corrine underwater, not coming up. Corrine lost. Corrine dead. Corrine gone forever and me too scared to help her in time.

I'm sobbing now, but it's self-indulgent and so I wipe my eyes, my nose. I swallow all this hurt up inside me again. My own Corrine, too. My own Corrine. I get my breathing back under control, and I go walking up the alleyway but not to my house or Booth's. I go to Mr. Butcher's house. I knock on his back door. He opens it and stands there with both hands, palms up, a man who doesn't know what to do with himself.

"She's gone," I say, crying again, my face wet and nose dripping. "She's gone and I'll never get her back."

Mr. Butcher's stubbly face crumples. He turns and leaves me here in his living room. I stand in the doorway a moment, ashamed to have been so thoughtless. I wipe my eyes, my nose, but the tears keep coming. I step inside and shut the door. There are dirty dishes on nearly every surface, old food grown fuzzy with mold. I take the plates to the kitchen. I scrape the food into the trash and leave the plates to soak. Years of dust coat all the surfaces in the living room, including Corrine's first-, second-, and third-grade pictures on the stone wall. Her in a green dress and pigtails. Her with French braids and a silly grin. Her in a light-blue top with colorful embroidered flowers, her hair cut short and pushed back in a white, plastic headband.

I check his refrigerator. There isn't much, but I thaw some ground beef in the microwave, brown it, and put together a lasagna. Once I get it into the oven, I wash and dry the dishes. Then I go looking for Corrine's dad.

"Mr. Butcher?" I call out, my voice quivering.

He doesn't answer.

I go upstairs, find him in Corrine's room, which is perfectly clean and just as it was when I used to come over to play and spend the night. He's sitting on the bed, his hands, palms up, on his thighs.

I stand in the doorway.

"At some point the world wants it to stop hurting." He shakes his head. "It never will. Not 'til the day we die."

I take a deep breath so I can make it out of here in one piece.

"Kayla," he says.

I'm backing out of the room. I'm running down the hall.

"Kayla!" He's coming after me. "Kayla, stop, please."

I stop on the stairs, my back to him.

"I meant that to be of comfort," he says.

"I made you a lasagna."

"Nobody's ever cooked for me—not since Norine left. Thank you."

I turn around and see his blue eyes are the color of Corrine's Texas-sky blue. I'd never noticed that before, and I suddenly realize I've been picturing my Corrine with eyes that same shade, and it's another little death again that those eyes are gone from my future now, too.

"What was she like that day?" he says.

I shut my eyes. Shake my head. "I hardly remember anymore," I say. "We were so young." I start down the stairs again.

He follows me down but lingers at the foot of the stairs.

"Was she nervous to do what y'all were doing?" His voice goes low and tight. "Was she afraid?"

"She was beautiful," I say. "She was fearless."

"Oh, God." He takes in a sharp breath and holds a fist to his mouth.

I go to the kitchen. "What would you like to drink?" I call. There's no alcohol anywhere in this house, no matter what my mother says. He doesn't answer, so I fill a glass of water. "Go sit," I call and take him a square of lasagna and a glass of water. Mr. Butcher stands wet-faced, fussing at the family table with the many piles of mail and paper that cover it. He lifts a few pages of one pile then sets them back down only to lift a few pages of the next pile and so on and so on, never moving any of the piles out of the way.

"Can we temporarily relocate one or two of these so you can eat here, Mr. Butcher? How about I just set this one on the floor here, and then we can set it back up here when you're all done?"

He nods, so I move two piles, and he sits.

"Aren't you having any?" he says. "Please, Kayla, share this with me."

"No, I made this for you to have leftovers."

"It's no good eating alone. Please." He picks up a pile at the next chair and places it on the carpet out of the way, too. "Besides, you're eating for two now."

I look away. "Right, OK."

I get a small piece, and we're quiet eating. When we're done, I take our plates and his glass to the kitchen and wash them.

"Have you looked through the box yet?" he calls out to me. "I don't remember Corinne's baby clothes much. It will be nice seeing them again on your Corrine."

I slip out the back door.

Out into the alleyway, where I stand stock-still, waiting to know which way to go—to my home, to Booth's, to the library's 155.937, to the mud pit. Or do I just go out to the front of our street, to my car, and leave all this behind me, heading out to a world where I might find a friend or a love without mud climbing inside. I slip my hand down into my purse, feeling around for my car keys, but what I come back with is the little yellow dress instead. Just barely big enough for two hands, the sight and feel of it makes clear to my heart.

I take out my phone and I call him, say for just the second time in our lives, "Booth, I need you."

Roseanna Alice Boswell

I Don't Know How to Tell My Father
He Didn't Prepare Me for the Real World

once a man watched me   from his truck

         I felt the translucent fish meat of me

    the tenterhooked bones

         on ligaments

            under skin

the way the pavement undressed my kneecap

        a blood-red blossoming   I hate

how clumsy   my body is when it feels afraid

      how could I possibly fight   or flee

on these legs   these watered thighs   my trick knee

     is the only thing I inherited   from my father

this unruly joint   never staying

     where it should   saved him from the draft

    but only made me fall

it never stopped him from finding a war

      I know what it means to let go of

   what holds you together   & abandon balance

Caleigh Shaw

Primitive Baptist Rules

Church means the month's first weekend,
    Saturday for business, Sunday for regular sermon,
        rules learned slowly, elder men and women on opposite sides,
            they are the old way, close my eyes to pray, follow along
      the hymn book, standing means something special,
  wait until service is over to visit the outhouse, must be quiet,
not even a whisper, don't cough too much, only play
    when they cry, the pew becomes my table, can't wear
      pants, not even a skort, cooperate with my brother,
        play tic-tac-toe and thumb wars, maybe rock-paper-scissors,
    don't kick the gravel, don't ask for the car keys,
  must talk to family after, talk about the school year,
we're always on the hamster wheel, don't go outside
    and fly among the lightning bugs, don't fan fast
      or the fan will wobble, rip from its post, sit up straight,
        can't show my shoulders or thighs, I'm old enough
    to pay attention, cannot play with my cousins anymore,
  must watch the moaning, the wailing, the snot, the spit,
the shaking, must babysit my brother, the saved
    are the only ones dipped in the river, don't live
      with a boyfriend before marriage or they'll threaten
        your status, they'll talk behind my mother's back,
      divorce makes you a leper, a woman who never loves again,
  even learns to fear to show her love, my mother
the only adult left not standing, don't cough too much,
    pray with the ones attempting salvation, and I decided
      to resist and manifest. Give up, please give up it's been

four hours and god ain't calling. I refused to wear hose,
    screamed at my mother I will not go, I followed
the wasps' threats as they flew across the pulpit, my early
routine was to take a nap in my mother's lap
    once the sermon starts, fanned as fast as I could, built my anger,
        imagined, hoped my cousins hated it, too, when I opened
            my eyes during prayer I found my brother the only one
        staring back at me. I couldn't believe in this anger and fear of god
    and sin, and my mother started her own revolution,
that singing was for everyone, to treat our cousins
    with kindness, to where she began to stand
        without the holy river.

Letitia Trent

My god is the episode of I Survived

where a woman recounts
her first date with a man later
shot in the head, a random
act of violence committed
by strangers in a pickup truck
but first, he takes her out
to the woods with
his camera: they're going
to photograph the full moon
she smiles as she recalls
those moments just before
the white truck pulls up, the smile
a groove in the record of this
moment she has played again
over and over (later, she says
she wishes she'd stayed
with his body instead of running
to the road, her side blown
open by hollow-point
bullets, she wished she'd stayed
by his body so he wouldn't
have been so alone)
she still remembers
that camera, that surprise
just for her, he was going

My god is the episode of I Survived

to teach her how to close
the aperture enough
to let that small nickel
of light in, though in person it
had seemed enormous,
the moon lighting up everything
around it, he explained it simply
wasn't enough light
to be captured, for complete
potential the eye
needs to be fully opened,
saying she wanted her freedom more than safety.

Gary Fincke

Missing

Had the boy, such a smart five-year-old, not unlocked a door and
walked away.
Had his mother not been bedridden by fever in their three upstairs,
rented rooms.
Had the boy, for half an hour, not bounced a rubber ball off a vacant
building.
Had his aunt not arrived to nurse her sister and noticed, at once, his
absence.
Had the boy, by this time, not been thirsty.
Had his mother not begun to cry.
Had the boy not asked for a free paper cup of ice water at the nearby
store.
Had the man who sold ice cream not refused, shouting, from behind
a showcase, "Buy something or leave."
Had the boy's mother not said, "Where on Earth could he have gone
to?"
Had he not meandered three blocks to the A&P to drink from its
ice-cold fountain.
Had his aunt not walked fruitlessly to each room's windows.
Had a creek and railroad tracks not been across the street from the
grocery.
Had the boy not followed them past the mill and picked his way to
the river.
Had his aunt, after an hour, not called the police.
Had she not been told to "give the boy longer to show up."
Had the boy, for fifteen minutes, not tossed stones into the reeking
water.
Had the boy's mother not read him his father's letters from Vietnam.

Missing

Had another boy, a year before, not drowned in that river.
Had the boy not retraced his steps from railroad tie to railroad tie.
Had those letters not taught the boy loneliness.
Had another boy, a month before, not fallen under a train.
Had those letters from Vietnam not stopped.
Had another boy, the week before, not been abducted and killed.
Had his mother not feared for the boy's life.
Had the boy not imagined being missing in action like his father.
Had his aunt not sat sentry for news.
Had a man not waved and asked the boy where he lived.
Had the boy, eager to be admired, not repeated his address perfectly.
Had the man not walked beside him along the tracks that led back to
   the three rooms.
Had the tracks not closely paralleled the creek and its flourish of
   undergrowth.
Had the creek not dipped into a narrow, shrouded valley.
Had his mother not listened, with diminishing hope, for a door to
   open.
Had a man not been fishing in the shadows.
Had she not imagined a future of bloodhounds.
Had the fisherman not decided what he saw was not a father and son.
Had he not called and scrambled up the weed-choked bank.
Had the friendly man not run.
Had the fisherman not held the boy's hand until the boy turned left
   into an alley.
Had the boy's aunt, waiting for "longer" to expire, not kept sitting
   sentry at the top of the stairs.
Had the alley not led to the house with three upstairs rented rooms.
Had there not been a bell that rang when the boy passed through like
   a customer.
Had his aunt not cursed, mistaking the stranger for a man with
   second thoughts.
Had that man not said he was a father, too, of three who were small.
Had the boy's mother not appeared, swaying beside his aunt.
Had she not caught her balance.
Had she not beckoned the boy, suggesting he choose between pizza
   and hot dogs.
Had she not embraced him, offering a cup of ice-cold water
Had she not kissed his cheeks, praising him with a promise of ice
   cream in a showcase of flavors.

Carolee Bennett

Why Having an Alter Ego Increases Your Chances of Fame, Fortune, and Really Good Sex

Rules for you: When they're ready for you, they'll call. Keep arms and legs inside. Prepare reasons you "couldn't possibly." On a scale of 1 to 10, your pain is never a 10. Take everything in stride and claim you're better for it. Get good at organizing pantries and baking scones. Whenever possible, google what's wrong, its symptoms and all invasive procedures that will be required. You must love juice cleanses and step goals. Type "Chronicle of Punishments" at the top of the page. Never get beyond a list of ways your mother's death fucked you up. Recognize *wife* as another word for *convenient* and *husband* as synonym for *the fix is in*. Romanticize everything until it's time to find parking. Grab your lunch pail. Get back to work.

Rules for your alter ego: There's only one route, and it's scenic. Love handles are sexy. Good plates are for everyday use, and there's joy in being on a first-name basis with your budtender. Go with your gut. Buy the merch. Keep a suitcase packed. It's nobody's business why you display the tumor in a jar between the homemade pickles and tomato jam. The answer to *How have you been lately* is *I ruined my favorite blue dress having a quickie beneath the sugar maple*. Practice throwing axes and hating holidays. When you pass dusty windows, give in to the urge to tease a cock out of the dirty film and tickle the balls with your finger. Anything that follows *You should* is bullshit. Want what you want. Tell him. Start with the toes.

Cathy Ulrich

There's a Joke About a Horse

Before your best friend joined a cult, she used to tell this joke about a horse walking into a bar.

For a while after (and she'd left her first husband by then[1], and her second husband, too, and her two children were living with her mother and father in that house with the same hardwood floors you remembered sliding on in stocking feet in your childhood, a little girl and a little boy with faces more like the husbands' than your friend's, and maybe that was why it was so easy for her to leave them, maybe she thought when she was putting her thirteen pairs of underwear into that raggedy suitcase, when she was taking all her savings from the bank in handfuls of twenties[2], *There is nothing left of me here at all*), you would get messages from her, little sparkles popping briefly onto your phone.

Today, the sky is blue!

The birds are singing!

You would think, *Yes, today the sky is blue; yes the birds are singing*, sometimes you would reply *I miss you*, sometimes you would say *Your kids miss you*, sometimes you would say *A horse walks into a bar, and the bartender asks what he'd like. The horse doesn't reply because it's a horse and obviously can't speak or understand English*, wait days and days for a response.

---

1 You were maid of honor at that first wedding, a salmon-pink dress still hanging in your closet; the best man's toast said he's a better man with her, your best friend's smile all tooth and shine.

2 The teller said she said *please* and *thank you*, the teller said she took the rubber bands off the money and laid them on the counter, she scooped some popcorn from the self-serve machine into a bag, she carried it out the door with her. The teller said *She looked happy*, the teller said *She looked joyous*.

And after that, there was nothing; you thought maybe it was something you did, maybe you pushed too hard, maybe you didn't push hard enough, maybe there was something about the photos you sent that made her hate the life she'd left behind; there was silence, silence and the empty cursed face of your phone. Silence until her parents telephone and say *It's on the news* and there are bodies being pulled out of a square concrete building, they show that sort of thing nowadays, bodies in stacks and piles; you see their curved little feet and their stiff arms[3] and you clasp your phone and you close your eyes and you think *A horse walks into a bar.*[4]

---

3 You don't know which body is hers, if any of them are really, but it doesn't matter. They are all her; they are all the things she has left behind; they are all waving goodbye from her window, all saying *today, the sky is blue.*

4 And several people get up and leave, sensing the danger in having a live animal in a bar.

Melissa Moorer

The Feral Dogs of Brooklyn

The feral dogs of Brooklyn dragged a baby out of the carriage and into the brownfields. The mother had only looked away for a second. The feral dogs of Brooklyn killed a homeless man sleeping in an abandoned Gowanus warehouse. They left nothing but his shoes. The feral dogs of Brooklyn are just urban legend. The feral dogs of Brooklyn are realer than the Empire State Building.

I'd heard the yip before late at night and I'd dismissed it the way you do in New York when you know it's nothing to do with you (you hope), but some part of me recognized it. The way anyone raised near the woods, in rural places, felt the sound of crickets, tree frogs, and maybe even the rusty-hinge call of a red-winged blackbird before it made its way into consciousness, before brains could put a label on it and file it away: threat or non-threat. Men were a threat in Brooklyn, animals not so much. People who'd lived in New York for years felt the danger before it was on them. Usually. Human dangers.

Tonight, the yip made my thoughts bounce between categories of threat and background noise. My dog, Zoe, whined low, her tail dropping as we crossed away from the deserted parking lot under the subway bridge to the brownfields with its sagging chain-link fence. Tall dead straw sprouted up from the bombed-out topography, a perfect blind for predators. Plastic bags caught what little wind there was, expanding and clenching like netted jellyfish, trapped by the chain link that seemed to go up and up almost to the concrete curve of the subway as it emerged from underground behind our block, arcing overhead, threatening to collapse on the deserted playground at the corner.

Broken glass carpeted the ground with a message: Brooklyn glitters sinister at night. Sometimes teenagers drank whatever they drank in the dark, sitting on the rusted playground equipment mocking each other and whoever walked by, but it was deserted. The night was deep dark the way the city does in winter. You go in to work in the dark, to your windowless office or cubicle, and leave again for home in the dark. Even if you manage to leave early, you're stuck underground on the train until the sun burns out.

You were sick so I was walking the dog alone and chose to go down to Smith Street with its still-abandoned brownfields holding the Gowanus safely at a distance. The Smith and Ninth stop ensured that someone would walk by inevitably if something went wrong (I hoped). The feral dogs must have used the unfenced run of the brownfields alongside the Gowanus to move north and south through our neighborhood like ghosts. No one would see them, much less believe in them, if they stayed in that liminal strip. On the other side of the Gowanus hulked rusting warehouses full of the evidence of old crimes and murders, and probably more toxic waste waiting to be dumped into the greasy depths.

Zoe and I froze as one dog stepped ahead of the other silent dogs to stare through the rusty fence directly at us in a way that no one in Brooklyn ever looked at you. After a low growl to the dogs who stood watching, she walked without fear to the chain link between us. These weren't wolves or even coyotes; they were clearly the discarded dogs of people who lived in Brooklyn, people who'd had to give them up or those who had thrown them away like trash, like old accessories. Or they'd escaped some terrible abuse, a dog-fighting ring or a studio apartment where they were kenneled twenty hours a day. Every size dog, every color and type of fur. The lead dog I remember now as a hyena even though I'm sure she wasn't. Her trash-colored brindle fur hackled like Zoe's, a perfect camouflage for her life in the night streets and rusted-out derelicts of Brooklyn's abandoned spaces. Here was a creature much better suited to New York City than I would ever be.

We stared at each other through the fence and I thought of the creeps I might encounter on the way back to our apartment, of the way I had to carefully plan every outing, plan for every possible violence. How I had to worry about my partner every time she left the apartment and even when she didn't. Nowhere was really safe for two women. Or even three or four. But this dog who had been abandoned, abused, this dog who was probably starving all the time and sick, stared calmly with a ferocious intelligence. Fangs and blood and the crack of bones to get at the marrow stared back, as well as abuse at the hands of an animal like me, and I knew I could be prey but for some reason wasn't. This was a potential violence I had never prepared for, but I wasn't scared even though I had no treats, no leftovers, no offerings with me for these wild gods. I felt unprepared, but I nodded, almost a bow, and she took that as some kind of answer, yipping something to the other dogs, who quietly slipped into the night.

It wasn't until we were almost home that I understood the danger, how close I'd come. The feral dog packs of Brooklyn were legendary urban monsters. Even if they weren't willing to attack an adult human, Zoe was a good target. But she was quiet as she tugged on the leash, pulling me toward home and you, asleep and safe (I hoped). I couldn't wait to get back to you and our soft, warm world, even as I thought about how close I had been to an animal violence. How close I'd been to running after them, shedding whatever made me human, feeling the crack of bone between my teeth, finally joining the pack and trusting you to recognize me anyway.

Nicholas Yingling

The Wild Kindness

All night we sleep as other people,
heavy, the tide beneath us
like a stranger's bed
we leave unmade. In time the waves return

our city, or at least the pieces
too big to breathe. We make small talk
over breakfast about phytoplankton
feeding off the ash

or how the yellow eel silvers itself,
its stomach dissolving
to make way for that final organ
as if love were some end to nourishment,

something cold and dreamless in our bodies
cutting through the current,
choosing for us
the one way we will empty ourselves.

In the distance two dogs
shake off the surf.
They chew through the new flesh
of their burns, knowing deep in their cells

somehow
the gold will grow back.

Nicholas Yingling

Seaside Apocalypse

All night we sleep as other people,
dreamless and on our backs. The monarchs
like an autumn of eyelids
drowse in their eucalyptus and we sip tea

and oysters at market price. We do our part.
We tip. In time the waves return
our bottles, full of yesterday's receipts.
You break even or open,

says the man burning plastic, and for a dollar
or a drink he can exchange our lives.
All night we watch the scale
turn and like a heart in fibrillation

turn back. It's just our way of saying, Yes,
we deserve this.

Ashley Hajimirsadeghi

landay of movement

There was once a woman with a vine tattoo
on her neck. It looked to choke her; my father called her

a Western ghost. I was born from dirt.
They named me wild rose because they didn't know what else

to call the girl plucked from the cracked earth.
There was a drought that year, so we moved. We were choking

on the lack of possibility. They called
us devils. My father checks off white on the census anyways,

as if it's some heavenly redemption.
We know our place. It isn't here; it's in migration.

Cut at the vines of an addicting life
here, the illusion of peace. Ghosts aren't bound by law.

Kimberly Lojewski

Spells to Unlock Your Inner Demon

A Charm for Forgetting
2 parts dried bluebell, 1 part sea salt, 1 part powdered sulfur.
Mix into the shell of an egg laid beneath a full moon.

We have always lived by the water. Rivers, streams, swamps, tidal marshes. Mamuna doesn't discriminate. If it is deep enough to wet her bones, any water is good water. In the old country, she says we might have had entire rivers to haunt for as long as we liked. Endless wetlands at our fingertips. But here, where things are new, constantly growing and expanding, we move around a lot. Here, people hunt you when your neighbors turn up dead. Mamuna says, in the old country, they would have left offerings just to appease us.

I never participate in the killings, and to be frank, it's something I have always found appalling. I don't share Mamuna's appetite for blood. I long for connection, not for slaughter. Her victims are often young men that I fancy from afar. I don't know if this is due to my tragic luck with romance, or if she kills them just to prevent me from growing away from her.

I can never remember these events, so I can never be sure. The holes in my memory are from a forgetting powder she blows into my ears. Whether this is a curse or a kindness, I couldn't tell you. At any rate, the morning the oysterman turns up dead, all tangled up in the feather-tipped mats of salt grass that line our shores, he joins the long list of wishful paramours that I mourn from the window.

"We'll have to move," I say glumly as a horrified crowd gathers around his body. I am sorry about this because I like our rickety stilt house that squats so silently over the teeming tidal marshes. I liked the oysterman, too. Actually, I think I loved him.

He was young and handsome, as most of Mamuna's victims are. Each morning, I watched him set out for his oyster beds in the quiet dawn, trudging through the gumbo mud in a pair of fluorescent hip waders. He whistled as he worked. He was gentle with the floating coot nests that bobbed about the reefs, making wide circles around any with baby chicks in them. This was a sure mark of a softhearted, principled fellow and one of the many reasons I cared for him.

I thought that maybe he loved me back. When he spotted me watching from the shore, he smiled and winked. Sometimes he waved or blew a kiss. Once, he even brought me a pearl, all folded up in squares of dried seaweed, to wear tucked away against my breast. On the few occasions we were near enough to speak, I crouched down low so that the hem of my dress covered my feet. Mamuna says that even the most red-blooded males find girls with goose legs repugnant.

"He was married, Nitsa," she says, coming to stand beside me at the window. Her massive body brims with disapproval at my sadness. She never has one single ounce of remorse for anything she does. Sometimes I think she finds pleasure in hurting me. "And with a wandering eye, too," she continues, spitting three times on the floor. "*Odrażający*. Look at his young wife down there. She's better off now, if you ask me."

It hurts to know another woman held the real space in his heart. My own grief is deflated by the lovely woman crying in the wet sand. Even through the comforting arms of folks trying to shield her from the sight of her dead husband, I can see the soft swell of pregnancy on her belly.

"Come away from the window now," Mamuna says. "They can see us watching."

Sure enough, we garner several darkly suspicious gazes from the crowd gathered below. She grips my arm and hauls me away from the window, as herons tiptoe delicately around my poor dead oysterman's body.

A Poison for the Lungs
1 part dried glasswort, 2 parts marsh marigold oil, 1 lung of fish.
Pierce the still-contracting lung with a thorn.
Coat with mixture.

The very next day, Mamuna falls ill. It is no kind of normal illness. She says it's more like the work of a powerful curse or the evil eye.

"Maybe it's the oysterman's wife," I say.

"Absurd," she sputters. "There isn't a hedge witch alive strong enough to take me down." And, "She is far too young and grief-stricken to have turned so readily to revenge."

That is true. Nevertheless, she is gasping and wheezing by sundown.

By midnight, just as a mighty intercoastal storm turns our marsh inside out, blowing out power grids and shaking thousands of iridescent ghost crabs up onto the shores, her condition grows dire. I rifle through books of spells and charms by candlelight as she flops about on the floor in a flowered housedress, sweating and gasping for breath. Her death spasms rattle the roof and rock the foundation of the stilts beneath us.

"I'm drowning from the inside out," she says thickly. "I'm suffocating inside my own flesh."

Indeed, her black eyes have lost their bite. Her hills of fat have lost their terrible strength and shake flaccidly beneath the force of her hacking. It's astonishing to see. In all our years together, I have only known Mamuna to be strong and evil and in control. She is a fearsome, murderous old witch who wreaks heartache and havoc wherever we go, but for the first time, I wonder how I will survive without her. The world is a difficult place for a goose-footed girl on her own. It is this truth that has kept me bound to her.

"Take me out to meet the tide," she commands after a particularly vicious convulsion leaves her breath rattling like an outboard motor run dry.

"Mamuna," I begin, but, terrible to the end, she uses the last of her strength to box my ears in.

"Take me now, Nitsa."

I roll her onto an old flour sack and tug and pull her wheezing bulk across the floor and down the steps. Outside, the moon hangs low in the sky, partially obscured with mushrooming storm clouds and starred by silver sweet gum leaves that slap wetly up against each other. Rain pelts us, icy and insistent, and the black waters of the marsh churn up tiny waves that hit the shore in a frantic cadence. The coots beat their wings, crying feverishly from their floating nests—a sure sign that death is coming to meet us.

I spend a long night wrestling her through the mud and against the wind. We are both soaked through, lashed by cordgrass and brined with salt, by the time I get her down to the edge of the water. She rolls herself over then, her dress transparent in the rain and moonlight, folds of blubbery skin slick and gleaming beneath. With her humped back rising up majestically from the mud, she looks as ancient and mighty and immoveable as a great white whale. It is impossible to think of her dying.

She holds her head up long enough to say, "*Idź dziecko.* Go forth, child, and find your home." And then plops down, face-first, into the water.

Road Amulet for Luck and Protection
Cut 2 inches from an elderberry bush and remove the core.
Mix equal parts powdered horsehoof, spiderweb, hair of a wild dog, and withered snakeskin.
Stuff the branch and seal ends with plugs of ash.

After Mamuna dies, I set our house on fire and take to the road. It's much dustier than I imagined. The intermittent stretches of hot asphalt wreak hell on my palmated feet. I have to stop every half hour or so and find a warm ditch to soak the tender webbing of my toes in.

It is the fear of the townsfolk finding me as I'm making my plodding escape that wears me down. Paranoia is rooted deep into my veins, implanted by years of fleeing. I weigh the terror of being made to atone for Mamuna's sins against the prospect of someone seeing my feet. In the end, I decide revulsion is better than being put on trial for murder. With my skirt pulled down low on my hips, I can pass for an ordinary girl. Comely, even. The trick is to keep my goose legs hidden.

In every television show I've ever seen, female hitchhikers use the sex appeal of their fleshy appendages to snare a ride, so I prepare myself for a good long wait. However, the third vehicle that passes, a pickup truck with a rusted-out bumper, pulls off to the side and then slowly reverses until it's flush to where I'm standing. I use my suitcase to hide the claws curving out from under my skirt. And then I smile.

I try to look coy. I try to look seductive. Mamuna always said that all men were perverts who want to be seduced to their deaths. But the man leaning out the window has a wide-open face and a sweet smile.

Not as handsome as the oysterman, but he does have a rather boyish charm despite being some years older than me.

"What are you doing out here on your own?" he asks. He looks genuinely concerned. "Taking rides from strangers is dangerous."

"I have an amulet," I say and lift my chin to show off my handiwork.

"Well, that's something," he says with a laugh, and I hear the thwack of automatic doors unlocking. "Better get in. Amulet or not, there are strange things happening around here. A man just turned up dead. It's not safe for a young woman alone."

I nod and graciously accept his offer. He takes my suitcase and tosses it in the back. When he helps me into the cab, his gaze goes straight to my feet. To the wide, flat webbing between my talons. The feathers tufting out at my ankles. The orange scales puckering my rail-thin legs. His eyes widen slightly, but he doesn't say anything.

It's a terrifying moment and one I have tried to avoid my entire life. I feel a wash of anxiety at exposing myself to a stranger. It goes against everything Mamuna has ever taught me.

"If they realize you're a monster, they will run from you, ridicule you, or hunt you extinct," she always said.

But this man doesn't run, and he doesn't look particularly hostile, though there is a tense air between us as we settle into our seats. I draw upon my own courage to break the silence.

"My name is Nitsa," I finally say. "I've got goose legs." It seems best to get it out of the way as quickly as possible. "I was born with them."

I cringe a little as I wait for his response. When his eyes meet mine, I only see kindness. "I have my brother's heart," he says after a moment. "I was born with a ventricular septal defect. He died in a car accident, and they transplanted his heart into my body." When I don't respond, he says, "It's nice to meet you, Nitsa. I'm Jackson."

We pull onto the road and head for the interstate. It takes a second for me to understand that I am finally on my way. And then my fears release and whirl away towards the suck of the outgoing tides. The feel of asphalt beneath the tires is pretty freeing. I begin to think that maybe the past is behind me. Mamuna is gone. The weighty ache of all those dead men I loved have gone with her. I take a moment to look back in the direction I came from. Plumes of smoke are beginning to rise up into the sky where the house in the salt marsh is burning.

☾

Jackson lives inland and to the south, in a town called Two Eggs. Since I have nowhere to go, I go with him. Just like the oysterman, he's married, except Jackson tells me all about his wife. Two years, he says proudly, and they have a boy and a girl. I can't stay with them, but he knows of a place I may be able to rent. We are bound by our mismatched body parts. Kindred souls of a sort. I can see he's determined to help me.

"How much money do you have?" he asks.

"None," I say confidently. "But I know lots of charms and spells that the townsfolk will want to buy." It's how Mamuna always provided for us.

Jackson laughs, which is something he does a lot of. "Not in Two Eggs," he says. "This is Baptist country. You'll need a real trade. Something useful."

It's bewildering that he doesn't consider magic a useful trade. If Mamuna were here, she'd find this outrageous. "I can catch fish and crabs," I say. "Trap muskrats. Gather eggs. I can shuck oysters faster than most men. I know how to tickle lobsters."

Jackson is laughing again, which makes me laugh, too. Even though I suspect I'm what we're laughing at. "Two Eggs isn't exactly an oyster-shucking-type of place," he says.

That sobers me right up. "Well, what type of place is it? Isn't there any water?"

I am seized with a sudden anxiety at the thought of a dry, dusty, waterless town. My toes cramp with dehydration.

"There are springs," he says. "Sinkholes. We get so much rain in the summer that fish walk across the streets."

That sounds OK to me. As if on cue, a light drizzle begins to splat against the windshield. Jackson laughs. He has an easiness I find more enviable than all the stilt houses in the world, and I'm sure that this is the new start I am looking for.

Spell for New Beginnings
Dry and grind old man's beard, fish scales, and elderberry.
Mix in equal parts.
Store in a pouch, along with 3 steel nails and whiskers of a white rat.
Hang over the door of dwelling.

47

My new home is a small cinderblock house that sits at the edge of a sticky, moss-draped forest. It is hot here. Hotter than I am used to, for sure. But the woods are old and dimpled with blue spring-fed holes connected by underground limestone tunnels. It is the oldness of the water running beneath the earth that makes me feel at ease. It's the wildness of the creatures that make their homes around it. There are otters, black crappies, snapping turtles, and spotted sunfish. There are great striped spiders the size of my hand. In the evenings, bats feast drunkenly on fat-bellied insects while whippoorwills sing laments to the stars, all set against the percussive din of prehistoric alligator-mating melodies.

I don't miss my old life at all. I'm like a fish in a new pond. Sometimes at night, when I swim beneath the moon, I think I can feel Mamuna's badness washing away from me.

The house is just dark and damp enough to suit. There is a plentiful variety of mold spores in the nooks and spiderwebs in the crannies. I delightedly scrape them off and store them away into jars. There might not be much of a seller's market for spells in these parts, but I'm not one to waste ingredients. Around the sinkholes I find all manner of useful things. There are red-tentacled sundews and water vipers with venom glands ripe for the milking. I disembowel a young alligator, grind up its organs, preserve its eyes, and stow away its bones. Then I fry up its tail for my dinner.

Jackson brings his wife over once to meet me, but she can hardly pry her eyes away from my feet long enough to hand over the clothes and blankets that she brought, and I can tell she doesn't like me at all. Her mouth grows slack when she eyes the alligator skin drying near the window. It's been agreed that once I settle in, I will work for them to pay off my debts. They own a small diner on the main drag of the town called The Two Eggs Café. I'll serve pancakes and coffee in exchange for my wages. It all sounds awfully human and civilized to me, and these qualities in themselves seem like an impossibility.

"It's mostly locals," Jackson says to assuage my trepidation. "They won't give you any trouble at all. Besides, you will be a help." At my dubious look he continues, "Since the second baby was born, Rosalie's been too busy to work like she used to."

He nudges his wife, who gives me an automatic smile. Then her gaze lands on my legs. On the alligator skin. On the jars of spiderwebs and snails stacked up in the windows. It quickly fades. "Of course, with those feet …," she murmurs. "You might trip and fall. Crash into things. Waitressing requires a certain amount of dexterity and social etiquette."

I feel a prickling of humiliation and anger that makes me straighten my spine with a show of pride that I just don't feel. If Mamuna were here, she would snap this woman's bones in half and smile about it afterwards. But what can I do? "I am very dexterous," I tell her. "I can swim faster than an anhinga."

Rosalie tries to hide her laughter behind her hand, and Jackson looks embarrassed, though whether it's for me or for his wife, I'm not certain.

"There's no swimming in restaurant work, you poor dear," she says, and Jackson murmurs, "That's enough Rosalie. She'll do just fine. She's not serving crumpets to the Queen of England."

They leave after that, and I rush out to the sinks. To the cold relief of the water against my burning cheeks. I dive as deep as I can. I rupture the filmy layers of duckweed growing over the surface. I thrash the water furiously with my flippers until my hair is green with specks of algae.

She can't do what I can do, I think to myself, holding my breath in great, gasping ten-minute intervals. Following lily pads down to their anchors. Tracing the crumbling tracts of the caverns beneath the water. Racing redbellies and bluegills through the tunnels until they're out of breath and heaving. Maybe she can look pretty and pop out kids. But she can't do all this.

"*Głupia geś,*" I hear Mamuna's voice echo in my mind, but this time the memory soothes me. "Of course, she can't. Why are you comparing yourself to a human, child?"

It turns out waitressing is harder than I expect. I don't take to it at all. For one thing, Rosalie was right: My goose feet skid on the linoleum floors, and they're pretty cumbersome when it comes to navigating around tables. I can't fit into any kind of traditional shoes. I have never had any need for them before. I take offense at the very suggestion.

But Jackson is good at explaining things in a way that disarms me. He has a calm kindness about him that is exceptional. Even after I've knocked down three customers, spilled a tray of tea into someone's lap, and dropped half a dozen plates of food, sure, he's a little red in the face, but even after all this, his voice is still soft and reasonable.

"It's all about adapting," he says. "I eat a heart-healthy diet. I jog to strengthen my muscles. Hot baths for circulation. I have an implanted valve that regulates my heartbeat. I'll never be exactly the same as everyone else, but with some extra tweaks to accommodate my differences, I live just fine alongside them."

Sometimes I feel like he speaks straight to my soul. Like he's the only one who has ever understood me. Because of this, I find myself considering his request. Perhaps he's right. Mamuna never taught me any coping skills. She only had three speeds: kill, flee, or remain hidden. I feel like fate has finally worked in my favor by bringing Jackson into my life. I tell him this. I am overcome with emotion.

"Aww," he says. His eyes crinkle up and his cheeks stain with color. "It's nothing. Let's see what we can do to give you some traction. I have some grip pads in the back that I use to keep the tables in place."

Despite some fundamental cognizance that feet like mine are just not made to be bound, I give in and follow him to the dry-storage room for a fitting.

Jackson devises a way of tying the foam pads around my ankles and then hooking them to my talons so they provide the extra grip that I need on the bottom. The diner is cleared out from breakfast and the lunch rush hasn't hit yet, so we have some to spare. I try not to blush as he touches the webbing between my toes. It feels intimate, letting a man touch this part of me that I've always concealed. I distract myself by staring at the top of his bent head, where his hair is thinning. I even find this imperfection endearing.

"There," he says, releasing my legs and straightening up to survey his work. "Custom-made non-slips."

I test them out and they work, although they make my feet look even more ridiculous. We laugh as I practice trotting around the restaurant. I even break into a wobbly, pigeon-toed sprint. He gives me a tray, shows me how to balance it on one hand, and we practice with empty plates and glasses.

When Rosalie shows up just before lunch with a baby on her hip and a toddler in tow, she is not impressed. "But, Jackson," she murmurs in a low voice that isn't quite low enough, "she already draws too much attention."

I ignore her, even though I can hear her just fine. I try to look dignified, despite the foam and string strapped to my feet. I adjust my ponytail, pinch my cheeks, and line up the pens in my apron, readying myself for the next wave of hungry customers. Mamuna always said I was pretty pleasing from the legs up. The skirt that Rosalie gave me for work is much shorter than I'd like; it reveals my bird hocks for sure. But I'll do what Jackson suggested and adapt. I'll use what I've got. I pull the neck of my shirt down lower to showcase some cleavage.

Rosalie's lips set in a grim line as the door swings open, ringing the bell that hangs over the top. I saunter over to the elderly gentleman as gracefully as I can and lean down low to take his order.

Talisman for Success
Drill 3 even holes in nutmeg seeds and string them on a green thread.
Tie ends together in a triple knot and hang from door of business.

Despite Rosalie's misgivings about me, the diner is busier than ever. Lots of folks come to gawk and stare, but I get used to that after a while. Eventually, they get used to me, too. The good people of Two Eggs are less concerned about my being a genetic aberration than they are with me accepting the word of Jesus Christ into my heart. I am waylaid with invitations to worship. While there is one school, one stoplight, and one general store in town, there are seven churches, and it is quite clear I'm swimming in Christ's kingdom.

On the odd occasion that someone insults me, Jackson shuts them down in that calm, steadying way that he has. But mostly, my lack of social graces doesn't seem to offend. They appear to find my naivete curious. Occasionally, even charming. As for the less-than-pious folks, they also approve. My top half is complimented on a daily basis, and that really makes me glow with pride. I bask in the praise and acceptance.

With some tweaks and adaptations, I become good at my new job. I pay Jackson and Rosalie back after just a few weeks of work and still have money left over to bury in the woods. I buy new clothes and burn Rosalie's hand-me-downs in my fireplace.

But most of all, I like working with Jackson. I like the moments when it's just the two of us sifting through a pile of receipts or cleaning up behind locked doors in the afternoons. I like his smile. I like his laughter. My poor dead oysterman is long forgotten. When I think of him now, it's only to realize that I never even knew him at all. How did I ever think love was watching someone whistle in the morning? How did I ever mistake a wink here or there for affection?

I buy a cell phone that takes pictures, mostly because I want images of Jackson that I can have for my own. I like knowing I have a connection to him in the literal sense. When I'm not working, I often sit with my toes dipped in the water, scrolling through his messages to me.

DON'T BE LATE TOMORROW

DID YOU TAKE THE FILET KNIFE HOME WITH YOU? PLEASE DON'T RETURN IT COVERED IN FISH BLOOD AGAIN.

NITSA ... THIS IS A FRIENDLY REMINDER TO NOT COME TO WORK WITH WATERWEEDS IN YOUR HAIR TODAY!!

There is a new feeling in my heart, and it is not always pleasant. It is a constant tingling. An excited fizzing feeling that makes me feel light and heavy at the same time. It makes me want to jump out of bed in the morning and also lie under the covers, paralyzed with anxiety. Occasionally, at the most unexpected moments, like when Rosalie walks through the doors of the diner or when Jackson's kids cling to his legs, it's also just terribly depressing.

It is not the feeling of unrequited love that has me so up and down. It is the feeling of something being returned. As improbable as it seems, something has shifted in Jackson's behavior. At first it is the long glances. The light in his face when he sees me in the morning. The unexpected smiles. The way his eyes track me around the diner while I work. I am sure that, despite my goose feet and even despite Jackson's familial devotion, I'm not imagining it. A real attraction is building. It is true that I am relatively inexperienced with men, but there are some things I know in my bones. I may have webbed toes, but I was always built for seduction.

There are moments—entire, long, heart-fluttering, stomach-dropping moments—where our gazes meet unexpectedly and my pulse begins to crash, and I know I'm standing at the precipice of certain disaster. One afternoon, when we have just closed the doors for the day, he reaches over to wipe a mustard smear from my cheek, and I close my eyes. I feel his breath grow close and feather-light on my face. Time slows. The world contracts until all I'm aware of is the heat of Jackson's lips hovering over my own. Then the shadows of all the dead men I loved before rear up between us, and I twist away in abject terror.

"Shit," he says. He's breathing shallow, and his eyes are more dark than light. "I'm so sorry. I don't know what I was thinking."

When I don't say anything, he says, "I'm married. I love my wife, Nitsa."

Well, I believe him. But I can see those aren't absolutes that exclude other feelings.

I begin having nightmares where Mamuna has come back from the grave and I find Jackson's cold corpse waiting for me when I clock in for work in the morning. And that's not my only concern. I am not a kind enough person that I care about Rosalie. I'm hardly human, after all. But I care for him. And I don't believe his brother's borrowed heart will hold up beneath the weight of our betrayal.

Time passes in this way for a while, and we remain in an uncomfortably charged holding pattern. The summer rains come, and just as Jackson promised, Two Eggs is pummeled with a thick and heavy onslaught of daily monsoon-level storms. It's more water than I've ever seen in my life. Catfish regularly amble across the streets, and alligators crawl up out of the ditches to scratch at the doors. The Spanish moss turns green and plumps up so fat and heavy it bends the tree branches. The town's single spotlight is blown away in a sudden gale. Fishing boats of parishioners and their families float down the roads when the school and churches close from flooding.

My dreams grow increasingly violent and disturbed. Something inside of me swells. I crave those moments where we get too close and Jackson's control almost slips. My emotions are reaching a fever pitch, and I wait for something to break down my restraint, even as we both struggle to maintain it. I am all filled up with the tempestuous wildness of these storms and held taut with a desire that terrifies me. All the while, the bell over The Two Eggs Café rings nonstop. They come by canoe. They come by kayak. They even come in hip waders.

Jackson and Rosalie grow rich and prosperous.

Spell to Break Attraction
Gather a handful of earth from a river bottom.
Sprinkle in witch water and ground alligator bones.
Scatter between you and the one you love.

I have never done a spell to release anyone, although I suppose I've done plenty the other way around. I've never had to let anyone go; Mamuna killed them all before things reached any kind of conclusion. She isn't here to put a stop to the destructive force of my attraction to Jackson, but I can still feel her weighty spirit pressing up against me under all this rain.

"*Głupia gęś,*" she says. Or maybe that's just the sound of rain sizzling on cinderblocks. "Why do you try so hard to fight your nature?"

Even knowing she's gone, even having watched her sink down into the mud myself, I can't shake the fear that something terrible is going to happen. Maybe it's the residue of so many heartbreaks and murders. Maybe it's a trick of my mind. Maybe it's a soul-deep knowledge that is stronger than forgetting spells. Maybe I'm just no match for the intricacies of human hearts. Either way, I mean to re-direct our romantic ardor.

I send Jackson a text from my house, asking him to meet me by the water.

Come quick, it says. There's something important i need to tell you.

The summer storms have flooded the sinkholes and turned them into a raging river that has washed away the duckweed and flushed out a multitude of blind, pale-skinned salamanders from their underground caverns. They flop about in the rain, gasping miserably. They remind me of how Mamuna looked in those final hours, and as I wait for Jackson to arrive, I kick them back into the river ignoring the accusations in their eyes. One latches sharp pincer-like teeth into my toes. After that, I spear them with my talons and fling them away to die. I take comfort in watching their death wriggles.

My emotions are mercurial. Heightened from the storm and stress. I vacillate from moment to moment. I throw the phone into the water to sever the connection to Jackson. But then I dive in right afterwards to retrieve it. I tussle with myself in the swollen current before finally bashing it up against a rock. It feels like a solid victory against my past. I can break phones. I can break cycles. I've started a new life here, and I will no longer run or hide. I remember the spell, diving down deep to scoop a handful of mud from the bottom.

When I emerge, Jackson is standing there in the rain, looking panicked as he scans the river for some sign of me. I frog-kick my way towards the shore, trying to still the blood coursing through my body. Trying to slow the heavy pounding of my heart. I have every intention of beginning the parting ritual the moment my feet touch ground. Of separating us for good. But there is something in his awed expression as I rise from the churning water, my long hair tangled and dripping down my back, that makes me forget everything new and remember everything from before. The pining. The loving. The wanting. But most of all, I finally remember the killing.

"Nitsa?" he asks, and his voice trembles over my name. There is only water and more water between us. He steps close to the edge of the river. The mud slips from between my fingers. It slides down my stomach. Trickles over my thighs. I must look different. My eyes have probably gone black. He doesn't even have the sense to be frightened of me.

There is utter wonder and yearning in his face, and I know that he is seeing me, really seeing me, for the first time. Not as Nitsa, some strange half-human that he has grown to care for, but as Bolitnitsa. Demon of Old. Mistress of Swamp and Sea and Tundra.

In the old country, everyone knows my name. Men fear me. They revere me. Mothers tell cautionary tales about straying too close to my waters. Travelers turn up drowned and bloated on my shores. Unfaithful lovers taste my lips as they die. I like to kill. I love to punish. Not even a creature like Mamuna could contain me.

"Now you see," I hear her say, as the rain sluices down between Jackson and me. I imagine a reproachful hiss to her tone as it hits the water, but I don't feel any remorse. Not even when I feel her death rattle echo inside the storm. "Now you finally remember."

I do. I remember exactly what comes next. Steam wraps around me. Hydrillas whorl around my legs, their delicate touch sending shivers across my skin. Sundews pivot their heads my way, shaking poison from insect-laden tendrils. Snakes hiss and alligators bellow. I rise up slowly, seductively from the raging current, finally feeling every bit as powerful as I really am.

"I've been wanting you for the longest time," Jackson says, in a voice so low I can hardly hear it over the rain. His eyes are thoughtless with lust.

There is a part of me that wants to stop. He's a good man. He loves his wife. He loves his kids. He's always treated me with such kindness.

But I can hardly hear that part over the thunder cracks and the roar of the river. I am blinded by a furious need that is much more ancient than anything that Jackson and I could ever create together. It is more powerful than good intentions, or forgetting powders, or new beginnings. It is love. It is not the sight of someone whistling. Not even companionship, or laughter, or acceptance of your flaws. Love is complete and utter destruction. It is the oblivion of all decent and rational behavior, and you have to answer whenever it calls.

I crouch down a little deeper into the water, my strong, sinewy goose legs ready to spring.

"Come," I say to Jackson.

Rachel Lloyd

Cock Block

In the woods behind the Cock Block—the strip in town with Pini's Pizza, Wang's Chinese, Johnson's Meats, and Woody's Liquors—there is a clearing overlooking the marsh—the clearing where they found Maggie Wood dead by alcohol poisoning and Anna Johnson's severed hand—where I go to scream. Today I'm screaming because I want to run away, yesterday because I peeled my knuckles shredding carrots. Last week because I overheard my father crying, saying with only daughters he'd have to sell Pini's.

On the Cock Block, girls are bad for business. We are by nature defiant, born in ironic opposition, the town's curse: The dance teacher's daughter has no rhythm, and both the blues singer's and the preacher's daughters have no soul. The daughter of a chef, I have no taste. The story goes there was once only one shop on the Cock Block—Standish's Steel—and when the blacksmith died, he left it to his talented daughter over her bumbling brother. Her brother, outraged by his empty legacy, worked to become a warlock, more than he had ever worked to become a blacksmith. He returned to the shop, burning with rage, and turned his sister's hands to iron, which melted to magma and slipped from her wrists like ribbons. The girls in town have been cursed ever since, while the boys follow in the footsteps laid forth for them by history. My mother says it's natural, that if boys take up the reins, girls must be the horses they ride. She says I will marry. "But not too soon," she adds. "You're still my baby!" She kisses my head and smothers me with her breasts. "Wait as long as possible. Children make you old," she tells me and my sisters, all sharing the same malady, ourselves those very children.

The men in my family have run Pini's Pizza for generations, the *Since 1925* sign as much a badge of honor as a mark of shame. Every shop on the Cock Block, this string of apostrophes and ownership, is like that: sons for decades, now only daughters.

I once used persimmons in the tomato sauce because I couldn't taste the difference, and we closed for a week. For a while, I tried spicy foods hoping to taste anything at all. I drank hot sauce by the bottle and Emily Wang brought me Tien Tsin peppers by the case, but all it did was give me acne on my forehead and eczema behind my knees.

Emily Wang has the opposite problem. Her taste is so sensitive she can eat only plain rice and chicken soup. During business hours, she stands in the alley flattening boxes and kicking trash because the smells inside are too strong for her. "I can taste with my nose," she told me, gagging on the pepper smell as I bit into one, and envy fell on me so strong I thought I was in love with her. Maggie Wood turned red and woozy at the smell of mouthwash. One day, stocking shelves in her family's liquor store, her touch turned the wine to water. Her father fired her, and the next day they found her dead, a half-empty beer in her hand.

When Anna Johnson, the butcher's daughter, showed talent for slaughtering animals, we thought she'd broken the curse. Before she lost her hand, I'd watch her wring the necks off chickens easy as squeezing water from a towel. Even without her hand, she was adept at killing, and I followed her to the marsh to see frogs flop over dead as she passed, their legs splayed open as slimy and unashamed as a seasoned hooker. When Anna's sister was born nurturing as a woodland fairy, Mrs. Johnson caved in with weeping. Anna's father was the vet all along.

Mr. Johnson had been angry, but not like Anna. She was not the girl who broke the curse, her casual killing not a gift. It was a reminder that the man who kissed her goodnight had no real claim to her. He still called her *my-baby-girl*, but her blood told her otherwise. Her father talked about her taking over the shop, but she was no longer satisfied watching blood drain from a freshly wrung hen, and every kill pillaged light from her eyes.

Anna is the one who told me there is "a rat" in *separate*. "It's spelled sep-a rat-e. Like how in your restaurant there is always *a rat* between the *separate* tables." I kicked her in the shins so hard I broke two toes. We made up before her bruises faded, and when they turned from green to yellow, I wished they would stay forever. I traced their irregular shapes with tongue and fingertips thinking, *I will brand her here with longing.*

When she cut off her hand, I asked her why, and she said she'd thought maybe that's where the cursed blood was, the killing blood. "I wanted to cut it out of me." Sitting in the marsh, silent with dead frogs, I told her I thought it hadn't worked.

"Maybe it was the wrong part," she said. "Maybe it's in my other hand."

She suggested I try it, saying, "You'd probably have to cut out your tongue."

"With no tongue, I still wouldn't be able to taste. Besides, I wouldn't be able to do this," and I got between her knees, which she spread for me like a dead frog.

That night, Anna undid her bandages and let me lick her stump, the stitches jagged like a zipper. They loosened as I passed my tongue over them and separated enough for her blood to leak out, redder and richer than any tomato sauce my father or his father or his father's father ever made, and for a moment I tasted a twinge on my tongue, a sting like the sound of bees and a deep vibration like the low-throated croaks of frogs. Her blood burning into dreams the tastes of salt and iron.

Joshua Jones Lofflin

The Museum of Small Tragedies

I got another two-star. I'm sure it was from Marla, whose own museum is sitting at a 4.2. Hers is a three at most. Yes, it's clean, well lit, her tragedies arrayed in handsome glass cases that she ordered from Amazon, the engraved brass plates a classy touch. But it's *too* polished—too posed—with its professional photos of her and Rod shouldered together in matching sweaters and Olan Mills smiles, her teeth digitally whitened while Rod's remained dull and yellowed.

(I met Rod only once before their divorce. He was cleaning his shih tzu's shit from my yard, said he heard about my museum, about me and Laura, and maybe he could take a tour someday? "Looking for ideas?" I asked. I meant it as a joke. But he said, "Well," then stared at the three oblong turds in his plastic bag as if confused how they got there.)

Some reviews say my museum isn't tragic enough. Describe it as "sad, and not in a good way." Complain that it's too stuffy, that the curator (me) hovers too much. I should purchase a review boost, like Marla did. Get it to four stars, maybe more if I update the exhibits and spring for full-color brochures. But most of my visitors appreciate the rustic touches. Homespun, they say. The living room arranged just how Laura liked it, her favorite episode of *Law & Order* on loop, her favorite sandalwood candle lit. And the sofa now covered in plastic, preserving all the stains of our marriage, including the last one, when Laura threw a steaming bowl of spaghetti at me. You can still see the lines where the pasta stuck, octopus-like.

There are photos of our dog, Melvin, a spastic thing, all wiry fur and drool, but Laura somehow liked him. She'd insist on taking him to the dog park downtown. I don't display the photos of Laura talking with other dog walkers, not even the one of the jogger who kept staring at her chest when she wasn't looking (though it's hard to tell; they were taken before I got my telephoto). Instead, I have one of Laura picking out Melvin at the shelter and another of just the three of us, labeled "Family Portrait." It hangs above the donation box that I prefilled with dollars. I always excuse myself to the kitchen at this part of the tour, after asking my visitors if they would like anything to drink. I offer only tap water, and they always refuse, but they appreciate the gesture, though I once caught a woman trying to pry open the donation box lid. She claimed she'd accidentally donated too much, that she put in a ten by mistake, and really the whole operation was a scam and I should be ashamed. She gave me my first two-star. I suppose I should be grateful it wasn't worse.

I'd hoped Laura would write a review, but she refused, even though I pulled out all the stops and gave her a private tour. This was after all the papers were signed, after she'd moved into her own place and we were cordial again, mostly. I told her it wouldn't take long, and then she could collect Melvin. She rushed through the exhibits, kept glancing at her phone, and I could tell she thought they were tastefully done. I still had plans for a wall installation of her childhood, if only she'd provide some archival footage, but she kept shaking her head no, saying she had to leave, though I knew for a fact that wasn't true. And I might've gotten sore, might've said some things I regret. I've never taken kindly to being lied to.

I told her to sit down. I told her this while she was trying to leave, Melvin squirming in her arms. I said, "Fine, keep your damn footage," and she kept saying, "Please, please," and tried to edge around me. I said, "Open your own museum: I don't care," and she said, "Please let go." I said, "Listen, I *want* you to open one. What don't you understand?" and I threw up my hands, knocking the plastic PLEASE COME AGAIN sign into the dish of individually wrapped breath mints. Then she was past me, trotting to her car with Melvin in one arm, a can of bear spray in her free hand. "I'm serious," I shouted as she peeled away and yelled at me to go fuck myself. And I was. She's creative. Smart. She'd get a four-star out of the gate. Wouldn't even have to buy fake reviews. Laura knows how to frame things. She's a star.

Joshua Jones Lofflin

Orange Fish

Orange Fish isn't looking so well. I tell this to my daughter, Ellen, who is trying to decide on another garish crayon—either laser lemon or atomic tangerine—her mouth pursed in indecision. I tell her Orange Fish is listing, that he looks like he's having trouble breathing. She doesn't say anything. Doesn't ask if he will die and go to fish heaven. She knows I don't believe in such things. She knows it's OK if she does.

She's almost eleven and has had Orange Fish since she moved back in with me. He came with five other fish, each one like it'd been dipped in DayGlo paint. Two greens, two blues, and the third one I forget. It didn't survive the first week. I had to flush it when Ellen was at school. She never mentioned its absence. She barely spoke of anything that first year.

She's drawing in a coloring book that's too young for her, that my ex-mother-in-law keeps sending even though I've told her Ellen's into adult coloring books now, or those extreme dot-to-dots with thousands of dots to connect. She has stacks of them on her bookshelf. I said we should throw them out—it wasn't like she could use them again—but her therapist says it's OK if she wants to hold onto them. Now Ellen's coloring in a farmyard scene with the tangerine crayon to go with a shocking pink cow and screamin' green horse. Her therapist says she's a strong artist. Uninhibited, she says, enunciating the word slowly as if I might not understand.

Will we have to flush him? she finally asks.

Probably. Unless you want to bury him?

She shakes her head, and I'm glad. I'm pretty sure the condo association frowns on that sort of thing. Besides, I don't have a shovel.

Maybe he's homesick? she says.

Her therapist says it's OK for me to tell white lies, to not always practice radical honesty—her words—though I don't think there's anything radical about dispelling myths like Santa or Jesus or that everything will turn out all right. Soften the truth. That's what she said. As if I could stuff cotton batting around it, gauze it up so you can't feel it anymore.

I'm not sure fish can get homesick, I say. I think he's just regular sick.

Will he infect the blueys and greenys?

I don't know.

We should set him free. So he doesn't get the others sick. So he can swim to the ocean.

If you want, I say and wonder if this is what her therapist meant. Not mentioning that Orange Fish would just get eaten, or that he's fresh water and couldn't survive in the ocean even if he managed to swim there. Though I'm sure Ellen knows all this. She knows about the water cycle and microorganisms and sex and even how stars die, that half the stars in the sky might be dead already. Ghost stars, she calls them. Just like real ghosts: electromagnetic echoes and resonances. Memories. She says I'm wrong not to believe in them.

There's a light rain—no more than a mist—and we drive in silence listening to the intermittent shush of wipers and NPR burbling in the background. Another story about another outbreak in a country I'd forgotten was a country. I turn down the radio, ask Ellen how Orange Fish is doing. She holds up his Ziploc bag, says he looks scared. I tell him to hold on, we're almost there. We pass the Health Department and their sign advertising the year-to-date opioid deaths—five more since I last drove past—and then we're at the park, almost empty but for a few miserable joggers and the remnants of a birthday party, kids with cake-smeared faces and sugar-glazed eyes.

Orange Fish is still alive in his bag. His gills pulse slowly as Ellen carries him toward the creek. It's not much of a creek. Just a man-made canal for flood management with faux stone bridges crisscrossing it. Reeds and yellowed grasses choke the concrete seams. The water is low and cloudy, a chalky gray.

Are you sure about this? I ask.

Ellen stands on tiptoes to look over the bridge's railing. Her face is pinched and serious as she fumbles with Orange Fish's bag. It's one of those baggies with a sliding lock that always seems to stick, and it's sticking now. Here, I offer, but she pulls away and keeps tugging at the bag's locking mechanism until with a click it finally opens, or I think it does, but the bag is falling, fish and all, into the flat, dull water below. There's barely a splash.

Shit, Ellen whispers, then shoots a fearful glance at me.

Shit, I agree.

The bag bobs up and down. A gentle current pulls it beneath the bridge and we rush to the other side to wait for it to emerge. The mist is now a rain, and drops pluck the creek's surface with faint ripples. When the bag emerges, it spins slowly like a dead jellyfish.

I think I can see Orange Fish swimming out of the bag, I tell her, and Ellen squints at the cloudy water where the bag has caught on some dried reeds. She doesn't contradict me. The bag twists in the current then breaks free, silently floating past Styrofoam cups, cigarette butts, a fading Doritos bag. Then, the shrieks of children, the barking of dogs. Rain hits our faces, and we know it's time to go.

Coyote Shook

The Gospel According to Sister Wendy

My sister brings me a DVD of Sister Wendy Beckett touring American art museums.

WELCOME TO FLORIDA

-Day seven in the hospital:

The doctor is in my room for all of three minutes. He politely asks me what my dissertation is about and nods with feigned interest when I talk about intersections of disability and ocean studies. He listens to my lungs and says he can hear them filling with fluid again even though we'd just drained them with a needle through my ribs that afternoon. I say that sounds like a greak first chapter topic, but he doesn't get the joke. Meanwhile, Sister Wendy visits the Boston Museum of Fine Arts. Sister Wendy visits the Met. Sister Wendy visits LACMA. As far as I know, Sister Wendy never once set foot in Florida.

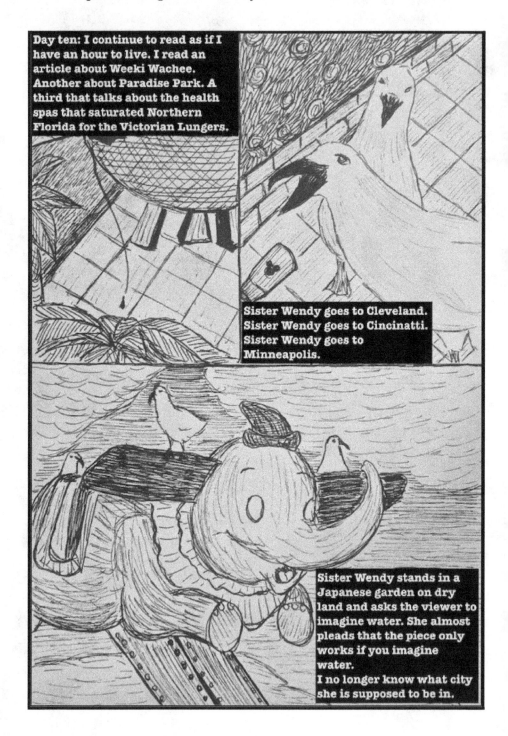

Day thirteen: I am thumbing through A River of Grass when the doctor tells me I can go home in the morning, but that I will need to schedule lung surgery within two weeks. Even then, I should not expect to ever regain full usage of my lungs.

Sister Wendy visits the ruins of some place I do not recognize, that could not possibly be America, and I realize that she's been fucking with me this entire time.

"Did you know," I say, as though it is an answer, "that Marjory Stoneman Douglas was a Quaker?"

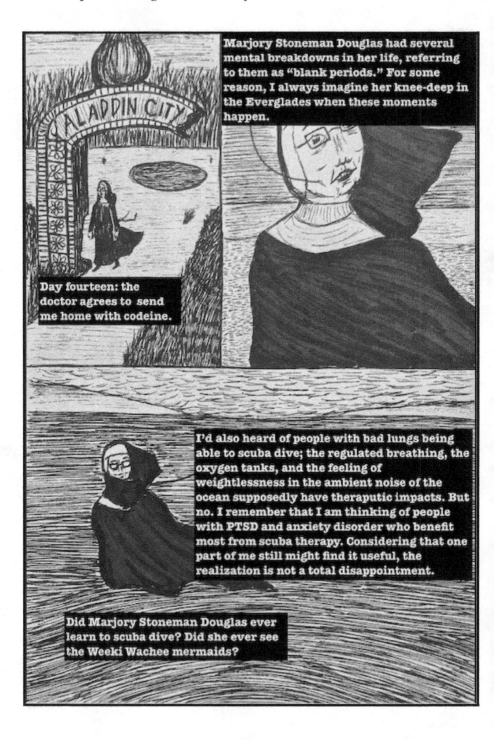

Marjory Stoneman Douglas had several mental breakdowns in her life, referring to them as "blank periods." For some reason, I always imagine her knee-deep in the Everglades when these moments happen.

Day fourteen: the doctor agrees to send me home with codeine.

I'd also heard of people with bad lungs being able to scuba dive; the regulated breathing, the oxygen tanks, and the feeling of weightlessness in the ambient noise of the ocean supposedly have theraputic impacts. But no. I remember that I am thinking of people with PTSD and anxiety disorder who benefit most from scuba therapy. Considering that one part of me still might find it useful, the realization is not a total disappointment.

Did Marjory Stoneman Douglas ever learn to scuba dive? Did she ever see the Weeki Wachee mermaids?

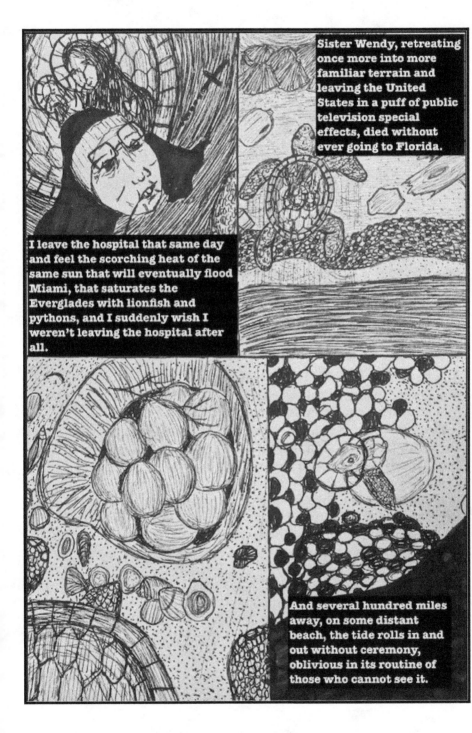

Sister Wendy, retreating once more into more familiar terrain and leaving the United States in a puff of public television special effects, died without ever going to Florida.

I leave the hospital that same day and feel the scorching heat of the same sun that will eventually flood Miami, that saturates the Everglades with lionfish and pythons, and I suddenly wish I weren't leaving the hospital after all.

And several hundred miles away, on some distant beach, the tide rolls in and out without ceremony, oblivious in its routine of those who cannot see it.

Gary Leising

Which Scares You More:
Dying or Going on Living?

The question you pose to the stink bug in your shower
before you scoop him up on a cloth
and shake his grip free so he falls down the drain.
What is that tunnel like? you follow up
as you turn the water to a trickle to wash him away,
and where will he go, you wonder, no longer
asking because he is out of range of hearing you.

You have been reading about people dying
and hospice workers comforting them.
Would anyone pay for end-of-life care
if the carer shouted at them questions like yours
to the stink bug? And in that moment you want
him back. Bug or not, you feel bad over your words

and maybe bringing him back could help you
understand how to better apologize for your wrongs
to everyone you've hurt, especially those closest to you,
who are, of course, the people you hurt most often.
You could help ease him out of this life, maybe,
but the thought in your head: When crushed, his kind
exudes a stink to fill the tub, the room, your house.
And you there without your scrub brush.

Gary Leising

The Old You vs. The New You

Someone complimented your poem
saying they had never seen the word "spike"
used as a verb before. Spike a volleyball,

spike your drink, spike the frog
and fry its legs for lunch. One version
of you thinks these things, one says them,

patting that person hard on the head
each time you say spike. The quieter
version of you nods and says thanks,

wry smile disappointed he doesn't,
after this poetry reading, buy your book.
You have your best signing pen out tonight.

You think about a scare-quote "friend"
who texts to say "I'm vibing on some
of those haikus you told me 'bout."

Every version of you wants to lean close
to him and say "spike spike spike,"
that weaponized word with two sounds

good for spitting, good for the old and new you,
a double-pointed nail binding two pieces of wood,
a carpentry miracle you'll never understand.

Frank Jamison

While Gardening, I Consider Redoing My Life

I'll shovel out
all my misspoken words
and never utter a sound
except to say I love you.
I'll cut the blossoms
of all the things
I should have said
but never did and place them
in vases on the mantle.
I'll banish all epithets,
root around in boxes
for pictures of the friends
I failed to keep in touch.
I'll line the hallway walls with them
and call each one each morning.
Then, after hanging up the phone,
I'll go outside to do the one thing
I have done right all my life,
put my hands in dirt
while listening to the birds.

Karen Zlotnick

The Bat

The morning I woke up to a little brown bat clinging to the curtain in my bedroom, I was supposed to lead a Name That Tree hike for first graders. I called Marti, and she reminded me that not more than a month before, the Ulster County news station reported the death of an old crossing guard. It was rabies, the result of an encounter with a bat found later at the foot of her bed. Dogged, Marti said I couldn't leave the bat in my house and risk losing track of it. She said she would cover for me and instructed me to grab my butterfly net and tennis racket.

Wide-eyed, the bat eluded every one of my attempts to snag it. Nothing makes you feel like an asshole as effectively as the swift, darting motion of a petrified animal you're trying to catch. At forty-seven, I'm still athletic, but my agility is waning. Panting and shaking, the bat understood the danger in the room, and every time I swiped, it sprang to another spot. Three holes in my sheetrock later, I gave up and called Marti's husband, the Bat Man.

When we were kids, I had a serious crush on Wayne. He had crazy green eyes and hair poking out of his collar by the time we were fifteen. He played guitar at our campfires and once dedicated a song to me in front of everyone. But I couldn't hold his attention the way sweet Marti could, so when they married under the autumn moon on the dock jutting out into the pond, I adjusted her veil and wished them a good life.

Just as well. Marti says Wayne is never home. As the Bat Man, he designs and sells bat houses, lectures environmentalists on the ecological importance of bats, and appears on TV to discuss the unfortunate prejudice against bats, which escalates with every case of rabies. Last month, when the news anchor asked him about the tragedy of the crossing guard, I was awed by his confidence, particularly when he looked directly into the camera and stressed that her death was "avoidable."

I knew Marti and Wayne would insist that the bat in my bedroom needed to be caught, beheaded, and tested. No question about it. It likely spent the night with me, and its tiny size made it possible for me to suffer a scratch or bite without knowing. Marti harped on the fact that rabies is fatal. "It's an ugly death, too." The tenderness in her voice irritated me. I thought of Wayne, the way he dances with the possibility of rabies every time he handles a bat.

Years ago, when I was jobless and Marti hired me to work alongside her as an outdoor educator, we came up with a saying that stuck: Nature isn't always kind. We tell the second-graders who visit our park, "Wasps are part of nature, but you don't want to get in their way." We tell our high-school seniors, "Marijuana is natural, but it won't take care of you while you're driving." One time, a smart-ass teenager—probably stoned—answered, "Weed isn't the kind of nature you have to worry about. It's human nature that's dangerous." Marti rolled her eyes when I told him he might be right.

The bat still on the curtain, I put Wayne on speaker and listened as he told me to leave the bedroom and shut the door behind me. "Most likely," he said, "the bat is terrorized and will stay in one place to rest once the threat is gone." It was uncomfortable to think of myself as a threat, but I went into the kitchen, poured myself a cup of coffee, and waited for him to show up.

I thought Wayne would have gear with him—some special bat-catching stick—but he said my net would do. He grabbed it and headed for my bedroom. His ponytail fell into a silvery wave between his broad shoulders. Just before he got to my bedroom door, he turned to me. "Didn't I tell you to shut the door behind you?" His tone was unfriendly. He peered inside the bedroom, stepped inside, shook the curtains, and, seeing nothing, chastised me further. "It appears the bat left the room."

I muttered, "Ugh. I thought I shut it."

Exasperated, Wayne left spewing strict instructions. "Keep all windows down. Make sure doors to the outside are fully closed after you sneak in or out. Finally, better hope that the little guy appears in the house over the next few days. Otherwise, you gotta call the health department about getting shots." With an appealing urgency in his voice, he added, "Fran, don't be stubborn about this. Think about that crossing guard. I know how you feel about shots, but if you can't find the bat to have it tested, you gotta get them. Period."

When I was in my twenties, I cut my hand on some wire fencing and developed a dangerously high fever after the tetanus booster my doctor recommended. Three immunologists assured me my fever was an anomaly, but I haven't agreed to another shot since. Every year after she gets her flu vaccine, Marti reminds me to wash my hands more frequently and stay away from people who have colds. "I don't want to hear that you're in the hospital with pneumonia just because some eight-year-old grabbed the museum door handle with his snotty hands." I'm always floored and a little annoyed by how much she cares. Once, in junior high, I convinced our teacher that Marti's science fair project wasn't ready because of a necessary "goodbye" visit with her grandmother in the hospital. The teacher got all sad and confessed to having to say goodbye to his grandmother at the same age. Despite her reservations about the lie, Marti allowed her gratitude to swell into a state of permanent indebtedness. A strange place for us to land, considering.

Determined to make its escape impossible, I checked the windows and looked for small cracks where the bat might have crept in. I ran my fingers along window frames and the duct-taped sides of my air conditioner, wondering not only where but when. Perhaps it was the night Marti and Wayne came over for beer around the firepit. Marti got teary and ran inside for some tissues. Maybe the little thing snuck in then, right through the door—on the breeze Marti's hair made when she whipped it around to apologize to Wayne and me. "I'm sorry," she said. "It's just such a hard date." Her voice scratched at my skin. It was the sixth anniversary of her last miscarriage, when she and Wayne finally agreed to stop trying. Marti was inconsolable—every year.

Suddenly, I felt mean. Marti had a way of doing that—making me mean and then sorry. "Tissues are on the counter," I offered, but I turned to watch Wayne chucking rocks into the woods before I could see if anything flew in after her.

When Marti returned with another bag of Doritos, Wayne extended his arm to help her maneuver around the fire and back into her Adirondack chair. When she moved toward his touch, I cringed a little and said I had to pee. Maybe I left the door open then.

☾

Marti and Wayne got married almost twenty-three years ago, on the same day I found out I was pregnant with Lila. Defiantly pregnant. I would have this child—despite the one-night-only-ness of her conception. As soon as the stick turned blue, I spoke to her. "We'll make this work. A giant fuck-you to anyone who doubts us." I was anticipating the are-you-sure lecture I was certain Marti and Wayne would deliver.

Lila was born June twentieth, just as the Earth would tip its days toward darkness. That's how I explained her leaning into it. In fourth grade, her strange drawings of the stray black cat who made its home under our porch. At twelve, her obsession with moon poetry. At sixteen, her new Wiccan identity. Though she liked to think it, Lila was no darker than any of us.

In spite of Marti's craving for a daughter of her own, she never betrayed our friendship by nourishing the resentment she must have held—of me and the child I never asked for. Instead, she became Lila's Mar-Mar, taking her into New Paltz to shop for poetry journals and mood rings. For Lila's fourteenth birthday, Marti invited her to Wayne's bat lecture at the nature museum, and Lila fell in love. She immersed herself in bat facts and vowed to travel to South America someday to watch the skies fill up with fruit bats. Wayne fed her interest and stopped by once or twice with a live bat he'd removed from someone's bedroom. He never told her they were on their way to the Department of Health, where their brains would be sliced up and tested for rabies. Instead, he said, "Most people are scared, Lila. But not you." But not *you*.

My indifference to all of this both surprised me and satisfied me. Lila's affection for Marti and Wayne should have bothered me. When it didn't, I wondered if maybe I'd actually grown up.

I arrived for work as Marti was finishing up with the first-graders, showing them her pressed flower collection. While she ushered the students to their bus, I found myself mimicking her, mouthing her parting words: "Remember, nature isn't always kind, so be careful."

The school bus gone, Marti turned to me and asked, "How's the bat? Did Wayne catch it?"

"No. I fucked up and left the bedroom door open. Hopefully, it's still in the house, but I lost track of it. Wayne isn't happy with me. He thinks my fate might be the same as the crossing guard's."

"He's worried. He says that almost always death by rabies is avoidable. You know, if you can't find it, you'll have to—"

I cut her off, my impatience simmering, threatening to boil over. "Marti, I know. Let's just see if I can catch it."

Marti, Wayne, and I met in Mrs. Wilson's third-grade reading class. I used to steal Wayne's primer so he'd have to chase me through the playground to get it back. Marti would scream, "Run, Frannie!" She thought it was hilarious that I was faster than a boy.

Once Mrs. Wilson figured out the key to Wayne's mastery of reading, there was no stopping him. While we struggled through stupid stories about families that would never look like who we would become—Marti, childless, and me, single and raising the Queen of Darkness—Wayne read about the animals of North America. Cougars. Timber rattlers. Grizzly bears. Coyotes. Bats.

In the last week of our third-grade year, when Mrs. Wilson took Wayne out in the hallway to tell him he won the reading award, I rummaged through his desk and removed a thin book about bats. I hid it in the sleeve of my sweatshirt, not quite sure how I'd use it but certain I would. Marti saw me, and I held my forefinger up to my lips to beg her silence. She giggled, but her eyes were conflicted.

On the very last day of school, Wayne told Marti and me that the bruises on his forearm were because his mom came down hard on him when Mrs. Wilson told her he'd lost one of his readers. My capillaries filled with shame. I dug a hole in my backyard with a beach shovel and buried the book. A week or so later, when Marti asked me what I'd done with it, I told her I didn't know what she was talking about.

When I got home from work, I searched the house and found the bat lying on the faded wood floor in Lila's bedroom. Half alive, it looked like a large, brown moth, wings hanging loosely from its tiny body. In my bedroom, the bat's presence seemed enormous, the threat of it existential. Here, I wouldn't need a tennis racket. I could have stepped on it and broken it into pieces.

Imagining what the bat must have felt—depleted, beleaguered, vulnerable—I worried that it might fly into my face and rip a hole in my cheek. I thought, That's what I would do if I were in its place. I'd take control. Find a soft spot and strike. The bat just sat there, its eyes squinting in the light.

I reached into the pantry in the hallway, grabbed a clear Rubbermaid container, and placed it over the bat. The bat lay mostly still except for the slight rise and fall of its back. I slipped a piece of paper under the edge of the container and then under the bat, who squirmed just a little, and tipped the container right-side-up. Once I secured the lid, I used the end of a knife to poke some holes so the bat could breathe. I studied it, wondering how so small a creature could command so much attention. I reached for the phone to call Wayne. And then I decided not to. Just like that.

The night we'd hung out around the fire pit, Wayne counted six bats in the sky above us, darting at moths and mosquitos. "That's what I love about them," he said. "Best bug control there is."

Marti stared into the fire, frozen in her sadness, so I overcompensated by asking Wayne for bat facts I already knew. "How many bugs does each bat eat?"

"Up to a thousand in an hour," Wayne said.

"Are they always nocturnal?"

"If they're healthy, yes."

"You're a wealth of information, Bat Man."

"I suppose I am."

I should have stopped there, but I didn't. "Do you still read about them, or do you know everything by heart now?" Marti looked up and caught my eye. I wondered if she could see what I was picturing—a thin reader, worn from Wayne's obsessive hands. *All About Bats.* Thrown into a hole in the earth in a dimly lit yard.

And I wondered what they said about the other time. If it ever came up.

Junior year, when Wayne's interest in Marti was growing beyond her collection of pressed flowers, I graffitied his name onto the side of the school building. Just beneath it, I included a symbol Marti had shown me, one they drew on silly notes they passed to each other all day long. I was the only one who knew of it. A flower petal with the zigzag of a bat's wing inside it.

Wayne was at a Scout meeting the night I spray-painted my jealousy onto the school's bricks, but Marti had gone for a night hike with her dog. The principal concluded that since other than Wayne, she was the only one who admitted to knowing that symbol, and since her dog couldn't vouch for her, it had to be Marti's artwork. Her weeklong suspension began after the principal made her scrub the bricks during a lunch period when all of our classmates could see. In addition, the boys in the grade went hard on Wayne. He never told anyone but us about the shoving that became a regular part of his school days.

Alone with my teenage brain, I wrestled with what I had done and why it backfired. I knew Marti would never tell Wayne that she'd shared the symbol with me, and I felt sure that Wayne would see— and hate—how Marti threw herself at him.

Instead, Wayne believed her when she said she didn't do it. She never suspected me, but she did say she thought that she was set up. That someone had gotten hold of one of their notes. That someone wanted her to look foolish.

Wayne comforted Marti in front of me. "I don't know who you're protecting or if you even know. But you're the most genuine person in this town, and whoever did this is messed up." I glanced down at my forefinger as it etched a zigzag into the denim covering my thigh. Then, fighting the burn in my throat, I brushed the denim clear and nodded to fake my agreement.

The flame settled low in the firepit. Just as we finished the Doritos, Lila's truck pulled into the driveway, sending bold light onto the pine trees surrounding the yard. Lila came around back, hugged Marti and Wayne, and dropped into my lap. She'd been home for about a month after finishing her degree. With her preventive rabies vaccine done, she was heading to Argentina to study the behavior of neotropical fruit bats. She had stopped by to pick up her backpack; Will, her boyfriend, was coming by in a few minutes to take her to the airport.

Wayne said, "That's how you know a bat lover. She flies at night." Was that pride in his voice or amusement? "One last chance, Lila. Come work for me."

"Aw, Wayne. Thanks, but not yet. There's a whole bat world out there for me to explore before I give up a real career to catch them in people's houses with you."

I winced, but that was Wayne. He could tolerate an insult.

"Ouch," he replied. "But I get it. You have to go see what night looks like somewhere else." His grin made him look proud.

I had to tell Lila that Marti was already crying before their good-bye hug. "Hard date for her."

Just as Lila closed the car door, Marti shouted, "Remember, nature isn't always kind!" before blinking the water out of her eyes.

From his seat at the fire, Wayne offered, "You did a good job, Fran. Lila is just great." His words lent a finality to her departure that I wasn't ready for.

Sitting on the floor with the bat, I acknowledged a painful silence that now reeked of permanence. I thought about Lila and how she made me believe that serendipity might actually be a thing. How one night with just the right person could offer you this: a perfect baby who grows up to study and protect a creature she believes has something good to offer the world, who grows up to nickname a tiny brown bat the Underestimated Rock Star of the Ecosystem. I wondered if her interest in bats was genetic. I wondered if she ever wondered the same thing.

An arrangement of my old album covers on Lila's bedroom wall caught my eye. Had *Bob Dylan's Greatest Hits* always been there? My eyes scanned the list. And there it appeared: the sudden memory of Marti and Wayne and me belting the song that Wayne once dedicated to me. *No, no, no, it ain't me babe. It ain't me you're lookin' for, babe.* So loud. So obvious.

Lila, now grown, had left me to deal with the loss of her, the gift of her, the improbability of her, the serendipity of her. But also the secret of her. The vast shame of her. Hovering over the Rubbermaid, I wrestled with the unavoidable truth that letting someone take the hit for your crime is another crime. And I was guilty several times over.

If Wayne ever thought it was possible that he fathered Lila, he never did so out loud. And Marti never seemed to suspect it—her ability to trust far exceeding her imagination.

The night Lila was conceived, Wayne and I were ruthlessly drunk. Marti was out of town for a few days, visiting her mom. I've always thought of that night as unavoidable. I asked Wayne to fix the drain in my bathroom, and I offered him some whiskey. And then some more. He slept it off on my couch, unable to remember ever following me into my bedroom.

I didn't tell them about my pregnancy until they'd moved up the road from me, and then I blamed a guy I'd met at a party months before. I kept his name from them, offering only that he was wildly irresistible. For a while Marti and Wayne insisted on tracking him down, on holding him accountable. But I said his absence was a gift. I'd make it work. Long after I headed home that night, I could hear their shrugs, their deep, doubtful sighs. What I didn't hear, what I never heard, was suspicion.

I lifted the Rubbermaid container to my countertop and turned it gently. The bat had shrunk itself into a tiny ball, no doubt protecting itself from its greatest threat—me. From one angle, it resembled a fallen leaf, perhaps a maple, all curled in on itself. But when I turned it around and could see its face, I recognized its fear. The poor creature had entered my house somehow and spent its last days trying not to be discovered. It was tired. Trashed, really. And, so, it gave up and lay down on Lila's floor, as if to say, You've got me.

The image of a motherly crossing guard took shape behind my lids. I wondered about her, if the symptoms took her by surprise. If she had time for regrets. If, like Wayne insisted, her death was avoidable. If she too made a choice.

Outside, the light faded, making the treetops look like shadowy knives cutting into the clouds. When I lifted the Rubbermaid lid and shifted the container, the bat lay still, refusing to budge. I thought it already dead, but all it needed was a little time. As soon as I turned the container on its side, the bat crawled onto the ground, lifted its tiny head, and took off to the trunk of a tree a few feet away. It was hard to see in the muted light of dusk, but against the bark, I could tell that the bat had spread its wings. It posed—as if to show off its zigzag. As if to remind me of why I decided to let it go.

Fannie H. Gray

When We Had Wings

Millard Fillmore loved the butterflies. He was confused at first, having never seen one. I struggled to explain that they used to be common; ordinary like birds, I said. That was a mistake since he'd never seen a bird. It took me awhile, but I told him all I knew about hummingbirds and roseate spoonbills, cardinals and woodpeckers, robins, eagles, and bluebirds. I waxed a little poetic on the bluebirds, I guess. Birds of happiness. Anyway, I started singing a snippet of some old song, a bluebird on my shoulder. At that point, Millard got bored and fell asleep.

That was months ago. Most of the butterflies are gone now, which is a bad sign and indicates we need to move along as well.

As I am packing our few remaining things, I say to Millard it's time to fly away. He eyes me warily and I admit it is a figure of speech but that also once people could fly. When water covered more of the planet than dust, when trees donned resplendent coats of many-colored leaves, when rain fell like tears and sometimes when it was cold, yes cold such a concept, and snow fell. At that time, so many years gone, we people, we were so clever, and greedy, we climbed into machines and dared to fly.

Millard does not think much of this story. He likes the stories about companions. I have shared with him tales I was told long ago, but by whom I can't even remember. A guardian? I would like to think I had a gran. Maybe I sat in a comforting, wide lap, listened raptly to a sonorous voice. Anyway, I like sharing the buddy stories with Millard. I tell him about Tom Sawyer and Huckleberry Finn. I tell him about Pooh and Piglet. He likes Bert and Ernie the best because he thinks it's funny that I don't know what they are. Once I said they were bears but last time I called them critters. So yes, I don't know how to explain to Millard what Bert and Ernie are, but I know they were close friends and I think that should be good enough. Sometimes he just misses the point.

I have packed up everything we want to take with us. After I have made sure we are leaving the place tidy, I realize Millard is not with me. I spy his fluffy ginger striped tail on the porch railing. This is unnerving and I feel a hot anxiety bubbling within me. I want to scream but at the same time a cautious voice is heeding me to approach quietly.

Millard, I practically whisper. He is vexed. I can tell from the twitching of his tail and the angry spitting noises he is making.

Millard, I manage it a little louder now. We no longer have wings, please, Millard. Please come back down.

When I am certain he will jump, when he has hinged up upon his back feet, I lunge. I have not moved with this kind of alacrity in months. I have not been chased or afeared for so long, but my muscle has memory and my body hurls me toward Millard, whom I grasp tightly around his midsection as we both hit the floor of the porch.

And then a thing so miraculous, I cannot believe my own eyes. At first, I think we are watching a dust devil; the air seems yellow. Then the thrum of hundreds of wings. Goldfinches! I say, Millard, I never mentioned goldfinches!

How can this be, I think. There is a veritable cloud of goldfinches hovering, swarming, surfing the breeze. They alight in the anemic branches of an old linden tree. They perch upon the ratty tatters of an elderberry bush. Their birdsong swells upon the break of the hazy dawn.

I sit on the porch with Millard in my lap. I think the warbling of the birds is moving through me before I realize that Millard is purring. There is a warmth, spreading over me, the way I imagined I would have felt in a gran's lap. I remember, if bluebirds bring happiness, goldfinches bring luck. Millard nuzzles my chin. Yes, I tell him; we will stay.

Laurie Blauner

The Fable

The small, furry creature with piercing red eyes arrives in my bedroom in the middle of the night. It perches on a nearby chair and asks if I want to hear the fable, explaining that anyone who hears the fable will experience new moments of extreme happiness.

I inquire, *What is it about?*

A man.

Of course it is, I answer, being a woman. *A war and money, too?*

Do you want to hear it or not?

I stretch and groan, waking up, and say, *Of course I do.*

The fable is long, complicated, interesting; things transform into other things, everyone changes, and too many people are involved with the story. I'm skeptical about its abilities, yet I feel it settling and finding a place within me.

Why me?

The creature blinks. *You are another place to hold it. And why not you?*

I'm tired afterwards and fall back to sleep. Later, in the morning, I sit up in bed. The rain outside is saying something that a bird might sing. So much is waiting for me to rise outside on the sidewalk, clouds huddling together against the wind, the voice of my forthcoming husband calling his dog, the good bits of my memory strewn in the high grass. Nothing is either right or wrong; it just is. I leap out of bed to meet my future, which is an exhilaration that is everywhere and in everything. Happiness turns off the television, opens a window, drinks tea, reads a book, forgets days at a time, and believes in all the possibilities. I am so excited by this I want to offer the fable every part of me. I remove my hair and my clothes and my jewelry and then begin with parts of my body, my ears, my nose, my fingers, and continue. In the end the creature appears and collects all these pieces of me. *Why me?*

Cherie Hunter Day

Animal Eyes

An animal's eyes have the power to speak a great language.
—Martin Buber

My mother said I was suspicious even as a baby. My green eyes fixed in a stare that made some adults uncomfortable. Trust is a lock that hasn't been tampered with. As it turns out, I was terribly nearsighted and it took eleven years for someone to notice. Then I became that owlish girl in class with glasses. Four eyes magnified that stay-away vibe. For my engagement photo I removed my glasses, glanced up, and looked right. It was the same soft scowl as in my baby pictures. Some neurobiologists dispute the lying eyes concept—looking right is the truth and looking left is a lie—as too simplistic. The rate of blinking during a story may have more credence. I still don't know why we close our eyes when we kiss.

John Cullen

The Planets

The nine planets strained wires
attached to the ceiling, spaced accordingly,
the universe scaled to the length of our class.
Attention on the heavens, I sat second
in the fourth row, directly under Mars.
Large forces swirled around me.
Today, I stare at that photograph
my mother took after delivering cupcakes,
Debbie Gilmore seated on my right,
blue blazer and starched white
button-down collar. Mrs. Johnson
stood behind us, one hand resting
on each shoulder, balancing planetary
forces the image can't contain.
Each of us looks straight ahead,
the moment barely capturing the strain
in our jittering orbits, our future
divorces and attractions all on track.

Julie Brooks Barbour

Dispatch From Planet H

A metal robot moves rocks from the flat terrain to my hungry mouth. Sometimes its thin arm feeds me only dust. I miss the lushness of Earth like one body longs to embrace another.

My ears fill with the recorded jokes, applause, and audience laughter I play on loop for effect. Ask a robot to tell a joke and it misses intonations of voice and artful pauses. I dig in the dirt and uncover animal bones, pebbles, a plastic fork with two broken tines (a useless tool). The robot erases my prints with a small broom.

In spring, when I lived on Earth, my neighbor's maple tree burst into the brightest burgundy. I wonder what might have opened in me if allowed. I might have uprooted what was planted. I never would have craved stones.

Michael Meyerhofer

Skeletor's Lament

At first, I mistook it for mercy,
all those times you let me skitter clear
of your friends' laughter,
the rest of my circus in tow:
the corseted witch, the cyborg
sans taste buds, the beast
with his glamorous eyeshadow.
But where I grew up,
mice take a long time to die
and there are no blazing swords
for whittling nightmares into confetti.
I wonder if you know how it feels
to hate something beautiful
just because it isn't you.
Didn't I keep your secrets?
Didn't I explain each of my schemes
slowly enough for you to follow?
Last night, I was trapped
in a drain and could only wait
for you to look down. Imagine
grade school with jaundiced cheeks,
crossbones set against your heart.
Imagine trying to wake up
when you don't have eyelids.

Whitney Collins

Dawn

Cole Harding was an opener at There's a Box for That!, which was indisputably the most ludicrous store in all of Pinesap Plaza. This was saying something, because Pinesap was also home to Banana Pants and The Pouchy Hut and Mr. Stupid. When people needed a box—"sized cough drop to coffin!"—they went to Cole's place of employment, and he or one of his despondent coworkers found a cardboard box suited to the customer's idiotic needs. In his brief time there, eight-ish weeks, Cole had provided boxes for toenail clippings, guinea pig ashes, an emotional-support potato, a surfboard, a Ouija board, a mounted boar's head, and a bored housewife's stallion-length autoerotic device, among other absurdities. In short, Cole had cashed out several dozen folks way sorrier than himself, which was also saying something, because just six months earlier, he had accidentally broken the neck of the homecoming queen by playing dodge-the-squirrel, and Cole didn't know what was sorrier than offing the local goddess. Well, maybe an imaginary fist fight with Henry David Thoreau. He'd been having one of those all morning, which was lamer than lame, but at least he was winning.

"Uncle!" Thoreau cried. Cole had the philosopher's arm pinned behind his back, his face pressed up against a sycamore's eye-pocked trunk. "You win! I give!"

Thoreau was wiry-strong but also, predictably, passive. He lacked an innate fury that Cole had in spades, and Cole, though fleshy and washed out and bedecked in a starched Starfleet Academy tee, was out in front thanks to his cornucopian rage.

"Is that all you got, H.D.?" Cole shouted, feigning aplomb. "Whatta you been eating? Beans?"

Up close to Thoreau's leathery nape, watching a bead of sweat travel south and magnify pores and hairs and moles, life's ugly minutiae, Cole felt the same in his make-believe world as he did in his real one: on the verge of total collapse. On the cusp of crumbling from wuss to puss. He was nothing more than a Pop-Tarts eater with chalky indoor skin. A boy fresh from bluffing his way through Death Camp, a bogus retreat for mourners that had done zilch to cure him of his survivor's guilt, but where, nonetheless, he had taken home the Golden Griever award for convincing staff and fellow campers that he was okey-doke with the horseshit life could strum up. Easy-peasy with Hannah being six feet underfoot.

"Uncle!" Thoreau shouted again. "U-N-C-L-E!"

Cole cranked Thoreau's arm an inch higher. He could sense the fellow's rotator cuff was on the verge of something dramatic and visceral, an osteopathic grand finale, but, still, Cole wasn't letting up. He would fight this fight for the same reason he'd sought out the job at There's a Box for That!—because Spectacular Cliff, his sorrow advisor at Death Camp, had told him to. And Cole wanted to wow Cliff the way Cliff had wowed him.

"Have you read Thoreau?" Cliff asked Cole on Day 1 of 28. "Because you should. You should read Thoreau and then do the exact opposite. Thoreau may have been hailed as the maestro of minimalism, but, in reality, he was nothing more than a campfire-building candy ass."

Cole knew Thoreau. Everything the man had done or stood for sounded sublime. A crude shelter? A hard cot? *Self-reliance?* To live in a place where hunger outweighed heartache sounded beyond idyllic. Maybe if Cole pulled a full-on Henry David, he could quit thinking of the car crash and start thinking of immediate things: the windchill, his thirst, a blister, the croup. Maybe the thunder of a melting spring pond could drown out the image of Hannah, passenger seat, eyes wide, soul gone, his fault. Too bad, then, that Spectacular Cliff was so spectacular. He had a way of doing something to—or undoing something inside of—everybody.

"Don't buy into the New Age goulash served up here, Cole Slaw. All the other sorrow advisors are filling campers' bowls with charlatan chili, and the campers are lapping it up. Grief and guilt make you a hungry, hungry hippo. But stay strong. Don't be a pantywaist," Cliff reiterated on Day 2 of 28. "Any old pansy can hide and deny. The only way to peace, Cole, is through chaos." Spectacular Cliff cracked his wide bronze neck and flared his nostrils in a decisive way. "Seek out the most maddening place you can think of. Then put your ass smack-dab in the center of it and let the pain pass through you like a sword. Pain kills pain, Cole. Invite torture into your heart."

Spectacular Cliff gave his mane a toss and stood Christlike in the middle of the archery field. Cliff was so fully Cliff that Cole wanted to please him the same way he'd wanted to please Hannah, who'd been so fully Hannah. Right then and there, on Day 2.5, Cole decided to do and say the things a boy might do and say to make an idol think he was someone other than who he was. Cole began fast, putting forth the illusion that he was fully capable of overcoming the insurmountable. That Hannah's death was a hill he could trot over in old sneakers, given a lazy afternoon and some granola bars.

"Uncle!" Thoreau shouted a final time. "Uncle Tom's Cabin!"

Cole, at last gripped with some sort of existential mercy, released Thoreau's arm. He opened and closed the drawer to the cash register. He wiped the counter with a wet wipe. He assumed the pronounced slump he reserved for first shifts. And then he stared, glazed, out into the mall. The first batch of Pouchies at The Pouchy Hut was being deep fried. Over at Shake Your Booty, the Doc Martens Cole had his eye on were still on display: soles soft, tongues wagging. In the Grand Atrium, the month's shopping theme was being assembled. This one, "Great Americans," thus far featured a half-inflated Muhammad Ali and an Abraham Lincoln scarecrow still facedown on the AstroTurf. Another laughable day at Pinesap was dawning. Just as the sun had risen over Walden, the singing fluorescents were starting their morning flutter above the mall's roaring chlorine fountain. Before long, someone wide and desperate would waddle to its concrete shores, toss in a penny, and sigh. Cole had done as Cliff had commanded. He had planted his ass smack-dab in the center of madness. But the pain was not passing though Cole like a sword. Instead, it was trapped within him, a short dagger twisting.

Halfway between agony and lunch, the girl appeared in the doorway of There's a Box for That! like some sort of savior from the psych ward. She wore a hospital gown, tucked madly into oversized cargo shorts, as well as a pair of disposable flip-flops, the sort Cole had seen scuffing out of Nail Perfecto at the dark end of the mall.

The girl's hair was the loud, artificial color of something tropical. Mangoes, maybe. Guava? Papaya? Whichever, whatever, Cole felt something expand in him when she appeared: relief, wonder, testosterone? He couldn't say.

"Here's the question of the day." The girl came up to the counter, breathless and darty-eyed. "What's your smallest of small?"

The question felt personal, and Cole shifted in his pants. Then he looked and saw: In the crook of the girl's left arm was worn white tape, on her wrist a blue, plastic hospital bracelet, of which Cole could read half. AURORA FLOO .... What sort of last name started that way? Floozy? Aurora reached down into her shorts pocket; then she brought out her fist, which she thrust toward Cole like she wanted him to guess what was inside.

"How small can a box be?" she said. "Because this here's as small as it gets." Aurora turned over her fist and opened her palm to reveal a black speck that Cole assumed to be a gnat, dead.

"A dead bug?" he said. "A box for that?"

Aurora shook her head aggressively. "It's a seed," she said. "And nobody so far has believed me when I tell them what it grows. At the hospital, you would've thought I had a grenade in my hand. They were all: 'Oh, sure, Aurora. That's a real nice seed you've got there. Real nice, sweetheart. And I'm sure it grows what you say it grows, but why don't you come with me for a minute after you finish your broth?' And then the next thing I know I'm going from the floor with the brain-deads to the floor with the nutjobs."

Cole looked down, but the girl's fist had closed back up around the speck, good and tight. The store was empty save for her. Earlier, there'd been a man looking for a box to hold a knife made from a deer antler. "Make a weapon out of the thing you've killed to kill another one of those things," he'd said. Then a woman had come in with seven bras the color of dough. "I want a box for each one. One for every day of the week." After the bra woman, there'd been no one for a long time. Cole had grown bored, then sullen, then panicked. He'd gone down to The Pouchy Hut and eaten two Pouchies: a "Frooty Tooty" and a "Hoomungus Fungus." He'd sat by the deafening fountain and crammed the strawberry pie and the mushroom pie into his mouth. Both had made him nauseous and sad. Eating Pouchies always brought him to the verge of vomit and tears. But now, here was Aurora with her mai tai hair and trembling voice, and the more Cole looked at her the better he felt. She put forth the sort of desperation Cole had packaged and frozen within himself, a roast wound and compressed in plastic wrap.

"I was in a coma for thirteen days after the fall. Fourteen is when they really start to freak out on you, but I woke up right before that because I've always been just decent enough to my parents." Aurora looked at Cole straight on. "You know where the comatose go? Because I'll tell anyone who'll listen, and you seem like a listener. Are you a listener? Don't answer me; just hear me out. The comatose live between this world and the next. You probably won't believe that, nobody does, but we go to the moon. To its dark side. Over there, there's a stadium. We call it the ComaDome. It's big and white and we're all just sitting there inside it, in our hospital gowns, waiting. Sometimes the person next to you disappears. Did they die? Did they go back? These are the things you wonder."

Now Cole wasn't thinking about boxes. He wasn't thinking about Hannah. He wasn't thinking about Thoreau or the dough in his stomach or the dough-colored bras or the deer knife. He wasn't thinking about how he'd picked up Hannah in the rain. How he'd convinced her to let him give her a ride to volleyball. He wasn't thinking about how she'd slumped down in the passenger seat so as not to be seen with him. He wasn't thinking about what happened next. And he certainly wasn't thinking about the visitation. About all the wailing and the glossy pink coffin covered in purple carnations and how Hannah's boyfriend, Dirk, had punched his fist through an oil painting of a Victorian woman holding two babies with bluebirds on their crotches. He wasn't thinking about all the people who hated him, who wished him dead. He wasn't thinking about pulling the dagger out of his insides and running it down his wrists. He wasn't thinking about how his father no longer spoke. How his mother cried when she looked at his face. Cole wasn't thinking about anything. All he was doing was watching Aurora talk. Her words were like a song he had heard a long time ago. A lullaby.

"Once, a girl who was sitting beside me in the ComaDome just up and vanished. Then two minutes later she was back. 'I died,' she said. 'I went to the next place,' she said. 'Heaven?' I said. 'No,' she said. 'The Garden.' 'Of Eden?' I said. 'No,' she said. 'The Olive Garden.' 'The restaurant?' I said. 'No,' she said. 'The Garden of Olives.' Then she held out her hand for me to see, and in her hand were two seeds."

Hannah held out her fist again to demonstrate, but she did not open it this time. Now Cole could read her last name on the bracelet: FLOOD.

"'These seeds grow the trees in the next place,' the girl said. And I said, 'Those don't look like olive seeds. Those aren't pits.' And she said, 'Not all the trees in the Olive Garden are olive trees, you idiot.' And then she gave me one seed and kept the other for herself, and we both sat there in our hospital gowns, staring straight ahead, with the seeds in our hands, and after a while she said, 'I can hear my mother begging. I can hear my father crying. Godammit. How selfish can they be? I cannot bring myself to go back to that place.' And I am wondering: Which place is she talking about? The next place? The Olive Garden? Or Earth? Is she talking about home? And then she turns to me and says, 'If you're unlucky enough to go back to the first place, you need to plant that seed I gave you. Plant it in the most terrible place you can find so that place stands half a chance.' And then she disappeared for a final time, and I knew she was at the Olive Garden, and I knew I was going back to the hospital before long with this seed. And that's why I'm here. The seed needs a box. I mean, I'm going to plant it, but until I find the most terrible place to plant it, I need a place to put it."

Cole stared at Aurora's mouth a final time. He wanted to press his own against it. Not so much for a kiss but so the story inside of Aurora could pass from her to him. So the story could go down inside him and pull out the dagger. Cole thought about this, the story and dagger battling it out, like he and Thoreau had, and Aurora just looked at him and frowned. She held out her fist again and then gave a little pound on the countertop. "You got a box or not?" she said. "That's why I'm here!"

Cole gave a jerk and apologized. He motioned down an aisle and nodded, and Aurora proceeded down the aisle and Cole followed behind. As the girl walked, her cargo shorts slipped a bit, and when she yanked them up, something dropped to the cold tile. Cole thought it was another seed, but when he bent over, he saw it was a pill. Bright blue, the color of a happy sky, and about the size of a small beetle. Aurora didn't notice, so Cole plucked it up from the ground the same way Thoreau might a berry. He'd save it for a time when he could really use it. He hoped it might do something to him that had never been done before.

((

Hannah hadn't had the luxury of going comatose. Her neck had snapped right after Cole had done his little zigzag game with the squirrel, right after the zigzag led to the elm. Cole and his zigging and zagging had sent the volleyball captain straight to the Olive Garden. He'd done the zigzag because that was all Cole had to offer someone like Hannah. That and math. Hannah had been assigned to work with Cole on a chemistry project. Hannah had made the gagging sign with her finger when Cole's name had been called by the teacher. Cole hadn't cared. He'd done all the work, all the research, all the writing. All Hannah had had to do was hold a poster that Cole had made and roll her beautiful eyes while Cole told the class everything there was to know about the project.

"I'm presenting the project," he said, "because Hannah did everything else."

He'd been willing to lie for her. To die for her. She was divinity; he was disciple. There was no god beyond Earth, Cole felt sure. But there were gods on Earth. Hannah, Spectacular Cliff. Cole had killed one trying to impress her. He'd kill himself trying to impress the other.

"It was a deer," Cole had told the cops. "Two," he'd said. "A doe and a fawn." This had been at the hospital. Cole had sprained his pinkie. Hannah's parents were in another room, on top of Hannah's lifeless body, flopping, heaving, like walruses. Cole had a little splint on his hand with bubblegum-pink foam to cushion his finger. "The fawn still had spots," Cole said. He'd heard somewhere that spots meant a deer was a newborn. "I swerved so I wouldn't kill it. Then I swerved again to miss its mother. Then I hit the tree."

The story played well to the police. Better than the zigzag would have. Better than him driving with his knees and him playing Pink Floyd and him not wearing his horn-rims and him all "Watch this!" would have. But Dirk & Company weren't the police. Dirk & Company let everyone know they would have chosen to hit the deer, to be on a different road, to go slower, to drive better, to own a safer, more expensive car. A Saab, Route 412, 25 m.p.h.

"Who swerves?" Dirk had asked.

"Who swerves?" everyone repeated.

WHO SWERVES? posters were hung at school. WHO SWERVES? was carved into Cole's locker with a key. His mother eventually pulled him from school to homeschool him, but all she did was let him sleep, watch *Star Trek*. His father had started drinking. His father knew nothing about alcohol. He was a short, shy computer programmer who stuttered. But he went out and bought rum. He drank the rum in a coffee cup and quit talking. His mother's lip always quivered when she smiled. At night, when he tried to sleep, Cole kept seeing the squirrel. Every time he saw it, he ran right over it. *Pip, pop*. Life went on as intended.

At the visitation, Cole held out his pink-splinted pinkie and shook Hannah's parents' limp hands. Hannah's father looked gray. Hannah's mother had white clumps in the corners of her mouth. Hannah's sister told him to go fuck himself. "With a fucking chainsaw." Cole's parents led him to a corner of the funeral home and gave him a small Styrofoam plate with three baby carrots and a circle of ranch on it. Cole ate them robotically and then regurgitated them into a peace lily.

When he went to Death Camp, Cole read *Walden* again when Cliff wasn't looking. Cole knew then who wouldn't have swerved: Thoreau. Thoreau wouldn't have zigzagged. Thoreau would have stopped the car. Good ol' Henry David would have put on his hazards and gotten out of the car and called to the doe, the fawn, the squirrel. The animals would have come to him. And when the animals came to him, Hannah would have come to him. She would have watched how the animals ate straight from his palm. When they were finished, she would have taken his palm and kissed it, pressed it to her heart. Hannah would have fallen in love.

Cole put the blue pill into the tiniest box the store sold, the coughdrop one, when Aurora wasn't looking. She put her seed into an identical box when Cole was. When Aurora bent down to remove her puka-shell anklet—"It's the only money I have"—Cole switched the boxes once, then twice, then six times, swirling them on the counter like a magician, until he didn't know which one held the seed and which one held the pill. He chose one and put it in his pocket.

"I might plant it right here in the mall someday," Aurora said, straightening.

She slid her anklet toward Cole, and he slid it back, shrugging. "This place is terrible, all right."

Cole didn't want to stop hearing the things Aurora had to say. He wanted to look at her cantaloupe hair and her chapped, wide mouth and scared, round eyes for as long as she would let him. Would he see her again? "Maybe at the real Olive Garden," he said. "I mean the restaurant one."

"What?" Aurora said. Now she had the box, the remaining one, in her fist. Her hand could almost cover it. It was a very small box. Cole had done a good job. He had done one thing right.

"The seed," Cole said. "You could plant it at the restaurant."

"Oh," Aurora said. She rolled her eyes like Hannah had holding the poster. "Right."

Cole wanted to say *You know where to find me*, but instead he said, "You should go now."

So, Aurora went. She shuffled back out into the mall in her disposable flip-flops and sagging shorts. Watching her go, Cole felt like he was at another funeral. This one was also his fault. He could smell another batch of Pouchies frying up. He could hear the roar of the mall fountains, a pond forever thawed. Even though his shift wasn't over, he went out into the mall. He went down to the Grand Atrium and saw that Muhammad Ali was now fully inflated. Abraham Lincoln was still facedown, but next to him, the display crew had set up a small pop-up tent. It was painted to look like a cabin: thick stripes of brown, thin stripes of white. Cole walked right into the display, right over Lincoln, and got down on his knees. No one noticed. No one cared. Cole darted his eyes like Aurora, just to be sure, then he crawled right inside the little cabin and lay with his legs poking out the front.

Inside the cabin, Cole closed his eyes and listened to the roar of the fountain, the periodic squeak of sneaker. He smelled the new batch of Pouchies and guessed they were Beefeaters. He tried to think of God. He saw the mall Santa Claus in his elastic beard. He saw Spectacular Cliff and Hannah. Maybe it would have been better if Hannah had gone to the ComaDome. If her parents had been put in the position of unplugging her. That would have taken some of the heat off Cole. Cole wondered what Cliff did the rest of the year. He remembered one camper had said he was a bartender. That from September to May, Spectacular Cliff was Shitfaced Cliff. *Don't tell me that*, Cole had begged. *Leave me with something.*

A tear rolled out of each shut eye. Cole let the tears roll into his ears. He thought of boxes. He saw Hannah in one of the surfboard boxes with seven bras and a deer knife. He saw the box get soggy, the worms get in.

"Don't think like that," a voice said. "Don't beat yourself up like you did me." Cole opened his eyes and saw Thoreau—his head at least— poking into the cabin. "Come with me," Thoreau said. "I'll show you which way she went."

Cole sat up as best he could in the little fabric cabin. He squeezed through the front flap behind and out into the maddening Grand Atrium. The people were as dense as a forest. They stared with big birch eyes. They talked, all of them all at once, like a murder of crows. Cole pushed through them, past the thawed-pond fountain, through more forest, more eyes. When he was on the verge of giving up, he saw her: a flash of her hair on the horizon. A slice of watermelon pink like the first glimpse of dawn. Cole quickened his pace. He threw limbs against limbs. He brought the tiny box from his pocket and shook it high above his head. Thoreau was nowhere to be found.

"Aurora!" Cole called. "It's me!"

Aurora turned and looked. She didn't see Cole, but he saw her. She was still within reach. If Cole could get to her before she disappeared, it would be the start of a new day.

Ryan Ridge

On the Horizon

When I opened the door, a tan man in a tan suit flashed a blue-and-gold badge and said he was with the government. Now it could've been my present hangover or my chronic insomnia, or the chronic I'd smoked in the night to end my stalemate with sleep, but still, this combination of fatigue seemed to break my brain as I couldn't think of a single reply to the government guy. For a solid minute, I stared stupidly at the street, listening to the neighbor's Pomeranian barking at nothing. Above us, a black hawk crested and dipped into a tilted pine at the edge of the dead lawn. The guy snapped twice in my face. "Are you with me?" he said, producing a little pad and pencil from his lapel pocket.

I yawned and stretched and nodded as I yawned. He scrawled something in his notebook. "What can you tell me about Morris Monroe?" he said.

I pointed across the street. "He lives there."

He nodded.

"Not much else to say," I said. "We sometimes wave to each other. He rides around on one of those electric scooters. You know the kind you rent with a credit card?"

The government guy motioned behind him with his tiny pencil. My eyes traced an invisible line to a scooter propped against the fire hydrant. "I ride one everywhere myself," he said.

"Which agency did you say you're with?" I asked.

"I didn't," he said. "I'll ask the questions. Would you say that Mr. Monroe is a trustworthy individual?"

"I've had like one conversation with him," I said.

"What was it about?" he said.

"He strongly cautioned me against painting brick," I said.

"And you didn't listen," he said.

"No," I said.

"The house looks great," he said.

"Thanks," I said.

"Did Monroe ever mention a coming revolution or try to coax you into participating in a bloodless coup?"

"No," I said.

"Would you partake in a peaceful upheaval or any sort of armed rebellion?" he said.

"Not today," I said. "I'm tired."

The government guy snapped his notebook shut and thanked me for my time. "You bet," I said as he walked away. When he reached the scooter, he pulled out a pocketknife and unscrewed the handlebar from the bike's base with the screwdriver attachment, and now he held the T-shaped bar aloft. "Oh," he said, "and there's one more thing." He aimed the T towards the upper branches of the pine tree and pulled hard on the brake grip. I heard a gunshot, saw a puff of dark smoke exit the end of the handlebar hole, and winced as a dead hawk hit the sidewalk.

"Look," he said. Soon I stood above the blasted bird with its mechanical guts spilling from its broken belly.

"What the hell?" I said.

"Drone," he explained. "And another thing," the government guy said, clawing at his face until his face came loose and fell off. He held the prosthetic mask in his hand, and his actual smiling face, I realized, was that of my neighbor, Morris Monroe.

"Nothing is as it seems," Morris said.

"Is your name even Morris?" I asked.

He lit a pipe, took a puff. "Doesn't matter," he said. "After the revolution, we'll have no use for names. We won't need words anymore, either." He exhaled thick smoke from both nostrils like an insane dragon.

"How will we understand anything?" I said.

"If we actually understood anything, then we wouldn't need a revolution," Morris said.

Next door, the Pomeranian continued barking, except now she was truly growling. On the horizon, a squadron of helicopters sliced through the sky.

Tom Kelly

Alternative Carls

Carl neither remembers dying nor feels dead, but when he wakes cramped inside a coffin. He doesn't need the scientific method to deduce an important funeral must've transpired during his afternoon nap. He kicks the wooden lid, stubs his littlest toe, and whines in meek resignation, what his wife calls a "Total Carl Move." He wants what he can't have: a lease on life and a microwavable chicken potpie from his toolshed's minifridge. While waiting for his vitals to expire, he tugs at the ends of the bowl cut he's worn for twenty years and imagines other realities in which he might've been a different Carl, better.

*

In one reality, Carl is a wealthy and successful private prosecutor who cannot read. All day, he signs important documents, says "Break it down for me in plainspeak" to his employees, and spies on the parking lot with a pair of Happy Meal binoculars. He lacks guilt over his unearned position and riches, because he believes his life of no consequence in the first place. In the mirror, he sees a nameless extra in a summer blockbuster whose years sum up to one high-stakes interaction with a hero he hasn't yet met. Death is inevitable, but well choreographed.

*

In another reality, Carl is bald with Empire State-sized ambitions of becoming a pastry chef. Carl can't cook, so he becomes a poet. Carl can't write poetry, either, so he becomes a tenured creative writing professor. At night, when he gets home from workshop, he tosses a stack of sonnets in the litterbox and wonders what he should bake for his students next week.

*

When Carl senses he's hitting his limit of possible realities, he envisions himself the face of a popular beer advertisement. Everywhere, a handsomer version of his mug beams off billboards, plasma screens, and frat kids' swimming trunks. Mostly, he cruises around town in the back of a stretch limousine and slurps Yoo-hoo out of juice boxes with his lover, Raymond Ramone. They both agree his photogenic grin makes up for a void of personality. This is the first time Carl's entertained life spent in the company of another man. He can't tell if he's attracted to Raymond Ramone. He knows he was never attracted to his wife.

*

Carl hasn't forgotten about the chicken potpie, but the alternative realities he's keeping in the dirt. Soon as he lost feeling in his spine, a seismic tremor split the ground and loosened the coffin's hinges from the lid. Now he pokes his head above the topsoil and greets crickets, a frog. He figures it best not to question how he got here. Tonight, in the delicious privacy of his backyard, he plays horseshoes three minutes past his appointed bedtime. When the metal loop catches on a neighbor's weathervane, he bows and blows a kiss at the yellow crescent moon.

James Harris

In the Clouds

Her casket was closed because they couldn't put her back together again.

My mom was the one who had to identify her. The tattoo on her right shoulder told her it was Monica. The rest of the body was ripped and torn, scattered around the intersection like discarded trash. Like the metal from the car, her muscles and bones were cut in jagged points.

"Mijo," my mom said to me, "it's like she blew up from the inside."

Acid built in my throat, but I held the vomit in. Stoic face. Straight back. Steady voice. "Shh, I know, Mom. I know." I felt each laceration like it was me being thrown around the car, not my twin sister.

When we were kids, around eleven or twelve, we used to play this game. There wasn't a name for it. It was stupid and, looking back, really messed up, but on sunny days, when the clouds were like pearls in water, we lay in the backyard and watched as they drifted past, slowly, without a care in the world.

Monica would jab at the sky and say, "An alligator! Do you see that cloud, over there? It looks like an alligator! That's how I'm gonna die." And I'd look where her index finger was pointing, and I'd nod.

"What do you see, Richard? What do you see?"

Monica saw everything in the clouds. Alligators, pirate ships, hearts, and cars, cars, cars. We'd come up with ways they could kill us. And we'd laugh because death wasn't real.

They buried her on a Saturday afternoon. Sweat stained the neck of my collar a mustard brown. There were clouds above, far from the sun. My mom cried until the tears ran black from her mascara, and then they ran clear. My cheeks burned and my throat pinched together. As they lowered Monica into the ground, we watched as parts of us were buried.

The reception was full of people I'd never met. Friends from college. Colleagues from work. Exes she didn't bother to tell us about. I shook their hands knowing I'd never see them again. They asked me idiotic questions. "How are you doing?" "You holding up?" "Do you miss her?" And I wanted to say that I felt like I was dying. My other half was ripped to fucking shreds and now I was alone, all alone, and soon I'd be nothing. I am nothing without her.

Everyone left the funeral home when the sun began to sink towards the horizon. The sky was a soft orange and purple, the clouds gargantuan. Finally, alone, I sat on the hood of my car and scanned the heavens. Maybe for Monica. Maybe for a sign. Maybe for salvation.

But all I saw were clouds and nothing else.

Just like when I was a kid.

Michel Houellebecq

The Crack

In quietude, there's an impalpable stillness,
I'm here. I am alone. If I'm struck, I move.
I'm trying to protect these bloody red hooves.
The world is a precise and persistent madness.

There are people around, I can feel them breathing,
their mechanical steps crawl across the barrier.
Yet I felt their pain, and their terror;
beside me, a blind man is heaving.

I have been surviving a long time. It's funny.
I remember the time of hope very well,
I even remember childhood's spell,
but I think this is my final journey.

You know, I understood it from the first second.
It was a little cold and I was sweating with fear.
The bridge was broken, it was seven, or near.
The crack was there, silent, unreckoned.

Translated from the French by Caleb Bouchard

Paul Rodenko

Bombs

The town is quiet.
The streets have widened.
Kangaroos look through the window holes.
A woman is walking by.
The echo is quick
to pick up her steps.

The town is still.
A cat slips off the windowsill, stiff.
The light has been moved like a block.
Three four bombs are dropped in the square, soundless,
and three four houses are slow
to raise a red flag.

Translated from the Dutch by Arno Bohlmeijer

Maria Zoccola

soft love

at five my favorite word was *please*,
but i grew up and learned it was the only word
that mattered. there is so much in this life
to eat: housefires and lucky dips,
gas-station trucker hats and dog tags
you find on the street. there is no end,
is the thing. is what i'm trying to say.
no place to sit down on the curb,
not even for a rest. think about a frog
the size of a plastic penny, traded
on the playground for all sorts of things.
gum wrappers. black magic. i think i want
to be held inside a child's hand,
kept warm by sweat and heat, by the heartbeat
in the thumb, laid down to sleep
on a cotton-ball bed. i eat
and then i'm hungry again.
my pockets overflow with parking tickets
and birthday candles and fistfuls of used
tissues. my frog was poison-dart yellow
and could hop so fast he could dodge raindrops
and cracks of lightning. so fast
he could split seconds, turn time gentle
as a warm breath. *please*, i said,
when paige traded him away from me
for a gel pen that bled on the page. *please*,
i say, crouching down on the curb,

heels sunk in an inch of dead leaves,
but my gut is empty and the wind
is a hand on my back, polite, insistent.

Philip Jason

The Woman Who Lives in My Bed

The woman who lives in my bed likes documentaries about nature and also ones about ancient cultures that did things we are unable to explain. I know this because she has taken control of the television and we've been watching these sorts of programs for months.

Tonight, we are watching a documentary about a system of tunnels dug into the earth by a culture so old, we don't know what to call it. What makes the tunnels interesting is their acoustic properties. The tunnels transport sound from one location to another location far off in the distance. Scientists believe they were used as an ancient telephone system but can't figure out how that culture was able to do this. In fact, they aren't sure that we modern humans can recreate it.

The documentary is fine, but I would rather be watching *Rim Shots*, a show about three astronauts in the future who travel around the galactic rim in search of the best jokes in the universe.

"I'm going to make some popcorn," I say. "Would you like some?" As always, the woman ignores me.

I get up from the right side of the bed, which is now *my* side of the bed, and head for the kitchen. With my back to the TV, I hear the documentary's primary archeologist.

"Isn't it amazing?" he says. "Even way back then in the dark, dark ages, people were trying to connect to one another across huge distances."

The woman who lives in my bed arrived on March 14. I don't know how she got into my house or where she came from. I returned home one night and she was lying comfortably on the left side of my bed, watching a documentary about a species of fish who have learned to eat man-made toxic chemicals.

What I do know is this: She's an avid reader, mostly self-help books. She reads two or three a week. I don't know where she gets them since she never leaves the bed. And I don't know where they go when she's done with them. I've searched my house but can't find where she's storing them.

While it's clear the woman who lives in my bed enjoys these books, they also serve a more nefarious purpose: She uses them to cancel me out. If I try to talk to her and she is not watching a documentary, she will pick one up from the nightstand next to her side of the bed and begin to read it.

For example:

One night, she was biting her fingernails and spitting the clippings across the room.

"Hey," I said. "Don't do that!"

But the woman continued to bite and spit.

"Hey," I said again. "Don't pretend you didn't hear me." I waved one of my hands in front of her face. "I'm talking to you." I started to snap my fingers. "Stop it."

She bit off three more fingernails. Then she turned to the left and picked up a book. It was called *Minding Your Own Business: An Entrepreneurial Approach to Managing Your Happiness*.

All in all, the woman who lives in my bed has read close to forty of these books since she arrived. Here are some of the other titles:

Secrets to a Casual Life
Big Heart, Purple Soul
You're Making Things Awkward
100 Tips for Superdates
Nobody Likes You

Sometimes I feel like she's trying to tell me something.

"*I Wish You Would Just Die?*" I said to her once. "How is that the title of a self-help book?"

The woman who lives in my bed is very different in the middle of the night. She likes to talk to me in her sleep. In particular, she loves to ask me questions.

"What do you think about people who live where there's no winter?" she asked me once.

"Like Pacific Islanders?"

"Not them, specifically, but people like them."

"I've never really thought about it."

"Do you think they like soup?"

"I imagine they're more interested in pudding."

"Oh. That's a good one. Pudding versus soup. Go."

Another time, she asked me this:

"Have you ever thought about what it would be like to throw your favorite thing in the world into a volcano?"

"No," I replied.

"Do it now."

"I'm not sure what my favorite thing is."

"Figuring that out is part of answering the question, silly."

"How much time do I have?"

"To figure out what your favorite thing in the world is? I don't know. Forever?"

I put a solid five minutes of thought into it. Every so often, I looked over at the woman who lives in my bed and saw she was making goofy faces at me (she's amazingly animated for a sleeping person; most of the time, if her eyes weren't closed, I'd think she was awake).

"I know what my favorite thing is," I said finally.

"What is it?"

"I don't want to say."

"You don't have to. But now you have to think about throwing it into a volcano."

"I don't know if I can do that."

"You have to try."

"But it really makes me sad."

"I know," she said. "Me, too."

The woman who lives in my bed doesn't perspire. She always smells pleasant. And she does not eliminate. I have spent a three-day weekend in my room, waiting to see if she gets out of bed to do so, and she didn't. She does eat, though, but only foods served in a large white bowl. She likes yellow things and green things and white things. Mostly, she eats bananas, kale, and marshmallows. I buy the kale once a week, and the bananas I buy every other day because she won't eat them once brown spots appear on the peels. I have sixty-three bags of marshmallows in my pantry, all of which were purchased on sale.

The first time I tried to feed her, I didn't know about her dietary needs, so I made hamburgers and salad.

"Everyone loves hamburgers or salad," I thought.

The salad was ordinary: romaine lettuce, cherry tomatoes, red onion, salt, pepper, oregano, olive oil, balsamic vinegar. I mixed it in a large blue plastic bowl and then dished her out a portion into a smaller bowl.

The hamburgers were also ordinary. They were premade patties I cooked until the centers were hamburger gray. I put them on whole-wheat buns.

When I brought the meal upstairs, the woman was reading a self-help book called *Adjusting to New Spaces*. She didn't look up. I put a TV-tray table next to her side of the bed, placed the food on it, and retreated to the kitchen, where I began to eat my own dinner.

I was halfway through my burger when I heard her scream. I found her curled up in the fetal position with a pillow over her head. The TV tray was knocked over. The food was on the floor.

"Are you OK?" I said.

The woman didn't answer, and I didn't ask again. I picked up the food and backed out of the room.

Hamburgers or salad? I thought. *I need to recheck my assumptions.*

The woman who lives in my bed used to make me nervous at night when I was trying to sleep.

What if I roll over and put my arms around her without realizing it? I thought.

In my head, I involuntarily imagined an electrified boundary that extended outward from her body about six to eight inches. Just being so close to this boundary made my entire body stiffen. I slept facing away from her, curled up into a tight ball.

Then, one night, she asked me what I was doing.

"Trying to sleep," I told her.

"You look like you're trying to fit inside a box."

"Sorry."

"For what?"

"I don't know."

"I'm going to try it."

The woman who lives in my bed pulled her limbs in and exhaled most of the air out of her lungs.

"Will I fit?" she said with the remaining air.

"Fit into what?"

"The box."

"What box?"

"The one you're trying to fit in."

I laughed and my body relaxed. I turned over to face her. Both of us were smiling.

"What now?" I said.

"You answer this question," she replied. "If you had to choose, would you spontaneously devolve into a monkey or evolve into a nebulous cloud of energy?"

The woman who lives in my bed guards the remote control fiercely. I learned this the hard way.

We were watching a documentary about an ancient culture that worshipped the mass of the sun, which this culture had somehow managed to estimate with a surprising amount of accuracy. The concept was interesting, but I wasn't in the mood to listen to the dull narrator talk about Sol-celebrating flatware for twenty minutes.

I get it, I thought. *The plates look like the sun.*

My attention drifted down to the bed, where I saw the remote control lying between her and me. The woman's attention was fixed on the TV screen.

Why not? I thought.

I reached out cautiously, my hand crawling across the bed like a Navy SEAL trying to sneak undetected into an enemy compound. I was expecting the woman to snatch it away suddenly, but her attention never wavered from the documentary, not even when I wrapped my hand around the remote and picked it up. For a moment, I savored its familiar mass, its power. Then I changed the channel.

Ha, I thought, *that was easy.*

I'm not 100 percent certain what happened next. I lost consciousness for a few moments, and when I came to, the channel had been changed back.

"Did you just hit me with a self-help book?" I said. Naturally, I received no response.

To this day, the woman who lives in my bed leaves the remote control in that same spot between us. Every so often, I reach out slowly and touch it. *Do your worst,* I think each time but never change the channel.

☾

The woman who lives in my bed keeps a list of things to think about. I know this because she told me about it.

"What's on it?" I said.

"I'm not ready to tell you that."

"OK, then, how many things are on it? Is that something you can tell me?"

The woman smiled.

"Ten things. That changes, though. A few minutes ago, there were twelve things."

On a regular basis, I like to get updates on what the number is. One time, she told me fifteen and a half.

"How can you have half a thing you want to think about?" I said.

"Sometimes, I want to think about something but not all the way."

"Like what?"

"Death, for one."

"Thinking about death is on your list right now?"

"Nope."

"So, what's the half a thing?"

She hesitated but only for a moment.

"You," she said.

The woman who lives in my bed receives postcards in the mail. They are all addressed to The Woman Who Lives in Your Bed. I try not to read them, but it's hard not to read a postcard without shutting your eyes completely. And these postcards usually don't say much. *Please come back to me.* Or: *I await your inevitable return.* They are signed, "The Man Who Loves You Most."

I've checked the postcards for postmarks to see where they're coming from, but they never have stamps. The image on the fun side of the cards doesn't tell me anything, either. It's always the same: a picture of a cowboy holding hands with a ballerina.

Really? I think every time I see it. *Who buys that kind of shit? And in bulk?*

The woman who lives in my bed is blood type B negative, which I know because she left a blood-donor card on my pillow while I was at work one day.

"What does this mean?" I said.

The woman was reading a book called *Sleeping Next to Morons*. She did not look up.

"You know," I said, "I don't really care about your blood type. In fact, I don't care about a lot of things about you."

I reached over to my night table and opened the small drawer where I keep my diary. I pulled it out, opened it to a recent entry, and began to read aloud:

"Things about the woman who lives in my bed I don't care about: what she got last year for her birthday, if she goes to the dentist for regular checkups, her thoughts on time travel, her handicap in golf, if she's ever had something in her eye, how much she weighed when she was born, if she's ever lost someone important to her—wait, that one's crossed out—her feelings on sales tax—wait." I grabbed a pen from my desk and crossed that one out. "That one's crossed out, too. If she's a good speller; the number of bees she's seen in her lifetime, approximately; if she has ever bounced a check ...."

The list went on for ten minutes. Not one to disappoint, the woman who lives in my bed didn't react.

That's OK, I thought. *If you're human, it has to hurt somewhere.*

The documentary about the "phone caves" is over. The woman who lives in my bed and I are now watching a documentary about depression in bears. It is mostly footage of sad-looking bears meandering aimlessly through the woods, interspersed with footage of even sadder-looking bears being poked with sticks by the documentarian.

"This bear lost its mate less than a month ago," the documentarian says. "I have been poking it with a stick for over ten minutes. As you can see, the bear does nothing."

It pains me to watch the bear being poked. I want it to regain its thirst for life and end the terrible documentary.

To my left, the woman who lives in my bed appears to be engrossed.

"How are you watching this?" I say to her. I wait thirty seconds for a response I know will never come.

I decide to try an alternate method of communication. I grab a pen and pad of paper from my nightstand and write the words, *How are you watching this?* Then I tear the paper from the pad and fold it into a paper airplane. I aim for a spot six inches in front of her nose and flick my wrist. The airplane soars majestically across her line of sight, landing on the floor a few inches from the bed.

The woman who lives in my bed doesn't even flinch.

I write out another message. *I know you saw that.* I fold it into a plane and sail it within inches of her face. Still nothing.

The woman who lives in my bed and I are at war.

For the next hour, I send squadrons of messages at her. One or two of them even hit her in the head.

You can't ignore me forever, I write.

And: *Your taste in documentaries is unforgiveable.*

And: *The forces of good (manners) will prevail over you!*

And: *I am not invisible.*

By the end of the documentary, the floor of my room is a paper-airplane graveyard, and my hand is cramped from all the writing (I was trying to ensure the messages were legible). Plus, I have several paper cuts.

"A battle scar," I say to the woman who lives in my bed as I show her the worst of them.

Her ignorance of me remains unconquered.

The woman who lives in my bed projects her dreams onto the ceiling whenever she is asleep and not talking to me. The first night I noticed this, I didn't watch them because I wasn't sure if it was ethical. I turned away and fell asleep on my side. I did that for almost a week before my curiosity got the best of me.

They're her dreams, I finally thought, *but it's my ceiling.*

The first dream of hers I ever saw was about a giant fortress filled with colorful objects and children. Each of the children had a favorite color, and they were able to use anything of that color as a portal that could take them to any other portal made from a thing of the same color. The children used this method to flit around the fortress. The woman who lives in my bed was trying to track them down and give them breakfast, but she had no favorite color, so she couldn't use the objects in the fortress as portals. Every time she tried, the object became a long, winding staircase that went up or down forever. She didn't seem to mind, though. The sounds of the children playing reverberated throughout the fortress and made her happy. Several times, she stopped chasing the children and sat down to listen to those sounds, but she was only able to stay still for so long because the breakfast she was carrying would start to get cold and she would panic.

I don't understand that dream. In fact, I don't understand most of them, but it's nice to watch something that isn't narrated by a lifeless academic or an actor who's only pretending to care about something. And the dreams she has aren't always so abstract. Sometimes, the woman dreams about planting tomatoes in a backyard garden or taking a walk in a park or watching fireflies through a window. And sometimes, the dreams include me. For instance, she has a recurring dream in which the two of us play tennis in a light drizzle. She has a monster serve I have difficulty returning, but I compensate with a relentless ground game that pleasantly frustrates her. On the nights I watch myself in someone else's dreams, even if I get no sleep, I feel fully rested.

The woman who lives in my bed is very fragile. I found this out when I accidentally touched her leg with one of my toes while she was sleeping. She yelped and her limbs exploded away from her body like a spastic fireworks display. She slipped a little too far left and almost fell out of bed. Frantically, she grabbed at the comforter. I grabbed at it also, and she used my weight to anchor herself.

"I'm sorry," I said. "I wasn't thinking."

"It's OK," she replied, still asleep but wiggling her way into a more stable position. "That was close, though. If I fall out of bed, I'll die."

"You'll die?"

"Yep."

"How do you know that?"

"It almost happened a lot when I was a kid."

"Well, I'm glad you didn't fall. Do you have any other weaknesses I should know about?"

"Oh, yeah. A ton."

The woman who lives in my bed can be destroyed by the following:

> too much talking
> overly critical people
> false teeth
> certain German dialects
> stillborn kittens
> sore losers

predictable ghost stories
the Department of Motor Vehicles
losing three times in a row at rock-paper-scissors
legitimate UFO sightings

The following things will only maim her:

bubble-gum-flavored toothpaste
antique piggy banks
white lies
nautical terminology
lightning
more than two minutes of elevator music
impersonal bouquets of flowers
decisions made through coin tosses
falsified UFO sightings
children raised by wolves

Naturally, I am very careful around her. I've abandoned my efforts to learn German, I make sure she wins at least once every three times when we play rock-paper-scissors, and I ended my friendship with Davie Wolf. Davie still calls sometimes and asks me why, but I don't tell him.

"Davie," I say, "we had a good run. Let's not ruin it at the finish line."

The woman who lives in my bed receives more than just postcards. She also receives phone calls. The first time, I found a message on my answering machine.

"Pick up, pick up," a man said. "I know she's there. I want her back."

Then he hung up.

He called back the next day. This time, I was home. I didn't answer immediately, but as he started to leave a message, I picked up.

"Who is this?" I said.

"I know you don't give her my postcards," the voice replied.

"I don't know what you're talking about."

"Of course, you do."

"Who are you?"

"She doesn't love you. You know that, right?"

"I think you should stop calling."

"Or what? What are you going to do?"

"I'm not going to do anything. Just stop calling."

"You really don't understand what's going on."

"I'm pretty sure I do. You want her back, but she lives in *my* bed now."

I hung up.

The man has called many times since, always between the hours of 12 p.m. and 7:30 p.m. He continues to leave messages.

"I know her blood type," he said in the most recent one.

The woman who lives in my bed turns all the food and water she consumes into evaporating self-help books. This, at least, is my theory. In an attempt to prove it, I installed video cameras in the bedroom. The job required a lot of hammering and drilling, which the woman who lives in my bed took no notice of, not even when I was drilling a hole right next to her side of the bed.

In total, I installed five different cameras that captured the bed from various angles, and though I primarily wanted to uncover the source of the books, I was also interested to see what it was she did when I wasn't around. It was a question that'd been bothering me since her arrival, one that followed me to work every day. I spent a good portion of my time in my office imagining what she was doing in the bedroom. I would love to say that in my fertile imagination the woman who lives in my bed behaved glamorously, that she called up her amazing friends and they congregated on my bed to solve mysteries or share slideshows that documented their amazing adventures in exotic locations like the Congo, but, sadly, I can't. In my head, the woman who lives in my bed enjoyed self-help books and documentaries created by my subconscious. The one I remember most was a documentary about the embarrassing moments in my life. It was pretty well scripted, but the narrator sounded too much like me.

Here's what I learned from the video camera footage:

1. Absolutely nothing that supports or disproves my hypothesis. In fact, I learned nothing at all about the self-help books.

2. At some point, the woman who lives in my bed donated blood. A nurse came to my bedroom with the proper equipment and extracted a pint from her. I don't know how the nurse got into my home (presumably, the same way the woman who lives in my bed did), nor do I have any idea who the blood was for. A sick child? A gunshot victim? An evil dictator who hoards every kind of resource? It could be anyone.

3. On a regular basis, the woman watches cartoons on TV. When I first found this out, I tried to talk to her about it.

"I like cartoons," I told her, hoping it would make a difference.

The woman picked up the remote and turned on the TV. For a moment, I was excited, but then she put on a documentary about an author who has written over two hundred self-help books on subjects ranging from coping with death to finding the perfect feminist hairdo.

"Did you plan this?" I said, "How is that even possible?"

4. The woman makes temporary sculptures out of the comforter. She's quite talented. She's created elephants, the Empire State Building, a 1972 Ford Mustang, a Mobius strip. I don't know how she gets the comforter to assume and hold forms with so much detail. It's another mystery, like the blood donation and self-help books, one I won't be solving any time soon. When she started making sculptures that looked uncomfortably like me and destroying them with flying elbow drops, I decided it was time to remove the cameras.

The woman who lives in my bed had fifty-three different dreams that I have watched and catalogued. They included the following:

The dream where she goes marshmallow picking in a marshmallow-tree forest.

The dream where she makes documentaries about herself, and they are are narrated with whale sounds.

The dream where she cuts herself and bleeds angry butterflies.

The dream where she and I are the leaders of a band of ninjas.

The dream where she sings "Happy Birthday" to everyone she meets.

The dream where she votes for me in a presidential election.

Of the fifty-three, the ninja dream is my favorite. The woman and I must lead our band of loyal ninjas across a field that's infinite so we can assault a rainbow. At the end, we realize we're going to die before we reach the other side of the field. It makes me sad when I think about it but in a good way.

My least favorite dream, on the other hand, is the one where she is kidnapped by a guy who doesn't know anything about her. He is crude and indelicate, and when she tries to tell him about one of her dreams, he sticks french fries in his ears. For some reason, though, she kisses him at the end.

Sometimes, I want to tear that dream out of the little notebook in which the catalogue is kept, but then I think about how empty my ceiling used to be at night and leave it where it is.

The woman who lives in my bed snores while she is reading.

The woman who lives in my bed likes to hold books in her left hand and turn the pages with her right.

The woman who lives in my bed laughs at footage of birds and squirrels.

The woman who lives in my bed keeps a drinking straw that I've never seen her use on her nightstand.

The woman who lives in my bed wears a polka-dot sweater.

The woman who lives in my bed never has more than twenty items on her list of things to think about.

The woman who lives in my bed always has braided hair.

The woman who lives in my bed has a birthmark on her shoulder that resembles a constellation whose name I forget and am too lazy to look up.

The woman who lives in my bed has left me with only one pillow.

The woman who lives in my bed usually has a small piece of kale stuck somewhere in her teeth.

The woman who lives in my bed blinks more than most people, but it's not Morse code.

The woman who lives in my bed has dry skin on her elbows and around her nostrils.

The woman who lives in my bed sometimes cries while she is dreaming.

☾

It is three a.m. The woman who lives in my bed and I are playing chess. She's been asleep for over two hours.

"This one has been on my list for a while," she says, "but I've finally thought it through. I think you and I should run away together."

"What?"

"You and I, we should go somewhere and escape all this madness."

"Where would we go?"

"Anywhere. It doesn't matter. Pick a place."

"I've always wanted to go to Greenland."

"Let's go to Greenland, then."

I laugh.

"We're not going to Greenland."

"Why not?"

"When would we go?"

"Right now."

"Impossible. It's extremely cold in Greenland. We don't have the right clothing."

"They probably have the right clothing in Greenland."

"True. But what about work? I have work tomorrow."

"Forget work. Work is humiliating."

"What about my house, then? What would I do with it?"

"Put a sign on it."

"That says what?"

"'FREE HOUSE.'"

"'FREE HOUSE.' I like the sound of that. Let's continue this when I get back."

I get out of bed and go to the bathroom. I'm gone less than two minutes, but I return to find the woman who lives in my bed is dreaming about birds laying eggs filled with peanut butter. On the night table next to her is a book titled, *Seriously, Why Don't You Die?*

Ha, I think and roll onto my back.

I watch the dream unfold on the ceiling, hoping to make an appearance.

Pedro Ponce

Field Trip

The time travelers are getting sloppy. They leave traces throughout my apartment—toppled glasses, blinking lights, car keys vanishing and reappearing in unexpected places.

Their carelessness suggests a pressing mission on which everything hinges. I can hear them scoff from the other side of their portal as I pour milk into cereal, squinting into harsh afternoon light.

No wonder the aliens took over so quickly, says the chief medical officer. His goggles make disapproving noises as they process my biometrics. I try not to take it personally and wait for my coffee to brew.

Maybe it wasn't aliens, speculates the lieutenant. Maybe he got lucky and heart disease did him in. Do we have a DOD?

Checking now, says the medical officer. I hear something like the squeal of a theremin followed by several light taps.

I'm losing the signal, says the medical officer, swearing at the fragile portal through which they scrutinize my breakfast.

We can project from DOB, says the lieutenant. She pronounces my birth date crisply into the void connecting us. The enunciated numbers prompt a series of grinding noises as paper ripples from a metal slot.

I remember that cereal, says the lieutenant. There's a box of it in the Museum of Early Man. We took a field trip there once for school. I've never seen one in such pristine condition.

Duly noted, intones the sober voice of the admiral, interrupting her. But your nostalgia has cost us precious seconds of infra-temporal integrity. Our connection won't hold much longer.

I hear the sound of tearing paper and then a deepening silence. The coffee is ready.

Tara Isabel Zambrano

Shameless

Nusrat calls me shameless. The way she says it, with affection and contempt. As if shame is a tandoori naan wrap holding all the feelings in, snug. I touch her cheeks, soft. We kiss again.

In an abandoned warehouse, Nusrat swallows me whole. Spit and sweat, my eyes misty. I am blank-faced, spent, while she adjusts her jeans and kurta, chameleons into a cool girl, puts her shades on. The joy I lose every time after I drop her home and drive back alone starts building up again. We walk outside; the clouds are sulking with rain. "Don't marry that asshole," I slow-mouth the words, the humidity stinging my skin like a thousand needles.

"Oh, you mean that middle-aged grocer, Rashid." She raises her eyebrows. I close my eyes and tighten my grip around her arm.

Nusrat is a little fucker I love, the way she struts in heels, the way she eats mutton and rice with her fingers, the rage she holds in because we cannot be together since I am of a lower caste than she is, the way she hollers, the agony and lust all released in one word, my name.

We motorbike around the narrow mohalla, our hundred-years-old neighborhood, in helmets. Nusrat is screwed to my spine, her arms around my stomach, pressing it, her chin digging into my shoulder. Old Delhi wraps us in its soot and nostalgia of sultanate and British raj, the aroma of its spice bazaar and sizzling jalebis on the surface of burning ghee, the shrill sounds of its hawkers, the prayer calls from the mosque, the constant ringing of the bells from the Hanuman temple. We chew the hours and pull the morning apart with the sound of the revving engine.

Nusrat skips town for a few days. When she's back, she is wearing the pink salwar and green top, an arm full of bangles. "Rashid's helping with Abba's debt. I am engaged to him," she says, looking at the ground. I start walking away. "It doesn't mean anything," she hollers, her voice cracked. I turn around and watch her run towards me, the slant of light on her neck.

I fuck Nusrat in my apartment. I ask her about Rashid; I ask her if I should talk to her father. "We can run away," I say.

"They'll find us," she begs, her eyes as large as a full moon, her kohl lining dark as night. I've heard about honor killings; I've seen pictures of bodies hanging from the banyan branches in the newspapers. I close my eyes and sing her favorite lullaby as she falls asleep on my bed. Then I gather my things and her things—a small mirror she kept by my bedside, her spare earrings, her single anklet; another fell somewhere while we were roaming. When I wake her up, the sun is crimson like a bride's attire, its gold splattered on the leaves, the roofs of houses.

"It's time for you to go." I whisper.

She looks at my packed bags. "Where are you going?"

"To find another Nusrat," I wink at her.

She hugs me tight. I inhale her scent and lick her neck.

"Shameless," she says, and pushes my mouth away. I grin. She cries. I caress her forehead like a child. We talk about finding a home with a veranda in Chandni Chowk, the one with long windows and high ceilings. Fireflies at night. We pretend we're going to the city fair the next day, and the day after that I'll teach her how to ride a motorcycle while her parents and her relatives watch, the whole Mohalla staring at us—the women in ghoonghats and burkhas calling on their gods to protect us. We talk about dying young from too much fucking. But the fact is: Nusrat would not die young. She'd learn to like Rashid. When she'd step into the storeroom where she'd keep the supplies and grains for the year, she'd inhale the musty smell of the sacks filled with grain, and she'd suffer my absence, if only for a moment. She'd postpone her thoughts for a later time when Rashid would still be at his shop; her kids would be running and screaming in the playground. Sitting outside in a veranda of an old-charm house with high ceilings and tall windows, she'd wonder if the handful of monsoons have washed her lust for me, if the tremors from the last earthquake in Old Delhi has swallowed the contours of my face, the structure of my body moving on top of her. Then she'd look up, leaning into the comfort of not missing me much, and the sky would descend to purple then navy and drop to her knees, lonesome.

Tucker Leighty-Phillips

Groceries

I've been trying to keep to the outer perimeter of the grocery store. Health websites say it's the best way to avoid processed foods. Most of the good stuff, milk and fresh produce, are along the border, like a moat or a barricade. Isn't that funny, all the good protecting the unsavory. Feels like a metaphor. To be honest, I stick to the outside because there's more space, less constriction moving around a table filled with peaches than, say, the cracker aisle. There is a sense of drowning among those center lanes. When I see a buggy at the end of one, I think of cage doors. Entrapment. The end of things. Which also makes me think of Jonah, you know, the guy from the whale, or, rather, the guy in the whale. I played him in a church production once. They asked me to do it because they could tell my faith was starting to teeter, cowering from the church bus when it pulled in the driveway, begging my mother to shoo it on from the window. They came back Monday morning, offered me the lead role. Jonah ends up inside the fish as a test of his faith, or something. That's how I felt, up on stage, in the center of a papier-mâché whale, newspaper articles about high school softball games bleeding through the blue paint. The whale was waiting for my re-devotion. In the grocery store, fish can be found on the outer barrier, usually in the back. Salmon, tuna, maybe haddock, depending on region and time of year. Sometimes there's one of those lobster aquariums. When I was a kid, I thought the aquarium was a magnifying glass, and the lobsters were actually much smaller than they looked. Little palm-resting crustaceans. Practically crawdads. I'll never know where I got the idea. Maybe I wanted them to be tiny enough to escape without notice. Maybe, to me at least, being trapped in something massive made you small by default.

Jim Daniels

Deep Silence of Sobriety

I ward off my personal vampire—the stench
of shadow beneath its black wings—
with warp-speed revolving clock hands
and the distant moan of a train
recorded and played backwards.
I nestle in the absence of the—
no, it's still there, sequestered
by the thin veil of years.
God's returned, wearing his crooked
hat, the clown nose and the permanent
surprised eyes regarding the calm statistics
of my recent life. *What's up, Big Dude?*
I ask, and *Why does that vampire feel more real
than you?* In that silence, he checks my breath.

Jim Daniels

Blowing Zero in Goudargues

We ate at a place off the main drag
        away from the tourists
on the canal, swans swimming
        with clipped wings.

Out back in a cement courtyard,
        a few tables next to a parking lot.
A group of boys sat on a high wall
        and watched us. They pushed

each other off the wall. We were boring.
        I'm used to boring people.
I quit drinking seven years ago.
        Knock on wood/a horn beeped.

A delivery truck circled the block
        for a phantom address.
My wife sat behind me sipping
        a polite glass of wine.

Flat water, I ordered, spreading
        my hands in the *safe* sign.
No bubbles. A helicopter hovered overhead.
        We looked up. Our server did not.

A bearded man tried to chase the boys away.
        They had their sour slouches on.
We ordered a mountain of shellfish. We plowed
        through it. We wore it down

to nothing. Our hands reeked of the sea.
> What's that word? Briny? I went for
the dessert sampler. They went for
> artisanal drizzled sauces.

Few vices fit in my small pockets.
> Another chopper.
What's going on? We all looked up.
> Takes more than knocking

on wood. Clocks tick loud
> in public places. We could have
stayed all night, but I begged for the check.
> We eased past the canal buzz.

Happy tourists posed and took photos
> of each other. The swans. The clear canal.
Blurry fish. Blurry selves. You can't be a snob
> about genuine happiness.

On the road out of town, two police cars
> were stopping everyone. Saturday night
drunk-driving checkpoint. Easy pickings
> in this tourist town.

I smiled and took the balloon,
> gave it everything I had.
> She sat beside me
in tears while I tried not to laugh,

giddy with seven clear years.
> Why was I so happy,
> the officer wanted to know.
You can't be a snob

about genuine happiness
> I almost said. He flashed
his light on the breathalyzer
> though I knew what it read.

He sent us on our way without warning.
      In between the laughing
and the crying, I blew my zero
      all the way home.

Daren Colbert

Silent Conversations With My Brother

How does a man build stone
on a body once so frail,
mold it like clay to move
like water? Where do the bones go

that belonged to the child
no longer there, the one who died
in the dirt of boys and their nature
that birthed the beast
standing before the world?

Vulnerability hides against his skin
like a shadow in the dark, like thorns
beneath his ribs that mar his chest
with every delicate move. His eyes
are blinded windows, shut
to all those hoping to enter
and witness the truths that lie
in their brown hue.

I look at the weight he carries
on his frame, the rigid lines
separating each pound from the next.
The taste of apple burns
against my throat, but all I do
is swallow it down and say goodbye.
He turns to leave and I watch his back,

how it is carved like a road map
to another time—

when he could be as soft
as wind, as pudding on the tongue,
as our father's kiss on his cheek
at night.

Brandi Handley

String

Ali didn't notice she was in the air until her head was bobbing gently against the ceiling like a balloon. Below her the sheets lay crumpled from where she'd slept. Or was she still asleep and in some strange dream where instead of falling she was floating? She swam through the air and flipped on her side, turning like a rotisserie chicken.

She'd been at her older sister Beth's house last night, eating spaghetti with mozzarella-filled meatballs and telling Beth how it seemed like she hadn't seen their dad in weeks. He got home after she went to bed, and he left before she woke up for school.

"Are you sure he's been coming home?" Beth had asked.

Ali hadn't understood the question.

But then Beth had said, "Dad's seeing someone." She'd hesitated before saying it and then had said it quickly.

Jeremiah, Beth's husband of one year, hadn't looked a bit surprised. It wasn't news to him.

Ali hadn't mentioned how her head had seemed to fill with air. Instead, she'd said, "That makes sense."

She pushed lightly against the popcorned ceiling. Her body sank for a moment before slowly floating up again. Little white ceiling flakes whirled past her head. Her eyes followed them all the way to the floor. If only getting herself down could be that easy.

She'd only ever floated in a swimming pool and knew only one way to sink to the bottom—she blew all the air out of her body until she could reach the top of her bookshelf. She used the shelves as a ladder to climb to the floor.

While she was changing from PJs to a T-shirt and jeans, she found herself up around the ceiling again. She pushed off from the wall with her legs, propelling herself forward and out into the hallway. She floated into Beth's old bedroom, where her dad had been sleeping for the last year, in search of something to weigh her down. She spotted a plastic cup from the gas station full of Dad's loose change. She poured all of it into her two front pockets. Instead of a balloon, she was an astronaut in space.

Astronauts didn't go into space without a tether. She looked around and found a spool of string, the kind she and Beth used to make into friendship bracelets, one of many items her sister had left behind.

She pulled herself down the stairs by the railing, grabbed her backpack, and bounded slowly through the front door to wait for the bus.

On the way to school, her backpack had weighed her down, but once she took it off in class to retrieve her math book, she rose in the air faster than ever. She tossed one end of the string down to her best friend, Lauren, who grabbed it and tugged Ali into her seat. Lauren held onto the string until Ms. Randal got tangled in it and told them to stop messing around. Ali, then, had to tie one end of the string to a chair leg; the other end she tied around her waist.

When lunchtime came, Ali realized she'd forgotten to pack anything to eat. She had to use some of the change from her pockets to buy a slice of pizza from the cafeteria.

After lunch, Lauren said, "You know, I can't really talk to you way up there. Were you even listening to me?"

Ali glanced down at her from where she had floated above their lockers. "Sorry," she said, "I'm running low on change." She unraveled the string from her pocket and let it dangle near Lauren's head. "I just gave you four quarters to buy chips."

Lauren jerked Ali to the ground. "You could try harder to stay put." She tied Ali's string to the handle of her locker. "There."

"I feel like I'm on a leash."

"It's better than floating out the door," Lauren said. Then she started laughing.

"What's so funny?"

"What if you got loose outside?" Lauren giggled. "That would be kind of hilarious. You'd look like one of those giant parade balloons. At a certain height balloons pop. Did you know that?"

Ali had never thought of that. She always imagined balloons just going up and up and up. How stupid. Of course balloons popped; they couldn't float up there forever. But where did they go then? Did the deflated skins just land in someone's yard one day? She should've seen at least one land by now, with all the balloons that had been let go all over the world.

She tried unsuccessfully to keep from thinking of what she would look like as a popped balloon as she and Lauren made their way to science class.

There were a lot of things she should've seen but didn't. Like her dad seeing someone.

"Your mom and I are working on it," Dad had told her when he'd first moved upstairs. "Nobody's going anywhere." He'd been upbeat then, optimistic.

When had he changed his mind? And why hadn't he said anything? He'd just stopped coming home. Surely, Mom had noticed, but she hadn't said anything, either. Ali had been the only one who hadn't known.

She was sick of being the baby of the family.

Mr. Johnson, her science teacher, had stopped talking. Ali had to look down to find him eyeing her. She'd never seen the top of his head before. From up where she had floated, his bald head was especially shiny.

"Ms. Lauren, help Ms. Alison to the nurse," he said.

The trip to the nurse was followed by a trip to the doctor's office. It was a relief to be in the car. The confines of the seat belt allowed Ali to relax for the first time all day. She sat in the back seat while her mom and sister talked nervously up front.

Mom squinted at Ali through the rearview mirror. "Have you been eating?" she asked. "You don't look like you've lost weight."

"I had pizza for lunch."

"I've been telling you to drink more milk. They say a woman's body stops absorbing calcium once she hits twenty-seven."

Beth twisted around and said, "Did you get bitten by a radioactive butterfly?" Then she pinched Ali's ankle. "Float like a butterfly, sting like a bee." She turned back to Mom. "Maybe she's training to be a boxer."

In the waiting area, while Mom persuaded the receptionist to bump up Ali's appointment with Dr. Mundhink, Beth draped one arm over Ali's shoulders and flipped through a magazine with the other.

"How do you feel?" Beth asked.

"I don't feel too bad," Ali answered.

"Weird," Beth said.

"Are you sure Dad's seeing someone?" Ali said.

"I'm sure."

"How do you know?"

Beth took her time picking another magazine off the end table.

"How do you know?" Ali repeated.

"One of Jeremiah's coworkers knows who she is," Beth said. "He handles her insurance. Dad's been paying for it."

"So? Maybe he's just being nice."

"Yeah, maybe," Beth said. "Mom's right—you need to eat more." She poked Ali in the ribs. "All skin and bones. We need to get you a steak or something."

Ali's arms were no longer resting on her lap but floating absently in front of her like two swimming pool noodles.

Beth glanced at them and said, "It's not like he's totally moved in with her or anything."

"Do you think he will? Move in with her?" Ali asked. "Where does she live?"

"I don't know—Jeremiah didn't memorize her address," Beth said. "Fourth Street, maybe? Somewhere near the Y."

Near the Y. Every time Dad hadn't been home, he'd only been a few minutes away.

Dr. Mundhink couldn't find anything wrong with Ali aside from the floating. Her heartbeat was steady; her lungs expanded and contracted smoothly; the full-body X-ray revealed her skeleton to be intact. The only other symptom Ali could think to mention was slight dizziness at times, but Dr. Mundhink attributed this to the constant change in altitude she was experiencing. Finally, he sent her home with a prescription for iron supplements.

At home, while Ali floated in her room, Mom sat like a stone in hers. Mom knew everything, Ali decided. She knew all about the other woman and the insurance and the house near the Y.

After several hours of hovering beneath the covers, Ali gave up on trying to sleep and let her body float to the ceiling. She kept thinking back to this past summer, now almost a year ago, when she and Dad had been at the mall, just the two of them. She'd needed new tennis shoes before school started. They'd parked outside Macy's, like usual, and once inside made their way past the purses and the makeup counters and the fancy shoes; the smell of leather and Estée Lauder perfume had made her mouth water. Then the quiet luxury of Macy's had opened up into the general chaos of the mall and the salty smell of the food court and the smooth speckled floor. They'd ridden the escalator down, gliding off the final stair before it disappeared into the floor. She'd felt the familiar bounce in her step, as if the escalator were springboarding her toward the Shoe Carnival.

She couldn't remember when she had taken Dad's hand—in the parking lot? After the perfume sample?—but she remembered precisely where and when she noticed she was holding it. They'd had to slow down their quick pace because a young couple was walking in the middle of the way, dragging their feet. It was a very young couple. They looked to be about Ali's age, and they were holding hands. As she and Dad went to pass them, she noticed she was holding Dad's hand.

The instinct to drop his hand immediately flashed through her. She would be thirteen next year. Teenagers didn't go around holding hands with their dad. But then a deeper instinct had made her cling to it more tightly. She'd felt defiant without knowing exactly what or who she was fighting against. She'd glared at the young couple, daring them to make fun of her, refusing to be embarrassed.

Ali had always worried about her dad, even when she was little. She'd lie in bed imagining him in a horrific car accident if he wasn't home before dark. She'd imagine a deer leaping into the road just as he was going around that last curve before their neighborhood.

He could be in the ditch at this very moment, maybe pinned in the cab of his truck waiting for someone to come. His cell phone thrown from the car—that would explain why he wasn't answering it.

He was either there or at another woman's house. It seemed more likely that he was in the ditch, despite what her sister had said.

Floating made it very easy to sneak out of the house. She drifted over the three creaky stairs and glided silently out of the front door. As she carefully placed one foot on the first of the porch steps, a gust of wind snatched her upward with a *swoosh!* She caught the top of the railing and gripped it hard as the wind pried at her fingers. Her legs rippled high in the air like streamers.

This must be how butterflies felt, completely at the mercy of the wind. She'd tried to catch the ones that seemed to be tumbling uncontrollably, to give them some relief, but she'd never been able to. They always kept fluttering just out of her reach. Then one giant gust would send them out of sight.

But butterflies could travel hundreds of miles. Monarchs migrated every year, somehow making it to where they needed to go.

Ali had a unique ability at the moment. If she just had more control, she could use the wind to her advantage. She could practically fly over the streets and look for Dad's white pickup from above. She was not a balloon—she was a butterfly.

Her body trembled. Her spine tingled. And her hands sweated until they couldn't grip the railing much longer anyway.

So, she let go.

The sky swallowed her. She whipped around in the air. She thought she might throw up. Closing her eyes, she took a big giant whiff of air through her nose and let it out slowly.

She would find him. She would be content just to find him and know that he was OK. When she opened her eyes and looked in the direction of the curved road, her body followed suit.

With some relief she passed over the curved road, finding all was dark and quiet. No skid marks, no wreckage, no white pickup.

She floated on. She floated along her dad's usual route to work at a surprisingly high speed. Treetops brushed her shoes. A few cars here and there followed the road, but none belonged to Dad.

Her body and brain seemed to be on autopilot. Soon, she looked down to see the YMCA below her, a big square building surrounded by streets that were lined with small houses. Houses near the Y.

She spread her arms wide and wheeled through the air. Her eyes followed each mazelike street, scanning for a flash of white. Any time she saw a white car or a white SUV or a white pickup, her heart would jump, bouncing her body upward.

In a cul-de-sac just a block away from the Y, she saw a white pickup and sank suddenly to the ground. But that could be anyone's white pickup, she thought. Even when she recognized the toolbox in the bed of the truck, she didn't believe it was his—not until she saw the coach's whistle around the rearview mirror. The truck looked enormous in the small driveway.

She felt embarrassed, like she'd walked into the wrong homeroom on the first day of school. Except there wasn't a classroom full of other kids looking at her, witnessing her embarrassment. She was alone and there was nowhere to go and no one to tell her where she should be.

Despite her lightness, her stomach felt heavy. She hovered a long time at the front door of this stranger's house, bouncing around in the air.

A window to the left of the front door was open, airing out a pair of sneakers. Sneakers that looked too small to be Dad's. Did this woman have kids? On an opposite counter, a dim light illuminated a spread of mail. Ali squinted but couldn't make out a name. To the right of the front door were two windows above the garage. From one of the windows, she heard the low murmur of a television, a sound that reminded her of her parents' bedroom at home.

She *could* simply turn away and float home and pretend that Dad would be there once she fell asleep. She started to follow her string back down the stairs. But if she left now, she wouldn't have the courage to come back. So, she knocked, her knuckles just grazing the storm door. Then she knocked harder.

The door swung open and a woman stood in front of her. She wore a large T-shirt and athletic shorts.

"Can I see my dad?" Ali said.

"Oh, my god," the woman muttered and disappeared back inside.

Then there he stood. Barefoot, ready for bed. He was looking down at her, perplexed, yet calm. He was thinking but not panicking. He knew what to do. He invited Ali in. She stood just over the threshold, pushing her hands down into her pockets, pushing herself to the ground.

Dad picked up his sneakers from the entryway, near where Ali was standing and took them over to the couch, where he sat down to put them on. He invited her in farther. She stood between the living room and the kitchen. She looked at the photographs framed and hanging on the wall. Bright, colorful, enlarged photos of two blond boys, maybe six and eight years old. The woman was front and center, hair gleaming bright blond, light-blue eyes, features Ali hadn't noticed when the woman was standing in front of her moments ago. Without the photographs, Ali couldn't have said what the woman looked like.

The woman had stayed out of sight—whether by request or by her own choice, Ali didn't know. But she was everywhere in that house, not just in the photos on the wall but in the furniture she had picked out for her home. In the ornamental wooden slats that declared HOME and FAMILY and proclaimed that readers should LIVE, LAUGH, LOVE.

Ali didn't see much of her dad in that room, besides him sitting in front of her, tying his shoes. This gave her hope that he didn't belong here, that he still belonged at home.

Ali was not surprised to be firmly planted to the ground. Her dad was there, and he understood the discomfort of her standing in a stranger's house. That was why he was putting on his shoes. He was taking her somewhere, somewhere away from this house.

Without a word to the blond woman, she and Dad left through the front door. Her feet landed hard and heavy on the concrete steps. She was in control of her body once more and easily hopped into the front seat of Dad's pickup.

She didn't know where they were going. She didn't care. The way the whistle on its long lanyard swung in circles around the rearview mirror was soothing.

A coach and a teacher, Dad kept people in line for a living. He knew how to handle chaos and noise. He knew about the human body. He'd be able to explain her floating. He would know it had nothing to do with what she had or had not been eating.

He pulled into the parking lot of the Waffle House—breakfast, their favorite meal. Inside, the greasy smell of the big metal grill behind the counter was thick. She could already taste the hash browns she'd order. She'd use the Waffle House lingo to order them "smothered" and "covered." She'd order a plate-sized waffle. Dad would get one of the meals that came with everything: eggs and sausage and hash browns, along with his own plate-sized waffle. Mom and Beth always ordered from the lunch menu. Lunch! At the Waffle House!

Dad slid into the booth across from her. He propped his elbows on the table and folded his hands in front of his face. He gave her a smile. She could tell because even though his mouth was hidden behind his hands, his eyes all but disappeared, crinkling and narrowing.

The waitress brought two glasses of water. "What can I getcha?" She looked at Dad first.

"Just some coffee," he said from behind his hands.

She looked at Ali.

Ali, with her mouth watering and about to say, "Hash browns smothered and covered," said, "Nothing for me."

"Are you sure?" the waitress asked. "We have some pie in the back."

"No, thank you," Ali said.

Ali could feel that her rear end was no longer firmly planted in her seat but hovered a little above it. She looked down and played with the frayed string between her fingers. When she looked up, she expected to meet Dad's crinkling, smiling eyes, but he was watching the cook scrape an omelet onto a plate.

Ali felt self-conscious, like when she suggested she and Lauren and Jessica go to the Pumpkin Festival last fall and it turned out to be lame and everyone was bored.

"I tried calling you," she said. "I was worried when you didn't come home."

"I'm sorry, honey," he said. "My phone was in the bedroom." He took a sip of coffee.

Once he had placed the cup back in its saucer, she expected him to continue, to explain the other unusual behavior, like his not coming home at night and the other times he didn't answer the phone this week and the blond woman in the house in the cul-de-sac and the sneakers in the windowsill. And her floating.

"I've been feeling kind of weird lately," Ali said. "Like sort of light-headed ...."

"Have you been getting enough to eat?" Dad said. "You should've ordered something."

"I don't—I don't think that's it," she said.

"Hm," he said. He didn't offer any suggestions or diagnoses. He didn't say anything funny. He didn't say anything at all. He was supposed to make sense of her floating. He'd always made sense of things, like why Brandon Berkman was always so mean to her and why her volleyball serve wouldn't make it over the net and why she couldn't do fractions.

"When are you coming home?"

"Ali," he said, "your mom and I ...."

"I know," she said. "You've been sleeping in Beth's room for a while."

He nodded his head.

"But when are you coming home? All your stuff is there."

He tried another smile. "Don't worry about that. I'll be by."

"But when?"

"Soon, honey," he said.

The waitress came by with the check. She'd meant to leave it discreetly on the table, but Dad was ready with his money and gave it to her before she could get away.

"You'd really like Sandra," Dad said.

Ali sensed that she should invite Dad to explain why, why Ali would like her. But what did Ali liking Sandra have to do with anything? What did it matter? What mattered was when he'd be by.

"I better get you home," he said. "Does your mom know you're here?"

She shook her head.

They walked out of the Waffle House, Ali clinging to her dad's hand, afraid if she let go, she would go up and up until she popped.

An older, rusted car pulled into the parking lot. Voices and laughter emerged from the car first, then three teenagers. They sounded like an absurdly loud commercial, blaring after a long dramatic scene on TV.

Ali didn't recognize any of them—these were older kids—but she liked the way they walked, swaying and bumping into each other, meandering through the parking lot. The instinct to drop her dad's hand came over her again. And this time she didn't resist and let her hand fall to her side.

Dad drove toward their house, following the same streets that Ali had followed from above, the same streets they'd driven down a thousand times together. But now it was quieter, except for the rumbling of the truck's engine, which sounded over-the-top loud in the silence of the cab.

After he pulled into the driveway, instead of opening the garage door to pull into his spot, he put the truck in park and turned off the ignition. The house looked strangely impenetrable with the garage door closed.

"Do you have your house key?" he asked.

She nodded.

"Let's go," he said. "Let's get you inside." He walked her to the front door.

Ali studied his face for some recognizable expression, but it looked not unlike the garage door. Locked tight.

She tied her string to the railing. She wasn't ready to go inside. They hadn't made sense of things yet. She was starting to feel defiant again, unwilling to let go of something she couldn't quite identify.

A gust of wind blew Ali off her feet and into the air, well above the roof. The string tugged at her waist.

Dad squinted up at her and pointed at the string, as if asking whether or not he should pull her down.

Ali nodded her head as well as she could while the wind tossed her back and forth.

From up there, the house looked small and seemed to be getting smaller. She glimpsed Dad briefly before he disappeared into his truck. The last of the string slipped from around the railing where he'd untied it.

The Missouri State University
Student Literary Competitions

On behalf of the Missouri State University Department of English and its creative writing faculty, the editors of *Moon City Review* are happy to announce the winners and finalists of the 2022 Student Literary Competitions in Fiction, Poetry, Creative Nonfiction, and Graphic Narrative.

Tara Isabel Zambrano, author of *Death, Desire, and Other Destinations*, judged this year's fiction competition. Zambrano decided on Meg Spring's story, "One-Way Ticket to the Big Pit," for first prize. Zambrano states, "'One-Way Ticket to the Big Pit' is a story with a lot of heart. Its deceptively simple language is daring in its core, meandering through the complex issues of relationships seamlessly." Fiction finalists this year were Hunter Adams, Taylor Barnhart, Steven Brymer, Sharon DeRubis, Jessica Flanigan, Blake Peery, Kathleen Powell, Habeeb Renfroe, and Shaina Thompson.

Nancy Chen Long, author of *Wider Than the Sky* and judge for the poetry contest, chose Katie McWilliams' poem "Please call me Katie with an 'e'" as this year's winner. Long comments on the winning piece, stating,

> There is much to admire in "Please call me Katie with an 'e'." At the poem's center is an invitation to experience the embodiment of contrasting voices: one loquacious, compliant, and youthful, while the other is succinct and authoritative—less wide-eyed. Through the poet's masterful use of form, rhyme, diction, syntax, and imagery, this winning poem interrogates the divergent aspects of identity, impressing upon us that one can indeed, as Whitman wrote, "contain multitudes."

We also applaud our poetry finalists, Molly Del Rossi, Abigail Jensen, Jueun Lee, Sujash Purna, and Eli Slover.

John McNally, author of over a dozen books of fiction, nonfiction, and pedagogy, served as this year's creative nonfiction judge. McNally chose Sujash Purna's essay, "A Colonized Essay with a Swollen-Leg Girl from Arambagh Intersection," declaring it, "… an impressive hybrid of the expository and the poetic, the didactic and the sublime."

Alexandria Clay and William Cole were named as creative nonfiction finalists.

"The True Story of My First Kiss" by Dez Pounds was selected for first prize in our inaurural graphic narrative contest by judge Josh Neufeld, author of several illustrated fiction and nonfiction texts. Neufeld says of Pounds' work,

> What strikes me most about the piece is the author's rhythmic poetic voice, which is well balanced by the storytelling and the pencils-only artwork. The story, though bittersweet, is sprinkled with much-needed humor and punctuated by a surprising/heartrending ending.

The finalists in the graphic narrative contest were Steven Brymer, Tara Doepke, and Katie McWilliams.

Many congratulations to our winners and finalists of these student competitions. We extend our gratitude to our guest judges and every student who entered.

Meg Spring

One-Way Ticket to the Big Pit

It is almost lunchtime. Mama is upstairs making love with Pastor Glenn. She has not cooked a meal in the last four days, but she cooked three meals a day for sixteen years—except on her birthdays and on Mother's Days because then Daddy or I had to do it. I think that it is fair that Mama is done cooking now.

Bobby's pudgy hand paws at my shoulder, so I reach a bit of ham and mustard over. His sticky-squishy fingers snatch it right up. I spread mayo on wheat, and I wonder how many ham sandwiches Mama has made. I think this is a teachable moment, and so I slap down the lettuce, and I turn around. "Robert, what is three hundred and sixty-three times sixteen?"

The ham juice makes Bobby's lips look slimy, like the time he tried to eat Mama's lip gloss when he was a baby. "It's somewhere in the ballpark of fifty-eight hundred, I think." He smiles all dimply, tongue pressed right up against his missing-tooth gap. I tell him he is correct because he always is and because I don't have a pencil to work it out for myself.

I give Bobby his sandwich on his triceratops plate. He does a joy-wiggle, his little butt scooting back and forth across the island. Bobby knows he is not supposed to climb on the counters, but I can hear Mama and Daddy's bed creak-thumping into the wall. Mama's too busy now to bother pinching my arm for not taking good care of Bobby, and I would never let him fall anyway. Besides, Bobby's not clumsy like other kids—not clumsy like me, either.

I fix a plate with two more sandwiches, stabbing five toothpicks through one. Daddy cussed at me yesterday because his provolone fell out before he had a chance to take a bite. It hurt my feelings, but I understand because provolone is my favorite, too. Nobody's cheese is escaping today.

Bobby asks me, like he did yesterday and the day before, if he can have lunch with Daddy, too. I scoop him up and plop him into a chair. "It's not safe in the barn. You could slip and fall."

"You could, too," he argues sweetly. He has a point, but climbing on the kitchen counter feels like enough danger for me. I tell him this.

"Eat your lunch in a chair like a human boy." On my way out, I grab a can of beer and turn on the television in the living room. Bobby likes to listen to the current events, and I hope it might distract him from the sounds upstairs.

I don't notice any new chigger bites on the way to the barn. Pastor Glenn mowed me a path through the pasture yesterday after he saw me scratching during Wednesday night service. He said I was distracting him during his sermon. I think I was only distracting him from staring at Mama, but I also think it's nice of him to mow the lawn now that Daddy can't. Daddy probably would not have mowed me a path if he could have, anyway.

I heave open the heavy barn door and tiptoe through. I am still worried that the echoes of my footsteps might be too loud and cause the whole floor to cave in. Bobby says our topographical region is called a karst and that sinkholes are not anything like avalanches, but I'm not taking any chances. I put Daddy's lunch in the bucket and unhook the rope from the wall, slithering toward the hole before laying down on my stomach. I lower the bucket as smoothly as I can, which is not really very smoothly at all.

"Hi, Daddy," I say. All the lights in the barn are on, so I'm able to make out the round shape of his donut floatie.

"What'd you bring me today?"

"Ham and cheese again, and a beer."

Daddy is mad when the bucket finally reaches him. "Why the hell is your mama buying Genny Cream? Genny Cream is for queers." Daddy is frustrated a lot lately, so it's easy to forgive his sour tone. I think that maybe I would complain, too, if I had to drink beer in a dark hole.

"Pastor Glenn's visiting." I don't think Pastor Glenn is really queer because I've seen him kissing Mama on the mouth, and also he came to our Sunday school class two months ago to warn us that if we ever thought about a same-gender person's body we'd get a one-way ticket straight to the lake of fire. Now, when I change out for gym class, I have to squint my eyes real tight so I don't accidentally think about the other girls' underwear.

Daddy grunts and reaches into the bucket for his lunch. He won't argue against Pastor Glenn because Daddy says that speaking ill of a pastor also buys you a one-way ticket to the big pit. I think that this is a good example of irony, and I wish Bobby were here because this feels like another teachable moment.

Before I eat my own sandwich, I sprinkle some feed down into the hole. Luckily, Mama was at the store and Bobby and I were both at school when the pit opened up, so it was just Daddy and a couple of hens who fell through.

"How are Penny and LV?" LV stands for Las Vegas, because Mama has always wanted to go to Las Vegas, but Daddy says it's too expensive and Pastor Glenn says gambling is a sin. Penny and LV are our nicest chickens. I thought about asking Daddy to put them into the bucket so we could scoop them out, but I think it must get lonely in there for him, so now I think it is better to let them swim together.

Daddy tells me that the hens keep trying to climb up onto his floatie with him and it's making it hard for him to sleep, so I promise the ladies that I will bring them their own blow-up raft. Daddy says that they would like an inflatable unicorn. Inflatable unicorns sound expensive, but I will ask Pastor Glenn for the money.

I ask Daddy what it's like, floating around all day. Daddy asks me to please be quiet except he does not say please, so I have to add it in my head for him. I finish my sandwich in silence, wheat breadcrumbs sprinkling down for the hens to peck out of the water. I want to ask Daddy if it was scary when the big hole opened up, but I already know in my head that it must have been, and I know that Daddy wouldn't admit to being afraid because boys aren't allowed to be scared. I imagine Las Vegas being swallowed up by the ground, wings flapping all useless. I hope she's happy being stuck down there.

The hole is not terribly wide—it doesn't even touch the walls of the big barn—but it is very deep. It took Mama and me a long while at the hardware store to find a rope that would be long enough for the lunch bucket. I asked Mama why we couldn't just use the rope to pull Daddy out of the pit, but she said he was too fat. Pastor Glenn agreed and said that it was an act of God. If God wanted Daddy to climb out of the pit, He would have built Daddy a ladder. This does not feel exactly correct to me, but I know not to argue with a pastor, and I don't know enough scripture to be able to anyway. I can't remember any Bible stories about building ladders.

I still know we are supposed to help others, even if we are not allowed to build them ladders, so I bring Daddy food and beer while Mama is busy with Pastor Glenn. Daddy was spitting mad, at first, that we couldn't just pull him up out of the pit, but he has been much calmer since Pastor Glenn shouted down a sermon just for him. I know I am supposed to act serious when he talks, but Pastor Glenn looked so silly shouting about the end of days with his hands on his hips, leaning over the pit with his butt crack poking out of his khakis. I laugh a little in my head, thinking about it. I know I am not supposed to laugh about the end times.

When Daddy finishes, he crumples up his beer can and puts it back in the bucket for me to throw away. Daddy grunts at me and I say goodbye to Penny and LV and head back toward the house. I feel a little pressure inside my chest, and so I take Daddy's trash and I chuck it real hard out into the pasture so I don't have to put it in the bin. I feel bad, though, for the cows, and so I have to search through the tall grass to find it again. None of the cows have ever left garbage in my house. I put the crushed can in the kitchen trash.

Mama and Pastor Glenn are kissing each other's mouths on the couch. It makes me feel a little sick in my belly, but it is an improvement over yesterday. Yesterday, I saw Pastor Glenn kissing a different part of Mama, right there on the couch, on my way back from Daddy's dinner. I don't know if what they were doing was a sin, but I know that I did not like having to see it.

I find Bobby in our room, reading today's paper. He has removed his little loafers and lined them up neatly at the foot of his bed. His proper white shirt looks almost ridiculous against his Snoopy sheets, like he's a little old man who really likes Charlie Brown. Ironically, Bobby has never cared much for the Sunday comics. This reminds me about my teachable moment from earlier, and I ask him if he thinks Daddy falling into the big pit feels like damnation-related irony, and Bobby says it does.

"I think there's a lot of irony occurring here lately." Bobby lowers the paper and props himself up straighter against his pillow. I have been working on teaching him good posture.

"Like what?"

"Haven't you thought about how funny it is that Pastor Glenn is having sex with Mama?" I am only mildly shocked to hear Bobby say the sex word. I am angry, for a minute, at both Pastor Glenn and Mama, though. I think that they should be more discreet around Bobby. He's so smart, but he's still only little. It's not fair that Bobby has to be so aware all the time when the most serious thing other third graders have to worry about is learning cursive. Bobby already knows cursive, and I think that should be quite enough. My cursive is not so great, so I have Bobby sign the checks whenever it's time to mail out the bill payments.

"I don't think it's funny at all. And I don't think you should say that word." I sit down on the bed next to him, squeezing his tiny knee. Sometimes, Bobby still looks like a little baby. I wish he could stay that way forever with me.

"I don't mean to be crass." Bobby pats my arm gently, and I feel my heart do a happy squeeze. "I just mean his involvement with Mama is ironic because pastors aren't supposed to be intimate with married women."

I think so hard about this that my armpits start to feel sweaty. I know that sex is not supposed to happen before marriage because Mama had me lie to Mrs. Kay from church when she asked about my birthday. That's how I found out I was conceived before Mama and Daddy got married. Conceived is a big word, but this does not feel like a teachable moment, and I bet Bobby already knows it. "Sex isn't supposed to happen *before* marriage. Mama is married."

"Yes, but not to Pastor Glenn."

"But does it count as adultery if it's with a pastor?" In my brain, I think that it probably definitely does count. But, also, I'm afraid about what might happen if I say something bad against Pastor Glenn. I tell Bobby not to answer because I don't want him to speak ill of Pastor Glenn, either. Shrugging, Bobby picks up the paper again, and I curl up next to him and watch his belly get big and small as he breathes in and out.

I try to think kind thoughts, but I cannot stop my brain from thinking about Pastor Glenn and Mama and Daddy and ladders. Wasn't Jesus a carpenter? Even if he didn't build ladders, I bet he probably built stairs at least once. I think that I do not like Pastor

Glenn at all, even though I know that it's wrong. I think his Genesee Creams probably taste bad, even if they don't make people queer. I think it's not fair to Daddy that Mama switched to Pastor Glenn's beer just as soon as Daddy fell into the big pit. I know that everything all the time is God's will, but I think God's will to have Pastor Glenn and Mama touch each other between their legs is gross. This whole house feels gross with their love in the air and all over the furniture.

"Bobby, do you wanna go to the store with me? We can buy some ice cream."

"I am amenable to that." Bobby is amenable to most of my suggestions. He is the most amenable person I know. I smooch his cheek for it. While Bobby slides his shoes back over his argyle socks, I head downstairs to ask Pastor Glenn for unicorn money.

Even the air around Mama and Pastor Glenn smells thick and I feel a little like throwing up. "Pastor Glenn, may I please have some money for an inflatable unicorn?"

He pulls his head away from Mama's neck and removes his hand from under her shirt jerkily, like he is surprised that I still live here. "You need money for what?"

"I need a unicorn for Penny and Las Vegas. They're tired of swimming."

He shakes his head and blinks big, like he thinks I am the one being unreasonable. He fishes his wallet out of the back pocket of his khakis and throws it to me, and I see his horrible butt crack again. How can Mama stand to look at his bare bottom? I suppose she doesn't technically have to see it to do sex with him. I mumble thank you and race away to the kitchen.

I feel spite blackening my heart, even as I see Bobby waiting for me in his tiny, fancy gray jacket. We used to be able to watch the evening news on that couch, and now Pastor Glenn's skin has rubbed all over it and I feel like a pile of vomit every time I think about sitting down there. I check Pastor Glenn's wallet. He has two credit cards and plenty of cash. I give it to Bobby to count and snatch up Daddy's keys from their wall hook.

Sweating again, I open the fridge and remove the rest of the pack of Genesee Cream Ale. There are eight left. I take the whole box with me as I leave through the side door. Bobby follows happily.

"Are we going to visit Daddy?"

"Yes, but you have to be careful, and hold onto me once we get inside." Bobby grins at me and his missing-tooth spaces make my heart less black.

Inside the barn, I don't even bother with the lunch bucket this time. Bobby and I sit close to the edge and he waves down to Daddy excitedly, wiggling his tiny bottom in my lap.

"I brought you more beer, Daddy," I say.

"Is it more Genny Cream?

"Yes."

"I told you I don't like Genny Cream." I pretend I don't hear this as I chuck the first can down. I also don't like Genny Cream, I have decided. And I do not want Genny Cream anywhere near me or Bobby. Genny Cream gets a one-way ticket into the big pit. I pass a can to Bobby, who tosses it down. Penny squawks from Daddy's lap, offended by the splash. I apologize, but I just keep throwing cans of Pastor Glenn's queer beer while Daddy yells out bad words. Las Vegas swims calmly. She does not care about flying aluminum even one tiny bit.

When all eight cans are floating in the hole, I scoop Bobby up and he waves goodbye, cheeks rosy like Mama's when she puts on too much rouge before church. Bobby is almost too heavy for me, and I feel lucky to be able to carry him like this for now.

I buckle Bobby snugly into the back seat of Daddy's rusty truck. I am barely tall enough to see over the hood even after I adjust the seat, but barely enough is still enough for me. I worry a little that I might get pulled over because I look young, but I am technically old enough to drive, even though I don't have a license. I already stole beer from a man of God. Driving without a license does not feel anywhere near as damning as that.

I am curious, and so I ask how much money we have in Pastor Glenn's wallet. "Three hundred thirty-eight in cash," says Bobby, blinking at me rhythmically through the rearview mirror.

"Sounds like enough for ice cream," I tell Bobby.

When we get to The General Custard Stand, I order a strawberry cone for me and plain vanilla for Bobby. I recognize the girl at the counter as Billie from church, a girl a few years above me in school. She used to wear lace dresses every Sunday until she stopped coming. There was a rumor that God handed her a one-way ticket after she got caught kissing a same-gender person. It is good to see that she is not actually stuck in a pit somewhere.

Billie's fingers brush against mine as she hands me my change, and I wonder if she ever tried squinting real hard in the changing rooms like me. I don't think Pastor Glenn tried squinting his eyes shut when he looked down at Mama from the pulpit. I think I would have seen it if he did. Billie seems nice, and I bet she has never rubbed her bare bottom all over someone else's couch. Her eyes are bluer than the sky, and looking at them makes me hate church for a moment. I don't even try to squint at her.

When Bobby's all finished, I clean up our trash and wave goodbye to Billie-from-church. As she smiles back, her lips curve upward all the way at the edges, the way I've only ever seen in movies.

The tank is almost empty, so I have to stop for gas. Bobby stays buckled in while the fuel pumps. There is a man, this time a person not-from-church, who is slumped against the convenience store wall like a big, lumpy doll. He is missing a shoe. I wonder if God really wants him to look so sad, but I decide that I do not care at all and so I march over and I hand the man one of Pastor Glenn's credit cards. Pastor Glenn always says that all good things come from God. Right now, good things come from Pastor Glenn's wallet.

I was too nervous to speak to the man and so I think that I might have been rude, but Bobby tells me that I did a nice thing as I climb back into the cab and so I feel fine about it. I sit, rubbing my sweaty palms across my skirt, before turning over the engine. "Bobby," I say, looking back at my favorite person through the mirror. "How eager are you to get home?"

"I am ambivalent." He grins at me, full of trust. "It might be nice to spend some time away from home and Pastor Glenn."

I agree. I put the truck in gear and roll us out to the road. "I read sinkholes can spread quick." This is a lie, but I know Bobby will not challenge me. "It's probably best for us to get somewhere safe."

"Indeed." Pastor Glenn probably should not have given us his entire wallet. This feels like a teachable moment, but I tell Bobby I love him instead.

Katie McWilliams

"Please call me Katie with an 'e'"

Adapted from Anne of Green Gables *by Lucy Maud Montgomery*
After Fred Chappell

Dear first-grade classmates,   *Slate*
as you stitch yourselves together like seams   *meets*
and line up your desks like red carpet rolled   *skull.*
out of a castle's doors, witness enchantment   *Repent.*
as your wands—number-two pencils—trace   *Embrace*
the dashed lines of cursive letters   *her*
with swirls and magic spells.   *spells.*
Now, my one wish for each of you   *Throw on*
is to use five simple letters when hand-   *an*
writing my name. K-a-t-i-e, not "K-a-t-y,"   *"e."*
which looks like "*cat*ee," sounds like my weakness: *Her fierceness is*
a kitten's pattering paws   *raw,*
and high-pitched "mews."   *spews*
If mice hear this mispronunciation, they'll drop their needles   *as*
   she reads
and cower behind sewing spools.   *"Ann" in chalk—a fool*
If I were Cinderella, I would soothe them to sleep   *sweeps away*
by singing of faraway dreams.   *her dreams.*

Sujash Purna

A Colonized Essay With a Swollen-Leg Girl From Arambagh Intersection

Therefore. The last time I used this word was probably back in Bangladesh, in my high school, in one of those meaningless letters we had to write in English class that followed very rigid, archaic, colonial formatting, disturbingly caring and yet aloof at the same time:

I, therefore, pray and hope that you would be kind enough to grant me a leave of absence.

We would start the letters like blind leading the blind:

With due respect and humble submission ...

It was like living in a black-and-white era movie with no background noise, our backs dripping with sweat of an eight-month summer as we quenched our thirst for a resolution with a stoic bliss from unctuous words serenaded into the deaf ears of our invisible lovers.

I actually *excelled* (another word I haven't used in a while) in it for the praise of my teachers. One of them was this guy with a beard that reminded me of Captain Haddock from *Tintin.* He was always angry with the way our country was running. *Our schools are importing monkeys trained to follow the circus masters! You are all those idiots! Monkeys screaming from the day one, and this system is telling you to say, "YES, SIR!"*

Therefore, I shared a bit of that anger with him, but mostly for my reasons to hate myself, that I wasn't a good enough student. I was wired to hate myself. I should have been much more *studious*. He was the epitome of a ghostly residue of our colonized mindset intended by our *glorious* oppressors, the British East India Company.

Therefore, I don't even know, as I write to you, reader, if I am actually showing you my true self or a colonized self. I am maybe using a walkie-talkie sealed with a British hallmark symbolizing the deaths and horrors of so many around the world.

The English teacher seemed *jittered* and *tousled* (two more words taught by my oppressors) all the time. I remember once I wrote a story about a man and his dog in his class. They go for a walk in the countryside, and the man somehow ends up in a river. The river is narrow and yet forceful in its currents, like the Buriganga. The dog is trying to help his master, but he is afraid of the water, and the man couldn't keep up with the streams, so he keeps crying out for help, but nobody is there. In most of my stories there is a drowning man. This probably has something to do with the fact that I am afraid of waters and drowning in general.

In the story I wanted to show the man's actions very vividly. *Therefore*, I remember I used the word "flail": The man was *flailing*. My teacher eventually read the paper and asked me what I meant with that word. I told him I just learned its definition in the Oxford dictionary. Maybe I am remembering it wrong, but I remember him telling me that I cannot use English words that people don't know, because they are not born in this language.

This was the closest I could get him to admit that colonizers built a system where a majority of people do not know what's going on because the system is written in a language they do not know. I only used a word in my tinkering little essay that my teacher could not grasp. Now think of a system that is written in an unfamiliar language and you're asked to learn it to navigate it.

A ponero koti manusher desh (A country of 150 million) is still trying to impress their colonizers by learning it, and some, while making mistakes, are resorting to hating themselves. Like me. *Therefore*, I pray and hope that you know I am not only flailing in this language; I am trying to express myself while acknowledging what makes me want to hate myself.

Our British colonizers were good at sowing seeds of doubt and judgment against our own people. Interestingly, I found the biggest example of that doubt through getting to know my own community, the Bangladeshi community in America, about eight thousand miles away from Bangladesh. My Bangladeshi side of the community is not a community at all. They are the *rankers*. They rank you based on how successful or rich you are. If you're working for a multinational corporation with a brand name, they will shower you with attention and gifts. If you're a poet like me, well, then you're just a nobody. It kind of helps if your father or mother back home are some big-shot people with power or money; then you could be redeemed. I don't have that, either. My dad's unemployed, and my mom's living on government pension after her forced retirement. She was crying on the phone the other day when she told me she wished she didn't retire early. She could have had the prime minister's "generous" bestowal of a higher cadre pension listing if she still held her job. But the men at her work were tiring her out with blatant misogyny. *Therefore*, she had wanted to quit for a long time.

Usually because of our hundreds of years of colonization, we love to idolize white people. In Bangladeshi communities in the USA, it is no exception. If you're a white man, you've won the jackpot. You are above all the misogyny or disregard. If you're a white woman, you're in purgatory, like my wife. They will not accept you among them until you make it big. Actually, even if you don't. You just have to wear brand name clothes, like Gucci or Kate Spade. Doesn't matter if you're furnitureless in your one-bedroom apartment or starving because you've dumped your last paycheck for an installment for a pair of Supreme shoes. Thrifting is a nightmare for these people. If you thrift, you are basically a street urchin in their eyes.

Therefore, you see, our colonizers were smart. They've egged on the model minority complex in us with a merit-based system. I myself occasionally have to fight with my Bangladeshi friends who have made it. *Trump is doing a great thing by calling out the illegals, deporting them! We waited in this line for so long, and they come in and just get in without waiting? How is that fair?*

I have no answer to their question. But I do know the *illegals* are not the enemy here. If you ever counted the amount of money the immigration system sucks off you and you happen to be living below the poverty line and death threats on your shoulders from the gangs of your local area and there is no protection, you wouldn't care what is legal or what isn't just to live one day at a time, anywhere.

When it comes to America, the meritocracy knows no bounds. With the steroids of capitalism, *therefore*, we've all become judgment junkies, salivating silently from a collective hysteria over our corporatized possessions.

When we talk about colonization, we talk about violence. My grade-school years were full of it, both inside and outside of the classroom. The ones outside of the classroom usually started with some cheap video game music in the background, like that 2D game Cadillacs and Dinosaurs. I remember passing by the market-side arcade gaming stores. There were shirtless boys, gaunt and skinny from lack of food, who somehow managed some quarters or some pintricks to give themselves credits and keep on playing for on and on. I was buying bitter gourds or tomatoes with my dad, and I could hear the cartoonish punches and kicks: Mustapha and his ensemble blessing the rogue dinosaurs with excessive force on a sliding stream filled with more goons and arcade props.

The boys would cackle like the hungry foxes. They would take out all the revenge they could on these little 2D monsters on the screens of the arcade machines. They were kicking and punching and fly-kicking, dreaming someday they could kick their abusive fathers out of their houses or their school teachers who won't let them come to school because they don't *fit* in. They were kicking their bosses who worked them to death for a few cents a day. I could see their sleepless, starving faces brightening up against the grainy, gleaming screens.

These kids are mostly homeless or sleeping in shanties. According to the World Bank, the estimation is that there are 4 million homeless children or street children in Bangladesh, and 75 percent of them are in Dhaka alone. The kids inside the arcade game store probably make a fraction of it. Rumor has it that many of these street children find themselves at the borders between India and Bangladesh and get sold and transported into the jockey market in cities like Qatar City or Abu Dhabi. One of my friends back in junior high school was once kidnapped and taken all the way to Benapole, but he made it back somehow, thanks to the intervention of the border police of India. Mustapha and his ensemble do not know that the young boys they are being controlled by with the help of fading colored console sticks are themselves in danger of being exploited by the evil system that corrupts them. Like the dinosaurs eating off the heads of the villagers in the game, the system eats away the hearts and the souls of these boys.

I don't even know what horrors their sisters or their mothers were going through. Women were always a mystery to most boys like me back in Dhaka. They somehow maintained a facade of patriarchy, or if they resisted they would get kicked out on the streets. I remember walking back from my high school on foot. I lived in an apartment building with my parents about a mile from where my school was. The apartment kind of looked over the busy Arambagh street that was flanked by makeshift fish and vegetable markets. And there were fleeting brothels in and around the alleyways that embraced the street like cobwebs. During rainy seasons, these alleyways were submerged in knee-length waters; catfish like darkest nightmares would spin in and out of these rivulets mercilessly, almost like valiant soldiers. There were rumors that these fish could give you rabies in some way, and for a kid like me who just recently grasped the differences between mammals and pisces, it was enough to scare the bejesus out of me.

In these alleyways during the winter and the dry summer season, there are women who sit by the pavements and in tea stalls, waiting for their clients, their bindis aglow with desperation, their faces whitened with talcum powder and standing out like searchlights for love, while their necks glistened with sweat and cheap jewelry. Their lipsticked lips spoke silent stories of horrors and violence from the men that are so desperately in need, and yet simultaneously full of hatred against women.

When one walks past these alleyways one can hear the clanking noise of bangles over the dry, lusty mud and garbage. There are vendors selling anchovies or rusting parvals in woven baskets. Farm chickens are clucking all day, despite the loud horns and yells from the vehicles packed like sardines in a crushd tin box on the Arambagh street. Pot calling the kettle black.

The women would give you coy smiles and sometimes they would end up on the streets as beggars after physical violence from their clients or pimps. There was this girl with a swollen leg (I can't remember which leg) who would sit in one corner of the intersection of the streets. When I would wait to cross at the traffic lights, I would notice her vacant stares glazing at me. I don't know any better, but from the stoic, glassy look in her eyes that I still remember, I think now that she probably hated how I had a place to go, an apartment home rented by my parents, a shelter filled with middle-class luxuries like buckets of water in the bathroom or stir-fried green beans on the kitchen counter, a TV with grainy broadcast of the FIFA World Cup or Bangladeshi cinema. I remember she looked like a bit of a spitting image of me, and it often bothered me thinking how my parents often told me they picked me up from the street just to mess with me. I often wished to sit down next to her and find out her story. Some days she would be gone and a part of me would be worried, wondering if her swollen leg from the infection she had for months finally got the best of her. My parents never knew I was consciously thinking about a girl back then, and I am glad I didn't tell them, because in their patriarchal, colonized heads a boy thinks about a girl for only one reason. They would have told me to focus on my studies instead, which I was already doing.

I often wonder about her name. I never dared to ask since the men around me would put two and two together and harass me to pay her, and I had very little pocket money to get by. Most of the money I had, I spent it on tea between my classes. I often wonder if her name was Rebecca or Sonia, very common female names in the part of the world I am from. I never saw any family members of the girl sitting with her, except this very ancient lady with a lot of lines in her face in her tattered sari. She would look at me suspiciously and I would avoid making eye contact with her. She could either be her grandmother or her pimp.

I often wonder about her whereabouts (another word I learned thanks to colonization!). She might still be sitting in that corner of the intersection as I write this, or she might be in the bed with a stranger, or she might be already dead from gangrene or some violent illness. There's no way to know. The other day I went on Google Street View to go back to Arambagh Street. I was virtually traveling around the city, and somehow I got to the intersection. The lights are still there, and there are many different kinds of vehicles caught up in the moment in the middle of the street. As you keep scrolling with the help of the mouse or the arrow keys on your computer, you can see the movement of these static vehicles and the hawkers hawking odd objects and bitter gourds inside baskets on their heads.

However, the girl, Rebecca or Sonia or whatever her name, with her swollen leg and her stoic, glassy stare from tired, doleful eyes, isn't there anymore. The crowd at Arambagh is caught in a time lapse.
The red light gleamd overhead below the smoke-filled sky.
There is no sign of her.

Dez Pounds

The True Story of My First Kiss

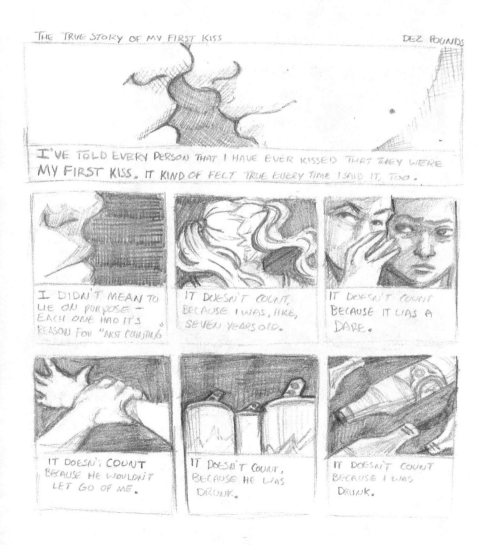

LOOKING BACK, HE PROBABLY LIKED IT BECAUSE IT WAS FAR AWAY FROM ADULTS.

AS FAR AS YOU CAN GET FROM ADULTS WHEN YOU'RE EIGHT, ANYWAY.

SEVEN-YEAR-OLD ME THOUGHT HE WAS SO COOL. IN A MEAN WAY.

LIKE, I'M PRETTY SURE HE CALLED ME STUPID RIGHT BEFORE HE KISSED ME.

AS FOR THE KISS ITSELF...

IT WAS PRETTY STANDARD FOR A LITTLE KID KISS. THE THING ABOUT THAT KISS WASN'T REALLY THE KISS.

THE THING IS THAT THAT BUILDING WAS DEMOLISHED A LONG TIME AGO.

THE THING IS THAT THAT BOY DIED AN EVEN LONGER TIME AGO.

THE THING IS THAT I DON'T KNOW IF IT COUNTS IF I'M THE ONLY PART OF IT THATS LEFT.

END.

Danit Brown

Jeopardy

In high school, Ms. Shaw, Owen's English teacher, tells the class she left her husband for a student. "I waited until he turned 18, of course," she said. "I'm not a monster." This is before Pamela Smart and Mary Kay Letourneau, before Facebook or MySpace. OK, Owen thinks. Mission accepted. He goes to the library and looks through old yearbooks, studying photo after photo of awkward teenage boys. Surely Ms. Shaw's student would stand out somehow: a full beard, maybe, or soulful eyes. He flips to the team photos and studies the members of the football team, who stand solemnly, helmets in hand, brows furrowed: meatheads, one and all.

Here is Ms. Shaw at her desk: Her hair is shellacked into place. Her nail polish is chipped. Her breasts sag. She is thin and forthright: "Leave me alone, guys," she says. "I'm on the rag." He tries to guess her age: Thirty-five? Forty? She is old in the same ageless way as his mother. By the end of class, there are circles of sweat under her arms. She fans herself and asks, "Is it warm in here, or is this a hot flash?"

Owen flips open another yearbook, working his way backwards. Ms. Shaw first appears in 1978-79, staring off into space, barely smiling. She doesn't look like a woman in love. In class, Owen watches her take attendance and wonders if her gaze lingers a few seconds too long on Conrad Hecht, the quarterback with hairy forearms. She calls the next name on the roster, which is Owen's. Her eyes meet his. She smiles. Her forehead glistens. They are studying figurative language. She is *literally* hot, Owen tells himself, but not *hot* hot.

At night, in bed, he tries to imagine it, him and Ms. Shaw, but the truth is, he can't imagine himself with anyone, not really, not yet. When he masturbates, it's his video-game self who gets all the action:

The real Owen watches from over his own shoulder, stalking himself from behind.

This is before Google but after Owen's parents get divorced. There are thirteen Shaws in the phone book, but only one named Georgina. She lives, he discovers, four blocks from the high school. He leashes the dog, an overweight corgi, and together they find the house, small and unremarkable. The blinds are down. The grass needs mowing. The dog pees on a wilted hydrangea. Back home, his mother has left a stack of neatly folded shirts outside his bedroom for the corgi to paw through. Owen undresses and lies in bed, studies his jutting hips, the spray of pimples across his chest. He should start doing pushups, he thinks. This is not the body of a man.

Weeks pass. Ms. Shaw cuts bangs, changes her nail polish from pink to red, from red to orange. On Curriculum Night, while his mother sits through a condensed version of Ms. Shaw's class, Owen picks up a Hot-N-Ready pizza at Little Caesars. He practices saying, "What do you mean, you didn't order this?" all the way to Ms. Shaw's house. "Be a man," he tells himself, then rings the doorbell. An actual man opens the door. He is as bald as a cucumber and short. Chest hair peeks out of the vee of his polo. He says, "I didn't order a pizza."

Owen forgets his lines, mumbles, "Keep it anyway." He hands the man the box and turns to go.

"Wait a minute." The man steps out of the house and onto the porch. "Want a piece?"

"Sure," Owen hears himself say. The two of them sit down on the front steps, and Owen helps himself to a slice.

"This is the guy who fucks Ms. Shaw," he tells himself, but even close up, he doesn't see it.

The man catches him staring. "Every year, at least one of you stops by. Sometimes it's a girl, but usually it's a boy. I should start charging admission." He shuts the pizza box without taking anything. "So what do you think?" he asks. "You want to feel my biceps? Check my teeth?"

Owen swallows, suddenly conscious of his own chewing.

"We could have a pissing contest," the man offers.

Owen stands up, and the man stands up, too. "Relax," he says. "I'm just kidding. Just having a little fun." He claps Owen on the back. "Seriously, guy, ask me anything. I'm the patron saint of lost high-school students."

"I don't know what you're talking about," Owen says stiffly.

"Delivery people wear uniforms," the man points out. "They drive cars." Then he asks, "What was your name again?"

For once Owen doesn't hesitate. "Conrad," he tells the man. "Conrad Hecht."

He walks away quickly until house and man are out of sight. This can't be right, he thinks. He had the wrong address, the wrong man, the wrong Ms. Shaw. He checks his watch. Curriculum Night is almost over. He is patient. He can wait. He returns to Ms. Shaw's and surveils her house from behind a parked station wagon. At 7:25 p.m., Ms. Shaw pulls up. She carries a lunch box and a stack of papers. She disappears inside, and then what? Does she hike up her skirt in greeting? Do the two of them do it right there on the floor? Owen knows better, sure, but just in case, he kneels on the sidewalk in front of the house and fumbles with his laces, hoping for a moan or gasp of pleasure. Inside, a blue light flickers on. Music filters out through the closed blinds. It's the theme from *Jeopardy!*

At home, Owen's mother is in the living room, folding even more laundry, also in front of Alex Trebek—there is no getting away from that man. "Who is Isaac Newton?" she asks the television. "What is Hawaii?" Watching her, Owen is overcome by a yearning so fierce that he almost doubles over: All that scandal, all that forbidden love, just to end up shouting questions at the TV. It isn't enough. It can't be enough. "What is guano?" his mother asks. "What is love?" Owen doesn't know the answer. He sits down on couch and waits to find out.

Garrett Ashley

Class Reunion

What's more is I can't look at their faces without feeling a sense of—everyone is here in the cafeteria, our small class of fifty-seven heads, like tulips, his head bulbous over the rest. You and I stay low, pretending to drink, talking to one another. I point and you point and we nod, talking—everyone does wrong by everybody—what is there to say when you ask why I'd not given you a chance to explain yourself? You were always the smell of burning plastic, of hair in my face, of humidity. I smoked cigarettes with you in a car, once, when we were both dating other people. There were good feelings, maybe somewhat harmful. In any case—the bulbous head, which belongs to the ex-NFL player, is connected to the widest pair of shoulders I've ever seen. He stands in front of us in the cafeteria, drinking milk from a box. He takes his shirt off, presumably so that we can see the marble of his skin, scars from a short stint of other NFL players plowing him into the earth. After a few years, he suffered some kind of debilitating leg injury. Got depressed, he says, and decided to do something good for the world, and so joined a growing land mine removal operation in Angola. He was the biggest white person they'd ever seen. They watched him coming from miles away. Shyly, he says he always took off his shirt there, too, working with the mines. It was hot and nothing fits him correctly anyway. Then there is the obligatory landmine story: His best friend of several years blew his arms off running wire. His friend, armless, learned to cook for himself with the nubs of his shoulders. The ex-NFL player got so depressed—for the second time in his life—that he stopped visiting his friend, and here he is now in the States, doing—he's talking about what he's doing when you get a phone call and answer it, leaving me with him, and I have to listen to the rest of our old classmate's story—what's there to say except you're doing what you have to do, walking away, and I'm doing what I have to do, staying here to listen, and I believe he did the right thing, too, abandoning his best friend of several years, abandoning that life. "How old are you now?" I hear myself asking. Do we age differently, the smaller we are?

Sudha Balagopal

Word of the Day

We stare at her long, long, legs, at the squares of skin peeking through the crisscross pattern of her pantyhose. We absorb the word she wrote on the board: adoration. We feel it in our cells.

We gape at the blue skirt that scrunches when she sits on her chair. We gawk at her face when she tells us there are many synonyms for the word affection.

We follow her golden tan to the cafeteria, to the library, to the teacher's lounge.

We horror-gasp when we see her with the maintenance man in the parking lot behind the school.

We hold our noses when he leans toward her, his paint-splattered hand touching her shoulder.

We place our index fingers into our mouths, make gagging gestures when he crouches to fix her wobbly chair in our classroom, underwear showing above the waistband of his jeans.

We huff when we hear the rattle of his tool kit and again and when he gives her a toothy grin, like a wolf's leer.

We drink in her melodious voice reading Shakespeare, toss notes seat to seat, saying she should be an actress on Broadway.

We memorize the way she loops the "d" and the "e" in the word of the day: endearment.

We disagree with her when she says attachment is not a synonym for affection.

We riffle through her desk when she's late from lunch, sigh when we find nothing but a handbag—red, big brass buckle, frayed handle—and a magazine.

We fall in love with the man on the cover of her magazine, a cross between a movie star and an athlete. We say: *This man, this man, this man should be her boyfriend.*

We decide so because she makes her eyes up like a model's, liner and shadow blending to illuminate the dark brown irises of her eyes.

We feel our hearts squeeze and hurt when she hugs the maintenance man in the back parking lot. We release trip-tripping breaths because she's with someone who fixes toilets, has stained fingers, and drives a clink-clanking truck.

We meet and plot and plan.

We paint his truck with the supplies from the art room. We fling bags of mud into his truck bed, smear leftover fries and ketchup on his windshield.

We throw rocks at the bathroom mirrors, leave jagged-sharp pieces in the sinks.

We meet and plot and plan and slide a note under the principal's door: *The maintenance man is dangerous. The maintenance man touches us in the wrong places.*

We huddle outside the principal's window, crouching, holding hands. We whoosh when the nun's face goes pale, then reddens as the blood surges. We slap palms when she stands, knocks her chair over, and strides out of the room.

We giggle when the maintenance man climbs into his truck.

We arrest the merriment when our blue-skirt idol runs into the classroom, hush when she grabs her bag.

We shout a collective *NO* when she slaps the metal of the maintenance man's truck. We let our heads hang when she climbs into the passenger seat, clench our fists when she slams the door.

We blink-blink like the signal on his truck, blink-blink as it leaves campus.

We blink-blink at the board and the antonym of the day: malice.

Megan Howell

Kitty and Tabby

Her full name might've been Catherine, but she went by Kitty when we were still failing out of Saint V's together. Sometimes our geometry teacher, Mr. Bell, called her Cate, and she wouldn't bother correcting him because she hardly came to class, anyway. That was the main difference between us: She was the type of slacker who skipped. I endured each test, failing miserably, never scoring anything higher than 55 percent in any of my classes. Not that the distinction mattered. Somehow, a fifty was just as bad as a zero, an F. The logic of the world evaded me.

She befriended me around April, I think. I was walking home, taking a long, winding route for the exercise. It was cool out but not frigid. When I took off my coat, I shivered, and when I put it back on, I felt suffocated. I undid the buttons and let the air circulate between me and the heavy, quilted fabric, hoping that the warmth and cold would cancel so that I'd feel nothing again.

Kitty came outside of the bungalow on Grant Street, the one with the purple shutters. I'd seen her hanging out in the yard during the warmer months, so I'd guessed she lived there. There was a guy who stayed with her, an older, goateed man whose face I couldn't remember. She was new to the area; she'd moved in less than a year ago, when she first transferred in the middle of the spring semester. Kids gossiped about her and the guy making out at the mall together.

Sweat shellacked Kitty's skin in a glamorous way that made her look as though she were made of fine, dark glass. She was taking out the garbage. A putrid smell kept me from going any closer. I watched as she hoisted the trash bag into the dumpster. The whole time, I avoided looking into her eyes. She was more popular than me. Consequentially, everything she did made more sense than my existence as Carissa Clearwater's ugly cousin.

"You're Tabitha, right?" she asked, dusting her hands, walking closer. "Carissa's cousin?"

I flinched. She was pretty and aloof like Carissa. She captured the attention of boys I used to fantasize about. I say "used to" because one of them, Uriel, my best friend in the whole world, a lifelong crush, ended my dreams when he said he could never love me—not because of my gender but my looks, which he said he found repulsive.

I stuffed my ruined hands into my pockets. I'd started biting my nails down to the quick again, piercing through the flesh until I tasted blood. I had no dreams or desires, only a vague urge to ruin myself. I wanted to bash my face against a steel door so that my mother would have no choice but to pay to fix the hump on my nose; hack the fat from my legs like meat off a rotating spit; jump off of city hall, the tallest building in our tiny hamlet, and be reincarnated as either a girl who was Victoria's Secret Angel: pretty or nothing at all.

"You should go by Tabby," Kitty said.

"No one ever calls me that."

"We could be Tabby and Kitty together."

"Sounds like the name of a cheesy sitcom."

"What's our theme song going to be?"

I laughed. When she didn't say anything and I finally realized she was being serious: "Something by Beyoncé?" I said.

"What's that one song? You have to know it. It goes: *People let me tell you 'bout my best friend.*" She started doing an awkward dance. "*Dun-dun, dun-dun.*"

"I don't know."

Silence passed between us. I wanted to leave but felt like the conversation was still going. Kitty swished her mouth from side to side like she was thinking of something serious to say.

"You know," she started, "I can't stand Carissa. She's not even that attractive, if you ask me. But your other friend. Uriel. Wow. If I didn't already have someone, I'd definitely want him."

"I have piano practice." The lie felt strange on my mouth as I turned to leave. "I need to go soon. My teacher, she's testing me on the scales or whatever."

Kitty called after me, her voice loud enough for people indoors to hear. "You should be careful. There's bad people." She paused. "You don't want to get hurt again."

Again. I started fast-walking. The word echoing in my mind: *again, again, again.* My heart felt like it was going to burst. What did she know? Had she talked to Uriel? Carissa? The principal's daughter who'd hated my existence since the second grade? Had the Discord of Saint V's students come back together to share more awkward, candid shots they took of me in P.E.?

My thighs chaffed. My chest swelled. Eventually, I struggled to do either. I stopped at an intersection and watched my mom's pet peacock, Percival, strut past me. He'd strayed too far again; my mom's house was almost a mile away. His sprawling train was folded in on itself like a closed fan. I petted his crown and he followed me all the way to the front porch, where my mom had laid out his dinner, candied yams in an old casserole dish.

Kitty was just playing mind tricks, I thought, as I watched Percival eat. She might know embarrassing things about me, but that didn't mean she knew me. My mind contradicted me, bringing up the look of knowing that had illuminated Kitty's eyes. I'd blocked it out when I first saw it, but my subconscious preserved the memory anyway. She'd been toying with me, treating me like some little kid who said funny nonsense that adults find amusing. Her eyes, an unnatural shade of green, were the only ugly thing about her. They were so scary, though I couldn't remember them well enough to describe them. Their shape resisted definitions.

I spent the weekend crying and, when I couldn't make myself feel anymore, rewatching a cooking show Uriel and I both liked. The feelings I still had for him softened the melodramatic music score, giving each episode a false sentimentality that I hadn't felt since we saw *The Notebook* with Carissa and her ex. I cried as a group of chefs struggled to keep a tiered cake from collapsing, thinking: How could he be so cruel? He'd been sleeping with my cousin Carissa for over a year, back when he still said he was gay and not bi.

My dad came home late in the evening from wherever he went now that he was jobless and without purpose. He threw his steel-toed boots onto the ground and chastised me for not greeting him like I used to. My eyes didn't break from the TV screen's glow. He was pointless to engage with, always punching walls when someone didn't say the right thing to him, so I didn't say anything at all. Dealing with his sour moods was like trying to fight a petulant toddler piloting the mech from that anime Carissa was obsessed with. He couldn't understand the fact that the degradation of our relationship had been a gradual progression that started years ago, before the hooker, when he cheated with an old neighbor and, before that, his coworker's ex-foster daughter.

I despised him not just because his crimes made the abuse that I faced at school worse but because I couldn't blame the bullying on him. My looks were what ultimately attracted their derision. Why else would Nancy Tadwater still be beloved by practically the whole school after leaking her best friend's nudes out of self-professed boredom?

"When's your mom coming home?" my dad demanded.

"Don't know."

"Yes, you do, bitch. Now, where's she?"

"A friend's house. They're playing cards together."

"So, you were just lying about knowing, then."

"You didn't ask me where she was. You asked when, and I said I didn't know."

"Such a liar."

"OK."

He trudged upstairs. My attention bounced from him to the TV commercial for vitamin-enhanced dog food to my phone. My iPhone's cracked screen kept lighting up with angry texts. Carissa was trying to guilt me over not speaking to her or Uriel.

I realized that I'd never liked her. Our two shared bonds, Uriel and a sense of obligation for the other that we mistook for love, had finally, mercifully broken. I deleted her messages as they came in, imagining that my phone was my memory and that I was slowly wiping all traces of her. *I didn't want to tell you because of Uriel.* Delete. *Ur seriously being so selfish.* Delete. *Uriel said he wasn't trying to hurt ur feelings. U literally were the one who kept pushing for details. U just can't accept hearing no.* Delete. *I'm done playing nice with people like you. You're a narcissist. Hope you flunk out of school and go to prison already that's what my mom thinks you'll*—delete, delete, delete.

Another message, this one from a number with a foreign area code: *It's Kitty! Look outside ur window* ☺. Carissa, I thought, my body growing hot with anger. I imagined one of her friends joining in on the fight just to make it more exciting for them.

I opened the blinds and studied the backyard. The grass was still overgrown and interlaced with weeds; the old playhouse basked in the sun, which had turned its hot-pink roof salamander over many years; empty Coke cans from Mom's birthday party collected rainwater on the deck. The striped umbrella leaned up against the fence, its wooden base snapped in two. Kitty must be playing mind games. I thought about blocking her.

Another message: *The front yard, dummie lol.*

I ran to the front door and looked through the peephole. Kitty was waving, smiling. In her small, blue-patterned package.

"Open up!" she said

My mind went numb with panic. While my mom hadn't banned visitors, she had an acute dislike of Kitty's type: wild girls, like the university students who lived two doors down from us and had parties practically every day, it seemed. Kitty was also black, very light skinned. Though my mom never spoke of race, her silence towards my older sister Melina and her Somalian husband screamed out. When she and my dad were still close, they used to threaten to drive me to the black part of town when I was being bad, making up impossible stories about giant poison octopi who lived in the dumpsters there. The latter would slow down his car when he passed through, even when I was saying nothing, putting the car in park and pumping the brakes like an expendable extra in a zombie film. Uh oh, folks, he'd yell over my screams, my mom's laughter, and my sister's silence. Looks like we're all out of gas.

I let Kitty in. She wore a floral dress that was too small on her, especially around the chests. Though she was tiny, she had mammoth boobs. She said that her back was hurting, then walked into the living room and plopped down miserably on my mom's recliner. I asked if she wanted anything to drink. She reached behind her back, digging into her dress to unclasp her bra's hooks.

"We have Diet Coke," I said because she was cool and I wanted her to be my friend. I prayed that she'd say no. We didn't have any Cokes. We could barely afford to keep the house, let alone waste food stamps on soft drinks.

"D'you have any beer?"

"No."

She peeled off her flats and sighed. Her expression stayed blank. She picked up the remote and turned the channel to the local news.

The anchors were talking about a dog who'd found half-eaten scraps of human remains at a landfill. She started channel surfing, whistling a tune that sounded made up.

"Oh, my gosh, I almost forgot!" Kitty said and pulled out a colorful package from her purse. "I got you a present. It's nothing extravagant. Just sweets."

"Wasn't Easter last week?"

"Yeah. That's why I got the stuff. It was on sale at Walgreens."

"But why?"

"Um, because I'm broke. I had to get rid of the guy I was dating. He was trying to kill me, and I wasn't ready for that. Not yet, at least."

"You should call the police on him. People like that only get worse if you keep them around."

"Nah."

"Oh." I looked down at my feet, trying to feel at ease while my heart cried out with anxiety. I was so lonely. Being around people only added to the pain, making me worry that I was always on the brink of losing a friend.

"Why did you buy me a gift?" I asked.

"I heard what happened with Uriel and was like, Wow, that sucks. He's so hot, too. I'd be pissed." She plopped her feet onto the coffee table, knocking over the small village of Precious Moments figurines. "I hate this body. It's been such a pain. It's not just that, either. I'm done with being a girl. It's too much stress"

"Me, too. I mean, like, I hate myself, too."

"I have a bunch of medical conditions because of this guy I was with before my new boyfriend. He didn't tell me how messed up he was before we got together."

"Did he have STDs?"

"No. Fibromyalgia. I thought it was an old-people's disease, but apparently not."

I nodded, assuming that whatever she was talking about was sexually transmitted. I lived in a small conservative town, very red, very religious. Carissa had informed me last week that it was possible to get pregnant while swimming in a pool with a chronic masturbatory because of how strong their sperm was, which was why she said she couldn't go to Davis Cottingham's pool party. Not because he'd spread a rumor about me being a pedophile freshman year for liking another freshman—no, she just didn't want to risk getting infected with super-sperm. The worst part was that I believed her until I googled the myth that she purported to be a scientific fact.

"I hate being pregnant."

Kitty delivered the words flatly as if she'd just said she hated waiting in line or going to the dentist. She didn't look it. Her stomach was flat. I started blinking hard.

"What're you gonna do next?" I asked.

She sighed and asked if I had anything that could treat pain. I brought her a bottle of aspirin and a cup of water from the tap. She took three times the recommended dosage of pills. All I could do was watch. She was strange in a way that made people want to get closer to her rather than pick her to pieces, which was probably how she'd made the Most Fuckable Seniors list at school. Or perhaps her strangeness elicited both desires, which was why she kept her distance from school: She didn't want it to destroy her. Yes, that was it. She and Saint V's were still in their honeymoon phase. The whisperings about her past—riveting tales of world travel and wealthy men, of a vague tragedy that couldn't be named and orphandom—hadn't had the chance to sour.

The way she shifted in her chair, wincing as she popped her spine, reminded me of my mom, who was complain-y and pretty and big-boobed like her. My mom did calisthenics to ease the pressure of what she coyly referred to as her "womanly afflictions." I was flat by comparison—not that I didn't mind. My dysmorphia concentrated around my face and weight. I didn't envy Tamara Russo or Emma Rosa, womanly-looking girls from school who people called slutty even though they were some of the more devout kids in the class.

I trained my eyes on the TV screen. A commercial for weight-loss supplements was playing. A fat cartoon woman unzipped her skin, revealing a thinner, bustier body underneath.

"If only people could actually do that," I said.

"Do what?"

"Just jump out of their own skin, you know? Like, it would be awesome if I could just pull all this pig fat off my arm and just be done with it."

"You could always have children. Live through them."

"That's a bad idea. For me, at least. Besides, even if my kids were way better than me, they'd just leave me eventually. And then my body would be in a million-times-worse shape than before, so I'd have nothing."

"Oh"—she popped her palm against her forehead—"I completely forgot. Sorry."

"What d'you mean?"

"I'm not like most women. I forget sometimes. I guess part of me wants to think there's other me's in the world, but then I have to tell myself: *No, dum-dum, it's just you.* I guess you just reminded me of myself. You look like someone who gets sick of being stuck in the same ol' skin every day. Not Carissa, though. Boy, will she be in for a shock when she turns thirty. Milky skin spoils. I learned that the hard way a while ago."

"How can you change yourself?"

"For you? You can get a name change, surgery. You can move. Or kill yourself. You have a ton of options. You could be like me."

"How're you different?"

"I can change form," she said as if the answer were obvious. "I've lived through all the women I'm descended from. My spirit can't rest until I have a boy, and then a new male spirit can finally take over until the next girl comes."

I tried to say something but could only open and close my mouth like a fish starved for oxygen. I'd read somewhere that pregnancy hormones could drive women crazy even after their babies were born. Sometimes, even the thought of being with child was enough to addle the mind, if the mere fantasy was strong enough. Maybe, I thought, Kitty was just in some niche religion I didn't know about. I'd once known a girl who was a Wiccan.

Kitty reminded me of a made-for-TV movie I'd watched with Uriel and Carissa. It was based on a true story, but the poor writing made all the true parts feel more funny than real. The main characters, a group of high-school girls, make a pact with each other to get pregnant. Carissa had purposefully chosen the movie to cheer me up, which it did because at least I wasn't a teen mom who had to deal with school. I temporarily forgot about all the rumors about me secretly getting facial masculinization surgery. We laughed at the stupid girls who'd willingly made themselves so vulnerable. How could they possibly think that having kids at their age would keep them and their boyfriends bonded to each other?

"Aren't you worried about people thinking less of you?" I asked.

"Why would I be?"

"Like, you don't want to be, like, a racial stereotype or whatever. Then people'll think of you in only one way."

Kitty snorted, making a theatrical display out of trying not to laugh. She thrust back her head, clasping both of her hands over her pursed mouth. Even as she got up and left, she laughed. She clutched her stomach as though the baby were already threatening to shoot out of her.

"What's wrong?" I asked.

"I'm not black," she said.

"Yes, you are"

"No, I'm not."

"Then what are you, then."

"I'm no one," she said and slammed the screen door so hard that it bounced back open.

I watched her waddle down the flagstone path my dad had installed the summer before his arrest. Desperately, I wanted to be her, only without the extra weight she carried. What I'm trying to say is that I wished I could be free, even though I obviously wasn't.

Carissa spread a rumor about me having limerence, a condition that I had to google. According to the internet, it was "the state of being infatuated or obsessed with another person, typically experienced involuntarily and characterized by a strong desire for reciprocation of one's feelings but not primarily for a sexual relationship." According to everyone else, it meant that I, Tabitha Drinkwater, had stooped as low as unrequited love or possibly even the lower, isolated hell of sexual predation where my father lived. I could normally alchemize other people's cruel words into flippant jokes I'd learned from fat male comedians. Now, there were too many to process. The rumors kept evolving before I could pin them down. They loved to see me in pain—"they," as in my schoolmates, who I repelled so hard that they all morphed into a single, contemptuous unit that was against me.

I tried begging Carissa and Uriel for help. I cried at our lunch table. Uriel hugged me, which only made me cry even harder. I viewed kindness as unstable energy that could collapse into hostility at any moment. I wanted to pull away, but the familiar scent of the lavender fabric softener his mom used made me feel nostalgic for a romance that had only existed inside of my head. I told him that I was sorry, that

I was happy for him because I loved him; I wanted him to be happy and everyone in the cafeteria to stop staring at me as if I were some wounded, dangerous creature on display. The rumors of me, which had existed since middle school, when my body first turned ugly, grew exponentially in size, threatening to break me down like a pair of giant breasts. According to the hivemind of my classmates, I was a barrel-chested lesbian who looked at other girls in the locker room, a maniac who wanted to kill Carissa so I could have Uriel for myself, a victim of incest, a product of incest, a whore, a prude, a homophobe. I could hear their voices, which felt so prominent that I could no longer tell what was my memory and what was happening in front of me.

"Are you really just gonna sit here and let her do that?"

"Look, she's doing it again."

"She's so creepy."

"Did you hear about her dad?"

"Yeah, he got arrested because the prostitute lady was, like, sixteen."

"I heard twelve."

"I thought she was fourteen."

For the first time since wetting my pants in elementary school, I decided to skip school and watch TV at home. I lied to Carissa and said that it wasn't her fault that people hated me a million times more than she had to. She gave a cautious smile. I went on, telling her that it was natural that she'd confide in her friends from the soccer team about Uriel and us. Never mind that the same group of girls used to dare each other to poke me with the sharpened tips of their pencils, trying to get me to "pop" and laughing when the teacher threw me out of the room for crying. I wanted to hurt her and love Uriel, an action that was impossible because they were now an official item, a single unit. He'd bought her a silvery locket, which shone brightly against her freckled décolletage.

Carissa called me that night to say that it was safe to come back to school, that I was no longer the target of everyone's ire because Kitty was pregnant. She didn't say that she was sorry. I pretended to be surprised by her anyway, then counted out the days that had passed since Kitty had come to my house. The last time I saw her was less than a month ago. Her stomach had been completely flat.

"It's so crazy," Carissa said. "One day, she looks completely normal, and then the next day it's like she's about to pop. She came into geography twenty minutes late, and Mr. P had to send her out of the room again when she saw her stomach."

"That sounds like BS."

"I was there."

"And that's supposed to make the story more believable?"

"Oh, my God, Tabitha, don't be like that. Do you have any idea what I'm going through right now?"

"I can't change myself for you. Sorry. I wish I could."

Carissa shifted the subject to herself again. I listened patiently as she told me about how she and Uriel were fighting. Apparently, Uriel thought she was controlling and manipulative. I pretended to care about her, my mind busy recreating the memory of him calling me repulsive. He told me after school, after confessing his bisexuality, which Carissa had slowly awakened. Something about her ethnically high cheekbones and long, dishwater-blond hair turned his envy for the features into a full-on make-out session in his brother's old Jetta. I joked about us having a threesome. He laughed and called me repulsive in a light tone that weighed down on me still. I made myself smile. I'd used self-deprecating humor as a joke for so long, laughing at myself the loudest to drown out everyone out. Still, no one had made him laugh all those times.

"Isn't that crazy?" Carissa said, breaking up my thoughts.

"It's super"—I stifled a yawn—"crazy."

"You were right about him. He's so fuckin' hurtful."

"Totally."

"I know, right?"

This went on for a while. When I hung up, all the light had disappeared from my window. I tried to look into the backyard again but could see nothing but blackness.

I went to bed early and woke up energized. I prepared an extravagant breakfast. I cut melon while uncured bacon cooked in the microwave under a sheath of dampened towel paper. At school, I came into math class fifteen minutes early and stayed long after the bell rang, staring at a midterm whose questions felt like an alien language. Kitty wasn't there. A boy had annexed her old seat near the helm of the class, the least popular one where the late kids inevitably had to go.

At lunch, Uriel and Carissa talked to me while ignoring each other. The attention felt flattering then quickly turned into an exhausting task that dragged. I gave up on trying to make myself eat the cafeteria food: watery creamed corn with undercooked, unseasoned chicken and milk.

When the subject of Kitty came up, the invisible, soundproof partition separating them disappeared. Uriel repeated what Carissa had already told me, only with new bits of information. He said that she'd thrown up by the soccer field, leaving a mealy lump of regurgitated food that someone posted a picture of online as a joke; that some thought she'd been wearing extreme shapewear all these months, which was why no one had noticed her baby bump until it broke through all constraints. Carissa took pride in Kitty's ostensible defeat. Though she didn't believe in God like her parents—she didn't think a benevolent deity such as Him would've let them lose their old house during the financial crisis—she still clung to all the puritanical aspects of her religious upbringing. She didn't think Kitty deserved to go to hell but rather the tangible, earthly equivalents of night school followed by a life of welfare, Section 8, probably jail.

I had the urge to kill my cousin. I winced and smiled, thinking: I should've drowned you in my uncle's swimming pool while I was still young enough to get away with murder. I didn't just want to kill her. I wanted to erase her from existence so that she'd never been born. The energy behind my hostility grew too large to contain, pouring over into my interest in Kitty. Guilt quickly followed. It was the worst type, the one that made me feel guilty for having sex with Uriel in my dreams.

"Where is she?" I asked. "Kitty, I mean."

Carissa turned to Uriel, who knew everything that went on at the school.

"I feel bad for her," he said. "It sucks to be in her spot."

"But why isn't she at school?" Carissa said. "Is she at the hospital?"

"I get what you mean," I told Uriel. I smiled for real this time, savoring the beauty of ignoring Carissa completely, a consolation prize for being denied her oblivion.

"I'm sorry," he said. "I didn't mean to hurt you."

"I'm sorry, too."

"I'm sorrier."

I laughed. Carissa rolled her eyes and tried to change the subject to a concert she and Uriel had apparently gone to last summer. Uriel ignored her, too, revisiting the subject of Kitty with a more sympathetic tone. He said he hated how the administration had given her the boot then made us both promise not to tell. He had a family friend who worked in the school's business office and didn't want her to get into trouble, even though the news would probably leak anyhow.

"It's all so hypocritical," he said, furiously squishing mashed potatoes with a spork. "Everyone here claims to be so compassionate, but they're lying."

"Definitely," I said.

"We should honestly create a petition for her."

"Totally!"

"I'm sure we could find a bunch of people who'd sign it if we can get just get it off the ground."

"Yes," I said, clapping, feeling my heart grow lighter with each suggestion.

Uriel asked Carissa if he could borrow a sheet of notebook paper to write down something that I can't remember anymore but felt important at the time. She swatted him away, giving him a pouty expression that looked more inviting than sad.

He put down his pen, drawing her into a hug.

"Carissa," he said. "What's wrong, girl?"

Her voice wavered, cracked. She broke down in tears. "You never pay attention," she said.

"That's not true and you know it."

She burrowed her face into her hands. "You're always leading me on like this. Why'd you bother sitting next to me if all you do is pretend I'm not here?"

For what felt like a million years, she cried into his chest. He cradled her head, burrowing his face into her hair, which had come undone from the French braids she'd worn that morning. I waited for him to bring up the petition again. The bell rang.

Another Saturday. The same message but from a different number with a foreign area code. *It's Kitty! Look outside ur window* ☺.

Kitty looked pale. Her glassy glow had become a curtain of sweat that dribbled down her face. Her stomach bulged through the cotton fabric of her striped shirt, which only made her look more inflated. She announced that she was anemic and let herself inside. This time, she opted to lie down on the low-slung couch. Both of her legs were wrapped in gauze and bandages. She said she was taking morphine that her boyfriend, a doctor, had prescribed.

I didn't mind the intrusion. I welcomed it. My mom was visiting a terminally ill friend from her childhood and wouldn't be back until early tomorrow. My dad was staying at his mom's because the rest of his side of the family found him too shameful to house. I'd thought my mind would mimic the calm of the empty house. Instead, it raced, filling with memories I hadn't had the time or concentration to think of for months, maybe years. People at school had finally stopped harassing me, at least for now.

"How's your back?" I asked.

"Awful. The pain's spread to my whole body now. I just want it to be over soon. I've been eating nothing but meat to make the pregnancy go faster. It puts my body in so much pain. Oh, Kitty, I'm just a mess."

She pulled off a large, bulging bandage from her arm. Underneath was a huge gash she'd stuffed with blood-soaked rags. She stuffed the wound with Kleenexes from the tissue box, forcing the rags deeper inside of her. I cried out for her.

"Don't be so loud," she hissed.

"You should get medical treatment. Maybe a surgeon."

"You sound like my boyfriend was. Except he was worse because I took the time to explain how my body works, but he just didn't want to believe me. He doesn't think I'm telling the truth. Hardly anyone does."

She put the bandage back on, slapping it down to her skin, trying and failing to get the weak adhesive to stick.

"Just go to your boyfriend or whatever."

"I already told you: He's gone."

"Go back to him again."

"Can you help me? I can't go to the hospital. I don't trust doctors. They have too much power."

"What do you want me to do?"

She rolled her eyes. "Help me give birth. I need him to help me speed things up. It takes so much more than pills to make new flesh."

"You're not in labor."

"Look. I just need you to make sure the thing doesn't choke on the umbilical cord. I don't want to go through this alone again."

Again. I said nothing. My hands felt clammy.

"If I wasn't so light-headed," she said, "I'd just rip your face off."

"I think you should go."

She stood still, staring at the fleur-de-lis-patterned wallpaper. She started biting her nails, chewing on them like I did. She swallowed, and I felt my stomach go sour. She did this for what felt like forever, prying each well-manicured nail with her teeth and devouring them. Blood dripped down her fingertips. She kept going, finishing off all ten fingernails so that there was nothing left but their bloody beds.

Then she ate her hands. I started to scream. There was so much blood, a cascade of it. Pools of red formed on the carpet. Her face looked pained. Devoted. She fainted, collapsing to the ground in a bloodied heap. Her head knocked up against the coffee table. A moment passed. She didn't get up. I looked into her face. Her eyes were open and glassy.

"Kitty?"

My voice sounded small, like it was coming from all the way upstairs. I couldn't make myself check her pulse, but I knew she was dead. My body started trembling. Though I couldn't move, the world around me surged forward. The phone rang. My next-door neighbor turned on his lawnmower. The leak in the kitchen ceiling was growing. The staccato rhythm of water hitting the pail grew faster. Children squealed at the park across the street. "Ready or not," one of them cried, "here I come!"

Red bloomed from between Kitty's legs, puddling onto the carpet. I heard the baby before I saw it. It crawled out on its own, its body wrapped in slimy tubes that looked too large and important for any of them to be umbilical cords. I made myself pick it up. I tried cradling her. It suckled my finger, then bit down hard on the flesh, drawing blood. The pain felt like a million electrified needles plunging themselves directly into my heart. I dropped her—it was a girl; there was no penis—and nursed the wound she'd left on my Mount of Venus.

The baby didn't cry. Instead, she crawled up to her mother's breast and bit through the cotton fibers of her dress and the skin, too. She suckled then ate, devouring the flesh with her incisors. I watched her swell in size. In my mind, her development happened all at once. There were no bright puffs of smoke, no explosions or awkward, liminal phases that temporarily left her with limbs of differing sizes. She was a baby and then she wasn't.

"What are you?"

The words felt like sandpaper against my throat. I was trembling so violently that I felt my bracelets clacking against each other.

"It's still me, Tabby. Obviously."

As she talked, I saw the semblance between the corpse and the new woman who stood in front of me. They had the same snub nose and big, anime-like eyes. Only, her skin was tan instead of brown. She was taller and thinner. Her chest wasn't as big.

I watched as the woman undressed the corpse of Kitty. Sweat drenched my shirt.

"Can I get some help over here?" she said.

I opened my mouth. No words. Only a cold, familiar silence. I watched as she put on the corpse's bloodied dress. She smoothed down her hair, smearing the auburn curls with her clean hand. The sunlight filtering through the blinds grew stronger. It hit the corpse, dissolving it into a bubbly red liquid that evaporated into nothing.

"Are you coming to school tomorrow?" I blurted out.

It was supposed to be a test. I wanted to know if she was really Kitty or some imposter. I'd seen it on cartoons growing up. An overly common cliché: two copies of the same person, one a doppelgänger who wants to destroy the world, and the other the true, original, benevolent character. The latter's friend, armed, had to shoot the former only to save them all. They asked the two a question that only the original would know the answer to. The copy falters.

Kitty laughed. "No way am I staying in this place, Tabby. I only came to get a break from city living. I think I might go to Paris. Or maybe London. I haven't seen the Thames since before The Blitz."

"Who are you?"

"I already told you: I'm no one."

"How old are you?"

She shook her head. "Even when you get it, you're still just as ignorant."

The time between Kitty's disappearance and Carissa's miscarriage was a blur. Of the events that I can recall: Carissa and Uriel fighting over some trivial misunderstanding that had to do with money; going to the grocery store and exchanging pleasantries with Katerina Nowak's mother, whose large, sun-spotted breasts reminded me of death; the Pabst Blue Ribbon I drank with Carissa and Uriel under the former's slatted roof; my dad coming back, leaving, coming back again, getting kicked out. I became especially numb to the changing seasons and silly school events. My dreams of Kitty devouring me whole felt more real than anything that happened when I woke up.

"Who gave you these?"

Carissa came into my room without knocking, her face still pallid and pinched from her hospitalization, which had allegedly happened sometime the week before. My mom must've let her in before leaving for her Saturday shift. She had Kitty's gift in her hands. I'd forgotten about the package until now. I wanted to ask if she'd recovered fully from the miscarriage, which I'd only heard about through rumors. But I decided not to. I didn't want her to feel more exposed than she already was.

I forced myself out of bed and watched my cousin devour the sour candies Kitty had gotten on sale. She threw the paisley wrapping paper into the trash bin then collapsed into the beanbag chair I'd stabbed with a pen upon realizing for the millionth time that Uriel didn't love me, that no one really loved me romantically. A steady stream of plastic beads leaked onto the carpet. I thought about blood again.

"No one," I said.

"Your mom said they'd been sitting on the coffee table forever. She was about to throw it out. Do you have a secret boyfriend or something?"

"No."

"An online friend?"

"No."

She started giggling. "Kitty?"

I paused, remembering: *I already told you, I'm no one. What are you, then? No one.* I still wanted to be Kitty, a formless blob that could use other people to remold herself differently, better. I wanted to be no one—not a nobody that everyone saw and ridiculed but a shape-shifter who could grow around the expectations of others that pinned me down. For the first time since discovering Carissa's relationship with Uriel, I let myself remember that time in middle school when

I'd let Uriel kiss me. He'd called me beautiful, and, though I knew this wasn't true, I felt the bones in my face reconfigure themselves into something beautiful. I let his tongue part my lips and infect me completely with his attraction. I didn't care that we were just supposed to be testing what it felt like to be kissed.

My eyes grew red. Tears rolled down my cheeks, wetting a dry, angry patch of stress acne that had been slowly colonizing my face since Kitty's self-cannibalization.

"Are you really crying?" Carissa asked. "Come on. I'm sorry. I can buy you more, I swear. You know I love you, cuz."

"It's fine. I don't care anymore. She's gone, anyway."

"She left a note. *To: Tabby*. Jesus, that's an awful nickname. Oh, my God, she's legit insane. Like, serious serial-killer energy. She didn't write her name or anything."

I jumped up, my heart racing. "What does it say?"

"*To a wonderful friend. I hope you have my future-son's daughter. You'll feel better when you learn to consume your old self.*"

I went to read it for myself, ripping the card out of Carissa's hand, feeling the bones in my face move again. The transformation felt more intense. Painful almost. I looked in the mirror and imagined my face slowly hatching like an egg. Gradually, a new life emerged.

Jeffrey Bean

Here Comes J., Back From the '90s

White shirt, blue smoke, black jeans, green smell of basil
in his armpits. He rib-jabs the dude who called me faggot.

Fingers scuffed from bass strings, calluses hard as bootheels,
his hands can crush a nose, then stroke my hair till I fall asleep.

Mornings, he turns kitchens into feasts of steam, tang of eggs
and hot sauce on his chin, French toast. His favorite sounds—

skateboards grinding half-pipe coping, coffee pouring
from carafe to mug, crackle of records between songs.

Look, he's shredding oregano, selling it to rednecks in dime bags.
Look, he's kissing me on the mouth.

Here comes his indignation, his rage when he's right
and I won't let him be right, when I hurt him

just to see if he can hurt. He's not taking my shit, magnificent
in his dragonfly robe. He licks syrup off his knuckle. Grins.

Jeffrey Bean

My Friends!

I love to walk past your houses and imagine you inside
      eating cereal or loading the washer or sleeping on your face,
and I love your yards, have I told you? Way better than mine.
      And the flowers! This time of year, anyway,
they are glorious and full of bugs and sometimes fluttering birds.
      I like how we have our shit more or less together now,
smoking weed (which is totally legal), then riding bikes
      with helmets and headlights, rushing home if it rains.
You are nothing like my old friends, who would sleep
      in dry fields with lit cigarettes and kiss me on the mouth
when they saw something beautiful, like a bank fountain
      late at night with redbud petals swirling around in it,
who would shit on the railroad tracks, drive to Kentucky
      for no reason, eat magic mushrooms with their guitar teachers,
and keep me up arguing about genetically modified potatoes.
      No, my friends, we are steady and talk about our new cars.
I will admit, yes, OK, you are all a little boring. No!
      I am boring, I mean, and pretty tired these days, and I like it
that way. It's peaceful; our kids are safe. I do, sometimes,
      wonder if—hear me out—we could, like, break into a liquor store.
Not to steal anything—just to do it, if, you know, we could
      find one with really shitty security, no video cameras or alarms?
And, OK, maybe we could have, like, *a* drink. We could
      leave money! Or not! What I'm asking you is, could we spend
one night, at least, in a closed liquor store (maybe we'd know
      the owner!) and wake up before dawn, well before it opens,
drive to Kentucky, where they have the best Waffle Houses,
      and get a huge breakfast, pancakes so big and syrup-soaked

My Friends!

they'd last us until bedtime, our kids' bedtimes, I mean,
  where we'd show up to sing to them, reeking of coffee
and sweet bready batter, the sunset out the window too much
  for one person to handle so we'd take them outside, hold their hands,
have them name the colors. Oh, and hash browns! Really greasy
  hash browns that would smell so rich on our breath our kids
would have to ask, and we'd tell them what they were, what we did.
  Everything but the liquor store. That we would keep between us.

Marci Rae Johnson

Hate List: Facebook & Summer 2020 Social-Distanced Visits

I hate how strawberries
collect the dew. The houses
we tore down, before. Hope.

I hate that work of art
that has significance for me,
or you. The games

everyone plays to keep the silence
at bay. I hate interesting facts
about birds, the thickness

of your neck, how I used to
watch you sleep when the night
was so deep not a single car passed.

I hate stout dogs barking
outside ice cream shops,
the masks on strangers

so I can never tell
which faces I used to love.
I hate small-town siren testing,

Robert Frost, the phrase
"from where I sit" & partially
opened chairs by the firepit.

I hate not knowing whether
you're out smoking on the porch
or writing that email to tell me

you're sorry. Sorry.

I hate that we're all in this
together. "Lean in." Forgetting
everything I read.

Having to breathe.

Bareerah Y. Ghani

I Was Never Yours

Dear Karachi, I'm sorry you're drowning—the pitter-patter of raindrops on gravel is loud, violent and booming—I wonder what you did now, who you made so angry now that they're hurling spit at you from up above—

Dear Karachi, I'm sorry you're turning to ashes as flames rise from burnt tires, kindled by the match curled in the religious fanatic's fingers; ribbons of smoke choke your airways, and a puff of black mist swallows your skies—

Dear Karachi, I'm sorry to have to break it to you, but you're not so dear anymore. To tell you the truth, you never really have been dear to me. I like to think it is because I wasn't born in one of your dingy hospitals; it's why I never felt an affinity for you. How could I have felt love toward you, like that of a child toward its mother, when Canadian snow imprinted itself on my rosy baby cheeks the night I was born? Doesn't matter that I never spent much time under the white sky. Doesn't matter that my parents left Canada a few months after my birth. What matters is that I was never really yours. You were never really mine. But that's the thing with you; you habitually take what's not yours. And so, as I sit here in a cozy little townhouse in Ontario's suburbs, scrolling through my Instagram feed, my insides squirm when I come across an entire account dedicated to you.

I click one post after another to find long and sweet captions under beautifully captured images of your sea, your streets, your sunsets. The account owner is pouring their heart out in these love letters to you. They say they are in love with the way you subsume them, with the way they find you in their blood and sweat. Each sentence I read scorches my gut, as if you, Karachi, are pouring absinthe into me, trickling it down my throat even as I gurgle and choke. The more I read such letters, the more I wonder about the people who write them. I wonder if they know your reality or are pretending to love you in spite of it. I wonder if anyone else can see that when it comes to you, Karachi, it's only a matter of time when the lovers turn to enemies, not because humans are hypocrites, but because you are a façade: the city of lights that emits darkness, the city of culture and diversity that breathes ethnocentricity, exhaling it so loudly, it consumes the minorities.

I was six when your slimy fingers, forked like a snake's tongue, grasped my body, claiming it as your own. Six is too young, Karachi. Too young for my mother to hiss at me to stay still, as she wrapped a scarf over my head for the first time, tying it in a knot too tight at my chin. She lathered layers of Johnson's pink baby cream over my cheeks and forehead while her face had settled in its perpetuity, creased, with a hint of a scowl right on her lips. I strained my neck, taking a peek in the mirror behind her as she fiddled with the scarf knot. I was disappointed to find that my skin looked the same. I had thought the pink of the cream would seep in, making my cheeks look flushed like my elder sister's, instead of the usual burnt brown. Unconsciously my hand flew up to the knot around my chin. My fingers tugged at it, trying to wrestle my mother's hand away.

"I don't want to wear it," I whined, wondering if my mouth turned the way hers did when she hated something.

She shot me the look: face pierced by a scowl, teeth gritted fiercely, her eyes popping out of their sockets, angry red lines streaking the whites. My hand fell to my side, and my eyes found the floor. She tightened the knot further, the scarf clasping my skull so desperately, as if hungry for the ideas inside, the daydreams, the imaginary friends, all the things I was told not to think about, all the things *you* labeled as distractions.

Next moment, I was yanked by the arm and shoved into the back seat of our car. I protested a little as it sped down the road, away from our house. I asked her why I needed to go, why she couldn't teach me herself, but she only responded with silence, her kohl-filled eyes glaring back at me from the slits in her niqab. Five minutes later, we had arrived at the destination.

The black, wrought-iron gate of the neighborhood madrasa gaped at me, its door left only slightly ajar. I was reminded of the countless times I had seen my sister disappear into the land beyond the gate. I had been too young then to follow. Now, I was old enough, but my sister was gone. She had learnt all she could from the place and moved on to the larger madrasa in another area. She had graduated, so to speak, except technically there were no graduations at the madrasa. With her gone, there I was all alone.

There was a puff and a hiss as the car came alive behind me. My head flipped to catch my mother's eye, my gaze full of desperation, begging her to take me home. But the white Suzuki Margalla sputtered away, and my mother kept shrinking in the distance and my heart sank deeper in my chest. My face felt sticky under the blistering sun. I turned back around and stepped inside, entering a white-tiled driveway where I was greeted by a woman, standing to my right.

She was wearing a long black chaddar, tiny curly wisps of hair peered out from under the fabric near her ears, her sweat making sure they stayed glued to her cheeks, obediently in one place. She smiled at me and told me to call her Baaji. She looked much, much older to be called my elder sister but I knew I had to comply. Then she gestured to me to follow her inside the small bungalow.

The entrance was just one screen door. There were murmurs on the other side, like cats purring in dark alleyways. We entered a lounge; ugly brown worn-out sofas lined the left side. On the right was a white door, in the front a staircase that led to the upper story. The air smelled sour, like sweat from the bodies inside had floated up to the surface and created a sheet that hovered above our heads.

Baaji handed me a thin, yellow book and I followed her inside. The room was brimming with girls, around fifteen to twenty bodies, crammed in the small space, some my age, others a year or two older. Eyes lifted off of the pages of books and widened as I entered, clutching mine to my chest, my heart beating in my ears. There was a consistent thump of the fan overhead. Everyone was seated around the room, in front of a wooden slat, a makeshift table that extended, making a rectangle that covered three sides of the room. The only side left uncovered was one where Baaji sat, reclining against a plush round pillow. She had a small plastic table in front where a Koran lay open, its pages fluttering every now and then when the fan blew air around. I was told to sit near her while the others returned to their lessons.

She opened my book for me and began to pronounce the Arabic alphabet, telling me to repeat it after her. I had heard recitations before, seen the verses written in black on yellowed, glossy pages, in thickly bound Korans at home. But there, under Baaji's gaze, the words on the page began to look like dark scribbles, swaying this way and that, with no meaning under their surface. But I did as I was told. Even at six, my default setting was to comply.

Every day at five in the evening, this was where I was left. For an hour and a half, my lips stuttered as my tongue rolled itself to form strange syllables and I took furtive glances at the clock. It helped a little when my cousin, Hafsa, joined the madrasa, too, a few days later. She and I would then sit close, whisper a little when Baaji wasn't looking. And when it was time to go home, we held hands as we walked out, our scarf ends happily swishing below our chins, bidding farewell to the white-walled, dreary bungalow.

One evening, my mother was meant to pick up both of us. We were waiting by the black gate, our fingers interlaced, our scarfs struggling to stay on our heads as we peeked out every now and then, waiting for the white Suzuki Margalla. A few minutes passed by, and then we heard Baaji yell, her lone head stretching out the screen door in the distance behind us. The sky was turning dark; mosquitos were buzzing in our ears, hungry for our blood. It made sense to wait inside.

The place had emptied. All the other girls had gone home. Baaji sat on one of the sofas, her chaddar a little loose now. Her hair was oiled, slick and gross, each strand so tightly pulled back as if disgusted by the sheen of sweat on her forehead.

There was another woman present, too, who apparently taught older girls in the upper story of the house but had walked downstairs now that everyone had left. The women talked loudly; the place cackled with their laughter while Hafsa and I stood meekly in a corner, sharing looks. One of them called us closer, asked us to sit on the sofa because it could be a long wait. It made sense.

But soon, nothing made sense. The baaji who taught us had pulled Hafsa into her lap while I sat next to her, sandwiched between her and the other woman, who had the exact black chaddar wrapped around her head. Hers was loose, too, the part draped over her chest bouncing as she giggled over things I could not understand.

Baaji was stroking Hafsa's milky white cheeks, asking her where she got the strawberry printed clip that held back her silky hair. My cousin replied in almost a whisper, her voice quaking, its tremor matching my heart's. Sweat clung to my pores as I felt the woman next to me shift a little closer. She walked her fingers above my arm,

Bareerah Y. Ghani

crossing my collarbone, finally reaching my earlobe. She said she liked the silver stud earring my mum had forced me to wear. Her breath was hot and smelly as if she had just eaten a while ago. She asked me where I got the earrings, if I would be happy to give them to her. I didn't respond. She then asked: Where did I live? I didn't respond to that, either. My gaze moved toward Hafsa, still in Baaji's lap. I noticed her strawberry clip was gone and Baaji was stroking her silky straight hair, telling her she doesn't know where the clip went. Then Baaji looked at the other woman, the two shared a look. They smiled a creepy smile as they said they didn't feel like letting us go home. They asked us how we would feel if they locked us in a room in the upper story.

I was six and I was scared. But that's all I remember. No matter how hard I try, I don't know what happened next. I don't know how Hafsa and I got home. I know that I never told my mother about the incident. What would I have said anyway? I still don't know what to say except that my insides squirm every time the memory surfaces. My skin prickles every time I think about the moments spent in that bungalow as if it knows something my mind doesn't. I wonder if Hafsa remembers it the way I do. I wonder if my sister remembers it the way I do. I wonder if the countless other girls who studied there had similar experiences; I wonder if they had it much, much worse. Outside of that madrasa, I know of some young girls who did have it worse because of you, Karachi. Zainab Ansari was one of them.

In 2018, Zainab was six, the same age as I had been when I entered the madrasa. But unlike me, Zainab wasn't lucky enough; she was on her way to a Koran recital when she was abducted. She had hazel eyes and silky hair parted exactly the way my cousin Hafsa's mother parted hers. Instead of a strawberry-printed clip, Zainab's hair was held back by a soft pink fuzzy pin. She was young but not young enough for the man who took her, raped her and then strangled her. When I first heard the news, my mind reeled back to a memory of the day when my mother had dropped me off for my Koran recital at the madrasa and the car sputtered away, but right then, I had realized that we had been given the day off.

There was no Koran class, it occurred to me. I had spun around and shrieked, waving my arms, watching as our driver turned the car left into the other street. Tears were streaming down my face as I ran after it. I knew the way home; I knew the turns the car would make, and yet I screamed at the rear windshield as I turned left. The sun was glistening on the glass, like a diamond sparkling in the distance, and I kept following it, like a man out at sea following the star, hoping my mother would just turn around once. But she didn't.

My slippers dragged against the gravel road as I tried to keep my pace, regarding the car as it made another left turn; I knew I had to go around that corner and one more to reach home, I knew I would be safe if I could just keep following the white Margalla even though my mother couldn't see me, couldn't protect me. Just the sight of our car, of her in the distance, made me feel safe. But the feeling didn't last long.

I was close to the street's end, about to reach the bend the car had just turned, when a man emerged from a nearby house. He hollered at me to halt, asked what the matter was. I slowed down, hiccupping as I told him my mother was in the car that went by and she had left me. I hadn't stopped; I knew better than that. I kept running, clutching my copy of the Koran to my chest, my scarf flailing around me. The man tried to jog a little to keep up with me. He told me to wait, take rest, saying he would call my mother. But I didn't listen. I don't know what would have happened had I stopped, had I listened to him. But I am glad I had the sense to sprint faster then. I wonder if my mother felt the same way when I reached home with tearstained cheeks and muddied slippers. I want to say she must have felt relieved nothing had happened to me, but I can't say it. Because when, at twenty-three, I left you, Karachi, and my mother asked me why, I told her you made me feel exposed, naked even with all my clothes on. Her face was blank, and there was only silence at the other end of the call. A little while later, she had asked how I could leave home just like that. And I think about that a lot—that conversation, that word: home.

When it comes to you, Karachi, I find the word "home" to be empty, devoid of all meaning. For isn't home supposed to be a safe haven? But you can't offer that. You can barely leave us alone, or the houses we call home. And don't you deny it because I have proof, proof that you pollute what is pure, puncture holes in what is guarded and secured, barge in on us like we are part of the property.

On Sept. 26, 2019, six men forced their way inside a woman's home at 12 p.m. In broad daylight, they raped her at gunpoint. But that's not all. They filmed the whole thing and then tried to blackmail her with the evidence of a crime they committed but *she* would be shamed for. And what is more is that when the woman plucked courage and reported the case, it turned out that of the six, two men were policemen—men part of the force that you call madadgar (helpers).

So tell me, Karachi, tell me how to not be so fucking angry at you?

Street corners, dark alleys weren't ever safe—for little girls or grown women—but you have stolen from us our homes, too. And it's not just strange men you let into our spaces, our rooms. It's uncles, fathers, and brothers, too. On July 4, 2020, a woman filed a first information report against her husband. His crime? He raped their fourteen-year-old daughter. Oh, but wait, that's not all. He had been raping her for years, and the mother had stayed silent because of the humiliation she knew it would bring her and her daughter.

These are the very men whose blood runs in our veins. The very men who tell us to be wary of the men *outside*. The men who command us to cover ourselves until no inch of skin is visible because of course it is our flesh, naked and out in the open, that entices innocent men. But tell me, Karachi: What do you have to say about the women in burkhas who are gawked at? Women with bodies hidden under layers and layers of clothes, who are groped in shopping centers? But wait, oh, wait. Let's come back to our homes. Back to the men within, who are meant to protect us. What about the women who are raped in their own beds, not by strangers who barge in, not by brothers or fathers who live in the next room. Raped in their own beds by husbands, because you, Karachi, you have made sure to declare at every point, at every such case: There's no such thing as marital rape. Section 375 is the only legislature related to rape crimes, but it includes no reference to marriage because a woman's "I do" is taken to extend to sexual intercourse, too, whenever, wherever, and however her husband wants it.

Consent as a concept is lost in your black smog, drowned in the fetid waters overflowing from the gutters you refuse to fix. It's a figment of our imaginations, you tell us. Another one of our feminist propagandas. When we come out on the streets for Aurat March, holding banners that say Mera jism, meri marzi (My body, my choice), you rally up men and boys, even the ones from elite institutions, the ones we think are educated, and they join forces with you and label us as whores who want to dance naked on the streets, when really, Karachi, all we're asking for, is to just. Fucking. Let. Us. Be.

But you don't listen. You punish women for exercising their right to say no. In 2017, Raheela Rahim was taught one lesson. She refused to marry her then-fiancé and he threw acid on her, disfiguring her entire face. She suffered scars on the left side, completely lost one eye and barely managed to keep some sight in the other one. With that on display, she walked into the courts demanding justice, but we all know how you work, Karachi. We all know the power you give to policemen such as her then-fiancé.

But perhaps what sickens me the most is that it isn't just men. Your poison seeped into the women, too; you were there watching from the shadows as the evening sun fell and the women at the madrasa who were meant to be mentors intimidated two little girls, closing in on their physical space, prickling their skin with their touch. You were there hiding in the crevice between my dresser and the bedroom wall every time my mum hurled her anger at me, weaving a mirror with her words, showing me my reality, my place: the fact that there was none. She told me you held no spot, no love for a dark-skinned girl like me, no marital bliss or even the potential for it, which translated into no future for a girl like me. But it wasn't just she who made sure I was aware of the color of my skin, the spots, the blemishes, the acne scars. It was also the billboards, doused in baby pink with models smiling down at me, their skin white and smooth. It was also the TV advertisements that displayed the woes of a dark-skinned girl unable to find love or acceptance from a man and his family until she lathered copious amounts of Fair & Lovely. Until she didn't look like herself anymore. But wait. While being dark was a crime, Karachi, you made sure to tip the scales for the fair girls, too, tossing them a bucketful of their own, special kind of mess. I witnessed it, secondhand, through my sister's account.

At thirteen, with skin the color of goats' milk, its texture like butter, my sister was learning how to make homemade recipes to tighten her pores, maintain her complexion. My dad bought her a treadmill that she used twice a day, with the time in between spent doing crunches, as my dad hovered over her teaching her the proper form. Right now, even after two kids, her core strength is better than mine. But that's not what impresses me. I am in awe of her resilience.

At fourteen, she was coerced into dressing up every other weekend. Rolling out a trolley filled with assortments, sweet and savory, she would enter the living room to find my mum and grandma perched on the sofas with some random aunty or two, who were meant to be her potential in-laws. Their faces beaming, their cheeks pink and rosy, their eyes would follow my sister around the room. One would think that after a few such unsuccessful meetings, my parents would give up on the ritual but that didn't happen. With every meeting that proved futile, there was another lined up real soon, and for each one, my sister was made to go through the same motions.

She would pour warm chai from a thermos, serve them to the guests first, making sure the dainty cup didn't rattle against the saucer, giving away the tremor in her fingers. She kept her head down, eyes on the ground, because girls who appear too confident don't make obedient wives or subservient daughters-in-law. After serving the snacks in our finest china, she would take a seat in a corner on one sofa. Sometimes, aunties would ask her to get up and show them how she walked. But most times, she would sit there, invisible, ignored as everyone else talked—about her, about what she was studying, about how many more years until she would be out of school. Our mother leapt in such conversations, immediately steering them in favorable directions. Her voice high pitched, excited, as she informed the interested aunties that oh no, our daughter will not go to college. We're not *that* kind of family. Her pride swelled and sputtered out in that declaration, pride over raising an obedient female who knew her responsibilities entailed taking care of her husband and his parents, and, eventually, bearing his progeny that would take his last name. Pride over raising a daughter who would know how to stay silent, crouched in a corner when her husband would lash out in anger. Pride over raising a teenager who wasn't even a grown woman but had the sensibility of one. Pride over having imparted the right values to her daughter: She must never walk out on her marriage; she must honor her commitment, display unwavering loyalty, never mind the fact that she will never be able to breathe, never mind the fact that she will only know love that equates to self-sacrifice, love that equates to shoving even her most basic needs down her very throat.

A week or two before every such meeting, my mum would begin pestering my sister over the clothes, the makeup, and the proper ways of conduct during such encounters. Most days, my sister could not resist. But then there was the odd day where she would straighten her back, stand tall, and flat-out refuse to go through it all.

Face red with frustration, she would yank the clothes off of the hangers, topple the items on the dresser. I was somewhere between the ages of five and seven, I don't remember exactly, but I do remember clearly what happened one night when my sister fought back.

I was in the lounge, playing or coloring. Again, I don't remember the minute details of myself, my surroundings. But I remember the shouting, the shrieks, the hiccups that erupted from the room my sister and I shared. The door to it was open, and I was only a few steps away. With each yell that came out louder, my heart began thumping in my ears; fear lodged itself in its crevices. I gathered the courage finally to leave what I was doing and tiptoe my way toward the bedroom.

My sister's face was tearstained, her fingertips white, curled around the fat bottle of some pills that stuttered inside as her hands shook. Her voice croaky and hoarse, her words sputtered out between the hiccups as she hurled threats that bounced off of the sharp scowl on my mother's face. The floor was vibrating underneath my tiny feet; the window in my sister's room shook violently as if someone outside were asking to be let in. But now, looking back, I think it was you, Karachi, outside, rattling on the glass in excitement for the havoc you were wreaking inside.

My mother's screams rose in pitch, but there was no hot lava spewing out of her lips, and I wondered if she was putting on a show. And I wondered why, because as the night darkened, my father whizzed past us, the wooden stick in his hand shaking right before it landed across my mother's back, my sister's arms. And I wondered why they put on a show that brought an angry mob of one, slicing their screams into pieces, their forms into what began to look like blots of ink splattered in a corner of the room while I still stood there, with my steady, tiny hands, perched on the doorsill, my body numb, my heart silent as if it had gulped all the fear that had been rising right before the first smack hit against my mother's bare neck.

This is how you raised me, Karachi. With a body so numb, a heart so silent, it accepted right from the start that there was no roaring— against men, against women you had poisoned, against you. You, who turned my house into a graveyard with dead women walking. You, who carefully crafted a mirage such that a silence pulsed when one crossed the threshold to my house, and to an untamed eye, it appeared peaceful, the house itself, the air and the people inside. But look at me; do I look at peace to you? Do I sound remotely calm? How can I when you never stopped spewing venom?

I was twenty-two, fighting to be independent, fighting for a freedom that was rightfully mine, but you made sure, Karachi, that I knew who I was rallying against. And so there I was, pleading for weeks with my dad to just let me go for one solo trip, let me taste a breath of air, fresh and unpolluted. But instead, I got a real taste of you, Karachi.

One night when the argument got really heated, my father's voice began booming through the house. It roared and resonated, growing into a mass of dark gray mist until it was all I could see. This time, my mother and sister had their fingers perched at the doorsill, lips pursed as they watched me crouch underneath the man I had spent years idolizing, silently letting him spill all of me like the worst batch of ink, thick and useless. I've never been the same since. The scars on my wrist, which had been lying dead since they had been carved at fifteen, began to sting for the first time. My skin prickled, the way it should've when it was touched inappropriately so many times. Goosebumps stretched and stretched as if ready to tear out of my flesh, the way they should've when I used to thread my way through the streets, feeling the leering male gaze on me. But you still won, Karachi. My body came alive, but my heart stayed silent. I was still a dead woman walking, but now, I was aware and there was no way for me to unknow what I knew.

You had my body, you had my heart, and you finally, finally, got to my mind, too. You made sure to split it into two halves, and a few months later, near my twenty-third birthday, my psychiatrist finally knew what was wrong with me. Bipolar, he said. And I accepted it, the way I accepted you, Karachi. The way I accepted your violence that surfaced firsthand at home. The way I accepted your poison that simmered on my mother's tongue and bubbled in her fingertips as she prodded my skin, my clothes, fixing and fixing a daughter that could not be fixed. I accepted it the way I accepted myself, my skin the color of burnt sugar, my body with its curves that can entice men if left out in the open. I accepted it all because you, Karachi, you have taught me well. You have drilled your mantra into us all too well: Someone else, somewhere, has it much, much worse.

But even after all that, you just couldn't let me be. I accepted everything, but you still wouldn't accept me. You made my mother tell me there was no such thing as depression, that maybe if I prayed enough, I wouldn't feel like shit the way I told her I did. You made my dad tell me there was no need for me to see a therapist because, you know, I could always talk to him. And I remember that moment crystal clear: He was in the doorway between his study and the lounge, and I was standing so far away but still in his line of sight. He said those words and I just stared at him, the words lolling on my tongue: I could talk, and talk, and talk, but would you listen?

It was a few weeks later when my dad lost his mother, the one person he held dear the most. He was broken, and for a while there, it did look like he would never recover. So my mother thought it best to take him away for a monthlong visit to family in the States. She said he couldn't stand to be in the place that reminded him of loss, of grief. And yet, when I moved away from you, Karachi, she couldn't understand why I couldn't stand you. What loss did you remind *me* of?

It was the week that my parents had left. I wasn't home alone; my younger brother was in the next room. And yet, the countless times that memory surfaces, all I remember is that I felt very alone. The lights in my room were dim, I had just the side-table lamp on, its deathly orange glow rising up to the ceiling in the shape of a cone. I was lying on my bed, feeling myself dissolve in the softness, and I wondered what it would feel like to dissolve altogether.

I looked around, trying to see if there was anything remotely close that I could maybe latch onto and pull myself out from the vortex that my bed felt to be. My new antidepressants were on the bookshelf, my books and teaching material lay scattered on the desk underneath it. My hands were trembling as I scrolled through my contacts, trying to see if there was someone I could call because I knew a part of me didn't want to do what my mind was telling me to. But there was nobody I could call, and the shooting ache in my chest, in my bones, pressed me deeper into the bed. I debated for hours and hours: What would my younger brother find when he opened my bedroom door the next morning?

You had scarred me, Karachi. You had my body, my heart, and my mind, and in that moment, you had my soul, too. You held it in your clutches, and you were digging your nails deeper and deeper into all of me. And even two years later, at a distance of 7,265 miles from you, it hurts just the same.

Francesca Mattei

Codling Moth

Yesterday Nonna told me to go get some wood, so I grabbed an axe and a wheelbarrow, and I went east. After a bunch of seconds, she came to the window and yelled at me to go in the opposite direction. *Not that way*, she said. *Over there it's all healthy trees; they bear fruit. Go to that orchard behind the abandoned church, with all the wild trees, the ugly ones, there. Cut 'em down.*

Nonna says that we should let the beautiful fruit trees grow, that we have to take care of them and love them if they get sick. Instead, the ones that give sour oranges or rotten apples are only good to make wood; there's not much to do if a tree was born that way, broken; it only takes up space, and it's just better to cut it down. So I went back and took the other way, the right one, like Nonna told me to.

The sun rose slowly and painted the evergreens yellow. The smell of mushrooms and moss was so strong that I sneezed. After less than half an hour, I arrived to the orchard and started working; I chose the driest trunks and the skinniest branches, and I dropped them in the wheelbarrow with a big handful of pinecones. I went back and forth many times, until the pile of wood on the porch was almost as high as the window.

Then I went inside for lunch, all sweaty and muddy, hungry like when you play all day under the sun, although it wasn't even noon. Nonna had made lentil soup and apple pie. As she gave me a slice, she congratulated me.

You did a nice job this morning; you're a man now. And how do you like the pie? She wiped a smear of powdered sugar off my cheek with her rough thumb and then started washing the dishes.

☾

Today is a big day because Papà is coming back. Nonna wakes me up early, even earlier than the usual, and she makes me wear my shirt, the same Papà had for his first communion. It smells all old and stuffy and it's itchy on my belly, but I'm not taking it off. Nonna starts cleaning the stairs with a rag and a bucket full of bleach, and then hands me a screwdriver to fix the kitchen cupboard. *Don't ruin your shirt*, she says.

I don't know what to do or how to do it.

Papà went to jail when I hadn't even started elementary school, and he's being released now that I graduated and learned how to make wood the right way. The cupboard is all smudged and crooked; the handle keeps coming off and falling on the floor, and I wonder why we don't just throw it in the chimney with the wood from the broken trees.

Nonna hears me grumble and yells at me from the stairs. She's out of breath for all the times she went up and down.

Come on, sweetheart, when Papà arrives, he'll find everything tidy and nice.

Tidy and nice. The coffee on the stove, the stairs all shiny, his son in his shirt, the good fruit on the table and the rotten fruit crackling in the chimney.

The handle rolling on the floor sounds like a walnut cracking on the path. I kick it away and I don't even know where it goes. I sit down, my elbows on the table, and count the stains on the wood.

The last time I saw him, I was with Zio at the family meet. Papà had just found out that his old cellmate, who had been moved to another town a couple of months before, had been found dead on his bed, his face all gray and blue. I knew what he looked like because all the newspapers talked about it and even showed before-and-after pictures of the guy. The news mentioned an accident and blamed "the usual rotten apples" among the prison guards. At the family meet, Papà and Zio spoke quietly and sometimes forgot about me. Papà said that the people who actually went bad in those places were the inmates, and that he couldn't imagine how someone had the guts to become a cop after seeing certain things. When we left, he gave me a kiss. That evening, at home, Zio and Nonna talked for a long time and told me that it was better for me not to see him for a while, at least not while he was *in that state*.

☾

It's been two years now, and I trust Nonna to make decisions for me, but I don't know if Papà looks the same as he used to; I can't remember the clothes he wore.

Papà spent all these years locked in a jail where prisoners don't die; it's a small institute with fifty cells, where inmates play soccer with the prison guards on the field by the street. On TV, they call it "the green oasis" of Tuscany, the showpiece of Italian justice. I know they have classes and shows and the inmates can edit a magazine, which they print out at a photocopy shop downtown and sell at fairs. They even have a garden, where they take care of plants and learn how to protect fruit from insects that eat them from inside, like the caterpillar that attacks apples or the fungus that spoils tomatoes.

People say, *Papà had it good.*

Nonna shows up at the kitchen door; her shadow comes forward and swallows me whole. When she sees my cheek on the table, she tells me off softly and laughs a little bit. She's carrying the water bucket in one hand; the other is holding the cupboard handle.

How did this end up in the hallway?

I raise my head to look at her properly and lean my body against the back of the chair. Nonna makes a hard face, but she doesn't look angry; she looks like she always does every time I scrape my knee or burn myself with the embers in the chimney.

Never mind. The cupboard is fine, even if it's a bit crooked. We'll just make do with it, right, honey?

My cheeks are blazing and I don't feel like looking at her big, saggy eyes. So I get up to go pee, and she doesn't object. As I sit on the toilet, I hear her messing with the pans and cursing at the cupboard. She moves the stools and opens and closes the doors of the pantry.

She controls and manages everything, like she always does, like she's always done.

I wash my hands and leave the bathroom. The kitchen windows are open, and Nonna wipes the glass with her blue scrub. I smell rubbing alcohol and fresh air, and the day feels like spring. When she's done cleaning the stoves, she goes upstairs to take care of the bedroom.

I look out and see Papà on the path coming from the highway.

He's walking, all hunched under the weight of a blue gym bag. He comes forward slowly, staring at his gray sneakers. He's skinny like a twig and he limps a little. He moves in a series of jerks, all stiff like a trunk.

Before coming in, he stops on the porch and sits on the pile of dry wood. From the open window, his thin back looks like a twig on top of the others. I try very hard not to make any noise and crouch down on the floor, and I don't really know if I'm happy or just scared.

He knocks three times and then pushes the door, which creaks open.

Nonna runs down the stairs while I get up and peek from behind the kitchen door. Papà drops the gym bag in the hallway and doesn't raise his head. His skin is stained like the wooden table; his hair is long. Nonna hugs him and his face disappears in her shoulder.

When he reemerges, he approaches me, kisses me, and messes up my hair.

He turns on the tap of the sink and fills a glass with cold water. He chugs it up and then grabs an apple from the fruit bowl. He chews it with his eyes closed, leaning against the fridge.

The light from outside shines on the dust mites, and no one says a word. Papà munches, fills his white, bony cheeks, and every now and then he wipes his lips with the back of his hand.

When he's done eating, he opens his eyes, walks across the room, and tosses the apple core in the chimney.

Translated from the Italian by Rachele Salvini

Michael Chang

Muscles

Person of good breeding: You're a dancer, always looking at your feet, studying your own form. You are monumental, already the best. The gift I can give you (let's be serious) is, I think, a sense of belonging. Someone who cares & consoles & celebrates with no expectation of return. You're soft & hard & smooth & rough. Your strength is magnificent like fog, like rain, like wind, precise as geometry, brutish yet tender. Don't know if you want me to go or tell you it's all right. I think I understand your tendency to retreat, your impulse to withhold, an *impulse* not to say anything (does that even square?). I've taken what little you've given me & cobbled together a sort of life. I'm capable of getting by, my existence a half-explored paradise, some vague satisfaction, a series of love letters to you, then a system of intelligent forgetting. You can't be resolved with reasoning, your own words killing any possibility of contentment. You don't believe in harmony, are done looking for it. We are green ghosts, delicate, dancing in our own air. We'll give it our all, get better together. The puppy-dog eyes, the shoulder squeeze, our madness.

Michael Chang

白球鞋
White Tennis Shoes

"poetry of the everyday" means boring poetry

foutez-moi la paix as in give me a break

u twirl the glass in ur hand, fingers deep inside

one sneakered foot perched on the other

sentences with no spaces

have designs on u

weather permitting, a/c on the beach

ppl write cronuts & frank ocean

i eat busily between ur legs

all-encompassing, so vantablack

i'm the best thing smoking thru ur life

a siren passing, there, then not there

i'm trying to fill my love empty

wink & a prayer

remember when kamala did an event with aka & her sorors went *skee-wee*

& a white reporter, not recognizing the calls, said they were hissing at her?

remind me what white reporters are qualified to write abt besides their too-big-to-fail?

immigrants never accidentally call their gf/teacher "mom"

are brazilian nuts from brazil?

no minor gods, ur major

i like how u take such good care of ur stuff

w/o u, no mathematics, no poetry

Travis Mossotti

Framework

We'd found ourselves in Memphis, Cologne,
Boston, then Lyon. We discovered churches,
escarpments, hillsides burnt to stubble and
the ruins of local bars flattened to rubble
for the onset of strip malls and boutique hotels.
We watched as trauma entered like detox
sweats on the third night, how it twisted
into a metaphor for the orchards and vineyards
and barnyards left to rot thanks to the usual
vehicles of displacement that rolled in from
out of state with bags of cash and bad plates.
We scratched like hens for love. We wasted
our time and money in the supermarkets.
We convinced ourselves that we knew
the firmament from the face of the lake
because that was a lie we could live with.

But suddenly the tone was all wrong. We
were midlife roustabouts debuting in white
at the dilettante ball. The salesman was our
father knocking on suburban doors with
tight knuckles and wrecking balls for fists.
We looked around in terror and saw the walls
were white as the emptiness surrounding
a stanza, and then we collectively blinked.
What changed in us was more feeling
than fact, more fog than mist. We lit a candle
in the basilica and flipped our collar up

as we pushed open the heavy wooden doors
stepped out into a street full of pedestrians
and shop windows refracting sunlight. It was
morning again, and each step forward
brought the world that much more into focus.

Michele Finn Johnson

General Considerations of Independent Living

As if this day didn't start crappily enough, waking up to yet another I-can't-do-this-boyfriend-thing-anymore text from Gary, I walk into my night shift at Danworthy Independent Living only to find out Mr. Spraker in 78A is dead.

Connie, Danworthy's administrative manager, tells me about Mr. Spraker on her way out the door. "By the way," she says, whipping her car keys around her index finger in a way that looks like she's planning to peel out for a joyride, "you'll need to make the arrangements."

"Make the arrangements? You mean, funeral arrangements?"

Connie laughs. "Jesus, Stephanie, you look pale. Is this your first no-show?"

I must be looking at Connie like my brain's gone pumpkin hollow. She lets go of the front door and heads back behind the counter. "Move over," she says.

"What do you mean, 'no show'?"

Connie grabs the mouse and flicks though computer screens. "A no-show for a meal. You know how old people are—if they miss a meal, they've either fallen and broken a hip or they're taking the 'Big Nap.' Spraker never missed the five-thirty dinner seating. That was the tip-off."

I think about Mr. Spraker, how he always wore a sweater vest, even in August, and how he'd salute me with his rolled-up *Wall Street Journal* every day after his 6 a.m. breakfast.

"Here's the checklist," Connie says, swinging the monitor towards me.

GENERAL CONSIDERATIONS UPON DEATH OF A RESIDENT.

I scan the list.

Connie points at item one. "Notify Danworthy's Director."

"Hal already knows. He said to leave Spraker in place until D'Angelo's can get here." Connie lifts her keys off the desk. "As if we'd move him. What is this? *Breakfast With Barney?*"

"Huh?"

Connie buttons her sweater so quickly it bulges with erratic misalignment. "That movie; you know, the one where they drive the dead guy around for a weekend."

"You mean *Weekend at Bernie's?*"

Sometimes Connie doesn't make any sense. I know she's worked at Danworthy for twenty-three years, but it's hard to connect the dots with her. It's like she's lost the perspective that in five or ten years, she could be the one moving in here, and she might want people like me, people like her, to have a little compassion. I look down at the lobby desk and see the mess of sudoku and crosswords that Connie's left behind.

"Just follow the checklist. You'll be fine." Connie tosses her permanent wave over her shoulders. "In fact, I can't think of a better person to handle death. You're so sympathetic."

Item two on the General Considerations Upon Death of a Resident checklist: "Do not discuss the death with any Danworthy resident until the body has been removed from the premises. Maintaining the privacy and dignity of the deceased is of paramount importance."

I reread Gary's text while I wait for D'Angelo's hearse.

I'm moving out while UR at work. We both know what's really going on. Don't make me say it. I'm the crappiest boyfriend ever. UR pathetic for taking me back so many times.

Wow. I'm pathetic and sympathetic, all in the same day. I'm about to tweet out one of Gary's dick pics when Mrs. Wobeser from 79A glides up to the front desk. I can't help but smile when I see Mrs. Wobeser—she's decorated her walker in a Hawaiian theme, complete with a fuchsia silk lei and a dashboard hula dancer perched on top of her accessory basket. She seems more with-it than most of Danworthy's residents; in fact, I think she might even get a kick out of Gary's dick pic.

Mrs. Wobeser leans across the counter. "Now tell me what you know about Terry."

"I'm sorry, Mrs. Wobeser; who's Terry?"

"Terry Spraker. 78A, my dear. My next-door neighbor. I thought maybe you'd heard if they found anything ...."

Her blue eyes seem to fade a bit and she stares beyond me for a few seconds. This happens a lot with our residents, and I've learned to be patient, wait it out.

"Did they notice anything unusual when they found him?"

Checklist item three: "Determine if the resident has passed under suspicious circumstances. If so, call the authorities and request, on behalf of Danworthy, that an autopsy be performed."

Mrs. Wobeser's face is unnervingly close; her eyes are back to solid blue and there's a clump of moisturizer stuck to the side of her nose. I'm considering what would be the most thoughtful response to her strange question when two men and a gurney enter the lobby. D'Angelo's. Mrs. Wobeser knocks on the counter three times—a call to order like the grade-school principal she once was. "Let me know what they find," she says. A command.

The problem with Gary is that I've known him since grade school. If I want tacos, he knows to order them on corn tortillas, not flour. He always has a minimum of $17 in his wallet because seventeen is his lucky number, and he can make me come, no fuss. Has all of my parts down pat. He's convenient, like so many of these Danworthy "sunset romances," as Connie calls them. Trapped in here like it's a submarine, what else is there for them to do but screw? I hate that Connie's put this image in my head, and now I can't help but imagine these old people in a myriad of complicated sexual positions. I found a Kama Sutra app three days ago on Gary's phone—asked him about it since we usually do the same three basic moves, but his face got all cabbage-sour. I downloaded the app after he left, scrolled through page after page of cartoon people—a bright pink man and sun-yellow woman—splayed out on floors, bent over chairs, bat-hanging over a couch or mattress or an exercise ball. Now I'm wondering why I've limited myself; what other ways can I curl and twist?

Once I open Mr. Spraker's front door, the guys from D'Angelo's tell me I can leave if I'd rather not see this. I think about the checklist. I think about Mrs. Wobeser's weird question. I think about the fact that I make twelve dollars an hour, which hardly seems like enough money when this death checklist gives me the authority to order Mr. Spraker split open like a lab rat. I think about Gary, how I'll have to make rent all by myself.

"No, it's OK. I'll stay."

The apartment is quiet, apart from the clicking of the grandfather clock in Mr. Spraker's entryway. The D'Angelo guys walk toward the back of the apartment, but I can't seem to move past the kitchen. This place smells like French toast and pork roll. Yesterday's *Wall Street Journal* is on the counter; the headline: "Domestic Forecast Upswing; GDP Extends Strong Stretch in Q4." Upswing, yeah, right. A crock of shit for Mr. Spraker and me.

"He's back here."

I want more than anything to run the hell out of here, out of Danworthy, anywhere—even to shithead Gary because if not wanting to see my first dead person is pathetic, then yes, I'm pathetic, but then I flash to Mrs. Wobeser's tap-tap-tap on the front counter, recall the steel determination in her eyes—*Did they notice anything unusual?*—so now I'm walking down the hallway, preparing to see blood and smell whatever it is death smells like—some combination of high school biology lab and Gary's laundry basket, I imagine—and instead, I see Mr. Spraker, naked on his bed, spread out corner to corner like a snowflake.

One of the D'Angelo's guys holds up a bottle from Mr. Spraker's nightstand. "Damn—KY lube! Look at this guy, still going at it."

Checklist item two—preserving dignity—swirls out of my throat. "Put that down." I don't recognize my own voice, the authority behind it.

"Sorry." The guys roll the gurney to the side of the bed. "You OK if we go ahead and move him?"

Checklist item three—suspicious circumstances? I survey the scene. Mr. Spraker's eyes are half-closed; his lips are purpled and parted. Both his arms are outstretched as if, at the very end, he'd been reaching for something.

At the edge of his bed, I see it. One silk, fuchsia flower.

By the time this night shift's over and I get home to my empty apartment, I'm dizzy from hunger and stress. I commandeer Gary's side of the bed, wondering if I can sleep him out of my system. Problem is, when I close my eyes, all I see is Mr. Spraker and Mrs. Wobeser flailing their arthritic limbs into positions that seem inadvisable.

Turns out that the Kama Sutra app, which I flipped through with fascination after the D'Angelo crew left with Mr. Spraker, is really more about love than sex—finding a life partner, maintaining an expanding love life, exploring the nature of love. I want to ask Gary if that's what he was trying to do—work on our emotional fulfillment, not figure out how to contort some other girl like a carnival balloon animal—but I know Gary. He likes Xbox games and sex with three-minute foreplay; he's not diving deep into self-work.

Checklist item four. "Complete the postmortem incident report." The questions on Danworthy's postmortem incident report keep rolling through me. The only answer I knew by heart was Mr. Spraker's apartment number—78A. The rest, I had to look up in his intake file. Deceased's full name—Terrance Andrew Spraker. Marital status—widower. He was a former wildlife manager for the State of Colorado; he'd been married to his high-school sweetheart, Madeline, for fifty-seven years; she died of cancer right before Mr. Spraker moved into Danworthy. His will was kept on file; he wanted to be cremated and have his ashes spread in the Platte River outside of Golden, Colorado.

Checklists aside, there are so many other things I could have asked Mr. Spraker—Why wear a sweater vest in August? Does the early bird really get the worm? Did you ever snowshoe through the Rockies? Live in a yurt? What do you think of Mrs. Wobeser in 79A? Have you ever been to Hawaii? Were the two of you in love?

This is progress—I don't actually want to talk to Gary. I want to talk to Mr. Spraker, ask him all of my Kama Sutra questions—the ones about the heart, the ones that might make a person sound pathetic: Was Madeline your great love? Did you only sleep with Madeline for fifty-seven years? Was it weird to sleep with someone new after fifty-seven years of Madeline? Would you ever take back a lover, again and again, even if they were a snake? Am I stupid for still thinking about Gary, even a little bit? If I'm asking this question, I'm stupid, right?

Damn, I just let Mr. Spraker walk past me every morning, saluting me with his rolled-up *Wall Street Journal*, never once considering that this man might hold the key to understanding happiness. Just some old dude in a sweater vest. My general consideration was to not consider him in any depth at all. Now, all of Mr. Spraker's wisdom will get dumped into the mighty Platte River.

Maybe I could create a new checklist—GENERAL CONSIDERATIONS OF THE LIVING RESIDENT. All of life's answers are probably right there at Danworthy under one roof, just waiting to be tapped. Maybe I'll start with Mrs. Wobeser—what a gutting thing it was, sitting at her kitchen table telling her the news. She'd made a show of acting as if Mr. Spraker's death was a shock and then asked me again if there was anything odd about Terry's passing. No, Mrs. Wobeser. He looked peaceful. It was like lying to Gary all of those times, telling him I could forgive his cheating while my insides filled up with puke. Well, at least that's something. Mrs. Wobeser sat up straight as if I'd given her a cue to end our visit. As she righted herself at her Hawaiian-themed walker, I reached into my front pocket, slid the silk fuchsia flower from Mr. Spraker's bedroom floor under a clump of placemats. Why I didn't just throw it in a trash can? Why hide it? I'm sure she'll find the flower one day—things don't ever straighten themselves up on their own. Or maybe they do. Maybe by then, I'll know Mrs. Wobeser's first name.

Lyndsie Manusos

This Is Not a Swan Song

A bevy of white swan paddleboats rubbed together on the dock. The necks arched up and down like a distorted willow branch before resting on the front of the boat.

My brother Jack allowed me to join him on the boats with his friends. Our parents were away for a long weekend. It was the first time we were left alone without having to go to Grandma's.

"This is our weekend," Jack whispered, as we heard our parents lock the door from the outside.

Ha. As if that could keep us in.

Every stolen moment was a spark to my brother, and he liked to share.

After our parents left, we hightailed it to the marina to rent two paddleboats with money we'd saved mowing lawns. I was twelve. Jack had turned seventeen weeks before, and despite promising our parents we'd only use the car for food and emergencies, there we were, screaming Nirvana songs out the rolled-down windows. A hot spark, thick and gummy as the heat.

Jack's friends Sonya and Louise met us at the marina. As we pulled into the gravel parking lot, the girls leaned their banana bikes against a large willow tree near the shoreline. Sonya saw Jack and waved. She wore a loose Port of Blarney's restaurant T-shirt over a bikini. Sonya had thin hair and a pointy chin, but her eyes were a bright greenish yellow. Cat eyes. Jack always had a thing for bright eyes to war with his own, his being as dark as the polluted lake water.

When we came upon the swan paddleboats, Louise insisted she ride with Sonya, probably because she didn't want to get stuck with me.

Once we cast off, we lulled to the pop-rock hiss of PBR cans thumbed open. We had stolen a pack from the back of our garage refrigerator, where our parents kept food they often forgot about.

Louis and Sonya raced us away from the pier, pumping their legs in the other boat.

We paddled after them, out into the middle of Grass Lake. Jack allowed me one can of beer. Of course, I was too young, but I held the can up like a knight might hold a sword before battle.

Jack had laughed and put his palm on top of the can to lower it to my lap.

"Don't get us in trouble," he said.

We paddled in a sparkling limbo, tossing beer cans in long arcs over to the girls. Jack flashed smiles at Sonya as we caught up and paddled side by side. He ruffled my hair while they spoke about school and where they'd go after graduation the following year. Eventually, I had to do all the pedaling, pumping my legs until they burned. Jack chugged his beer and wiped his lips with the back of his hand.

"Marry me, Sonya," he called.

"Never," Sonya shot back, grinning.

Still paddling, I tried chug my beer like Jack's, a fluid motion of the throat, his growing Adam's apple bobbing in rhythm. Instead, I hiccupped. Foam spouted up my nose.

"You can't marry," I said, wiping my face. "You're seventeen."

He patted my back, but his eyes locked with Sonya's, summer-drunk with beer and cat eyes. The way he stared announced he was growing apart from me, growing spectral limbs and wheels that would spirit him away, eventually. He'd go somewhere. When he did, I wondered what would happen to me.

It began as an aura.

We watched it loom, a humming bee of blue and yellow fiberglass. We expected the boat to go around us. All the others did. We expected its wake to splash us, and then we'd hold our middle fingers in the air, defiant as revolutionaries.

I heard laughter rise and circle the boat in a halo. Sonya whooped from the other paddleboat. Jack held out his hand and she reached out to meet him, their fingers a sliver out of touch. Louise stood up next to her and started waving her arms.

"Stop rocking the boat," Sonya snapped, reaching for Jack.

The laughter grew louder as the speedboat approached. Louise smacked the beer out of Sonya's hands.

"Wake up," Louise screamed.

Jack lowered his own beer can, and with his other hand slowly took the life vest at my feet and set it on my lap. I glanced at it, then stood up at the oncoming speedboat.

"Jack ...," I began.

*

I surfaced in a plume of mud. The neck of one of the plastic swans floated beside me. White plastic everywhere. Egg shells. Confetti.

I held the swan's neck under my chin, shivering despite being hot. I lifted my head and screamed for Sonya. Her name first. To this day, I don't know why.

Across the lake, from the shore, or maybe one of the other dozens of marinas along the Chain o' Lakes, I heard a shriek.

"Not it!" It sounded like Jack from yesterday. It sounded like Jack from last night.

Next time, I promised Jack and I would stay home. We would play video games in the basement, punch each other to bruising over Knockout points, and chug cherry soda until our stomachs boiled.

From across the sugar cubes of debris, a beer can rested on my butterflied life jacket. It wept condensation but stayed impossibly still. I laughed. Ha, that was exactly what Jack would do. I laughed and laughed and laughed. It was as if Jack had placed it there, a beacon for us, before diving below.

Tommy Dean

An Announcement of a Certain Kind of Embarrassment

They took turns tacking the foreclosure notices on the dining room wall. They'd been coming in the mail for months. At first, they used tape. Mindful of the paint, the lack of holes in the wall. The spiderwebs of crayon drawings long pained over. Their children—thank the heavens—in their own houses or condos on the beach. Rooms with views. A parent's dream of a certain kind of success. How many nights had they whispered these aspirations to each other, had hoped for them together on college visits and vacations to historical sites.

Even now, these parents keep the regrettable news to themselves. Parents aren't supposed to become burdens. Parents are meant to be forgettable, tucked safely away in childhood homes with dry basements and stable foundations. Their issues should be petty and inane: a new librarian who hoards the new Danielle Steele novels and neighbors who cut their lawns too short. Barking dogs and potholed streets and tree branches that fracture in wind storms. Never the threat of lost houses.

It's his idea to pay the bank sporadically, in random sums of money, with checks and cash, with refunds from the hardware store and twenty-dollar bills found in yellowing birthday cards. Little surprises that used to make them smile, that drew them closer to each other at night—security as a thoroughfare toward intimacy.

It's her idea to purchase the darts, to make a kind of gameboard out of the mailings, spiking the name of the bank their new bullseye. Hitting any dollar amount was worth something, a jeer, another shot of whiskey, anything but tears. Weathered and withered, they agreed.

Eighteen months they survived, plucking each monthly notice and eventually stapling it to the wall. She ignored the holes created by his fists, the way he wanted her to think he was out of control, but he never hit a stud. Never angry with her. This only made her love him more. The way he kept her from embarrassment. No rushing to the emergency room, not another bill they couldn't afford, not another lie to tell their children.

The day before the sheriff was scheduled to arrive, the house was still unpacked, a showroom of their lives. Americana knickknacks and fake potted plants, dust of their former selves frosting the counters and crevices of peeling wainscoting. The holes aren't enough. The warped floors and peeling linoleum didn't tell their story. Her rage the melted wax around a burnt candle wick, easily ignored. She said they needed more blood. Something haunting. A reminder to the bank executives and the realtors, the house flippers, and the new homeowners. The consequences of stealing.

He volunteered by flexing his wrists, popping out his veins and arteries like a carnival show. She promised not to cut too deep, to skate the razor across the tributaries under his skin. Something wordless passed between them as she let the blade glint in the light. They enjoyed the show of it, the drama, even if no one else was watching.

But the blade was nicked, chipped from tape and cardboard, haphazardly maintained, so it cut in jagged breathes, the skin weeping. His uninjured hand reflexing to the cut, holding himself in, forgetting to splash it against the wall. The X-Acto knife dropping from her fist, daggering into the plane of her foot. Blood dotting the carpet.

They bicker over who should call the ambulance, neither wanting their voices recorded, each of them gesturing with their hands, the pressure from their wounds gone, their hearts pumping out puddles.

We watched from fogged windows, the sirens calling us to witness, the red lights washing the neighborhood in scarlet, as we waited for the next foreclosure victims to appear.

Nan Wigington

Invasive

The arborist knew why the oak bled, but his wife? She'd had what she had needed. Lots of water. The right amount of sunshine. Good food. Good family. But. He saw her face in the trunk, the paper-thin skin, the lesions growing, cracking open.

The arborist snapped a twig from the oak. He held it out to the client who looked down and did not take what was offered. The woody bulges at the joints must have seemed part of a whole, new buds … although it was late August, almost September.

The arborist picked a bulge from a joint, popped it like a pimple. The honeydew spit, oozed onto the arborist's thumb and index finger.

"It's an insect," he told the client. "Kermes scale. It's killing your tree bite by bite."

He would recommend a treatment, a systemic pesticide. Most clients would shiver, shake their heads. Pesticides had a tendency to unbalance, eliminate one bug, open the door for another—heal one tree, harm three others.

"It'll be safe. I'll inject it at the crown," the arborist lied.

He gave the client a quote, urged careful thought, never admitted he'd make more money cutting the 45-foot tree down.

At home, the arborist found his wife sitting in the backyard. The treatments had taken her hair. Brown curls had fallen like frostbitten leaves. He wished there were something he could do to bring it back. Maybe fertilizer? Sea kelp? Could he inject it in her foot?

Her red metal chair rocked.

"I can't do it," she said when he was close enough to hear.

He looked down at her garden, the pumpkins spilling into the tomatoes, the dried peapods knifing at the bolted broccoli. A grasshopper sailed from the radish tops to the wilted spinach.

"I'll help," he said.

"I'm not talking about the garden."

He looked at the insects hovering close to her exposed hands.

"This cure," she said, "is worse than the disease."

He thought of his clients, the dull comforts he always gave them. *It's just drought stress. Water the tree enough and the armies, the ants, the aphids, the beetles, the borers will all go away.*

What could make this mad production of his wife's cells go away? What could melt a tumor?

The arborist had no trees in his backyard. When they had first moved in, there had been a paradise tree. It was fat and industrious and tall. He watered it, pruned it as much as he could. No insect fazed it—no caterpillar, no beetle or bagworm. It would be immortal.

His wife had called it a ghetto palm, had wanted him to get rid of it.

"But it's so healthy," he had said.

"It's invasive," she'd answered. "Its roots are burrowing into our sewer line."

In the end, he had obeyed. Now there was no shade for her to sit under, nothing to shield her from the day's onslaught. He looked down at the sore near her jaw, black streaks like rotten roots to her chin. Even with his best grub hoe, he wouldn't be able to pull it loose. He had a vision of cutting his wife's dead body down, arms first, then head and trunk. He looked up, the overgrown world around him teemed with menace, tongues and stingers, wings and teeth.

"Let's go inside," he said at last.

Alanna Shaikh

Carrying

The bullet hit my ribs, shock first then
I thought, this will be so useful.
Carrying a new wound, I can cry on cue again
and it will be good for my art. I'd
almost forgotten the smell of fresh blood.
I'd almost forgotten how to carry lead.

Cynthia Marie Hoffman

Trigger Warning

How fat the nest is getting year after year. The extra tuft of dangling twigs that swung in the wind for weeks before finally dropping to the deck. You swept it away. Loving anything. Loving this world. Your mother hoisting her bird feeders on a pulley in the forest where you were once young. Her house wreathed in flowers like a horse with the winning garland hooped around its neck. Your own dry garden, a shy blush of pink by the stairs. The neighbors who turned off their nature camera after all the eggs were taken from the nest one by one. Ghosts you called for reassurance but never answered. Those you know by name and those you don't. The bird your sister rehabilitated in the bathroom until the final day it winged into the trees and did not return. The squirrel you've watched tending to her babies splayed out flat on the porch. You scare her away just to know she is alive. Bird fountain glowing like a silvery coin of riches. The time you thought you had so much of.

Zhang Zhihao

Poetry in the Open Air

Wild ducks in Dusi Lake had never
    swum with such ease
one family of five paddling back and forth on surface water
or tumbling up and down underneath the water, repeatedly
    repeating acts of intimate love
The morning sun stretched the in-patient department
    of Renmin Hospital
The afternoon sun stretched the dawn redwood trees
The wild ducks swimming from morning till afternoon
For the first time they covered the whole lake solely as theirs

Translated from the Chinese by Yuemin He

Allison Parker

Phantom Place

My husband opened the Phantom Place five years back. His collections have grown from the first couple of spirits to what it is today: two rows of Tupperware containers with cages around them, twenty-five ghosts in total, and a wall of artifacts owned by these ghosts. The Tupperware containers hold the ghosts, because ghosts can't slip through plastic, and the cages are there to keep visitors from opening the containers and letting the ghosts out. The business started because my husband had a buddy who had a ghost infestation at his house. My husband went to his friend's house, and his friend said the ghost liked to hang out in the pipes in the shower. My husband, being a very resourceful man, took a plastic grocery bag and tied it around the showerhead. Then he took a hammer and beat on the pipe and yelled at the ghost until it slipped out of the pipe and into the grocery bag. From that point on, he's been helping other folks out with their ghost problems, collecting the ghosts, and arranging them into a museum.

He and the mayor are talking upstairs in the dining room now. The mayor asked him if she could put the Phantom Place on the county's website to attract tourists. They're discussing the plans, and she's trying to help him make his website more user-friendly. I'm tending to the museum down in the basement while they chat. If the ghosts aren't tended to at least once a day, they get cranky and start moving things around and do things like making visitors trip or suddenly feel sick. If they're tended to properly, we'll get a playful light flickering every now and then to keep the visitors interested but not scared out of their minds.

Each ghost is tended to in a different way. They don't need food and water, obviously, but they need spiritual sustenance. Some like poetry; some like to hear a particular Bible chapter read over and over again; at least five like to listen to the same bluegrass CD. I tend to Mae first. Mae is a sweet little thing. She fits into a 16-ounce Tupperware container and never misbehaves. My husband says she's making up for past wrongs. The family he took her from said that, according to family legend, she was a hell-raiser. When her father told her she couldn't do something that she wanted to do, like hang out with her friends or have a glass of wine, she'd set a piece of furniture on fire. The family had to replace every piece of furniture in the house at least three times before she was shot by the boy her father had forbidden her to spend time with. My husband says we have to keep Mae happy or she'll burn down our house, but I know she wouldn't. She's not like that anymore. I know her better than he does.

Mae likes it when I sing the old hymns to her. I was raised in a small country church where our hymnals were at least sixty years old, so I know all the old songs. Sometimes I'll sit and sing to her for an hour before I tend to the others. When I do, I can feel her peace falling on my head like rain. This is the first time I've felt it in a little while, so I keep singing, forgetting to take care of the other ghosts. I sing "Victory in Jesus" and "How Great Thou Art." Our favorite, though, is "Farther Along."

Father along we'll know all about it.
Farther along we'll understand why.
Cheer up, my brother, live in the sunshine.
We'll understand it all by and by.

I sing her favorites to her while my husband and the mayor talk business in the dining room. It goes on so long the other ghosts are starting to get testy. Someone just threw a book at my head.

Two weeks ago, I believe I disappointed Mae. I've been trying to make it up to her ever since. There was one day that I didn't feel like singing, and she's been giving me the silent treatment since. After that day two weeks ago, and before today, she stopped sharing her peace with me, but gave me this feeling of discomfort instead. It's like when my husband pouts if I annoy him. He'll sit there and watch the TV and only answer my questions in short one- to two-word answers.

I had been helping my husband build the new cages to put around the ghosts. The old ones were made of chicken wire and were easily bent up by visitors trying to push themselves as close to the ghosts as they could get. We decided to build new cages out of metal bars like you'd see in a Western movie jailhouse. My husband thought he could save some money by using the rebar that was sitting in the shed. He bent the rebar while I tied the steel connecting the bars into a cage.

I liked watching him work. I always have. When we first got married he was surprised by how much I wanted to help him with the outside chores. He said his mom never helped his dad on the work outside, and he thought it was strange that I wanted to help. I helped him anyway in whatever way I could. In a couple years I learned from him about changing the oil in a tractor, repairing roofs, using the tiller on the garden, and tying steel. I learned that he couldn't fully get into the work until his skin started sweating. I learned how he leaned to one side with a hand on his hip when he was assessing the work he'd done and the work that still needed to be done. I saw how a curved board or a crooked nail didn't make him huff and throw things like it did for my father. Instead, ornery materials gave my husband focus and determination. Building the rebar cages for the ghost museum wasn't very challenging for either of us, but I still watched as he slid the metal pipe over the end of the rebar, placed his hands on the pipe, and shoved his body against it just enough to bend the rebar to a perfect 90-degree angle.

We built five cages by lunchtime. After lunch, I told my husband I'd better go tend to the ghosts. He asked me if I'd come outside to help him build more cages instead. He was always one to ask instead of command. That's another way he's not like my father. I was finishing the last bite of my soup.

"If it's OK with you, I'll tend to the ghosts first. Or else they'll get fussy," I said.

He sipped his lemonade, and I could tell it was not the answer he wanted to hear.

"This is our business, after all," I said. "We can't just neglect them."

My husband shook his head and took his glass to the sink. "The cages are also important for the business," he said.

"I'm going to look after the ghosts. You can continue with your cages, and I'll be there in a little bit." I never could stand being pressured.

He walked to the living room without looking at me and turned on the TV. As I walked toward the basement door, he called out, "I guess we'll do the cages tomorrow." I'd put him in a mood, and when he gets like that, there's nothing to do but wait for him to get over it.

There are some things you just can't do when you're upset. Singing is one of them for me. Singing and having sex. I put a hymns CD in the CD player and set it beside Mae's cage. I read a quick poem to Bertie and a chapter from Corinthians to Gustie and swept the floor. I couldn't tell if Mae was pushing a bad attitude at me or if I was just in a bad mood on my own.

Mae didn't even get cranky like that five months ago when my husband threatened to switch her out for a "more entertaining exhibit." We were standing close to her cage when he said it, so I know she heard. I told him to lower his voice and that we should go upstairs to continue the conversation.

Upstairs, we sat at the little table in the kitchen while he told me why he wanted to switch Mae out. He said Mae was so quiet from her guilt that she wasn't interesting to the visitors anymore. She never nudged her container over an inch while a visitor was watching or flickered a light while a visitor read her plaque or even sent chills over to a visitor. She wasn't pulling her weight, he said.

"We can't turn her loose. She has the most interesting story. Everybody loves her story," I said.

"She don't act like that anymore, and people don't believe it." He meant people wanted her to burn things like she used to when she was a girl. They wanted her to be a rebel like the plaque said she was. When she sat there quiet without ever acknowledging them, they felt cheated. They lost faith in the whole shebang. That's how my husband explained it. The business only works if people actually believe that we have ghosts in the containers.

"What'll you do with her?"

"Take her off somewhere and turn her loose," he said.

Like what you do with a racoon or possum that gets caught in the traps behind the house, I thought. Like an unwanted, wild animal. I begged him not to. I grabbed ahold of his forearm that was resting on the table and begged him to let her stay. I told him we couldn't do her like that after we're the ones that took her from her home. She might even come back and burn our house down out of spite if we turned her loose. She might burn his car down on the way to wherever he would take her. I knew in my heart she wouldn't, but I said that.

He looked annoyed. He always had a business mind. I didn't let up until he broke a small smile and said "All right, we'll just move her to the corner so people will walk past her without seeing her."

We had sex that night for the first time in a while. Before that, I told Mae she would always have a home here and I sang to her our favorite hymn over and over because it felt just as good to sing it the tenth time as it had the first.

The day I found out that Mae loved hymns was about a year ago. I had been trying to figure out what she wanted for a while, but nothing I tried worked. She didn't like any other type of music I played for her. She didn't like anything I read to her. I even tried a few dances in front of her cage, but nothing took. She sat in her Tupperware container and spread a feeling of discontent that agitated the other ghosts. I knew if she kept causing problems, my husband would get rid of her. But he'd told me her story, and I felt sorry for her.

I tried to please her for weeks. Every time I came downstairs, I could feel her unhappiness all around the basement. It made the visitors grumpy and confrontational. Somehow, it brought me closer to her. Mae could alter the mood of everyone in the museum. She must have been a very passionate girl in life, full of emotion and spirit, to be able to affect the people around her so heavily.

My husband was growing concerned. He told me I was spending too much time on a lost cause. He accused me of caring more about Mae than I did about him. He said she was a liability; she was bad for business. It was an argument he repeated the whole time we had Mae, but that was the first time. With a little bit of effort, I convinced him to let her stay until I could bring her around. She was so close; I could feel it.

One night, after Mae had agitated a visitor into threatening my husband with a gun when my husband refused to give the man his money back, I went to the basement. I wanted to talk to her, let her know that that kind of behavior was unacceptable. Her bad attitude affecting the visitor could've killed my husband, and she needed to know the seriousness of that. I tried turning on the lights, but they wouldn't come on. I complained to the ghosts, telling them to stop making things difficult, but they kept the lights off. I stumbled my way to where Mae's cage was and opened the door. I felt around for her container so I could hold her close while I talked to her. When I felt it, I found it unsealed with one corner lifting up.

I immediately closed the container and made sure it was tightly sealed. The ghosts were flicking the lights on and off at that point. My husband had been the last one in the basement that day. I didn't want to believe he would've let her go like that, trying to make it look like the lid just became slightly unsealed either by itself or because of Mae. I marched to the door and prepared myself to let him have it. Halfway to the door, though, I realized I didn't have it in me anymore. I dropped to the floor and crawled my way back to Mae's container. I held it in my arms and sang old hymns for no other reason than that they came out of me in the moment.

I immediately felt peace falling all around me. The lights turned on and stayed on. Everything was quiet while I sang. I imagined this was the feeling that hymns were supposed to create, but I'd never felt it until I held Mae and sang them. I knew Mae hadn't left, and just as importantly, I knew I'd broken through. I'd found what it was that would calm her.

Mae wasn't the first ghost I had cared for. She was the second. The first was Tommy. We got Tommy from an old woman four years ago, shortly after the museum opened. The old woman said there was a ghost on her property that kept killing her chickens. My husband had a doctor's appointment that day, so I went to collect Tommy on my own. It was my first time going on a ghost collection. Since the ghost liked to kill chickens, I brought a large plastic container, the blue rectangular kind used to store clothes. When I got to the old woman's house, she was standing in the yard waiting for me. I got out of my car and headed toward her with the plastic container.

"What do you want?" she asked when I walked to her.

"I'm here about the ghost." I held up the container as proof.

"I thought you were going to be a man," she said.

"My husband has an appointment. But I know all the tricks," I assured her.

She looked at me skeptically before turning to lead me toward the chicken coop. She told me that the ghost killed one chicken most nights around nine. The ghost had gotten at least five of her chickens so far. I asked her if she was sure it wasn't a fox. She told me if I didn't believe her I should be getting the hell off her property. It took me several minutes to convince the old woman that I did believe her.

Since the ghost liked to kill chickens, I suggested we put a chicken in the plastic container and put chicken wire across the top so the chicken couldn't get out. Then we'd wait for the ghost to take the bait, just out of hiding, and catch it. She thought my plan was sensible, so we moved all the other chickens to the barn and kept one chicken in the coop. We placed that one chicken in the container and put the wire over the top. We sprinkled some feed in the bottom of the container so she'd be content. Before we went to hide behind the shed to wait for the ghost, the old woman bent down close to her chicken. She mumbled to the chicken and placed her hand on the wire. The chicken was a necessary sacrifice to protect the rest of them. I couldn't tell for sure, but I don't think that she said that to the chicken. Whatever she said sounded sweeter than that.

It wasn't long before we heard the chicken rustling around in the container. She sounded agitated, and we knew the ghost was close. The old woman looked determined now, with her lips pressed tightly together and her eyes never moving from the container. As soon as we heard the chicken scream out, I pounced from behind the shed with the lid of the plastic container and slammed it down tight. There was some rustling and shaking, and then all was quiet.

"It's done," I said. "What's this ghost's name?"

"How the hell should I know?" the old woman answered. "I didn't stop to ask its name while it was killing off my animals."

On the drive home, with the ghost in the trunk, I tried to open my mind so I could hear the ghost's story, if it wanted to share it. The name that came to me was Tommy. I imagined that Tommy was so angry because he'd been bullied and mistreated in his life. I imagined he hung himself over a creek in the dead of summer when he was just 12 years old because the other boys had held him down and put dozens of spiders down his pants. It never does much good to try to figure out if the images that come to mind when I'm near a ghost are from the ghost or if I'm simply making them up. All that's needed is to accept the story. That's all the ghosts really want: someone to accept their side of the story.

I felt responsible for Tommy. I had saved him myself, and I had accepted what he had to tell me. I knew him in a way my husband did not, just like in time I would come to know Mae in a way that my husband did not and did not care to. Tommy liked for me to read Zane Grey novels to him. We started with *Riders of the Purple Sage*, then moved on to *The Heritage of the Desert*, then *Forlorn River*. I read so many novels in the short time that Tommy was with us.

The problem was that the chicken was starting to stink. I acclimated to it quickly, but the visitors did not, and neither did my husband. According to my husband, it hit him and the visitors in the face like a ton of bricks as soon as they opened the basement door. I said if it smelled like death, then it fit the theme of the place. It was an immersive experience for the visitors. He let it go on for a while, but when I started to bring the smell with me to bed at night, he said something had to be done. I moved Tommy outside and built a lean-to over his container to keep the rain off it. I knew Tommy didn't like being cast off like he didn't matter. I could feel his anger coming back, even as I read him the Zane Grey novels. It was affecting my husband, too. The smell wasn't a problem anymore since I'd moved him far enough away from the house, but Tommy's anger was far reaching. My husband got mad any time I went out to spend time with Tommy. He threatened to throw Tommy away. When he got started, he'd throw fits like I'd never seen from him before. He'd throw things around the house, slam the dishes around in the kitchen, and cuss out the visitors for the smallest comments. He was right: Something had to be done.

Two weeks after I moved Tommy outside, I loaded his container into my car. I drove him to the mountains and set the container down on a small peak overlooking a field full of wildflowers. I knelt by the container the way the old woman had knelt by it the night I captured Tommy. After a moment, I opened the container and walked away without looking inside.

My husband and the mayor are talking in the dining room while I sing to Mae. They've been talking for a couple hours now. I should offer the mayor something to eat or something to drink. She declined when I offered her a piece of buttered bread and some lemonade when she first arrived, but she might be getting hungry or thirsty now. I know my husband wouldn't think to offer her any unless he also started to feel hungry or thirsty. I think of getting up, but I want to sing our favorite hymn again, at least once more before I leave. I sing to Mae. *Farther along we'll know all about it.* Sweet Mae. I'm sitting on the floor in front of her cage, and she sits curled up in her plastic container. *Cheer up my brother, live in the sunshine.* We are wrapped up in this melody together. *We'll understand it all by and by.* We pull this melody up over our heads like a blanket.

Anthony Immergluck

A City Without Money

I think I would be lonely
in a city without money.

To not be known by name
at any taqueria, to never wave
between those effervescing
vats of aguas frescas.

It's not an insignificant thing,
I think, to pat the staffy
who guards the bar.

To shoot Malört on
a mutual dare, to relish
the fwift of darts implanting.

I have taken my wages
and whatever time is left
and I have mashed it all
into some theater of love.

So how hard, really,
could I be to hold?

My head has been so
delicately shampooed by
the barber with the ear tattoos.

And how hard, really,
could I be to get to know?

I am privy to the traumas
of the laundrywoman.
Together we have wept.

I think I would be lonely
and I think I would be hungry

because this is how we eat
in a city with money. This
is how we eat each other.

J.L. Conrad

Miracle Town

in which we count ourselves lucky

They finished the time machine on a Friday, ahead of schedule. The invitations to gather had gone out, but by the time everyone convened, bearing platters heaped with steaming meat and casserole dishes weeping cheese, they were gone. No point in waiting, they had said. Time to save the world. There was, in that season, a general consensus that things were going badly. We checked the knots of hollow trees for messages that failed to show up and kept the muscles of our shoulders tensed and ready for flight. The boy who hid himself at the edge of the clearing said that the machine folded into itself. Or that the edges grew dim, the bulk of the machine transparent. Later, the crowd could agree on very little, except for the sound, which was like glass breaking in a small room. We do not know if they succeeded in their mission. The fact that we are still here speaks volumes. Each night we wash the dishes, then sink into our slightly concave mattresses when words on the page begin to swim past each other like errant minnows. We murmur to one another *May* _____ *save you for another day*, though what we mean by this is *May the swift horse of the week carry you past the next crossroads*. We could be forgiven for thinking that we had more time.

Liz Robbins

This Game Is a Rip

The city I come from was split into parts
by a river, its tributaries. Everyone knew

goodness, gauged how deep its well
in everyone else. A black dog, Rover,

stalked the night streets, lining the minds
of housebound women. Watery circles

on tables where glasses of gin had been.
The heart, stopped at the start of an engine.

At sixteen, I owned nothing. Fear, gone,
stuck back in the heads of mothers.

I confessed, gave myself away at makeshift
fires in the woods. So many fallen dead trees.

If I owned things, I didn't know it or love
them enough. Instead, I developed habits.

Cranked heavy metal, inhaled and coughed.
Anything to step deep into the boats

of boys, the boats of their fathers, anything
to flee, though the river whirled endless,

dark. My face burned by the sun, all the tiny
whispers. My town, where boys gauged me.

Then the girls. Now I wake to what sounds
like a shot, like a coin dropping into a slot.

Lucy Zhang

Cutting Ties

Sister tries to pay Mom back for her college tuition on Mom's birthday. I stab a wax candle into a peach because there's no cake besides the mooncakes, but Sister wants to bring the cakes back with her, and Mom should avoid overly sweet, overly oily foods like that, like swallowing solidified spoonfuls of grease that cover the beef stock like a layer of ice. If a peach can become Momotaro's amniotic sac, why can't it also be a cake? Lyrics and music mow over rage. We sing stilted to the peels of apples rotting outside by the garden of loofah that has overtaken the evergreens, to the spotted lanternflies decorating every window mesh and screen. After we sing like parched sparrows, Mom confronts Sister, and I try (not) to listen, plucking the plastic out of Jersey peach flesh, scratching wax that has dropped and hardened on the fuzzy peel. Sister thinks money can free her from familial expectations. *I want my children to have fulfilling lives*, Mom says. *You just want me to get married and have a baby*, Sister, thirty years old, shoots back. The end of peach season nears. I can't be sure if the fruit will be grainy without tasting it. I stretch my jaw and try to mimic the way a snake latches onto its prey many times larger than its body. I'd eat the pit if I could, let it settle in my stomach, see if its endocarp can withstand the hydrochloric acid and sprout up my esophagus—a blossoming tree protected by human shell, human sarcophagus. I chew so I cannot hear Mom refuse the money already wired over to her account. My jaw emasculates Sister's voice, crushes fibers and squeezes out juice—I'm sure this peach between my teeth couldn't live the life it wanted, either. Sister flies back to Albuquerque on Monday to her white, helicopter-flying boyfriend from Alabama whose dad speaks in baseball and beer. From the open window, I listen to cicadas and crickets buzzing and clicking, the kitchen light luring critters close, and slap my arm too late after a mosquito has its fill. I douse the swollen spot with methyl salicylate and eucalyptus oil. I'd thought age would make me less attractive to bugs as it does to humans, less fragrant, more stale as time demands penance from those who bleed but don't birth. Mom likens our bodies to Earth, though I instead think of the god who raced the sun and drank an entire river only to die from thirst. I wonder how Earth will feel after we suck carbon from the air and bury it under the ocean floor. Sister tells me she finished a small watermelon while watching her rabbit roam outside so coyotes won't gobble it up—*Albuquerquean coyotes are sneaky*, she tells me. They'll wag their tails to lure dogs over as a next meal. That plump rabbit is asking for it. I've got to save my maternal instinct for later. If one daughter goes free, the other is left coughing in dust. I steel myself, count the days between menstrual cycles until one day, they must stop. I used to play DVDs, watch the Monkey King chomp through a peach of immortality, wonder at what cost. It's why I eat so many peaches.

A.J. Bermudez

Picking the Wound

She monitors the opalescent ticktack of a scar like the first-time owner of a desert plant, standoffish and anxiety-ridden.

Each morning, with the precision of clockwork, the curvature of her ankle bleeds like a waterfall, a Tarantinan-Elizabethan deluge of blood, inevitable and inexorable.

The phone rings, again. The display reads DREAM GIRL, an alert hyperbolized by the tinny glissando of a mawkish ringtone.

She mops up the blood with her whitest towel, like a moron. Waves of red lap at the pocky hardwood, wet and indifferent. Through the excitement, fingers of panic claw their way up her aorta. She fantasizes about cleaning up some fabulous, more serious crime.

Between calls, the silence festers like a blister—best left alone, impossible to ignore.

Rinsing the towel, she thinks: This is *red*. She cross-checks the towel against her ninety-six-pack of Crayolas and discovers that it's more like bittersweet. Possibly brick red.

She reads up on the anterior tibial artery, the posterial tibial artery, so recently, recurrently ruptured by her negligence. She considers whether she'll do it again, contemplates her next shower with the splanchnic, sickly sweet feeling of staring downward from a height.

Dream Girl stops calling. (This, of course, is to be expected.) She feels the thrill of having done this, having put to death an entire alternate reality.

She scours a very long article about the ankle-brachial index, courtesy of the Mayo Clinic, but is betrayed by its irrelevance.

She takes a walk, up and over, block by block, listing slightly to the left (to accommodate the wound), toward one particular upper-story window where the lights switch on and off with disciplined, enviable regularity. Somewhere above, Dream Girl looms like a ghost, omnipotent and immaterial, beneath a wash of Ikea lighting.

Four stories below, the cotton rim of her sock plumes in a blossom of bittersweet (possibly brick red) blood.

She limps. Conjures magnitude. Takes credit for the failure of her tools—a most excellent carpenter.

She wishes, intently, for everything to mean something but must admit that this means nothing. That sometimes one is simply terrible at shaving.

It is unlikely that she will try a different type of blade, or alter the angle at which she shaves the doomed swerve at the base of her calf.

She will, instead, glide the tip of her nail beneath the scab and invite the wound again.

Julia Brush

Calf

Bad luck
the knowledge of beasts
won't sate me.

Lord knows
my appetite
grows feral
and my commandments
lost their silver scales
among desert and drought.

Back in the curtains of the sea,
I saw only bottom-feeders.
Make me no prophet, but
this must have been foresight.

Holy of holies,
you struck me
in muscle memory,
called me
home—honey,

mine
is a mistake of faith,
forty years wandering
and no gold
to show for it.

Julia Brush

Cibola

For fear of colonization,
I fashioned my left ribs
into a multiplication table
lest I forget how to take stock
of daily madness.

For quite a while now
I have been trying to name
conquistadors before I sleep.

For I am only just past my youth and
it's hard to keep track of every bad man
I've ever heard of or the ones who walk
behind me at night.

I am my own island and I am calling
a new world to my shores and I am loss
and I am memory, and bone, and my name
you won't ever know.

Ifeoluwa Ayandele

The Boy Who Carries
the Eyes of the Owl on His Journeys

The iroko tree in your front yard hoards
an owl on its body as you hoard your dreams
in your eyes. The eyes of the owl become

the eyes of the tree as your eyes are the vision
of your body, of your dreams & of your longings.
The iroko tree is wrapped in myths of ancestral

visitations & you find a future wrapped in owlish
memories. Your grandfather nursed the iroko tree
in your front yard as an emblem of life & the owl

is a carrier of your ancestral vision forged in dreamlike
pursuits of the vastness of your roots. The owl is a gift
of the reminiscence of your roots & before you joined

the train waving home goodbye, your father brought
you before the iroko tree & spoke the language
of your ancestral tree while the owl flapped its wings

over your head. *Your future is insured in this tree*
& your journeys through unknown roots are held
in the eyes of the owl. Your father's words were

departing echoes in your ears as the train tracks
become a flitting shadow of home you are leaving
behind, but you carry the eyes of the owl in your eyes.

Sean Thomas Dougherty

Faded Map or Historiography at 3 a.m.

The past pulls
& ebbs like tide,

saltwater flats,
marshes

where Napoleon's
soldiers froze

in the bog,
or it is the voices

of women
keening

over the ditches
or at the wake

of the boat's
keel catching

the muddy river bottom
lined with the bones

of our dead
with their constant

listlessness—shades
my eyelids droop

as I trace my finger
along the map

that no longer
has meaning

except for the mountains
etched dark.

What treaty
changed the name

of the city
where my ancestors

baked bread,
birthed calves,

bowed the violin
in the hay barn,

carried the awl
and the prayer

rug?
There now no one

speaks my grandfather's
tongue.

How could they
once their throats

were cut?
Their neck wound

made a new kind of mouth,
spoke a new not-

sound, but something
not silence

finds me at 3 a.m.
What did I expect?

When I too have traveled
like the dead

through countries
that no longer exist?

Ben Freedman

Roadkill

I

I hate the smoke. Feels like every summer now, Idaho or British Columbia or somewhere is burning. Planetary destruction aside, it sucks to drive in. Things emerge from nowhere.

Our reason for travel is a relaxing weekend in Walla Walla—where the town is small, the wine plentiful. The problem: We're not relaxed and I prefer beer. Grace and I are struggling. I forgot her birthday, work too much, have been acting "rob-tronic." So she tells me.

Still, her hands aren't clean. A few weeks ago she killed my dog, Rudy. Legally speaking, it wasn't intentional. But who goes leashless during rush hour? In a park without gates? With a dog who loves the chase?

Grace tells me to stop. Huh? I was *thinking*.

Oh.

She means the car. I pull over.

"What was that?" I ask.

"Coyote," she says.

I squint at the road.

"Possum," I say.

Turns out we're both right. The top half of a possum hangs from a coyote's mouth, like those pictures of anacondas swallowing deer. The difference here is the possum-coyote lacks a third dimension. I guess highways will do that.

Grace notices my glazed eyes.

"What are you thinking?" she asks.

"About Rudy," I say.

On the road, my thoughts return to possums and coyotes. For some reason, I imagine a coyote with the head of a possum. Then vice versa. Other variations, too.

"Um," says Grace.

The road. There's something else. What the hell is that? It's large, but the form is obscured by smoke.

I slow, then stop, then reverse.

A cow? Yes. Bloated. Mangled.

The animal is split down the center, resembling something from a horror flick. Must be the work of an eighteen-wheeler. It's the level of gruesome where you need to laugh. Nervously. I do just that.

Grace, ever a fan of the morbid, gets out and pokes the cow with her foot. Its intestinal tract is strewn about in tangled heaps.

"Cool," she says.

I've always admired her unrelenting positivity.

"Looks like it got cut by one of those ancient devices."

"Ancient devices?"

"Torture devices," she says. "That giant saw they used back during the time of knights and shit—to slice people down the middle."

"Oh," I say.

"Can you imagine? Fastened snug, upside down, the blood rushing to your head so you stay awake longer during the—"

"—Jesus, Grace."

She takes the driver's seat with renewed vigor. That's fine by me. Let her brave the smoke-filled skies.

We cruise off. It's quiet but a different quiet than before. Now, she's thinking.

"I bet there was a guy whose job was saw-sharpener," she says.

"Can't be working with dull equipment," I say.

"They thought it was a normal job. Imagine that. *Honey, I'm hooome!*"

"We have things like that now."

"Not as gruesome, though."

"Guantanamo?"

"Sure. But that's different."

"I bet there's a guy whose job is to optimize waterboarding."

"Oh, God."

"A career devoted to improving the essentials: better seal, increased discomfort, low risk of death."

"...."

"He's got a family, too."

"...."

"His kids attend nice schools with the waterboarding money. It pays well."

Grace shifts in her seat.

"They're socially minded, the kids. Want to grow up and make things better for folks."

"True progressives," she says.

The land has changed. Once you're across the Cascades, Washington becomes a different state. The trees disappear and the ground flattens into rolling hills.

Smoke is thicker. I have to stop myself from looking at the sun, which is softened just enough to allow relatively painless glimpses.

Then I see something.

Grace gasps. Brakes hard. I fly forward, my seat belt snapping taut. Something rumbles under the tires.

"Shit shit shit," she says.

I open the door.

A guy is facedown in the road.

That takes a moment to settle in.

He's an older man with long gray hair and a beard. His right arm turns in a strange direction.

"He was just lying there," says Grace. "On the highway. There was so much smoke I could barely—"

"—I know, I know," I say.

I crouch beside him. The arm's broken. No question there. But he's breathing and the rest of him seems OK. We missed the important parts. I notice a tattoo of roots curling down the base of his neck.

"Is he alive?" I ask.

Grace checks his pulse. I'm about to dial 911 when his eyes shoot open. He blinks. Looks at Grace. Coughs.

"My God. Are you OK?" she asks.

He stands up.

"Easy," I say. "You're in shock."

His eyes open further. Seemingly confused.

Then he darts across the road. Grace follows him. I hear feet crunching dirt, her voice shouting questions after him.

The next part is difficult. Somehow, my brain figures things out before I do. The way he's running. The thoughtlessness of it. The direction. What's in front of him. It's all been precalculated. I feel a tightness in my gut.

We see the edge of a ravine.

I yell for him to stop. She yells for him to stop. Or maybe she does first. I'm not sure. Time feels slippery.

His legs keep chugging until the land ends and daylight shoots beneath his feet. For a moment it looks like he's flying. He actually flaps his arms.

Then he drops.

Grace is on her knees, peering over the edge. She makes a low moaning sound.

I stare at the boulders below. Feel the tightness turn into a jagged pang along my stomach. Every rock has oddities about it, little grooves and places where water or wind have chipped parts away. Eventually, I can't look without feeling it: the jagged sensation. Like it's been infused into the rock itself.

I put my hand on Grace's shoulder.

"What do we do?" she asks.

"I don't know."

Silence.

"He was drunk," I finally say.

"...."

"Probably lost his mind, too. Lying in the sun like that."

"...."

"The pavement can fry eggs. Imagine what it does to a brain."

"So?"

"And the smoke? You couldn't have seen him. I wouldn't have, either."

"Yeah?"

"We tried to *help* him."

II

Things we should do but don't: Call an ambulance. Stop in the nearest town. Tell someone. Tell anyone.

Things we do: Get in the car. Drive in silence. The farther we go, the more our decision solidifies. Becomes part of the environment around us.

When we arrive, Walla Walla is smoky as hell. We say maybe three words checking into the bed and breakfast. A kind woman named Laura leads us to our room.

She sees our faces. Asks if everything is all right.

Grace nods.

I wince when our host opens the door. Champagne and flowers remind me I got the Lover's Deluxe.

"Enjoy yourselves!" says Laura.

I put the champagne and petals in the trash. The scented candles on the table can stay. No reason our guilt can't have fragrance.

We collapse on opposite sides of the bed and don't sleep.

Next morning is rough. Grace and I hurry past Laura and a continental breakfast sufficient for a small militia. Rarely have I witnessed such disappointment.

"Fresh-squeezed OJ," mutters Laura.

We still haven't talked, really, until that afternoon when our stomachs have us faking normalcy with bagels and coffee a few blocks away. Grace cries in line.

"He should be alive," she says.

"Careful," I hiss.

I glance around. Nobody seems to be listening. A kid with a bowl cut talks about another fire in Oregon.

"If it wasn't us, he'd still be lying on the road," I say. "Another car would've come."

"I see him everywhere," says Grace.

She turns towards me.

"Even when I'm looking at you."

"Yeah?"

"My memory of his face stretches over yours."

"Christ."

Grace nibbles her thumb.

"Can we try something?"

"I'm open to suggestions."

She leads me to a secondhand store. The place is filled with racks of clothes and miscellaneous items. A lanky woman with pink hair waves from behind the front desk.

Grace tells me I should dress as the guy. I stare long enough to confirm she's not kidding.

"If you could just ... I wouldn't have to keep imagining him. My mind could rest."

So we buy a gray wig.

I pull it on. Feels like I'm in a children's Halloween costume.
Grace smiles.

"Perfect," she says.

Then it's the flannel. Grace helps me into the sleeves. It doesn't
look half bad. Her face lights up when I turn. My jeans already look
the part.

"Wait," she says. "You're missing the tattoo."

"Grace."

"Don't worry," she says, pulling out a Sharpie.

She draws the roots with care. My skin tingles. I take a picture
and look. Grace beams. Despite the strangeness of dressing as
someone we recently watched die, it does help. For me, it feels like I'm
displaying the secret for everyone to see. I notice a shift in Grace as
well. When she looks at me, she's actually looking at me, not through
me. She talks more. It feels nice. Her renewed energy is infectious.
I speak without thinking, enjoying the lightness of spontaneity. We
both laugh for no reason at all.

Our improved moods act as a feedback loop—a recursive little
process where she makes me a bit happier, and I'm doing the same to
her—which in turn bumps me up another level, back and forth like a
Slinky dragging itself down a staircase.

In a few hours we've bootstrapped ourselves into alarmingly
high spirits. With a fresh outlook on things, we join a wine tasting.
The pourer gives me a double take but says nothing. Other couples
surround us, telling stories about jobs and family life and a time one
of them met Ichiro. He was so *nice*, says the man.

After a few drinks, my brain hums. I gaze at the glass, noticing a
tiny chip along the lip's far edge. The voices around me recede. Words
slur together, losing their discrete edges. The content of the voices
grows increasingly distant until the meaning drops off altogether. All
I hear is babble. Rough, overlapping, loud.

I watch their useless mouths open and close.

My mind returns to the road. I remember the way his arms flailed
as he dropped. The thud. The jagged pang in my gut. How the rocks
held it.

I drink another glass until the sensation fades.

Grace puts her hand on my thigh. I look at her. She looks at me.
I wink. She gives my leg a squeeze.

Then we're speed-walking back to the room, not through the door before we're kissing and ripping off clothes.

I reach for the wig.

"Leave it," she says.

We try new things from new angles for longer than normal, finishing breathless and sweaty and alive. I feel myself floating above the bed.

Grace traces the roots down my neck.

"Are we bad people?" she asks.

"Depends on your definition of bad," I say.

"Guantanamo-guy bad?"

"No, that's different. We didn't try and do this. It just sort of happened."

"Right."

"And there was smoke."

"There was."

"And he was just lying there."

We grab the champagne. When we're finished, Grace tosses it. The bottle spins end over end, exploding on tile.

III

Sunday comes and goes. Neither of us mentions work. Given our circumstances, it feels like a fictional concern. Part of a former life. We book the room for another couple days.

Even the beard and wig start to feel normal. Besides a singular shower, I haven't taken them off yet. I don't even want to.

During the day I say things that make Grace shudder. A detail from before the trip. Something about our families. Our time at college.

She tells me she sees the old guy in me. And when I talk about things before the accident, she remembers he's not here. The distance between the two, of seeing me and seeing him, of shifting between the visions, hurts her.

I try to be more careful, but the slipups keep happening. Eventually, I stop talking about myself altogether. Sometimes, Grace will ask me (but directed at the old man) what I was doing before the road. I make stuff up, tugging on my beard and speaking in generalities about work or hobbies or my prostate, which I say has grown considerably in recent years.

She asks for my name.

Um.

John, she says. Too generic. Lenny comes to mind. Ehh. Dopey. Then Grace says: Stuart? That one clicks. I say he's from Minnesota. Rural Minnesota, she adds. One sister? No. Only child.

We buy some beers and lock ourselves in the suite. Then we're off, firing away about Stuart's life.

His parents were a couple of bastards, we think—the product of long winters, not enough opportunity, and too much to drink. And with no siblings or pets or other sources of companionship, from an early age Stuart (or Stu, as he was called in his youth) was the sole victim of his parents' benders. Things were thrown. They called him names not meant for developing young minds. Sometimes forgot about him for days. As it happens with children, Stu internalized this anger. It became his way of existing in the world, which was devastating precisely because he couldn't recognize it for what it was. Anger.

And so Stu was not only routinely agitated and sad but profoundly confused, you see, since the rejections and lost friends and angry teachers that defined his childhood seemed to come from nowhere— simply more examples of a life in cahoots against him, a life hell-bent on ensuring loneliness.

Without access to the little fact that something was wrong, that the bruises Stu hid on his arms and stomach were not—as he had come to believe—normal or justified, he turned the blame inward, says Grace, shaking a bit now, realizing (as I do) that what we've started has a real inertia to it. For me, this manifests as a clicking sensation. A Geiger counter sputtering away in my head, urging things forward.

Stu has some good memories, too—playing ball on the weekends, running down pop flies and spitting sunflower seeds into the cement dugout floor. Or the way tree limbs looked during winter. Like veins running through the sky, he thought, we think. Sometimes, he'd spend hours sitting on the porch, admiring them, thinking how similar-shaped roots tunneled underground. During winter, you could flip the tree upside down and conserve its original form.

As he grew older, Stu's anger softened into a kind of bitterness, a boogeyman within his psyche that injected pangs of longing that made his skull ache deep within itself. In time, his world began to feel like a shell of the world—as in, he could talk in an intellectual sense about the wonders of friendship and love and being an alive/ conscious thing and yet feel none of it.

We continue how the drinking was a momentary solution for Stuart (as he was called from adolescence onward). It fractured his pain into manageable pieces, beginning in the afternoons, or mornings, on the bad days, up until the beer was gone and he was feeling numb and could settle into the couch or ground or wherever and gently fade into the world. At this point in the story, Grace trembles, body facing me but head cocked away, hands moist and correcting my suggestions with phrases like *That's not something* you *would do*, finger digging at my chest. I madly catalogue every detail in a notebook, terrified we'll forget something.

I follow the Geiger counter into Stuart's early adulthood, and one night in particular when he felt especially low, sitting on a curb and watching blurry visions of cars float by, listening to the sounds warp as they approached, and considering the merits of drinking until the whole show was over. And it wasn't sounding like a terrible option, really, until he remembered this stupid book he had as a child, and its picture: a thousand-year-old tree that survived storm after storm, with roots that grew miles underground. And in a slightly clichéd but personally meaningful moment, Stuart told himself to *Get up, you bitch*. If a fucking tree can last a thousand years, he could eke out another thirty. The next day he got the tattoo.

It's also clear we're rapidly approaching the present. My Geiger counter is beeping like crazy. Grace begins adding extraneous details, something about pancakes Stuart had in the morning, a walk, arthritis in his left knee, etc.—a sort of narrative filibuster to hold off the end we both see coming.

Given enough care and attention, I think, any chunk of experience can be indefinitely expanded. As soon as you feel it's pinned down, a perspectival shift happens: An unconscious rattling flicks the ground beneath your feet. The world becomes a great kaleidoscope. You're still in the same spot, but things are rearranged ever so slightly.

Grace's eyes are red. I'm crying, too. She keeps telling me she's sorry. Stuart, I'm sorry, she says, grabbing my wig and dabbing her eyes and repeating it again, sputtering like a record and clawing at my arms until she draws blood. I observe from a point just above my head, watching myself say it's not her fault. That we couldn't see.

Grace shakes her head. Tells me she can't finish.

"We owe him that," I say.

I continue on how Stuart rides with a friend heading west on I-90, drinking from a bottle he finds in the car. They argue. Stuart says a one-liner that's some combination of personal and accurate and cruel that makes the friend go pale. Tells Stuart to go fuck himself and stops the car. Stuart walks, bottle in hand, with his tired eyes and body feeling increasingly untethered.

He thinks about all the trees burning. Charred bark and water sizzling. Smoke blurring the images around him.

Decides he can continue after a nap.

Grace closes her eyes.

I take her hand in mine. She squeezes me. Hard.

"I'm not going anywhere," I say.

Stuart finds a nice flat space and sleeps with his arms outstretched. Wakes to some glassy-eyed kids. His arm feels funny, too, but he's mostly just groggy and disoriented and spooked to hell. So he runs, not noticing the voices behind him or the ground shift or the edge even after he's left it. Then: the sensation of weightlessness. And boy does it feel nice.

Reviews

Eternal Night at the Nature Museum by Tyler Barton. Louisville, Kentucky: Sarabande Press, 2021. 214 pages. $16.95, paper.

Tyler Barton's *Eternal Night at the Nature Museum* places the reader in a colorful yet parched geography of no place. They paint a landscape that is still generally ignored; more than being what has been derisively labeled "flyover," the settings for these stories are the kinds of places that have been nearly scrubbed off the map by interstates and more or less erased by GPS. The narrator in "Watchperson" personifies and articulates the core problem that drives all of these stories: "My weakness is being unsure of what's essential."

The style itself is pared down and essential; there isn't a word that isn't necessary in the whole collection, and we are told—from mostly first-person points of view—only what we need. While there are longer stories, like "Once Nothing, Twice Shatter," they resonate with the same sharp impact of the shorter selections like "County Map (Detail)." The result is that the readers get a sense of the no places as much as the people who inhabit them. There's a small-town, rural, Midwestern sensibility to the descriptions: "The west Best Western is the best Best Western." The story from which the collection title is derived, "Eternal Night at the Nature Museum, a Half Hour Downriver from Three-Mile Island," is one such no place: In the shadow of a manufactured disaster, the narrator lives in the midst of a dystopia that isn't so far removed that it would make for one more *Blade Runner*-inspired Netflix movie. This is the dystopia we live in now: not memory, not forgetfulness, just the impact on others of someone else's inaction:

> What I mean is the museum belongs to, I don't know, some kid? The one I sensed hiding in every building I ever closed down for the night. The same kid I imagined stowing away inside the tree trunk, or the shark's mouth, or the trash tote in the mop closet—this milk-mouthed kid with nothing to lose, too spooked to say uncle after having chosen hiding, now living out what was never a Disneyland fantasy but rather the lesser of two letdowns.

In the midst of this landscape that lends no hope are people crippled by their inability to decide or having to bear the consequence of forced action. The narrator—let's call him Todd—in "Once Nothing, Twice Shattered," for example, sells his car to Luther, a psychotic, New Age deliverance-selling owner of a demolition derby track.

> You have to remember, I was trying so hard not to want anything. I helped the food crew with their gardens and tried to practice detachment: If the tomatoes ripened they ripened, and if they rotted they rotted. Some were stolen in the night, and I failed; I cared. What Luther preached was the abdication of attachment. No more clinging. I gave his weekly speeches to the crew. *You must detach from your sense of morality. Without bad there is no good; all good creates all bad. There is no hippie without a cop. The goal here is to start sensing all phenomena as one—no good, no evil, just is.*

Todd's life before selling his car (and consequently, his home) to Luther was a series of consequences. His home and career lost to addiction, his dealer essentially owns him, thanks to extortion and dependence. When he embraces Luther's bubblegum mantras, he finds what he thinks is freedom but ends up being forced to decide whether to "take the demolition to the customer" and make "gone" his dealer—let's call him Colt—so that he can be, under Luther's tutelage, "free."

In "Spit if You Call It Fear," our narrator, Greg, is trying to let go of his bother, Waylon, who "still ain't over Y2K" and believes he somehow kept it from happening. In a harebrained scheme to either meet a woman from a prepper dating app or to steal her massive supply of laundry lint, Greg ends up leaving his brother in the woman's care and escaping to Alaska (maybe), in one of the few instances of action in the whole collection. Hope here is escape, though there is no certainty or enlightenment to it:

> But when they move into the light of the window, it's just a dance. They're dancing. He's terrible. His eyes are closed. She's teaching him to trust another person. He's teaching me to trust my convictions, to live in exactly the way I see the world. Or at least he's trying, and maybe he has been forever. I close my eyes too.

Every narrator in this collection is the carnage left after being fed into a culture machine. "Cowboy Man, Major Player" is a stark and absurd example of this. An aging and nearly out-of-circulation musician is given new life when a meme using his image goes viral. At first he tries to remove it; then he sees people imitating him, not even knowing it's him they're imitating; and finally, he embraces his own erasure, becoming a caricature of himself in a way that's reminiscent of Philip K. Dick.

The dystopias offered up here, though, have a gritty realism to them that is both unsettling and unrelenting because they reflect what is outside our windows every day.

—*Mick Parsons*

The Burning Light of Two Stars: *A Mother-Daughter Story* **by Laura Davis. Seattle, Washington: Girl Friday Books, 2021. 368 pages. $17.95, paper.**

Too many women know the shame their families laid on them as puberty set in. Announcements at family dinners. Comments such as "You really should wear a bra," or "You've got nothing to put in one." (my grandma's contribution to the oeuvre.)

As Laura Davis tells it in her new memoir, *The Burning Light of Two Stars: A Mother-Daughter Story*, when a girl in her family began developing, the females surrounded her. The pubescent girl's shirt was removed to allow the patriarch, Poppa, to inspect her breasts.

Davis' grandfather had been molesting her since she was three years old. No one in the family knew—least of all Davis, who represses the memories. Even so, when the women in her family insisted Davis bare her breasts to her grandfather, Davis came up with the word every survivor who wasn't able to, at her own critical moment, wishes she could have found.

Davis said, "No."

No one in the circle of female relatives took her side. Davis' own mother said, "We all did it."

"No."

Her shirt stayed on

Laura Davis grew up to write, with Ellen Bass, the book many survivors call our bible: *The Courage to Heal: For Women Survivors of Child Sexual Abuse.*

It is impossible to overstate the international political and sociological impact of *The Courage to Heal*. It debuted in 1988, a time when few said at any volume "rape," "sexual abuse," or—God forbid—"incest." No one was a "survivor." We were victims.

In the first third of *Burning Light*, Laura Davis deftly covers the above, and more. There is the time that Davis and her coauthor, Ellen Bass, are targeted by an also-worldwide faction of folk who don't believe in repressed memories, who whine that *The Courage to Heal* ruined their families, their lives. During one interview, this happens:

> Ellen remained steady, looking straight into the blinking red light above the camera, ignoring the men and talking only to the survivors she knew were watching at home on TV. "You aren't alone," she said to the blinking red light. "Healing is possible," she told the women. "It wasn't your fault." And "I believe you."

As electrifying as it was to have Davis bring me into the room where it happened, I was feeling a mite antsy as I approached the hundred-page mark. Though well written, the material has a too-familiar vibe. Some scenes bring nothing new, such as a rollicking but "Why?" description of San Francisco Gay Pride parades in the 1980s.

In German, "Temme" means fierce. According to Vedic astrology, Temme has a fire element. Temme Davis, the author's mother, is a small-time actress with big-star narcissism who knows how to blow a gasket to great effect. Faced with the "my daughter/my father" breakdown, Temme chooses Poppa. She and the majority of the family strive to erase Davis—even Davis' dear brother Paul, shown as a hopelessly earnest enlightenment seeker. (When Davis reveals the incest, Paul responds, "It must have happened because of something terrible you did in a past life.")

This is where Davis chomps into the story and shakes it like a slipper. Mother and daughter stitch together what Davis calls "love with a hole in the middle of it." She moves to Santa Cruz, eventually to settle down with her spouse, Karyn, and their two children. Karyn is training to be a yoga teacher. Their family bruises homegrown peppermint leaves to steep for tea. They watch surfers. Then, the Drama Queen of New Jersey calls. She is declining. She wants a relationship with her grandchildren; she wants to get along with her daughter. She will be moving her nails-done, pocketbook-carrying, my-father-is-not-a-pedophile self to Santa Cruz. She is not asking.

How mother and daughter pass through the hole and into respect, then to love, and ultimately into total acceptance makes up two hundred pages of dropped-jaw, wiped-eye, "Did that happen?" story not often found in a book.

Davis has the ability of the excellent memoirist to tap into a universal through relaying the personal. During one rainy car drive, Temme comes close to acknowledging the probability of her own abuse, only to retreat to yet another cigarette—more proof that this mother will never be able to say that which every adult child yearns to hear: "It happened. I am sorry."

For her part, Davis overworks, ignores her spouse, bails on her kids' activities, and takes a few too many solitary tokes. She overeats. All this as we witness Temme's painful slide from independent to assisted living, then to nursing home, then to hospice. (Reader beware: There are fluids.) Following Tenne's death, Davis and her brother watch their mother's cremation:

> The attendant wrenched open the heavy metal door. The blast of heat made us gasp. Mom's bones lay scattered across the floor of the crematory, but her skull glowed red with fire. Lit up till the end. She looked great. She looked ... beautiful.

Laura and Paul don't waste the four hours they sit in front of the crematorium as the corpse becomes ashes. Looking directly into each other's eyes, they apologize. They ask each other to be his sister or her brother with the tenderness of a couple taking vows, without an ounce of ick factor. At this point, *Burning Light* brings in what can only be described as grace: the moment we understand that while our efforts with our parents might not achieve all we hope for, in our generation, healing can happen.

—*Alle C. Hall*

Three Urgent Chapbooks Confront Dangers, Seen and Unseen

Covenants by Tommy Dean. Washingtonville, New York: ELJ Editions, 2021. 27 pages. $10.00, paper.

Tommy Dean's slim stories take readers to the edges of the end. With vivid description and emotionally weighted action, Dean pushes his characters to face final moments, rising dangers and the things that are slowly slipping away. Characters succumb to flood, drought, and flames licking the sky.

In one story a character says, "Fighting never looked so much like defeat." In another, a character resolves that "collapse is eminent."

Most of the dialogue in the stories match the tone of immediacy, and the actions hold the weight of the inevitable in these worlds quickly rolling to a stop. In "Slipping" a couple is on the edge of divorce and the children want to keep looking up at the blimp overhead instead of going inside the house to face a family falling apart.

"We refused to come back into the house, necks angled backward, hips swiveling to keep the balloon ship above us, wondering what would happen if it popped."

Boys come of age in worlds where guns are always needed and the fighting goes on and on. Hope is hard to find in these stories, and they are hard to piece together as one cohesive whole, but the individual pieces offer their own insights. One story, "The Wave," offers insight on why the speaker is fixated on broken pieces: "Anything unbreakable I find endlessly irritating. Maybe love is one knob turn of agitation away from complete surrender, but that would be too easy for people like us."

Maybe surrender is the best way into and through this collection that asks readers to hold an armload of endings in mind as they move toward their own fragile future.

Breaking Points by Chelsea Stickle. Mount Vernon, New York: Black Lawrence Press, 2021. 57 pages. $9.95, paper.

Breaking Points is the debut fictioin collection by Chelsea Stickle about young women who want to break free from their angst, their relationships, their families, and the dangers they face—real and imagined. It begins with an abandoned car and a mystery of a missing woman—a new mother and wife of a husband who "doesn't understand." Yet, the reader knows the woman has left her car and her life behind for something else, possibly "a cave that echoed so she could finally hear herself."

Stickle's characters run, scream, or break things to escape societal pressures and the threat of erasure or violation. In "The One Who Gets Away," the speaker suggests reality checks can be one way to avoid the snare of sexual predators and toxic, socialized womanhood: "The adrenaline of having narrowly escaped a closing cage keeps you up past when the other girls stumble home, eyeliner smeared and unclear about what happened."

Stickle leans into social commentary about women's safety and autonomy and plays with form as containers for some of the inner dramas coursing through her characters' minds—a recipe, a flowchart, and a quiz carry the weight of their own narratives. Stickle's stories build in intensity until she deftly unravels them at the end with a character who becomes undone.

Lovebirds by Hananah Zaheer. Durham, North Carolina: Bull City Press, 2021. 49 pages. $12.00, paper.

Romantic love is hard to come by, and birds' necks are intentionally broken in Hananah Zaheer's collection of stories where women are the caged birds trying to break free.

Set in Pakistan, each story is a fully rendered and immersive. Zaheer is a master of characterization. From the first sentence of each story, the reader is placed beside each new character navigating a life within the context of firm cultural norms and strict gender roles. Control is the love language of men in Zaheer's stories, and the women look for a new form of speech beyond the walls built around them. One woman forms an intimate attachment to a willow tree. Her attachment becomes so strong her husband decides to cut it down: "It was just like him to try to take away the only thing I did without permission."

A story set in a post office delves into one woman's loneliness that eventually morphs from fixation and desperation to madness and self harm.

There is so much violence in Zaheer's stories, but so much beauty in the way she pens them. One clear example is in story where a mother feels the impending danger of her son becoming a religious zealot, or murderous monster made from a mob of men shaping his morality and manhood. She leads the reader down to a winding conclusion that hits as hard as cannon. This is the power of Zaheer's prose. Her lines are immediate, varied, and engaging, and her dark stories keep you locked in until the very end.

—*Yolande Clark-Jackson*

The Great Indoorsman by Andy Farkas. Lincoln, Nebraska: University of Nebraska Press. 174 pages. $19.95, paper.

The Great Indoorsman is a menagerie, and a smart one at that. Topics of the book include the hunt for the perfect video store; a discourse on nothingness; filk music; legends you've heard, maybe, but not like this, or not this way, not so mesmerizingly introspective and bizarre, yet somehow still registering as familiar; the belief-in-God found dead at a kitchen sink.

Perhaps the best way to put it is to think of it as a tome of *weird*, and I mean that complimentarily. All of us find ourselves at the apex of strange experiences, now and then; Andy has kindly given us a wonderful portrait of some of his strange experiences. The true beauty in it, though, is how relatable it all feels. I've never drunk Kool-Aid at a coffee shop, nor been approached by a Christian teenager sporting a jacket bearing the Soviet hammer and sickle. But you know who has? Andy Farkas. And he's here to tell you about it. And somehow, by the end of it, I come away thinking I was wrong. Didn't I do that last week? Well, no, of course I didn't do that last week, that was *Andy's* story. But now it feels a little like my story, too.

This familiarity between Andy and the reader is its strongest quality. Think of a friend, a specific friend: that one who always has the best stories. Sure, maybe the last time you saw them was a few years ago, but when you meet up for a drink after years apart, you're excited because you just know that friend is going to have some wild stories. And why? Because, somehow, they seem to have odd experiences and interactions at a much higher frequency than most. Now, having imagined that, you understand this book.

When you read *The Great Indoorsman*, you're sitting down with Andy for a drink. Maybe you don't know him at all, or maybe you're a close friend, but whatever the case, you're glued to your barstool by his stories. His *actual* stories. Elements of them may be exaggerated, or mildly altered, sure, but we shouldn't care, don't care really, because these are damn good stories.

This is a collection of confessions—confessions of the absurdity and comedy life thrusts upon us, willing or not. I could break this book into its parts, be more analytical about it, but then I think that sort of defeats the purpose in the first place: having a drink with Andy. We don't, or at least I don't, tend to sit and pick through the quotidian happenings of a drink at the bar. Because a drink at the bar is to see a friend, to catch a long-awaited update of their life. Still, decorum and conventions of expectation mean I will, against my better judgment, spend some time analyzing.

At times, more often than not, this book lingers around the idea of identity. Andy asserts the absurdity and randomness of life, yes, but it goes beyond the assertion. Coupled with this chaos is a want for order, or at least an assurance of meaning, an assurance that Andy seems hard pressed to give. Rather, this book assures that, whatever happens, whoever you are, there is something about telling the story of our lives that fills them with meaning.

One of the essays, "Somewhere Better Than This Place," demonstrates this meaningful meaninglessness quite well. Andy is taking stock of the city of Tuscaloosa, Alabama. In it he places some furtive hope, a hope for progress and change in the city, that it will breathe with new life. Except, the problem is, it never does. The town continues onward, into the unending future, no more or less than what it's always been: a place some people live. The final line of the essay puts it nicely: "[Tuscaloosa] would never change."

Now, I did just spoil the ending, and the ending says nothing happens. But in his evaluation of the city of Tuscaloosa, Andy has brought the city to life. It's a brief moment, a quiet one, but he has immortalized the sheer Tuscaloosa-ness of Tuscaloosa, and in such a captivating way. In Andy's Tuscaloosa, readers will find their own city, their own neighbors, their own groanings. And isn't it nice to know that Andy Farkas is out there, somewhere, probably on a barstool, waiting to tell more of his stories? Stories that, even though they didn't happen to you, they might as well have? Do what you will, but I'm sitting down (metaphorically, but still) for a drink with Andy. And boy, does he have some good stories to tell.

—*James Heil*

Weird Pig **by Robert Long Foreman. Cape Girardeau, Missouri: Southeast Missouri State University Press, 2020. 263 pages. $18.00, paper.**

From Nilsen Prize-winning author Robert Long Foreman, the novel *Weird Pig* is titled after the antihero the narrative follows from adoption to near-death. The minimalism of the cover is a complete juxtaposition to the complicated world residing within; it gives readers no warning for the shock and awe that awaits them. This novel illustrates a reality where animals can speak for themselves, yet their lives are no less cruel. The world where *Weird Pig* exists is chaotic and absurd, much like the reality it satirizes. Despite these conditions, he never looks for meaning in the uncontrollable life he leads; instead, Foreman makes himself comfortable wherever he goes, following impulsive desires into decisions that nearly always have dire consequences.

In a novel riddled with consequences, Weird Pig never learns a single lesson from his actions—as if nobody told him he's supposed to be self-actualizing. With no moral hang-ups on murder or massive crime sprees, Weird Pig embarks on adventures that quench his various appetites for recognition and destruction. He isn't loved or admired, yet he's generally accepted by communities wherever he wanders. Unrestrained by ethical consciousness, the antihero stirs antics within the publishing industry, higher education, and the military, among other industries in his journey across America. Fueled by various drug addictions and weapon fascinations, he moves from one unpredictable, absurd scenario to the next. Weird Pig says it best himself: "I leave only wreckage in my wake."

Adopted by a suburban family at the recommendation of a sitcom marriage counselor, Weird Pig watched TV to learn English and social cues. The adoption of a pig was supposed to make the Mayhews closer as a family, even though they only like pigs for dinner. Weird Pig learned to walk on two legs in order to fit in among humans. Craig, his older brother, impressed upon him that the best way to learn to walk is on a skateboard:

> It's how all people learn to walk, he said. It's how I did it. It's how Mom and Dad learned. Come on, Weird Pig, just put one foot in front of the other, on the skateboard that the state government provided you, so that you may learn to walk with grace and efficiency.

Following Weird Pig's traumatizing and unconventional formative years, he finds a home at Dan Farm, where he begins his life as a sociopath extraordinaire. After settling into his life on the farm, he decides to take up writing. Shortly into this newfound obsession he makes an enemy of author Lexie Glass after mailing his magnum opus about the burdens of manhood to New York for her Year in Reading list. The author fails to feature his poem, so naturally Weird Pig winds up in a position to confront her after traveling to New York in a stolen car:

> The first thing Weird Pig did in New York City was ditch the Focus while it was still moving. He dove out the window so it careened into a busy intersection and collided with a truck large enough that no one in it was hurt, thank goodness.
>
> The police searched for the driver, but their search was limited to human beings. They failed to consider the possibility of Weird Pig.

As a negligent father, Weird Pig would do anything to avoid his children, whom he makes deeply uncomfortable. The most displeased of all his children is the Sun Pig. Born in the darkness and captivity of some stranger's basement, the Sun Pig contracted a god complex from his tragic childhood. Not even the morally bankrupt Weird Pig can interact with him without being restrained. The dynamic between Weird Pig and his son captures what can only be described as generational trauma.

Weird Pig's story is told in episodic chapters that explore the different, sometimes disturbing facets of his world. Aside from fatherhood, Weird Pig encounters caricatures of prostitution, police work, and industrial farming along the way. His world is a self-aware spoof of American culture that stupefies readers with captivating moments of stark realism.

Recommended for readers who enjoy witty humor, nothing is sacred in this dark satire. Foreman delivers an entertaining experience that confronts the horrors of American culture with endless nonchalance. Designed to violate all expectations, *Weird Pig* is truly one in a million.

—*Sidney Miles*

Wind Farm: Landscape With Stories and Towers by **Jeff Gundy.** **Loveland, Ohio: Dos Madres Press, 2021. 157 pages, paper.**

"How should one describe a landscape that has not only changed, but been erased as it changes?" In other words, as Philip Metres is asking in one of the epigraphs to poet Jeff Gundy's excellent collection of essays, "What countries could we see, and what countries could we make, if we erased the erasures?"

Wind Farm is a slim book with an ambitious goal. Gundy endeavors to both consider the land of his childhood in rural Illinois and to "erase the erasure" of that land, to consider what it was once, and what it may become.

Gundy writes in both a considered, mellow first person and as the persona of "Wind Farmer," whose exploits he describes more whimsically in the third person. The Wind Farmer essays let the author pluck memories from his past and tie them to his larger rumination about the communities that have disappeared from the Midwestern landscape over the past few generations. The new innovation dotting the vista is wind farms, representing both progress and something bittersweet, an emptying out.

The bigger the machines, the fewer farmers it takes to run them. We drive past the farmsteads where the house is gone or falling, where the barns are slumped and rotten, where a few trees wave vaguely at the wind which is the only thing that changes without growth or decay, the only thing that comes and goes as it will.

Gundy was raised as a Mennonite and made a career teaching poetry at Mennonite colleges, and his narrator comports himself with a noticeably humble air. Take in "On the Wind Farmer's Youth: Football," when he writes about his difficulties relating the intense physical and communal experience of high school football to a skeptical feminist friend: "It didn't fit her narratives about men and patriarchy and violence, as it fits only awkwardly into mine."

Whether writing about turbines or "The House of the Rising Sun" or the Lenni Lenape prophet Neolin, Gundy approaches subjects with infectious curiosity and relays memories with a sharp eye. From his vantage point, the wind farms become a jumping-off point to consider everything from nostalgia to climate change, when he condemns his own generation's inaction: "The wind farmer is white and getting old and knows that his generation has unforgivably squandered its best chances to keep the planet from crisping and drowning at the same time."

The only true qualm I had with the book was with the photography. Every single essay begins with a photograph, many of which are pictures taken of the windmills he writes of so compellingly. At one point, he admits his photographs don't do the majestic, weird turbines justice, and I have to agree. While perfectly good in the context of amateur photography, they distract somewhat from the elegant prose Gundy uses throughout. The archival pictures included in the second half of the book do more to illuminate the subjects being discovered, but overall, I thought the book could have used some restraint around their use of imagery. On the other hand, it leans into the unpretentious nature of the book, giving it even more of a scrapbook quality.

When a poet writes essays, they often find ways to bring a poet's directness to their prose, as Gundy does when describing the stench of chicken manure he encountered working on a farm as a kid: "The smell was almost pure in a way, immediate and overwhelming, with an intensity that olfactory fatigue never really overcame."

What stitches all the disparate elements of this book together is the force of Gundy's imagination. Each short essay touches on a topic or two, and before you know it, the whole book has snowballed into a cumulative meaning and clarifying insights. In an otherwise mellow essay on a less-than-rousing high school love affair, Gundy ends with a deceptively simple message: "The world gives some of us more than we deserve." It is a noble thought, and one that I felt often as a reader I rode shotgun with Gundy eon his literary tour of the heartland, past, present and future.

—*Timothy Parfitt*

***Proof of Me* by Erica Plouffe Lazure. Milwaukee, Wisconsin: New American Press, 2022. 252 pages. $17.00, paper.**

Erica Plouffe Lazure's short story collection, *Proof of Me*, exhibits her expert skills in weaving together characters and tone into a gripping prose that leaves little to want except to keep reading. Winning the New American Press fiction prize, Lazure showcases a range of circumstances throughout the collection, each unique and new, but with characters that are open in their voices and familiar in a way and that inspires deeper connections.

Proof of Me unfolds across five sections of stories. Some are linked through their reused sets of characters, forming a chain of stories that tell the larger tale of those involved. Many also connect through the central point of fictional Mewborn, North Carolina, but oftentimes it is a sense of theme that drives these connections. Although *Proof of Me* is used in reference to the story of the same name within the collection, many stories throughout the book are characters in search of proof for something, whether it is proof of themselves, proof of family they have lost, proof of their connections, or any of the other various proofs they search for. Although they are separate stories and sections, they wonderfully compose a collection around this idea of searching for proof, for validation.

Lazure incorporates the perspectives of each character, whether first-person narrator or third-person protagonist, as vital factors of each story. The stories are defined by their tellers in a beautiful way that strikes a balance on how the events are displayed and perceived through the influence of the narrator's psyche, the characters around them, and the reader. Some of these narrators, such as Quinn from "The Ghost Rider," tell their own story, walking the reader through their struggles one painful step at a time.

Lazure builds Quinn's story through one night of playing in his band, being left by his girlfriend Sage, picking up the pieces to figure out why, and going through fragmented memories of his past with Sage. She situates the narrative deep within Quinn's first-person perspective, letting the reader see both the reality of the situation as well as how Quinn desperately denies that Sage left him and clings to misguided hope that she will return to him. Lazure holds the story through a delicate balance of the other characters who do not believe anything is wrong, Quinn who cannot accept that his relationship has fallen apart, and the reader who knows it has.

This is a careful back-and-forth of hope and despair in the narrative, as in one moment "The contract said it all. The contract said, Fuck you, Quinn," but soon after hope resurfaces with "Or maybe Sage was home by now. Maybe I'd try the bench outside her apartment, play a song or two on my guitar, and see what happens next." It is a compelling pull throughout "The Ghost Rider" and other stories in the collection, such as "Gestate," "Freezer Burn," and "The Cold Front," as characters search for proof that their relationships are not lost yet, that there is still a connection, even if at times it is already gone.

Theme and place intertwine throughout the collection as most characters connect to Mewborn and become attached to their own piece of it throughout the book's sections. Each connects to the same place but also gives a new perspective and feature to the town than the one before it. Lazure never seems content to reuse and rehash what she has written for Mewborn. Instead, she always adds something new to it, expands into an unexpected direction of life.

Lazure also utilizes recurring sets of characters across her stories. Some occur in smaller, more loosely connected pairings, such as "Cadence" and "The Ghost Rider" or "Freezer Burn" and "The Cold Front," but the second section of the collection, Stitch, chains five stories around the character of Cassidy Penelope first through her mother, then her uncle until following her as she grows up and strikes off on her own away from Mewborn. Lazure develops a larger narrative through her chain of short stories, allowing for examination of the characters across multiple points in time, from varied perspectives and with different temporary characters to reflect on the main cast and the central character of Cassidy.

One story in this set is the titular story, "Proof of Me," following Cassidy's life in San Francisco after leaving Mewborn. Lazure builds on Cassidy's search for connection from the previous story, "Selvage," as Cassidy searches for a proof of her own existence in her unfamiliar environment through fake tattoos, her lover's artwork, and social ties. Eventually, it comes to a point as she is asked,

> "What's you, then? You spend the day killing trees for peep shows, scribbling all over yourself, thinking you're going to get to the meaning of life from some stupid drawing of a duck on your ass," Amar said. "And here, you deny something that actually contains a piece of you?"

It is this unabashed prose that drives characters throughout her stories, confronting characters like Cassidy directly and looking for their answer. What Cassidy must discover for herself is what that answer is, what the proof of her is, and while that is not a question answered in any one story, Lazure gives us a world of stories to move among and find an answer in their complexities.

Each of Lazure's stories can stand well on its own with driving characters, prose, and plots, but as a collection, they are able to highlight the depth in Lazure's range from San Francisco to fish festivals, Broadway music, and a trip to the metaphorical center of the universe in "Object Lessons." *Proof of Me* wonderfully arranges these stories to guide us through their nuances and show shifts in the characters over time and their searches for validation.

—*Sean Turlington*

How Far I've Come by Kim Magowan. Des Moines, Iowa: Gold Wake Press Collective, 2022. 199 pages. $14.99, paper.

The best pieces of art show us a reflection of who we are and who we could be given any choice that we make, and Kim Magowan's collection *How Far I've Come* holds a mirror up to readers and forces them to look not just at what they are, but what they can be, even if the reflection isn't always present.

The stories in this collection are short, many nearly microfiction or flash fiction, but each paints a portrait of a different woman and how that woman is managing her relationships, her career, or her internal struggles. Each woman portrayed is flawed in her own unique ways, but because of these flaws, the reader has a chance to see themselves in different characters repeatedly throughout the collection.

In "Ice," the readers can examine their relationships to their siblings when the forces that necessitate those connections are gone. Does the connection between siblings have to last once the parents have passed away? Do adult orphans still owe anything to each other besides what is in the will?

"Tapped" allows the reader to be a mother in a struggling relationship with a daughter preparing to go to college. The contemplation and the honesty the mother character feels while thinking about her daughter and all that went wrong in her marriage and with the loss of her other daughter builds to the ultimate showing of restraint and giving kindness when it is not deserved.

On the other side, there are stories that revel in the pettiness of withholding undeserved kindness. "Dear Dave" is a small vignette that in its one page punches the reader with such feelings of backhanded kindness that you cannot help but to support the unnamed protagonist in support for why she wrote the letter. "Ninth Stepping" has a similar feel to it, this time a woman recklessly attempting to make amends as part of her AA program, but instead of fixing bridges, she burns a few more without much care for if she will need those bridges again.

These vignettes and stories don't paint the whole portrait of the female experience, nor do they try to. Magowan restrains from such ambitions and instead opts to portray a moment in each woman's life, giving just enough detail to understand the woman and to sympathize with her, even if we disagree with her choices.

Oftentimes women are painted as the better, purer sex, shying away from masculine sins of adultery, greed, and drink. This collection, instead of painting women as angelic and sinless, dwells in the brokenness of humanity and shows how women are part of the problem. The women in this collection are equal parts victims and perpetrators of the brokenness that they face. They are the reasons their marriages fail at the same rate that they are the victims of poor husbands.

Magowan achieves this resonance through poetic prose, many of the shorter pieces reading as prose poems. Themes of love, family, loyalty, ambition, desire, and surrender woven throughout, these stories interrogate what it means to be human from the female perspective in a way that men can relate to as well. This collection is perfect for anyone who can read only in micro doses and is looking for masterfully written examinations of femininity and its relationship to every part of the world therein.

—*Josh Springs*

Mad Prairie **by Kate McIntyre. Athens, Georgia: University of Georgia Press, 2021. 176 pages. $19.95, paper.**

The Midwest is filled with sprawling plains, hardy farmlands, and a generally congenial populace. In Kate McIntyre's *Mad Prairie*, readers are transported to the rich landscape of modern Kansas, where the plains sprawl with "wheat fields like quicksand," the hardy farmlands are hardly inhabitable, and small-town residents smile while plotting how best to keep their secrets intact. We are treated to a wide cast of complex characters throughout seven short stories and one novella, with Miriam Green as our central protagonist weaving each of their lives together. Themes of corruption within society and within humanity, toxicity in gender roles, and trust for others and oneself all coalesce into a masterpiece that keeps the reader turning to the next page well into the night.

The short stories in this collection don't have captivating endings. They do end, of course, but the finality of the stories isn't quite what we'd expect. At first, it was difficult to resolve the idea of the short stories not having resolutions or distinct endings, with the exception of "New Man." However, upon realizing that the purpose of these short stories is to build aspects of the whole story, their lack of succinct endings propels the narrative forward. We're given a polyphonic narrative that's less cohesive than a traditional novel, but no less captivating for its disjointed storytelling.

For the reader looking for a nice short story collection where you don't have to put much thought into what you're reading, this probably isn't the book for you. This collection will have you cozying up for a long night in, and its nuanced writing will have you trying to find the connections among the characters and the overall plot as you read each story. Can it be read superficially? Of course, but we wouldn't recommend it. The small details that hint at something darker and more sinister are tucked away in expertly crafted sentences that, for the discerning reader, unravel a more intriguing look at the inherently flawed world in which we live.

Mad Prairie most often bends reality discreetly with vivid descriptions and gripping introspection that leaves the reader suspending disbelief without realizing it. What we may see as absurd feels much less so with the emotional connection built between the reader and the characters, and among the characters themselves. With

Jim and Patty in "New Man," we see the effects of a longtime marriage withering away and culminating in a newfound sense of freedom as Jim moves on, leaving Patty to a life she never would have taken for herself.

McIntyre's writing toes the line between grotesque curiosity and absurd obsession as Elizabeth wonders whether her drinking really affects her liver, and Vern contends with his fear of losing his wife Della after he's laid off from the quarry. "The Moat," specifically, grapples with an exploration of problematic characteristics in marriages, and the ways in which we deal with them (or don't). Vern isn't entirely unlikeable, but it's difficult to find redeeming qualities as he wades through his own sudden lack of purpose that manifests itself in a moat around the house to keep his wife trapped there, unable to leave him or their children behind.

This book treads the line between a short story collection and a novel with how intertwined the stories are; however, what's most compelling about the storytelling is the underlying tension that builds with each piece. McIntyre masterfully keeps each story contained within its own central conflict, but by the time we reach "Elegy for Organ in Ten Parts," the connections among the stories become clearer, and the larger implications of the characters' relationships sink in.

McIntyre also sprinkles in hints of pop culture references that readers with a keen eye will pick up. The toxicity of some of the relationships gives a raw, unfiltered perspective to the stories we encounter. Most importantly, *Mad Prairie* offers a poignant look at the relationships we build with one another and the effects that ripple out from our existence in the world. By the end of this collection, we are left with a full understanding of "a true Midwestern impasse: Everybody was smiling but nobody meant it."

—Alyssa Malloy

They Kept Running by Michelle Ross. Denton, Texas: University of North Texas Press, 2022. 240 pages. $14.95, paper.

Fiction editor of *Atticus Review* and author of dozens (and dozens) of published stories, Michelle Ross has quickly established herself as a master craftsperson of "small fictions." Her three story collections have all been prizewinners: the Moon City Press Fiction Award for *There's So Much They Haven't Told You*, the Stillhouse Press Short Story Award for *Shapeshifting*, and the Katherine Anne Porter Prize for her latest collection, *They Kept Running*. The majority of the stories in the new book feature female protagonists whose lives have been affected—often outright damaged, some subtly twisted, still others simply framed—by their relationships with men. It's possible to viscerally feel the pressure these characters are under to somehow re-see themselves in new ways, to push beyond emotional and social boundaries created by men and seemingly reinforced by nearly everyone. The tension, the deep desire to construct an identity outside of these restrictive terms, is palpable.

The story that contains the line from which Ross takes her book's title is called "Binary Code." Here, a group of women have decided to run a loop in the desert before the season becomes too hot and therefore too dangerous. They want the beauty of the landscape and the warmth of the sun, but it's also understood they want the solitude. They want no—or at least fewer—eyes watching them as they move. The park ranger warns them about mountain lions, about heat. They already know about the heat; they're not afraid of mountain lions. What he doesn't warn them about is a group of men in a Jeep who slow down to sound the horn three times and catcall the group before speeding off. The real danger here, Ross shows us, is that sudden jolt of fear that comes with each blast of the horn and the reminder that the male gaze only sees their bodies. Nahala, who does what she can to hide beneath old, formless T-shirts, says of women's predicament, "Being female is like operating with a wonky binary code. We may have infinite choices in how we present ourselves and conduct ourselves, but in the end, men read the same output regardless." The tone of the piece is one of resignation, a version of "We've seen all this before, ladies; there's nothing new under the sun," and an admission that the only thing to do is exactly what they have been doing: enjoying each other's company and getting some exercise. Ross end the story with, "As slow as the women were moving up that hill, they knew they'd probably make the same time if they walked. But still, they kept running."

In further stories like "Binary Code," Ross sometimes turns down the temperature of the misogyny, but sometimes she turns it up. In "Killer Tomatoes," the sexism, the wanton nature of the male gaze, and the harassment of women operates at nearly quid pro quo levels. Here two teenagers, Lindsey and Cheyenne, are home alone watching cheesy horror movies when there's a knock at the door. The reader knows the trope and so right away begins to feel a vicarious dread. And indeed our worst fears are seemingly realized. On the other side of the door is

"Uncle Rick"—an on again/off again "friend" of Lindsey's mother. We know not to let him in, but the girls are bored, and at least one of them is ready to test out the power of her new sexuality. On a previous visit when the mother was at home, Rick noticed Lindsey, saying,

> "I remember when you were no taller than my thighs. Now look at you. You have ten boyfriends?" She pictured herself sawed into ten equal pieces, like a piece of lumber. Her mother said, "She's barely thirteen." He said, "That don't mean a thing."

Before long Rick and Cheyenne, who plays the flirty ingénue to foolish perfection, have begun to discuss the recent and mature development of Lindsey's breasts, to which she responds with "Stop talking about my body" and a reminder that her mother isn't home. Nevertheless, something compels Lindsey to follow Cheyenne and Rick outside to where his car awaits. He pauses for a moment on the porch under a red light bulb still left over from the Christmas decorations, but which may have beckoned him here, and at least casts him in an appropriate light. Like the women in "Binary Code," Lindsey adopts a tone of resignation, understanding that she's in danger but not knowing what can be done about it. "She can't know for certain what will happen, but she is learning to anticipate the unthinkable."

Significantly, Ross can also dazzle with a lighter touch. In "Cubist Mother," a daughter finds her mother hurling dishes at a mortar wall at the back of the house, the shards scattering in small explosions. Immediately, the reader wonders about the cause of this violence. But then we realize we know. The scene doesn't need to be explained. Just in case, the daughter helps a little. She looks at her mother, the dynamic movement of arms and legs and hips and buttocks as she hurls plate after plate, and is reminded of a Duchamp painting, *Nude Descending a Staircase, No. 2*. The flurry of movement seeming to bring all these parts together—unless she's wrong. And maybe she is wrong, the figure could just as easily be *disassembling*, shattering. Her mother invoking whom? The anonymous model Duchamp disfigured, just as Picasso disfigured Dora Maar, Marie-Thérèse Walter, Françoise Gilot?

Chief among the achievements in *They Kept Running* is that Ross compels the reader to look closely at the women into whose lives these awful men—absent fathers, sexual predators, gaslighting morons with fragile egos—enter and asks us to assess the damage they leave behind, physical and emotional, visible and obscured. This can be heartrending work, and there aren't many opportunities for redemption in this prizewinning collection. However, the stories do bear witness. They will leave you thinking and feeling at a fever pitch, then turning back to read them again and again.

—Jeffrey Condran

How the Moon Works by Matt Rowan. Denver, Colorado: Cobalt Press, 2021. 200 pages. $16.00, paper.

Matt Rowan has written a collection of short stories reminiscent of French surrealist Boris Vian or absurdist master Franz Kafka, creating in many stories a world not quite like our own while allowing us to recognize some profound truths about human nature. The universe he propels us into is often raw and cruel, but not so cruel that the setting and plot twists seem gratuitous.

The cruelty of the world is most in evidence in "Grizzly 25," but it is also the story with the biggest redemptive qualities: a point of view that spares us gruesome details of children being slaughtered in a maze, a satire on the world of small business, and a spot-on, satisfying ending. It is also one of the stories where Rowan's deftness at handling fantastical elements is most in evidence. The author has a unique voice that keeps the reader engaged, as well as sharp insights into all his characters while he presents deeply original storylines.

While "Grizzly 25" certainly is most memorable, the universe in all the works contained in this scintillating collection is populated by protagonists who struggle with alienation, as well as loners, misfits, and nonconformists. Many of the stories contain a phantasmagoric quality; for instance, the first story, "No me say it," focuses on the love that a character with knobs for hands has for his daughter.

The world Rowan has created provides a respite from the pandemic and deeply politically divided landscape while asking probing questions of the society we live in, a society where we select heroes and spit them out, exploit workers, condemn many to loneliness, and cause silent despair or even mental illness; yet, Rowan's world never comes across as completely bleak, thanks to his incisive commentary on society, his keen observations on human behavior, and, most importantly, the excellent endings, which keep the reader turning the page to the next story instead of putting the book away.

The best story after "Grizzly 25" might be "The walk-in-their-footsteps historical footsteps museum," about a museum employee who must take the place of a colleague in a historical recreation of

Commander George A. Custer's last stand at the battle of Little Bighorn, after the star actor decides he is through with the show. That story is told in the first-person point of view of the museum employee thrown into the performance, and the narrator's inner dialogue is entertaining. The story also represents an interesting reflection on the vagaries of fame and success in theater and shows Rowan's range with an example of a story that does not have an absurd element.

The title story, "How the moon works," provides an unusual twist on unrequited love by considering unrequited friendship and a loner's need to seek salvation from his elderly neighbor. The collection may have been better served by picking a different title that conveyed more sharply its central themes of surrealism, alienation, and absurdity.

Other signature stories are "Not the actions of a hero who must be nice," which—under the pretense of showing the narrator's obsession with eradicating feral dogs—provides a pointed critique of our tendency to worship heroes, and "Blurring it so clearly," about a pathologist who invented or not the illness that the narrator has been diagnosed with. Rowan demonstrates great deftness. in making us suspend our disbelief to follow his characters on their adventures.

—*Aurelie Thiele*

Sin Eaters by Caleb Tankersley. Fairbanks, Alaska: University of Alaska Press, 2022. 185 pages. $21.95, paper.

Sin Eaters by Caleb Tankersley is an impressive debut collection of stories. They're like Kelly Link meets Mary Oliver but with more Jesus and set in the Midwest. In these stories, the city of note, which is referenced in several of the stories, is not New York, but rather Kansas City. This big city offers a contrast to the more rural location in which several of these stories take place.

The stories alternate between those that focus on people facing everyday dilemmas and those that center on people of faith. For me as a reader, the stronger stories were those focusing on ordinary people. But, in this collection, even the ordinary isn't mundane, and some of the stories dwell firmly in the magical realism/fabulist tradition.

"Swamp Creatures," the first story in the collection, focuses on Karen, a disaffected wife who was recently laid off from her job at the dry cleaners and who may just be the world's worst babysitter. Her marriage to Gary isn't much of a comfort, but the swamp in her backyard is. Karen notes, "The swamp is impressive, a gargling pool stretching as far as we can see." Likewise, "Trains" tells the story of another unemployed woman, who moved to a new place with her boyfriend Gregory and who's trying but isn't really trying to find a job. Just as Karen obsessively focuses on the swamp, the main character in "Trains" obsessively focuses on the trains that run right by their rented apartment. Karen states that "the noise moved in waves, steadily more forceful until I could see the train, a shadow of gears and iron between flashes of light."

While many of the stories in this collection examine the lives of characters who make devastatingly bad choices, two of my favorite stories deal with people who were doing the best they could in spite of facing grief and loss. In "Never Been More in Love," Dean struggles with meeting his own emotional and sexual needs while caring for his declining wife, Barbara, whom Dean and really, truly loved. However, he considers abandoning his wife because though he and Barbara used to love frequenting the foodie scene, things are different now. "He has to do everything—clean, cook, give her medication, help her across the room. Dean can't wrap his head around the idea that this is his life now." Likewise, in "Candy Cigarettes," school-aged Mellie is also coping with something she can't control, the death of her beloved grandpa, a man whose lessons were intended to get her "ready to face the goddam world" but bordered on abuse. "Grandpa believed people good at poker were good at life. He gave her lessons in the cards, flushes and pairs, what beat what, how to shuffle and deal like a pro. But mostly the training was on keeping your face still."

These stories were like truffles infused with bourbon; even the ones I didn't like I thought about and kept on thinking about. These were stories with a kick. In "Apparitions," the main character, Logan, sees an image of Jesus in the bathtub but pretends otherwise to his significant other, David. David's rediscovered faith makes Logan uncomfortable. Logan notes, "We're in a nice apartment complex that I can run laps around, but this morning I round a few corners and enter the real suburbs, houses like a hall of mirrors, sameness down to the welcome mats. These are the Jesus people."

Like Logan in "Apparitions," Gertrude in "Sin Eaters" is looking for a more quotidian explanation for her extraordinary experiences. When Gertrude's jaw drops to the floor and stays there one morning, she wants to find a rational, scientific explanation. But when she consults Doc Parry, the local dentist, he tells her something unexpected. He says he thinks that she's a sin eater, one who is meant to eat the sins of others, thus taking on those sins. Gertrude's response to Doc Parry's explanation is less than grateful: "I expect this nonsense from a Christian Scientist, but Doc Parry's a relatively reasonable man. I'm agitated and about plain done with him." For me, another memorable character was the title character in "Uncle Bob," who is stuck in a subpar nursing home but who isn't meek and feeble. He tells a visitor who is trying to save his soul, "This place is close enough to a fiery pit. Why don't you go peddle lies down the hall?"

Sin Eaters contains fourteen stories in all, ranging in length from flash fiction to full-length stories. The main characters include children, the elderly, and even a ghost. Previously, Tankersley published a chapbook, *Jesus Works the Night Shift*. On its acknowledgements page, he thanks some of his literary heroes, including Kevin Wilson, whose influence is notable here. Like Wilson's *Tunneling to the Center of the Earth*, this is a collection that keeps the reader wondering and leaves her wanting more.

—*Lori D'Angelo*

Groundscratchers by Gabriel Welsch. Flagstaff, Arizona: Tolsun Books, 2021. 192 pages. $20.00, paper.

Gabriel Welsch's collection of fourteen short stories, titled *Groundscratchers*, offers honest portrayals of multifaceted characters. This is highly commendable, especially given the range in character background, motivations, and struggles. Each character is sympathetic, despite his or her flaws. There's a tantalizing depth of emotional resonance found in each character's tale, and personally I could not peel myself away from the stories, as I needed to discover how each story ended.

"Twins" is an affecting story in this collection. It depicts the peculiarities of a set of twins, in their seventies, that reside in the town of Walkchalk. The twins sleep in "… barns, in detached garages, underneath decks, in hunting cabins—their resourcefulness is almost equal to that of a cat or a rodent." Further into the story, readers learn a few girls in the town have gone missing. The townsfolk worry, uncertain where to place blame. The protagonist has twin girls of his own, and throughout the story, we follow their growth, and well as the narrator's increasing apprehension of the other twins; fear brings this story to a chilling and heavy conclusion.

Another story in the collection with a cold atmosphere is "Prayers." Welsch writes, "She would find him some nights standing naked in the light of the refrigerator, the hair covering him blue from the light there, and she would take his hand and lead him to bed." Though the piece is short and succinct, the story is seamlessly layered with glimpses into the fictive present and the past. While intensely heartbreaking, the writing is gorgeous. Welsch creates stories that both satisfy and sting.

Like "Twins" and "Prayers," many of these stories center on themes of loss. This is a theme in "Nguyen Van Thieu Dies at 78" and "Visions of Edwin Miller" as well. In these short stories, Welsch crafts fiction strongly rooted in history and in science respectively.

In truth, Nguyen Van Thieu, ex-president of South Vietnam, fled his country and lived the remainder of his quiet life in the United States. Welsch takes this time of exile and creates a fictional story. One of the many enjoyable aspects of this story was how Welsch used Nguyen Van Thieu's quietness to add complexity to this tale. Sound is mentioned many times in "Nguyen Van Thieu Dies at 78"—what is heard versus what is seen. Welsch writes, "Sound was, for a long time, all I knew about the accident. Visual memory I have had to build myself. I remember hearing their garage door go up, since it seldom did."

In "Visions of Edwin Miller," Edwin struggles with trusting what he sees:

> As he started class, an opening equation on a theoretical valence level of the particles he and his peers suspected to work about the atoms, he felt a splash of seawater against his face, up off the iron prow below. The air shoved at him with the force of explodings every few seconds, and behind him, the crew was screaming his name. ... Edwin whirled ... and found only chalk in his hands and a group of startled faces
> ....

Edwin's home and work life are masterfully interwoven with scientific fact throughout the piece, creating a multilayered narrative that is engaging to read. While readers join Edwin in his failure to bring balance into his life, the depth of the storytelling and characterization facilitate compassion for Edwin while also allowing us to empathize with his frustrated wife. This story is relatable and timely.

Throughout his *Groundscratchers* collection, Welsch's sentences are lyrical and sharp. In each story, his identity as a poet is evident.

The characters and their situations are accurate renditions of reality, making the fiction feel like it could be nonfiction. I admired the work and the other stories in the collection. These stories explore themes of loss—loss of life, country, temper, marriage and innocence. While not peppy or feel-good, this collection captures humanity and makes *Groundscratchers* an unforgettable and poignant read.

—*Lauren Voeltz*

Contributors' Notes

Garrett Ashley's work has appeared in *The Normal School*, *DIAGRAM*, *Asimov's Science Fiction*, and the 2020 issue of *Moon City Review*, among other places. He lives in Alabama and teaches creative writing at Tuskegee University.

Ifeoluwa Ayandele was born in rural Ago Are, Nigeria. He received his master's in English literature from the University of Lagos, Nigeria. He is a *Best of the Net* nominee. His work is published or forthcoming in *Borderlands: Texas Poetry Review*, *Cider Press Review*, *Harbor Review*, *Rattle*, *Verse Daily*, and elsewhere. He tweets @IAyandele.

Sudha Balagopal's recent fiction and nonfiction appear in *CRAFT*, *Native Skin*, *SmokeLong Quarterly*, and *Split Lip Magazine*, among other journals. Her novella in flash was published by Ad Hoc Fiction in 2021. Her work will be published in *Best Microfiction 2022*. More details can be found at sudhabalagopal.com

Julie Brooks Barbour is the author of two collections, *Haunted City* (2017) and *Small Chimes* (2014), both from Kelsay Books, and three chapbooks, including *Beautifully Whole* (Hermeneutic Chaos Press, 2015) and *Earth Lust* (Finishing Line Press, 2014). She teaches writing at Lake Superior State University where she coedits the journal *Border Crossing*.

Jeffrey Bean is professor of English and creative writing at Central Michigan University. He is the author of the poetry collections *Diminished Fifth* (WordTech Communications, 2009) and *Woman Putting on Pearls* (Red Mountain Press, 2017), winner of the 2016 Red Mountain Prize for Poetry. His poems have been featured in the *New Poetry from the Midwest* anthologies and online at *Poets.org* and *Verse Daily*. More details can be found at www.jeffreybeanpoet.com

Carolee Bennett is a writer and artist living in upstate New York, where—after a local, annual poetry competition—she has fun saying she has been the "almost" poet laureate of Smitty's Tavern. She has an MFA in poetry and works full time as a writer in social media marketing.

A.J. Bermudez is an award-winning writer and director. Her work has appeared or is forthcoming in *Chicago Quarterly Review*, *Boulevard*, *McSweeney's*, *Story*,

Creative Nonfiction, and elsewhere. She is a recipient of the Diverse Voices Award, the Page Award, and the Alpine Fellowship Writing Prize. Her first book, *Stories No One Hopes Are About Them*, will be published as winner of the Iowa Short Fiction Award in fall 2022.

Laurie Blauner is the author of eight books of poetry, five novels, and a creative nonfiction book. Her latest novel is *Out of Which Came Nothing* (Spuyten Duyvil Press, 2021). Her nonfiction book, *I Was One of My Memories*, won *PANK*'s 2020 Creative Nonfiction Book Contest.

Arno Bohlmeijer is a poet and novelist, writing in English and Dutch. He is winner of a 2021 PEN America Grant and runner-up for the 2018 Gabo Translation Prize. His work has been published in five countries.

Roseanna Alice Boswell is a queer poet from upstate New York. Her work has appeared or will soon appear in *Driftwood Press*, *Jarfly*, *Capulet Mag*, and elsewhere. She is a doctoral student in creative writing at Oklahoma State University. Her chapbook, *Imitating Light*, was chosen as the 2021 Iron Horse Literary Review Chapbook Competition winner. Her first full-length collection, *Hiding in a Thimble*, was published by HVTN Press in 2021.

Caleb Bouchard lives in Atlanta. His poetry has recently appeared in *As It Ought to Be*, *Dead Skunk Mag*, *MORIA*, and *The Pointed Circle*. His translations of the French poet Jacques Prevel have appeared in *AzonaL* and *Black Sun Lit* and are forthcoming in *Poet Lore*. "The Crack" is his first published Michel Houellebecq translation.

Danit Brown is the author of *Ask for a Convertible* (Anchor Books, 2009), a *Washington Post* Best Book of 2008 and winner of a 2009 American Book Award. Her stories have appeared in numerous literary journals, including *Story*, *One Story*, and *Glimmer Train*, and have been featured on National Public Radio. She teaches at Albion College.

Julia Brush is a doctoral candidate and teacher at the University of Connecticut. Her poetry has appeared in *8 Poems*, *The Malahat Review*, and *Nightjar Review*.

Michael Chang is the author of several collections of poetry, including *Boyfriend Perspective* (Really Serious Literature, 2021), *Almanac of Useless Talents* (CLASH Books, 2022), and *Synthetic Jungle* (Northwestern University Press, 2023). Tapped to edit Lambda Literary's *Emerge* anthology, their poems have been nominated for *Best New Poets* and *Best of the Net*. They were awarded the Poetry Project's prestigious Brannan Prize in 2021 and are a poetry editor at *Fence*.

Yolande Clark-Jackson's essay "How You Get There" was among the top twelve awarded in the 2021 Winning Writers contest. She is a 2021 Eckerd College McCartt Fellowship awardee and one of seven artists awarded the 2022 James Weldon Johnson Foundation artist-in-residency fellowship.

Daren Colbert is a writer and filmmaker from Missouri. His work has been published or is forthcoming in *superfroot magazine*, *Puerto del Sol*, *Unvaeled*, and elsewhere.

Whitney Collins is the author of *Big Bad* (Sarabande Books, 2019), which won the 2019 Mary McCarthy Prize in Short Fiction. She received a 2020 Pushcart Prize and the 2020 American Short(er) Fiction Prize, and she also won the 2021 ProForma Contest. Her stories have appeared in *AGNI*, *Gulf Coast*, *Shenandoah*, *American Short Fiction*, *The Pinch*, *Grist*, and others.

Jeffrey Condran is the author of two story collections, *A Fingerprint Repeated* (Press 53, 2013) and *Claire, Wading Into the Danube at Night* (Southeast Missouri State University Press, 2020), and the novel, *Prague Summer* (Counterpoint, 2014). He is an associate professor of creative writing at the University of Arkansas at Little Rock and the cofounder and publisher of the independent literary press, Braddock Avenue Books.

J.L. Conrad is the author of the full-length poetry collection, *A Cartography of Birds* (Louisiana State University Press, 2002) and the chapbook, *Not If but When* (Salt Hill, 2016). Her poems have appeared in *Pleiades Magazine*, *Salamander*, *Beloit Poetry Journal*, and *The Laurel Review*, among others. She lives in Madison, Wisconsin.

John Cullen graduated from SUNY Geneseo and worked in the entertainment business. He teaches at Ferris State University and has had work published in *The American Journal of Poetry*, *The MacGuffin*, *Harpur Palate*, *North Dakota Quarterly*, and other journals. His chapbook, *Town Crazy*, is available from Slipstream Press (2013), and his poem "Almost There" won the 52 Annual New Millennium Writing Award.

Lori D'Angelo is a fiction writer whose work has appeared in literary journals such as *Drunken Boat*, *The Forge*, *Gargoyle Magazine*, and *Potomac Review*. She lives in Virginia with her family.

Jim Daniels' latest book of poems is *Gun/Shy* (Wayne State University Press, 2021). Other recent books include his fiction collection, *The Perp Walk* (2019), and his anthology, *RESPECT: The Poetry of Detroit Music* (2020), coedited with M.L. Liebler, both published by Michigan State University Press. A native of Detroit, he lives in Pittsburgh and teaches in the Alma College low-residency MFA program.

Cherie Hunter Day lives in northern California. Her short prose pieces have appeared in *100 Word Story*, *KYSO Flash*, *MacQueen's Quinterly*, *Mid-American Review*, *Quarter After Eight*, and *Unbroken Journal*. *Miles Deep in a Drum Solo* is her latest poetry collection (Backbone Press, 2022).

Tommy Dean is the author of two flash fiction chapbooks, *Special Like the People on TV* (Red Bird Chapbooks, 2014) and *Covenant* (ELJ Editions, 2021). *Hollows*, a collection of flash fiction, is now available from Alternating Current Press (2022). A recipient of the 2019 Lascaux Prize in Short Fiction, he is on Twitter @TommyDeanWriter.

Sean Thomas Dougherty is the author or editor of twenty books, including *Death Prefers the Minor Keys* (forthcoming from BOA Editions, Ltd.) and *The Dead Are Everywhere Telling Us Things*, winner of the 2021 Jacar Press book contest. His website is seanthomasdoughertypoet.com.

Gary Fincke's latest collection of stories is *Nothing Falls from Nowhere* (Stephen F. Austin, 2021). His full-length and flash stories have appeared in journals such as *The Missouri Review*, *Kenyon Review*, *Crazyhorse*, *Wigleaf*, *CRAFT*, *Atticus Review*, and *The Best Small Fictions 2020*. He is coeditor of the annual anthology series *Best Microfiction*.

Ben Freedman is an MFA candidate in fiction at Colorado State University. "Roadkill" is his first published story.

Bareerah Y. Ghani is a Canadian-Pakistani writer, an MFA candidate at George Mason University, a book reviewer at *Publishers Weekly*, and the assistant fiction editor at *Phoebe Journal*. Her work has appeared in North American and Pakistani literary journals such as *Defunkt Magazine*, *Kalopsia Literary Journal*, *Desi Collective*, and others. She is on Twitter @Bareera_yg.

Robin Gow is a trans poet and young adult author from rural Pennsylvania. They are the author of *Our Lady of Perpetual Degeneracy* (Tolsun Books, 2020) and the chapbook *Honeysuckle* (Finishing Line Press, 2019). Their first young adult novel, *A Million Quiet Revolutions*, was published in 2022 by Farrar, Straus and Giroux Books for Young Readers.

Fannie H. Gray writes fiction inspired by her Southern American upbringing. Her published works, along with her poetry, can be found at www.thefhgraymatter.com. She is on Twitter @fannnster.

Ashley Hajimirsadeghi is a multimedia artist, writer, and journalist. Her writing has appeared in *Barren Magazine, Hobart Pulp, DIALOGIST, Rust and Moth*, and *The Shore*, among others. She is co-editor-in-chief at both *Mud Season Review* and Juven Press. More of her work can be found at ashleyhajimirsadeghi.com.

Alle C. Hall placed as a finalist for 2020 The Lascaux Prize and won the Richard Hugo House New Works Competition. Other work appears in *Tupelo Quarterly, Creative Nonfiction, Necessary Fiction, Brevity* (blog), *Another Chicago Magazine*, and *The Citron Review*. She is a current reader for *Creative Nonfiction*. A Best Small Fictions and Best of the Net nominee, Hall's first novel will be published in spring 2023.

Jacob Griffin Hall was raised outside of Atlanta and lives in Columbia, Missouri, where he is a doctoral candidate and works as poetry editor of *The Missouri Review*. His first collection of poems, *Burial Machine*, was selected as the winner of the 2021 Backlash Best Book Award and is forthcoming with Backlash Press. His poems have appeared or are forthcoming in *32 Poems, New South Journal, DIAGRAM, New Orleans Review, New Ohio Review Online*, and elsewhere.

Brandi Handley's work has appeared in *Post Road, The Laurel Review, Adelaide Literary Magazine*, and *Wisconsin Review*. She earned an MFA in creative writing and media arts from the University of Missouri-Kansas City and teaches English at Park University, a small liberal arts college in Parkville, Missouri.

James Harris is a Black, Mexican, and white writer who writes speculative fiction with a literary twist. He currently resides in Kansas City. More information is at jamesharrisstories.com

Yuemin He's poetry translations appear in anthologies and magazines, including *Oxford Anthology of Modern and Contemporary American Poetry, Metamorphoses, The Northern Virginia Review, The Cincinnati Review, 91st Meridian, Rattle*, and *The Tiger Moth Review*. She is an English professor at Northern Virginia Community College.

James Heil recently graduated with his MA from Missouri State University, where he served as an assistant editor for *Moon City Review*.

Cynthia Marie Hoffman is the author of *Call Me When You Want to Talk About the Tombstones* (Persea, 2018), *Paper Doll Fetus* (Persea, 2014), and *Sightseer* (Persea, 2011). Hoffman is a former Diane Middlebrook Poetry

Fellow at the Wisconsin Institute for Creative Writing, Director's Guest at the Civitella Ranieri Foundation, and recipient of an Individual Artist Fellowship from the Wisconsin Arts Board. Her poems have appeared in *jubilat, Fence, Blackbird, diode, The Los Angeles Review*, and elsewhere.

Michel Houellebecq is the author of several poetry collections and nine novels. His most recent novel available in English is *Serotonin* (Flammarion, 2019). A book of selected poems, entitled *Unreconciled: Poems 1991-2013*, was released in a bilingual edition by Farrar, Strauss and Giroux in 2017. He lives in France.

Megan Howell is a Washington, D.C.-based freelance writer. After graduating from Vassar College, she earned her MFA in fiction from the University of Maryland in College Park, winning both the Jack Salamanca Thesis Award and the Kwiatek Fellowship. Her work has appeared in *McSweeney's, The Nashville Review*, and *The Establishment*, among other publications.

Shen Chen Hsieh is an illustrator, instructor, and art director in Missouri. Shen studied and graduated in the MFA in Visual Study program at Missouri State. She currently works as an art director in the local design industry.

Anthony Immergluck is a poet, publishing professional, and musician with an MFA in poetry from New York University-Paris. Some of his recent work has been published or is forthcoming in *TriQuarterly, Beloit Poetry Journal, Tahoma Literary Review*, and *Copper Nickel*. Originally from the Chicago area, he now lives in Madison, Wisconsin.

Frank Jamison is a graduate of Union University and the University of Tennessee. His poetry, essays and children's stories have won numerous prizes. More details are at jfrankjamison.com.

Philip Jason's poems and stories can be found in *Prairie Schooner, The Pinch, Mid-American Review, Ninth Letter, The Summerset Review*, and other journals. He is a recipient of the Henfield Prize in Fiction. His first novel, *Window Eyes*, is forthcoming from Unsolicited Press, and his first collection of poetry, *I Don't Understand Why It's Crazy to Hear the Beautiful Songs of Nonexistent Birds*, is forthcoming from Fernwood Press. More information is at philipjason.com.

Marci Rae Johnson is an editor and writer. Her poems appear or are forthcoming in *Image, Main Street Rag, The Collagist, Rhino, Quiddity, Hobart, Redivider, Redactions*, and *32 Poems*, among others. Her most recent book, *Basic Disaster Supplies Kit*, was published by Steel Toe Books in 2016.

Michele Finn Johnson's short fiction collection, *Development Times Vary*, was the winner of the 2021 Moon City Press Short Fiction Award and is forthcoming in 2022. Her fiction and essays have appeared in *A Public Space*, *Colorado Review*, *Mid-American Review*, *DIAGRAM*, *SmokeLong Quarterly*, and elsewhere. Her work was selected for the *The Best Small Fictions 2019* anthology. Find her online at michelefinnjohnson.com.

Tom Kelly is earning his doctorate in creative writing from Florida State University. His fiction and poetry appear in *New South Journal*, *Ninth Letter*, *LIT Magazine*, *Redivider*, *Passages North*, and other journals. He is on Instagram @tomkellyyyyy.

Tucker Leighty-Phillips is a writer from southeastern Kentucky. His work has appeared in *The Adroit Journal*, *The Offing*, *The Forge*, and elsewhere. He received his MFA in fiction from Arizona State University and works for Roadside Theater, a division of the Appalshop film workshop in Whitesburg, Kentucky. His website is TuckerLP.net.

Gary Leising is the author of the book *The Alp at the End of My Street* from Brick Road Poetry Press (2014). He has also published three poetry chapbooks: *The Girl with the JAKE Tattoo* (Two of Cups Press, 2015), *Temple of Bones* (Finishing Line Press, 2013), and *Fastened to a Dying Animal* (Pudding House, 2010). He is a professor of English who lives in Clinton, New York.

Rachel Lloyd is a two-time winner of the Sultan Short Story Contest and the recipient of the Virginia Mason Vaughan Prize. Her work has appeared in *The Capra Review* and *The Next Chapter*. She has studied and taught in Boston, the United Kingdom, and Shanghai. Her website is rachelloydwrites.com.

Joshua Jones Lofflin's writing has appeared in *Best Microfiction 2020*, *The Best Small Fictions 2019*, *The Cincinnati Review*, *CRAFT*, *SmokeLong Quarterly*, *Split Lip Magazine*, and elsewhere. He lives in Maryland. His website is jjlofflin.com.

Kimberly Lojewski's first story collection, *Worm Fiddling Nocturne in the Key of a Broken Heart* (Burrow Press, 2019) won the 2018 Gold Medal in General Fiction in the Florida Book Awards and was a Rumpus Book Club selection. Stories from that collection won a Best of the Net and were included in Ellen Datlow's 2019 *The Best Horror of the Year*.

Alyssa Malloy is a graduate student at Missouri State University, recently finishing a master's degree in English with a focus on creative writing, and will start an MFA in dramatic writing this fall. She is originally from Tampa, Florida.

Lyndsie Manusos' work has appeared in *Barrelhouse, Passages North, The Magazine of Fantasy & Science Fiction*, and other publications. She lives in Indianapolis with her family, works as a bookseller for her local indie bookstore, and writes for *Book Riot* and *Publishers Weekly*.

Francesca Mattei's short stories were published in Italian magazines such as *Malgrado le Mosche, l'Elzeviro, SPLIT, Clean Rivista, Narrandom, La Nuova Verde*, and *Voce del Verbo*. Her first collection of short stories, *Il giorno in cui diedi fuoco alla mia casa*, was published by Pidgin Edizioni in 2021.

Katie McWilliams graduated with her bachelor's degree in English with a creative writing emphasis from Missouri State University in 2021 and writes for the MSU admissions team. Her poetry has been previously published in *Loud Coffee Press* and *Furrow*.

Michael Meyerhofer's fifth poetry book, *Ragged Eden*, was published by Glass Lyre Press (2019). He has been the recipient of the James Wright Poetry Award, the Liam Rector First Book Award, the Brick Road Poetry Book Prize, and other honors. His work has appeared in *Hayden's Ferry Review, Gargoyle Magazine, Ploughshares*, and other journals. He is also the author of a fantasy series and the poetry editor of *Atticus Review*. More information is at troublewithhammers.com.

Sidney Miles' work has been featured in the news column of *The Standard*, a Missouri State University newspaper.

Melissa Moorer's work has been published in such journals as *Electric Lit, Hobart Pulp, The Offing, Lady Churchill's Rosebud Wristlet, The Toast, Flapperhouse*, and *Vestal Review*. She was assistant editor at The Toast and is on Twitter @knownforms.

Travis Mossotti's third full-length collection, *Narcissus Americana*, was selected as the winner of the 2018 Miller Williams Poetry Prize (University of Arkansas Press, 2018). Mossotti has also published two chapbooks, and he lives and works in St. Louis.

Derek Otsuji is the author of *The Kitchen of Small Hours* (Southern Illinois University Press, 2021). Recent poems have appeared in *32 Poems, Beloit Poetry Journal, Rattle, The Southern Review*, and *The Threepenny Review*.

Timothy Parfitt is a Chicago-based writer. His essays and criticism have appeared in *X-R-A-Y Literary Magazine, Contrary, LIGEIA, Punctuate*, and *Newcity Lit*.

Allison Parker is a third-year MFA candidate at the University of Memphis with a focus on fiction. She holds a bachelor's degree in English and philosophy from Austin Peay State University and is the online editor for *The Pinch*.

Mick Parsons' work has appeared or is forthcoming in *SmokeLong Quarterly*, *Contemporary Haibun Online*, *Thimble Literary Magazine*, *Poetry Flash*, *The New Southerner*, *Pegasus*, *Antique Children*, *The Smoking Poet*, and more. His work published on semantikon.com is permanently archived as part of a group of writers representing the Ohio Valley at the turn of the century.

Pedro Ponce is the author of *The Devil and the Dairy Princess* (Indiana University Press, 2021), winner of the Don Belton Fiction Prize. His short stories and flash fictions have appeared in numerous journals, including *Copper Nickel*, *Split Lip Magazine*, and *The Florida Review*, as well as in the anthologies *New Micro* and *The Best Small Fictions 2019*. He teaches writing and literature at St. Lawrence University.

Dez Pounds is twenty-three years old, born and raised in the Ozarks. They are a drawing major at Missouri State University.

Sujash Purna is a poet and photographer. He is the author of *Epidemic of Nostalgia* (Finishing Line Press, 2021). His poetry appeared in *The South Carolina Review*, *Hawai'i Pacific Review*, *Kansas City Voices*, *Poetry Salzburg Review*, *English Journal*, *Stonecoast Review*, and others. His photography can be found on Instagram @poeticnomadic

Noley Reid's third book is the novel *Pretend We Are Lovely* from Tin House Books (2017). Her fourth book, a collection of stories called *Origami Dogs*, is forthcoming from Autumn House Press. Her fiction and nonfiction have appeared in *The Southern Review*, *The Rumpus*, *Arts & Letters*, *Meridian*, *Pithead Chapel*, *Confrontation*, and *Los Angeles Review of Books*. More information is at NoleyReid.com

Ryan Ridge is the author of five chapbooks and four books, including the story collection *New Bad News* (Sarabande Books, 2020). An assistant professor at Weber State University in Ogden, Utah, he codirects the creative writing program and edits the literary magazine *Juked*. Ridge lives in Salt Lake City and plays bass in the Snarlin' Yarns.

Liz Robbins' third collection, *Freaked*, won the Elixir Press Annual Poetry Award (2015); her second collection, *Play Button*, won the Cider Press Review Book Award (2012). Her poems have appeared or are forthcoming in *Denver Quarterly*, *Kenyon Review*, *The Writer's Almanac*, *The Missouri Review*, and

Rattle. She lives in St. Augustine, Florida, and works as a poetry screener for *Ploughshares.*

Paul Rodenko (1920-76) was a Dutch poet with a British mother and a Russian father. An essayist who made surrealist and experimental poetry accessible, he wrote extensively about Ezra Pound's work. During World War II, Rodenko went into hiding and worked for clandestine literary magazines.

Rachele Salvini is a bilingual Italian writer based in the United States, where she is working toward a doctorate in English and creative writing at Oklahoma State University. Her translations and work in English have been published in *Lunch Ticket, American Book Review, Necessary Fiction, Modern Poetry in Translation,* and others. Her first collection of translations is forthcoming in Italy.

Alanna Shaikh is a first-generation American who is the daughter of a Pakistani immigrant. Her poetry has been published or accepted for publication in *The Examined Life Journal, Fatal Flaw,* and *Gordon Square Review,* among others.

Caleigh Shaw is a poet from Canton, Georgia. She is an MFA candidate at Oklahoma State University, where she is an editorial assistant at *Cimarron Review.* Her poetry has appeared in *8 Poems, Ghost City Review, Roanoke Review,* and *Maryland Literary Review.* She is on Twitter @caleighcal14.

Coyote Shook is a doctoral candidate at the University of Texas at Austin, as well as a cartoonist. Their graphic essays and comics have been in *Kenyon Review, The Puritan, The Tupelo Quarterly Review, The Tampa Review, The Portland Review, Shenandoah,* and *Salt Hill.* Their first full-length graphic novel, *A History of Jellyfish in Wyoming,* is now in production with Really Serious Literature.

Meg Spring is winner of the 2021 Student Literary Competition in Fiction for *Moon City Review.* Raised in the Ozarks, she has always enjoyed feeding pears to cows and writing stories about regular people doing irregular things.

Josh Springs is a middle school teacher based in South Carolina with an MFA in fiction from Converse College. His work can be found in *Best Emerging Poets,* the *Mountain Laurel,* and other places online.

Aurelie Thiele teaches engineering and writes fiction, paints, and has a passion for the performing arts.

Letitia Trent's work has appeared in *Diagram,* *Waxwing,* and *Ghost Proposal.* Her most recent books include the poetry collection *Match Cut,* (Sundress

Publications, 2018), and the chapbook, *the ghost comes with me* (ghost city press, 2019). She lives in the Ozarks and works in the mental health field.

Sean Turlington is an assistant editor for *Moon City Review* as well as an English MA student and graduate assistant at Missouri State University.

Cathy Ulrich's work has been published in various journals, including *Puerto del Sol*, *Ecotone*, and *Reservoir Road Literary Review*.

Lauren Voeltz's work is at *Youth Imagination*, *trampset*, and *TL;DR*. She is on Twitter @mattnwife.

Nan Wigington works in an autism center for primary grade students. Her flash fiction has appeared in *The Best Small Fictions 2019*, *Microfiction Monday Magazine*, and *The Ekphrastic Review*.

Nicholas Yingling's work can be found in *Poetry Daily*, *The Missouri Review*, *32 Poems*, *Colorado Review*, and elsewhere. He lives and teaches in the San Fernando Valley.

Tara Isabel Zambrano is a writer of color and the author of a full-length flash collection, *Death, Desire, And Other Destinations* by Okay Donkey Press (2020). She lives in Texas and is the fiction editor for *Waxwing* literary journal.

Lucy Zhang's work has appeared in *The Offing*, *The Rumpus*, *EcoTheo Review*, and elsewhere and was selected for *Best Microfiction* and *The Best Small Fictions*. Her chapbook *Hollowed* is forthcoming in 2022 from Thirty West Publishing. More information is at kowaretasekai.wordpress.com/

Zhang Zhihao is author of ten poetry collections and several books of fiction and essays. His Chinese commendations include the People's Literature Prize (2004), the annual October Prize for poetry (2011), the Chinese Literature Media Award for poetry (2014), the First Chinese Qu Yuan Poetry Award (2014), the Chen Zi'ang Poetry Award (2016), the Luxun Literary Prize for poetry (2018) and the October Literature Award (2019). He is editor-in-chief of *Chinese Poetry*, a quarterly poetry magazine in Wuhan, China.

Karen Zlotnick was born and raised in New York and lives in the Hudson Valley. Some of her work has been featured in *Pithead Chapel*, *Typishly*, *jmww*, and *Stonecoast Review*, and one of her stories was nominated for *The Best Small Fictions 2022*.

Maria Zoccola is a queer Southern writer with roots in the Mississippi delta. She has writing degrees from Emory University and Falmouth University. Her work has previously appeared or is forthcoming in *Ploughshares*, *The Iowa Review*, *The Cincinnati Review*, *The Massachusetts Review*, and elsewhere.

CPSIA information can be obtained
at www.ICGtesting.com
Printed in the USA
JSHW051858230722
28440JS00003B/11